D0652668

A DARK GUARDIAN

The man made no reply, advancing. His eyes were like live coals burning into Cora, holding her gaze relentlessly. She couldn't tear herself away from the mesmerizing look in them. They were transporting her to a place far away—a dark place crimsoned with blood; he was covered with it. The room swam as he approached, and she groped for the foot of the sleigh bed for support. This didn't seem real, yet there was no question.

Screaming at the top of her voice, she tore the yards of gauze curtain draped over the sleigh bed, and threw it over the advancing man. Then screaming again in multiple spasms, she raced through the door she'd left flung wide—right into the cold, wet arms of Joss Hyde-White.

How safe she felt in those arms. That struck her at once, and it shocked her given the circumstances. Perhaps it was the suddenness of the impact that took her guard down. He was soaking wet, his fine woolen greatcoat spongy where she gripped it. He wore no hat, and his dark hair was scattered across his brow, combed by the wind. He smelled of the clean, fresh North Country air. She inhaled deeply, but the indulgence was short-lived. Screams from below funneling up the staircase called her back to the urgency of the moment, and she strained against his grip.

"No!" he said, holding her at arm's distance. "Do not go down there. Do not move from this spot!"

Other *Love Spell* books by Dawn Thompson:

BLOOD MOON
THE FALCON'S BRIDE
THE WATERLORD
THE RAVENCLIFF BRIDE

Dawn Thompson

The Brotherhood

LOVE SPELL NEW YORK CITY

*For DeborahAnne MacGillivray,
in heartfelt appreciation. For all of her unending help and
support, I am eternally grateful.*

LOVE SPELL®

August 2007

Published by

Dorchester Publishing Co., Inc.
200 Madison Avenue
New York, NY 10016

ISBN-10: 0-505-52726-X
ISBN-13: 978-0-505-52726-4

The name "Love Spell" and its logo are trademarks of Dorchester
Publishing Co., Inc.

Printed in the United States of America.

Visit us on the web at www.dorchesterpub.com.

PROLOGUE

Whitebriar Abbey, Cumberland, England
May, 1812

Jon paced the Oriental carpet runners outside his wife's bedchamber like a caged lion until he tripped on the mess he'd made of them. Did all babies take this long in coming? Cassandra had been closeted in that chamber for hours—nearly all day, with Dr. Fenimore from Carlisle, and Grace Bates, the housekeeper at White-briar Abbey.

Jon plopped himself down on the hard wooden set-tle beside the door and dropped his head in his hands. A blood-chilling scream came again from inside—then another. He vaulted off the settle and kicked the wrin-kled carpet runners out of the way against the wall. Whose idea was it to lay down runners in the first place? What colossal dunce dictated that? Why wasn't there regular carpet on the floor in the corridors? Good God, the Hyde-Whites certainly had enough blunt to afford carpet. The halls were more frequently traveled than any chamber in the Abbey. He was surely going mad.

Another scream pierced the quiet, and Jon groaned. Raking his hair back ruthlessly, he began pacing again. The heels of his top boots rang on the bare wood underfoot. The runners he'd kicked aside had absorbed some of the noise; now, between Cassandra's screams and the racket he was making, he thought his brain would burst. There was nothing for it; if something didn't happen soon, he was going to barge straight into that chamber like a juggernaut and see for himself what was taking so bloody long.

This was no ordinary baby being born. They had both agonized for seven long months over this birth. The child would either be normal . . . or like they were, infected with the unspeakable *condition.* Jon hadn't spoken its true name—not even in his mind—since he and Cassandra returned from Moldovia. She had put up a brave front, trying not to worry him with her fears, but he saw through her thinly veiled attempts just as clearly as he saw through the leaded panes in the window at the end of the corridor. No light passed through that window now; night had fallen—dark, bleak, moonless night. The blood moon had saved them, but no moon would shine upon the birth of this child. Was it an omen of ill-boding that it be born during the dark of the moon? Cold chills snaked their way up and down Jon's spine at the thought. What else could it be? The baby was coming nearly a month early.

Hours passed. Grace came and went, bearing soiled bedding and clean linens. Bates, her husband, the butler at Whitebriar Abbey, carried kettle after kettle of water up from the kitchen, but neither would let Jon into Cassandra's chamber.

"Bear up, sir, 'tis almost over," Bates had said the last

time he barred him in the doorway. That was over an hour ago, and save Cassandra's screams, which seemed closer together—and growing weaker, God help her—there hadn't been a sound in the Abbey since.

Just when he feared he could bear no more, a lusty cry from inside ran Jon through like a knife blade. Was it born? Was it finally born? He pounded upon the door with both fists. There was a moment before it came open. Grace's plump face was flushed, and beaded with sweat. Her apron and hands were streaked with blood. There was a time when the sight and smell of blood—especially Cassandra's—would have brought on the feeding frenzy, the accursed bloodlust. Jon scarcely gave that a moment's thought. His eyes were riveted to the housekeeper.

"Is . . . is . . . ," was all he could get out. It was as if his tongue were paralyzed.

"Aye, it is," she replied. "Ya have a fine son, sir, and the mistress is restin' easy. 'Twas a difficult birth, but she's goin' ta be just fine."

She didn't have to tell him it had been a difficult birth. Cassandra's screams would pierce his heart and live in his mind until doomsday. But he had to see for himself.

"May I see her . . . uh, *them* . . . ?" he asked, craning his neck to see past the woman into the darkened room.

"Once we've cleaned them up," Grace replied. "Now, sit you back down and give us a couple o' minutes."

The door shut in his face, and he did as she bade him, dropping his head into his hands again. He had a son—*a son!*

It was only minutes, as the housekeeper said, but it seemed like forever before she opened the door again. This time, she beckoned. She needn't have bothered.

The instant the door left the jamb Jon streaked past her with a crashing disregard for her bulk and knelt down on one knee beside the bed, where Cassandra lay propped with down pillows, cradling the child in her arms.

Outlining instructions for his patient's care, the doctor took Grace's arm and led her away. Jon studied the child in his wife's arms. How tiny it was, and how fair complexioned for one come so recently through such an ordeal; Jon could see the tiny blue veins through the baby's translucent skin. How dark the eyes were, like two midnight sapphires, only showing the faintest trace of blue.

Jon leaned nearer, a close eye upon Grace and the doctor behind, and spoke in a stage whisper. Neither was aware of the situation, and it wouldn't do to have them find out what he feared they had just brought into the world.

"Is he . . . ?" he murmured.

Cassandra stared. How lovely she was with the candlelight picking out the sun-painted streaks in her honey-colored hair, with that touch of color in her cheeks and her hooded eyes glazed with the shimmer of leftover tears.

"I see what you see," she said. "It is too soon to tell. It may be years before we know for certain. If Milosh were here, perhaps he could tell us. I miss our Gypsy friend, Jon. He knew I was with child before I did. . . ."

Jon embraced mother and child. He had a beautiful son, and his wife had come splendidly through a difficult birth. What more could he ask for? It was enough for now, and he thanked Divine Providence through a deep, heaved sigh. He would not share his morbid thoughts about the birth occurring during moon-dark.

Cassandra was radiant, gazing down at their infant son. He would not spoil her euphoria. It was contagious. He had a son—a beautiful, healthy, perfectly formed son. Yes, it was enough . . . for now.

CHAPTER ONE

Cumberland, England
January, 1841

Joss should have stayed in London. Here was the worst snowstorm in history, and he was abroad in it—on horseback, no less. Madness, but necessary madness, at least the way he viewed it. It would have been worth it all if his efforts had borne fruit, but they hadn't. His parents, Jon and Cassandra Hyde-White, weren't at the townhouse when he'd reached it. None of the servants knew where or when they had gone. It was passing strange; they had vanished in the night, and Joss was right back where he'd begun, with nothing resolved. He had to find them. Though he knew he'd been tainted in the womb, that he wasn't exempt from the curse, he wasn't a blood-lusting vampire as they were before the blood moon ritual, either. Now, there were new symptoms. Something in him was changing. He needed answers. Hence his journey back to Whitebriar Abbey in what had had all the earmarks of becoming a blizzard, in hopes that they had tired of Town and decided to winter in Cumberland after all. This didn't bode well. Only a Bedlamite would venture forth in such a storm, and at this moment, battling the cruel north wind, that was exactly what Joss considered himself to be.

His head bent low in the gale, he urged his mount onward. He might have stopped at an inn along the way, but the snow had just begun again—one storm having bred another—when he'd passed the last public house, and he'd been so close to home, he'd decided to press on. Now, his multicaped greatcoat and beaver hat were caked with snow, as were his eyebrows and the woolen muffler wrapped around his nose and mouth. Freezing moisture crackled in his nostrils, and he cursed the air blue. Cold melting snow was trickling down his back beneath his coat collar.

Night was falling, and the road was no longer visible. Joss had no choice but to press on. He would have known the terrain blindfolded, but it had disappeared; the swirling blasts of blowing snow had whitewashed the earth and sky into one continuous blue-white blur. The snowflakes, driven by the wind, stung like thousands of needles piercing what little of his face was still exposed. He began to daydream of the welcoming hearth in his study at Whitebriar Abbey, of propping the feet he could no longer feel up up on the little tapestry-covered stool before the fire and sipping his favorite French brandy, warming himself from the inside out.

Lost in those fantasies, he came so close to the obstruction ahead that he nearly plowed into it before he realized it was there: a carriage—a brougham, by the look of it, its horses standing like two ghosts, washed white in the snow. A faint snort from one as he climbed down from his mount was the only evidence that the animals weren't frozen statues. He had considered taking a carriage home. Now, looking at this, he was glad he hadn't.

His top boots had scarcely sunk to the calf in the snow when something shaggy and black against the white world all around bounded through the open coach door and lit out over the drifts to disappear in the night—an unusually large dog, by the look of its paw prints, or a *wolf*. But that couldn't be.

Joss reached beneath his coat for the pistol in its holster strapped to his leg, but the animal had disappeared behind a whirling curtain of snow by the time he'd taken aim. No use to waste the bullet. He jammed the pistol back in its holster and plowed through the drifts toward the carriage, dreading what he would find inside.

Hard-packed snow from the previous storm underneath the fresh blanket kept his feet from sinking too deeply. He lost his balance nonetheless in the slippery stuff, and floundered several times before he reached the gaping carriage door. It had been thus for some time, judging from the way the snow had drifted inside and begun to mount up and spill onto the floorboards.

It was moon-dark, and there was no light save what reflected eerily from the snow. The coach lanterns had all but burned out, and he took one out of its bracket and held it high, peering inside. It gave off no more light than a firefly. Why did everything of a catastrophic nature always seem to happen to him in the dark of the moon?

There were five passengers in the coach. The coachman was nowhere in sight. Perhaps he had gone for help. There were no footprints in the snow, but that wasn't unusual. The way the stuff was falling now, it would have covered any tracks recently made. Jon's heart sank. The passengers were all in a jumble on the floor of the carriage. Had they passed out, or fallen to the floor when the coach abruptly stopped? There was no use trying to make sense of the situation, so he set the lantern aside and began lifting the passengers back on the seats one by one.

There were three men and two women. How long could they have been bogged down there? They seemed to be frozen stiff. By the look of it, the wild dog had gotten to four of them; they were dead, covered with blood. The woman at the bottom, to Joss's profound surprise, was alive, and she didn't seem to have been bitten, though it was hard to tell in the bleak semidarkness called by the storm, through a veil of falling snow and so much blood.

The salty, metallic smell rushed up his nostrils despite his muffler. It was happening again—the same surge of euphoria, the same strange reaction to the scent of blood that had driven him to London seeking answers. He beat the bone-chilling sensations back. The woman needed tending. The others' bodies had kept her warm by the look of it, and more than likely kept her from freezing to death. The carriage had evidently been bogged down there for some time.

All at once, the carriage lurched as one horse's forelegs buckled and it fell forward, then onto its side in the snow with a mournful whinny. Dragging his feet through the drifts, Joss unhitched both animals, but the fallen horse would not right itself. Its crazed eyes were bulging, and its tongue had slipped out between its teeth and lay like a ribbon in the snow. Its breathing was heavy and labored.

The animal could go no farther. Joss couldn't leave the horse at the mercy of wild dogs like the creature he'd just frightened off; that one would be back with the rest of the pack the minute he moved on, and the horse was in no condition to defend itself. His hand gripped the pistol beneath his greatcoat. He withdrew it, running his all-but-numb hand over the cold steel barrel, hesitating, but only for a moment. The horse was in pain. There was nothing for it, and so he raised the weapon and fired. The horse went limp in the snow.

A groan from the coach turned him back toward it, but when he returned the woman showed no signs of coming around. She was a little thing, wrapped in a chinchilla-lined hooded cloak, which had also spared her from the cold, and he hefted her over his shoulder, collected the other carriage horse's bridle, and trudged back to his own mount. Laying her across the horse's back before the saddle, he swung himself up and lifted her into the crook of his arm, meanwhile setting his mount in motion. The snow was falling more heavily now. He couldn't see two feet in front of him. With a firm grip on the carriage horse's bridle, he called out to the steed underneath him: "Home, Titus!" praying that the animal knew how to get him there.

Titus labored up the tor and into the flaying wind. They reached Whitebriar Abbey an hour later, and not a minute too soon for Joss. The carriage horse plodding along behind, they struggled to the flat summit, where he left both mounts in the hands of Otis McFee, the stable master, and plowed through the drifts carrying the woman to the Abbey.

It wasn't until the door came open in the hands of Jonathan Bates, the antiquated butler, and lamplight flooded the Great Hall, that he got a good look at his charge. She was as white as the snow swirling in around them, and caked with it just as he was. Her lips were tinged blue, the starkness of her whole countenance a shock against the wisps of chestnut hair spilling out from beneath her hood. She looked to be in her early twenties.

Limping on his lame leg through the little white whorls dancing over the threshold, Bates struggled with the wind in the doorway until he'd slammed the door. Joss was already streaking up the stairs, leaving a wet trail of melted snow and solid clumps that had fallen from their clothes behind him on the terrazzo.

"I shall take her to the yellow suite," he called over his shoulder. "Send Grace and Amy up straightaway to attend her. The poor gel is nearly frozen stiff. I suppose we shan't have Dr. Everett?"

"In this?" the butler barked. "You dream, sir."

"I thought not. We shall just have to make do, then. Don't just stand there, man! All four of her companions lie dead in their bogged-down carriage on the moor. Let us see if we can save this one, eh?"

The butler loped off at a pace consistent with his age and disability despite the directive for haste, and Jon carried on to the yellow suite and burst inside. Stripping off the girl's snow-caked mantle, he laid her on the sleigh bed, trying to ignore that her frock beneath was covered in blood; he prayed not hers. Chucking logs into the hearth, he engaged the tinderbox on the mantel, producing a spark that ignited the flammable bits inside and singeing his numb fingers in the bargain. Cursing, he dropped the flaming tinder on the hearthstone and waved his hand about, making matters worse. Sucking on the most painful of the burns, he fed the ignited matter into the pile of logs with the help of a hearth shovel.

He was breathing life into the fire with the bellows when Grace Bates, the butler's wife and housekeeper at Whitebriar Abbey, marched over the threshold, through the door he'd left flung wide, with the housemaid, Amy, in tow.

"What on earth are ya doin', sir?" the old woman asked. "That's no chore for you. Get up outta there afore ya burn yourself." Then to the maid: "Don't just stand there, girl. His hands are like two cakes o' ice. See to that fire before he does himself a mischief."

"We shan't have the doctor till the roads are passable," Joss said, straightening up and slapping ashes from his buckskins. "So we must make do. The young lady has been exposed to extreme cold for God alone knows how long a time in this blizzard. Do what you can, and report to me once you've done. I shall be in the study after I've changed. See that there's a fire there as well. I'm chilled to the bone."

Shuffling to the bed, Grace Bates threw up her arms and screamed. "Heaven save us! Where is she bleedin'?"

"I do not know that she is," Joss said. "The others in the coach with her were drenched in blood and she was underneath them; I believe it's theirs. Just . . . do what you can, and burn her clothes—all but the mantle, which can be saved. You may fetch some of Mother's things; they should fit. Are they at home: Mother and Father? Have they come on from London?"

The housekeeper gave a start. "In this?" she said. "No, sir. We've had no word to expect them."

Joss nodded and said no more. Briefly, his gaze fell upon the huge sleigh bed and the unconscious girl covered with blood, and his nostrils flared with the evocative smell. His heart began to race and his sex leapt with an unexpected arousal. He dared not remain. It was happening again.

Riveting chills raced along his spine, setting him in motion. Streaking past the slack-jawed servants, he marched down the hall to his own apartments, flung open the door and stripped off his wet coat, muffler and beaver, which he left in a heap on the floor for Parker, his valet, to deal with. The soggy top boots and hose came off next, and he chose a clean shirt and trousers from the armoire. His wet ones soon joined the pile. Then, shrugging on a bottle-green satin dressing gown over the dry togs, he went straightaway to the study, drawn by visions of that French brandy he'd been fantasizing about. Minutes later, the dream was a reality. He had done all he could for the gel. Lounging in his favorite wing chair before the fire, with his long legs fully stretched out, the neck of his shirt undone, feet propped up and snifter in hand, he viewed the world through the amber liquor in his glass and waited.

Slowly, his toes stopped tingling. Feeling was returning in his numb limbs, and with it, pain—throbbing, aching pain. At least his sex was behaving. Away from the scent of blood he was no longer aroused, though the sight of the girl in the yellow suite upstairs literally covered with it would not fade from his mind. What had she been doing out in such a blizzard in the first place? Who were her companions that now lay dead for their foolhardy decision to venture out in such weather? The other woman in the party had been older; a plain-looking woman with a large hairy mole above her upper lip. From her black twill costume, Joss assumed her to have been the girl's abigail. Two of the dead men were portly, considerably older as well, and the third was a

younger man who appeared to be in his late twenties—
younger at least than Joss's thirty. The dead youth was
well-dressed gentry from the look of him: a country
squire, perhaps, or the son of one; or full-fledged aristocracy. It hardly mattered now. They were all dead, and
horribly. The strange girl upstairs in the yellow suite was
the sole survivor—if indeed she survived. One thing was
certain; she would have met the fate of her companions
if he hadn't blundered onto that carriage when he did
and chased off the animal that had savaged the others.
He would just have to wait to see if he'd been in time to
spoil Mother Nature's assault.

Lulled by the snapping and crackling of the logs in
the hearth, he began to doze. Sleep dulled the pain and
his fingers relaxed on the glass in his hand. When the
knock came at the study door, the snifter slipped from
his fingers and shattered on the floorboards that edged
the Aubusson carpet, scattering glass shards and what
remained of the brandy in all directions.

Joss lurched erect, his sleep-dazed eyes trained upon
the study door. "Come!" he said, clearing the thickness
from his voice. He vaulted upright in the chair. For a
moment he was disoriented. His sleep had been sound.

Grace entered, sketching a curtsy—no mean task, he
observed, considering her age and circumference. *She
must be nearly seventy now,* he thought.

"The young lady hasn't come 'round," she said, "but
we done for her as best we can, and she appears ta be
restin' comfortable. Cook is fixin' an herbal draught ta
bring the fever down, and we'll try to get her ta take it,
but she needs the surgeon, and there's nothin' for it till
the snow stops fallin'. 'Twill be a miracle if the poor lass
don't take pneumonia."

"The blood . . . Was she . . . injured?" Joss said.

"There was some bruises on her, and a real bad lump on her head, which is probably why she ain't come 'round. Cook's makin' a poultice, but there was no wounds ta cause blood the likes o' what was on her frock."

"There were others in the coach that had been savaged by a wild dog. The blood was evidently theirs," Joss explained, ignoring the woman's gasp. "Did you burn her things?"

Grace gave a crisp nod. "Tossed them straight inta the kitchen hearth, I did. Her mantle's dryin' out below stairs."

"Good," he replied. "I do not want her left alone. Have Amy stay with her till she comes 'round. Her companions are dead. It must have been a terrible ordeal for her. She is bound to be frightened when she wakes."

"Yes, sir."

"I'll look in on her before I retire."

The housekeeper opened her mouth to speak, but a hollow pounding on the front door echoing through the Great Hall and along the corridor brought Joss to his feet, and he streaked past her. Bates had shuffled to the door and opened it by the time Joss appeared with Grace in tow. A man stood on the threshold dressed in coachman's togs, a green coat with a wide skirt, a wide-brimmed, low-crowned brown hat, cord breeches and top boots—all caked with snow. The only thing that wasn't was the bright red traveling scarf he had tucked inside his coat.

"Beggin' your pardon, gov'nor," the man panted. "I've lost my way. My coach bogged down in the snow. I went off afoot to get help . . . and got lost in the blizzard. . . ."

He hadn't crossed the threshold. Snow was swirling past him in little whorls, and his caped coat was flapping in the wind. Could this be the missing coachman from the carriage on the moor? If it was, he knew naught of the fate of his passengers. Something didn't ring true. He was either a colossal dunce, or there was more to it than he was telling. Why hadn't he un-hitched one of the horses to go for help instead of trudging through the drifts afoot? Still, the poor man looked done in, and Joss could hardly turn him away.

"Come in, man," he said. "I believe I have given one of your passengers sanctuary."

The coachman stepped inside and jumped out of the way as Bates slammed the door shut on the storm.

"Only one?" the man said. "There were five in that coach."

"The rest are dead," Joss said. "I came upon them just after dark."

"How dead?" the coachman queried, doffing his hat. He was a man of middle age, clean shaven, his dark wet hair plastered to his head. He was tall and thin, with an-gular features and the sharpest pair of black Gypsy eyes Joss had ever seen. "They were alive when I left them."

"They were attacked by a wild dog," Joss told him. "I chased it off, but not in time, I'm afraid. How is it that you didn't take one of the horses instead of floundering about afoot in this blizzard?"

"I thought I saw lights off to the east, and I was sure I could reach them easily enough afoot. I was mistaken. 'Twas will-o'-the-wisp, no doubt; the fells can be deceiv-ing at night. Where is this place?"

"Whitebriar Abbey," Joss said. "I am Joss Hyde-White. This is my home. And you . . . ?"

"Owen Sikes, at your service, sir," the coachman said, sketching a bow.

"Well, Sikes, you look about to drop in your tracks,

and there is naught to be done tonight. Go along with Bates and Grace here. They will see you have something to warm your belly and a place to sleep in the servants' quarters. Then, in the morning, once the storm has passed over, I will take you to your coach. I managed to save one of your horses. The other had to be destroyed, I'm afraid."

"Thank you kindly, sir," the coachman said, sketching another bow. "You're a fine gentleman to be givin' shelter to a total stranger on such a night as this is."

"I wouldn't turn a dog out in such a storm," Joss said.

The coachman smiled, but it did not reach his eyes. "I was banking on that, sir," he said, giving a nod and following the Bateses toward the servants' quarters behind the green baise door under the stairs.

CHAPTER TWO

Amy was nodding in the chair when Joss entered the yellow suite. That wouldn't do. When he shut the door behind him, the mousy little maid scrabbled up, wide-eyed, squaring her posture, and she surged to her feet as if she'd been launched from a catapult as he prowled closer to the bed.

"She hasn't come 'round?" Joss said.

Amy cleared her throat. "N-no, sir," she replied. "She's limp as a rag poppet, she is. The fever seems to be goin' down some, though. We give her some o' Cook's herbal tisane, and it's took hold right nice."

Joss stared down at the unconscious girl. How pale she was. There was no trace of the blood now, but he could still detect the odor of it lingering in the air. How strong his senses were becoming: he'd only just begun to realize. Cold chills riddled him. He didn't need to think about that now, but the unanswered questions kept gnawing at his thoughts, prying their way into his mind. What was happening to him, and why?

A hitch in the girl's breathing brought him back to

the present; a gentle, barely audible groan, though she didn't move. He stepped closer. How frail she looked, dwarfed in the huge sleigh bed beneath the mound of quilts and counterpanes Grace and Amy had heaped upon her. Circulation must be returning. That had to be a good sign. He studied the planes of her delicate face, the high cheekbones and wide-set eyes whose dark sweeping lashes rested on the alabaster flesh beneath. Her gently bowed lips were still tinged with blue. How lovely they would be tinted with the color the cold had robbed from them. And her hair, long and wavy, was a rich shade of brown, like chestnuts warmed by the sun, drifting over the eiderdown pillow. Something pinged in his sex. It had been a long time since he'd been with a woman.

He turned to the maid. "Go and fetch Grace," he said. "Tell her I want her to spell you and remain here in this chamber with the young lady through the night."

"But I thought I was ta—"

"No," he interrupted. "I caught you nodding when I came in just now. We cannot have that. Our guest has just come through a horrendous ordeal. When she wakes, she will be frightened to find herself in a strange place. Grace will be better at dealing with that than you." No doubt the silly chit had been looking forward to a comfortable night beside a roaring fire in the well-appointed chamber. Grace would be the better choice.

"Yes, sir," Amy said, pouting.

"Run on, then, girl, and tell Grace to bring the poultice. That's a nasty bruise on her brow."

Amy grumbled another "Yes, sir," bobbed a careless bow, and quit the chamber.

Minutes later, with the girl's care resolved and Grace in Amy's place fully instructed with orders to fetch him at once if she regained consciousness, Joss dragged himself to his own chamber and his warm bed. Yet, exhausted though he was, he couldn't stay in it.

Outside, the storm showed no signs of stopping. The hissing of the blowing snow assailing the mullioned panes in his bedchamber window, and the howling of the relentless wind, screaming like a woman, gave him no peace. It reminded him of the strange young lady down the hall in the yellow suite. Cold air was seeping in through the panes, teasing the fire in the hearth, and tall flames leapt into the air trailing smoke, casting grotesque shadows on the walls and ceiling. Was the chimney clogged with snow? The heat of the fire would eventually melt it if that were the case. But he'd scarcely completed that thought when a heavy clump of the stuff plopped into the middle of the flames in a hissing, spitting whoosh of ghostly white that all but put the fire out.

Hissing within, hissing without. It seemed as if he had been cast into a pit of angry snakes. It was no use. Surging out of the bed, Joss padded toward the window and parted the heavy gold portieres. Below, the tor was a solid mound of white tinted blue in the darkness. The driving snow was impossible to penetrate with the eye. Joss couldn't even see the courtyard, much less the kirk in the valley below. A run on the moor would be welcome right now. That would tire him enough to sleep, but the prospect of going back out into that frozen wilderness—even in wolf form—after finally thawing out was unthinkable. Besides, he couldn't take the shape of a wolf now, not with strangers in the house, in any case. But he could go abroad in the house as he was. Something was not as it should be. He had, since a child, been able to perceive when things weren't just so, when a threat of danger or deception was near. That gift was awakened now, detaining him from his sleep, preventing it. It had activated earlier, when he'd found Amy nodding in the chair in the yellow suite. What would he find if he went there now? There was only one way to know for certain.

Shrugging on his dressing gown, he cinched it about his waist and burst through his bedchamber door barefoot. The Oriental carpet runners he remembered crawling over as a babe had been rendered to threadbare tatters. They were taken up by the time he was breeched, and the floor was cold against his just thawed bare feet. Riveting chills shot through his body, causing him to misstep. Maybe he should have shape-shifted into wolf form after all. He never felt such things in his wolf incarnation, or if he did, he took no notice.

That part of the *condition,* as his father called it, had always appealed to him. The shapechange had manifested itself early, when he reached puberty. He never could fathom why his mother and father were so upset over it, since they, too, possessed the gift. Why hadn't they ever told him about the rest? If only they had been at the London townhouse. But they had not, and now he was on his own, with strangers in the house, and something untoward was about to happen; he could feel it in his marrow-chilled bones.

Those thoughts had gotten him to the yellow suite without realizing it. Lifting the latch soundlessly, he opened the door and stepped inside only to pull up short on the threshold. Now Grace was asleep in the chair, and a strange, dark figure was stooping over the girl in the bed. At the click of the latch, the figure spun toward him. It was the coachman.

"What are you doing here, Sikes?" Joss said. His voice had all the subtlety of a thunderclap, but Grace didn't move, curled in the large old wing chair beside the hearth. Was the woman drunk?

"You startled me, sir!" the coachman gushed. He nodded toward Grace, laying a finger across his lips. "Shhh . . . or you'll wake her. I've taken great pains not to do that."

Joss paid him no mind. Let Grace wake. She had some explaining to do. "You dare to 'shhh' *me*, sir? Why are you in this room—in this part of the house, come to that? You were given accommodations in the servants' quarters. You weren't given leave to prowl about the Abbey."

"Forgive me, sir," the coachman gushed again, "I could not sleep without seeing that the young lady was resting comfortably with my own eyes—not after hearing that all the others . . . are dead."

"Well, you have seen. Now I must insist that you return to the servants' quarters, and kindly remain there until I send for you. Morning comes quickly, and we have your other unfortunate passengers to deal with once the snow stops falling." What was the matter with Grace? She should have wakened by now, considering their raised voices. If she weren't snoring, he would have thought her dead, slouched as she was in the wing chair.

The coachman bowed. "Of course, sir," he said. "Dreadfully sorry if I've erred and overstepped my bounds. I meant no harm."

Joss studied the man, looking deep into his dark eyes. Something in them made him uneasy, and drove his gaze away. Perhaps he should have shapeshifted into the wolf after all; his intuition was always heightened when he took that form. He heaved a sigh. His imagination was running away with him. After the events of the past few hours, he shouldn't wonder.

"Wait," he said, arresting the man with a firm hand on his arm as he passed. "She was your passenger. You should know something about her. What is her name? Who were her companions in that coach? Where were you taking them?"

The coachman hesitated. A smug smile creased his lips. He'd smiled that smile before. There was neither warmth nor good humor in it, but rather a patronizing air of superiority that was most annoying. The man was working class, after all.

"She is Miss Cora Applegate," Sikes said. "Her father, Algernon Applegate, hired my coach. The young gentleman was her intended. I do not know his name, nor that of the other elder gentleman, his father. We were headed for Gretna Green."

"I see," Joss said, though he didn't see at all. His eyebrow lifted, and his forehead wrinkled in a thoughtful frown, narrowing his gaze. "All haste to the anvil, with both parties' fathers in such a storm? An odd business, I daresay. Why not a cozy drawing room, or a church wedding? Or was this the sort of wedding that is prodded by the barrel of a gun?"

"I wouldn't know, sir," said the coachman. "My coach is for hire to any who can pay the price. I do not make it a practice to meddle in my passengers' affairs."

"Mmm," Joss grunted. "I shall see you below. This time, stay there, if you please. Miss Applegate is in my care now. I will see to her needs from now on. You are obligated no longer."

With no more said, Joss led the coachman below and remanded him to Bates's keeping, with a warning that he'd best see that the man stay below stairs. The butler, having been awakened from a sound sleep by the reprimand, took charge, and Joss padded back to the yellow suite for a word with Grace.

The housekeeper was still snoring in the chair when Joss entered. He didn't dare call out to her for fear of waking her charge. Granted it was late, and Grace was certainly past her prime and overworked in an understaffed house, but that had always been the case at Whitebriar Abbey, and he couldn't remember her ever failing him before. Gripping her shoulder, he shook her gently. She didn't respond, and he shook her again. Bending close, he nudged her a third time, whispering her name. This time, her eyes popped open. It was a moment before they focused, and she vaulted upright in the chair, her bleary-eyed gaze sliding back and forth between him and the inert figure heaped with quilts in the sleigh bed across the way.

"Can no one in this house be trusted to stay awake?" Joss gritted out through clenched teeth.

"I dunno what happened," Grace said. "I was wide awake, and then . . ."

"You let that coachman, Sikes, into this room. What were you thinking?"

"I never done no such, sir!" Grace defended.

"Lower your voice," Joss warned. "I just found him stooping over that bed"—he made a rough gesture toward it—"and you snoring like a bear. You don't remember him being in this room?"

"I do not! I'd have died o' fright if I seen 'im in here."

"What am I to do now?" Joss said, low-voiced, waving a wild arm in the air. "I cannot very well remain in this room in your place without compromising the young lady, and I cannot trust you to stay awake. Something is not as it should be, and I mean to get to the bottom of it, but first we must get through this accursed night. So! Here is what we shall do: You will remain here, and I will camp on the settle outside in the hall—"

"Beggin' your pardon, sir," Grace interrupted. "Ya can't! It'll break your back, that hard old thing!"

"Better than having more harm come to the poor unfortunate girl in that bed." The housekeeper opened her mouth to speak, but his raised hand and rigid posture would brook no opposition. "You're certain you do not recall that man coming into this room?"

"No, sir, I do not!" Grace said, indignant.

"Hmmm. Well, he shan't do it again. Now then, carry on, and call me at once if she comes 'round."

Joss didn't wait for an answer. Stomping past her, he quit the chamber and paced a bit to calm himself before plopping down on the settle. Seldom used, it groaned with his weight. Thirty years ago, a hall boy would have been posted there . . . and then again, maybe not. The Abbey had always lacked servants; there were too many secrets to keep. How he'd managed to keep his own secret from the household was a bona fide miracle. They would all run screaming from the house if they knew the heir to Whitebriar Abbey had the power to shapeshift into the form of a wolf whenever he pleased, not to mention this new development, whatever it was. But that was largely due to the fact that he never stripped off his clothes, streaked through the air, and hit the ground running on the pads of a huge gray wolf. At least, not in front of the servants. Bates was the only one that knew. Bates knew *everything*. How the butler had managed to keep it from his wife was a mystery.

Inspiration struck. Did the faithful butler know what he did not? Had the answer been right there under his nose all the while? A ray of hope. He would wait until the present dilemma was resolved, and then have a nice long talk with Bates. The butler wasn't getting any younger, and if he did know something, he wasn't going to take it to his grave if Joss Hyde-White had anything to say about it.

Dawn was still a ways off, and the sharp edges of those rambling distractions finally dulled. Could no one keep their eyes open in the Abbey tonight?

Joss tried first one position and then another on the hard old settle, until he finally found a bearable one, arms folded, with his long legs stretched out before him and his head cushioned on his shoulder. Trusting Bates to hold the coachman below stairs, and counting upon Grace to at least sleep with one eye open so he could close both of his, he slowly began to unclench his mind and drift away. . . .

CHAPTER THREE

Cora's eyes came open to shadow-steeped semidarkness. The fire had dwindled. The only light was issuing from a candle branch on the nightstand, where the candles had burned down to stubs dripping tallow on the embroidered linen runner. What was that wet, foulsmelling rag doing on her forehead? The liquid from it had dampened her hair and begun to trickle down her neck and into her ear. That must have been what woke her . . . unless it was the rotund woman snoring in the wing chair beside the hearth. Cora slapped the folded scrap of cloth away with her hand, as if it were a creepy crawly spider or worse, and vaulted upright in the gauze-draped sleigh bed. She winced for having grieved the lump on her brow that the poultice had covered, not to mention her aching muscles. Her whole body throbbed with pain.

Where was she? She threw back the counterpane and glanced down at the all but transparent voile nightdress clinging to her body. It was the color of melted butter, and just as soft to the touch, with a neckline that bared her shoulders. Whose was it? Certainly not hers. She brushed the hair out of her eyes. Her amber combs were gone. In their absence, her long chestnut mane fell over her shoulders and arms from a center part, and puddled in her lap. She flung it behind her shoulders and eased her feet over the edge of the mattress to the floor.

Eyeing the sleeping woman across the way, she wondered, *Where have they taken me, and what evil are they plotting now?* She wouldn't be a party to it, whatever was afoot. That resolve summoned strength she never would have believed she possessed, and she surged to her feet, glancing about for some object she could employ as a weapon. This time, she would not be beaten into submission—never again!

Her eyes flashed at once to the hearth and the pokers amassed there. Tiptoeing to the hearthstone, she hefted one. Why was it so heavy? It took all her strength to lift it with both hands. Her whole body was trembling and vertigo starred her vision. She set the poker back in its bracket. Her tiny wrists weren't strong enough to wield it. Anyone could easily wrest it away from her. Staring at it longingly, she sighed. In her present condition it was useless.

Turning back, she glanced about the room again. There had to be something. . . . Yes! She lifted the porcelain pitcher from its bowl on the dry sink and tested it in her hand, assessing its weight. Perfect. She could wield it easily enough to do damage if needs must; at least, whoever happened to be on the receiving end of it would be hard put to escape unscathed. And if it were to break . . . Yes, it would do nicely, indeed.

Wasting no time, Cora padded to the door and lifted the latch. It creaked open a crack. The candles in their sconces, like the ones beside her bed, had burned low, and the hall outside was in semidarkness. Where was this place? Nowhere she had ever been before, that was for certain. Surely not Gretna Green. There wasn't one familiar thing about it. Without hesitation, she floated over the threshold only to pull up short before a tall dark figure rising stiffly from a settle beside the door. Who was he? No one she knew. When he took a step toward her, she uttered a strangled sound and wielded the pitcher. It struck the man hard on the head, making an awful sound, and broke, raining porcelain shards over the corridor floor.

The man swayed, and Cora made a bold attempt to race past him, but several porcelain slivers pierced her feet. She cried out in pain, and again in shock as he captured her with a strong arm wrapped around her waist and hoisted her over his broad shoulder. She fought against his grip.

"Put me down, you great oaf!" she shrilled, beating his back with her fists, kicking whatever she could reach. "Put me *down*, I say!"

"And have you cut your feet to shreds?" he growled. "I think not. You're bleeding already. Hold still! I'm not going to hurt you."

"Where is this place? How have I come here? Who are you?" she rattled on as he gave the porcelain shards a wide berth and carried her back toward the bedchamber she'd just quit. "Where are the others? Ow! You are hurting me, you brute! Put me down, I say!"

"You are hurting yourself, Miss Applegate," he replied. "If you would cease thrashing about, you will come to no harm."

She let loose a shrill, bitter laugh heavy with scorn and unshed tears. *Come to no harm?* she despaired. It was too late for that. But it wasn't going to happen again, and she fought him like a tigress until he burst through the chamber door and literally dumped her on the bed.

"Grace!" he roared.

The housekeeper vaulted erect in her chair, clearing the sleep from her throat.

"Ring for Amy! We need warm water and dressings. She's cut her feet, thanks to your vigilance."

The housekeeper gasped. Both hands flew to her mouth. "You're bleedin' yourself, sir!" she cried. "What's happened to ya?"

He wiped the blood out of his eye, and Cora gasped in spite of herself. She'd given him a nasty scalp wound.

Struggling to a standing position, Grace started shuffling toward the door.

"No!" he barked. "I need you to stay here. Someone must remain with her at all times for propriety's sake. I shan't compromise her."

"Will somebody please tell me who you people are and where I am, sir?" Cora demanded. Glancing down, she realized he could see through the thin nightdress he was staring at, and yanked the counterpane up to her chin.

"Well, my little spitfire," he drawled, wiping more blood from his forehead. "If you hadn't tried to murder me in my own house just now, I'd have introduced myself long ago. "Joselyn . . . *Joss* Hyde-White, at your service, Miss Applegate," he said, with what would have been a heel-clicking bow if he weren't barefooted also. "You are at Whitebriar Abbey, my Cumberland estate . . . at least, it will be mine one day."

Cora stared. He seemed like a gentleman, and he had mentioned not wanting to compromise her, but someone else had said that, hadn't they? And then . . . No, she wouldn't think about that now—*couldn't* think about it. She stared up at him, into eyes that shone like molten silver with a hint of blue steel. He was handsome enough, the blood notwithstanding, tall and well muscled beneath the bottle-green satin dressing gown now stained with crimson splatter. His face was a study in finely chiseled angles and planes that collected shadows about his deep-set eyes, sensuous mouth, and the thumbprint dimple in his chin. A dark mask of stubble was beginning along his jawline, where stiff muscles had started to tick, and his thick dark hair was matted with blood.

He brushed it out of his eyes, examining the blood on his fingers, then threw the counterpane back and reached for her foot. Why was he trembling so all of a sudden? Instinctively she yanked her foot away, and drew them both up, dragging the counterpane up to her chin again.

"I want to see if the cuts are clean," he said. "If there are no slivers in the wounds, it is a simple matter of cleaning and binding them. My housekeeper, Grace here, is an able nurse. She has cared for you since I brought you back yesterday, but she is in her seventies and her eyesight isn't as sharp as it used to be. Mine, however, is infallible. May I?"

Cora gave it thought. Reaching behind, she pulled her long hair in front and draped it over her breasts. Let him see through *that* with those roving eyes. Then, curling her toes defensively and fixing in place what she hoped was her most fearsome glower, she nodded her assent and let him move the counterpane.

How gentle his hands were as he examined her feet. A strange sensation rippled through her at his touch. Making matters worse, his fingers tickled her, and she wiggled her toes. How could she even think of laughing in such a circumstance? He didn't seem to notice. He seemed more interested in the oozing blood than probing for shards. After a moment, she drew her feet up beneath the nightdress, again out of sight and out of his reach.

He replaced the counterpane and stood up, raking his hair back into more blood. His hands were covered with it by the time Amy knocked at the door.

Ignoring the maid's gasp, Joss rattled off instructions that she stoke the dwindling fire, then fetch warm water, some of the cook's healing balm, and bandage linen. That done, he dismissed her, crossed to the window and pulled the draperies aside. The gray streamers of first light were showing no break in the storm. The glare hurt Cora's eyes, and she diverted her gaze. He seemed to be deep in thought, but she wouldn't stand for that. She had too many questions demanding answers.

"How did I come here?" she said. "Where are the others . . . my father? How do you know my name?"

"All in due time, miss," he said, stalking toward the door. "Rest assured that you are perfectly safe in my care. Let my servants minister to you. We shall talk once you've rested."

Joss reeled out of the room and stumbled along the hall in the direction of his chamber. He hadn't taken two steps when he backed up a pace. He'd forgotten about the broken pitcher, and he cursed under his breath as some of the slivers pricked his feet. One by one, he brushed them off, then skirted the rest and staved off toward the sanctuary of his apartments.

What a wildcat! Cheeky little slip of a girl. What could have provoked such a display? Just minutes in each other's company and they were both bloodied. That was another thing: there was no mistaking the strange phenomenon now. The scent of her blood was still with him—on him, in him, mingled with his own. He tasted it on his fingers. How salty-sweet it was, thick and red and heavy with the taste of precious metal. The thrill it gave him rocked his soul. And then there was the physical attraction. Her strange, hostile behavior was part of that. Granted, she had come through a great, nearly fatal ordeal, but something horrendous must have occurred in her life for her to fly at him in such a way without provocation.

There was no denying her beauty—the alabaster skin and large, almond-shaped eyes glazed over and dilated with rage. Oddly, he couldn't recall their color. And her hair! He had never seen the like: thick and lustrous, the color of chestnuts kissed by the sun. How long it was, falling about her like a wavy curtain fringed with tendrils. It had taken all of his willpower to keep from reaching out and stroking it. He'd curbed those urges, however, and stroked it with his eyes instead. She had already wounded him once; if he had done otherwise, considering her demeanor, he would have put himself to the hazard again.

Underneath the compelling scent of blood, his extraordinary sense of smell detected the faint aura of lemon verbena and roses. A soft moan escaped him as the ghost of it threaded through his nostrils. He had reached his suite without realizing it or remembering stomping there. All he saw was her exquisite image in the sleigh bed, with that incredible hair cascading to her waist. He had already seen what lay beneath—what she tried to hide from him—perfect breasts, young and firm, their pink buds stressing the thin voile nightdress. He couldn't help but stare. She was exquisite. Despite the palpable rage in her, the hostile attitude that brooked no room for opposition, Cora Applegate was the most desirable woman he had ever met.

Thinking on that, he burst into his bedchamber and slammed the door behind him, which brought Parker, his valet, shuffling through the door that led to the adjoining chamber. He'd evidently roused the man from bed. Clad in his wrinkled nightshift and plaid dressing gown, Parker was a comical sight, with his mouth agape and his sparse gray hair fanned out about him like a slipped halo, for the top of his head was bald.

"Heaven stone the crows!" the valet exclaimed. "What catastrophe has befallen us, sir?"

"A catastrophe by the name of Miss Cora Applegate, Parker," said Joss.

The valet swallowed audibly, and his scalp shifted. "You'll want a bath," he said, shuffling off. "I shall see to it at once, sir."

Joss crossed the room and pulled back the draperies. The view was just as bleak from his window as it had been from the window in the yellow suite. Blowing snow erased the terrain at the foot of the tor from view. Land and sky were whitewashed so severely that he couldn't detect where one stopped and the other began.

Turning away from the frosted glass, he drew a ragged breath. He would not be able to send the coachman on his way until the snow stopped, and it didn't show signs of letting up any time soon. It didn't matter about the girl, but something about Sikes did not sit well with him. It was ridiculous, of course, but still, the man made him ill at ease, and he would be glad to see the back of him.

No matter what happened, Joss had his work cut out for him. It still remained to tell Miss Cora Applegate that her entire entourage had perished, and horribly. He did not relish that chore. Considering that he'd come away from their meeting bloodied, he shuddered to wonder if he would survive their next interview without broken bones.

But not even that was paramount. He needed answers about the strangeness that kept coming over him. His parents were the key to that, but in their absence, there was Bates. He was anxious to question the butler, but not while the coachman was in residence. It had to be done in secrecy. It had been difficult enough over the years keeping his secret from the rest of the staff, let alone attempting to do it with an outsider of dubious origin underfoot. There was that nagging suspicion again, and again he shrugged it off. Whether he liked it or not, Joss was shackled with two houseguests until Mother Nature decreed otherwise. Deciding to begin preparations with a nice hot bath and a hearty breakfast before he bearded the lioness in her den again, he stalked off toward his dressing room to put that plan into motion.

CHAPTER FOUR

"The young lady did this, did you say, sir?" Parker asked, doctoring the cut on his brow. He clicked his tongue and shook his head, making an attempt to cover the angry-looking gash with Joss's hair. It was to no avail; Joss's hair waved naturally in the opposite direction, and the valet soon threw up his hands in defeat. "Whatever provoked her?"

Joss's eyebrow inched up a notch. "Not I, Parker, I assure you," he said. "Leave it. I shall have to go down as I am."

"Scalp wounds are nasty bleeders, sir," the valet offered. "Take care not to stress the mend. It won't stand opening, else I have to stitch it closed, and that will leave a nasty scar. Even as it is . . ." He clicked his tongue again. "Time was, young ladies of quality *behaved* like ladies. And that is all I have to say in the matter."

Joss suppressed a smile. Over the years, Parker had said much about many matters. Hearing the words that had become his mantra—especially now, when things were so unsettled—put the situation into perspective.

"Don't worry, old boy," he said. "Believe me, I shall keep my distance hereafter."

The valet nodded and said no more, attending to his chores. A quick glance in the cheval glass and Joss was on his way to the breakfast room for fortification before the dreaded interview with Miss Cora Applegate.

What did one say to draw such a person out? She was like a cornered animal—a lioness with sharp, hooked claws poised to pounce. How could he put her mind at ease? Hah! How could he hope to range himself close enough to attempt it?

Such were the thoughts that ruined his breakfast. He was scarcely aware that he'd downed two cups of coffee, and a plate of Cook's best coddled eggs and ham. He asked twice for reassurance that Miss Applegate had been likewise fed, and almost asked again, though he did agree to a third cup of coffee to delay the inevitable. Preoccupied as he was, he was painfully aware that all eyes were directed toward the nasty gashes upon his scalp and brow. Thankful that the servants were well trained to keep their place, he finished his third cup of coffee, and quit the breakfast room.

Outside the yellow suite bedchamber door, he hesitated. He raised and lowered his hand several times before his knuckles addressed the wood. At first, no answer came. *Grace can't still be sleeping,* he thought. The sun had risen hours ago. He rapped again; still no answer. He waited, his hand hovering over the door handle, but only for a moment before he gripped it, turned it, and stepped inside.

A gasp from the bed stopped him in his tracks. His eyes flashed toward the wing chair. It was vacant. Anger flared his nostrils. Why had they left her alone? His first instinct was to close the door behind him. That would be a mistake. Instead, he left it ajar.

Cora vaulted upright in the bed, yanking the counterpane up to her chin. "Do you make it a habit of barging into ladies' bedchambers, sir?" she snapped at him. God, she was beautiful with the snowy dazzle streaming through the window picking out the coppery lights in her chestnut hair. It was painful to gaze upon.

"What have you done with my housekeeper?" he asked.

"Done with?" she said. "I dismissed the poor woman, you tyrant. She was exhausted. I am hardly in need of a nursemaid."

"You can trust me when I say—"

"I trust *no* man, sir," she interrupted, narrowing her almond-shaped eyes. Blue. They were blue. He had wondered about that. How could he not have noticed? They were the color of the bluebells that carpeted the fells in spring.

"—when I say," he went on with raised voice, "that Grace was not stationed here for that. She and Amy, my housemaid, were instructed to stay with you in shifts so that you would not wake alone in a strange place—and for propriety's sake, lest you be . . . compromised."

"Where is Lyda?" she demanded.

"Who?"

"Lyda, my abigail," she said. "It is her function to see that I am not compromised, sir."

Joss's shoulders sagged. They were down to it too soon to suit him. He'd been hoping to make some kind of peace with the girl before breaking bad news. This did not bode well for a favorable first impression. She had already drawn blood, and now as he took a step nearer, he saw her eyes flash in all directions in search of something else she might hurl at him. When she reached for the porcelain basin on the nightstand that had once held the splintered pitcher, he stopped in his tracks.

"Your abigail . . . has not survived, miss," he said. "I had not meant to break the news to you this way. I know you have been through a terrible ordeal, and—"

"You have no idea what it is that I have 'been through,' sir," she snapped. "What of the others—my father . . . the Clements?"

"I'm sorry," Joss said, avoiding her eyes. They were riveting. A man could drown in such eyes, even as they were now, spitting blue fire. God, she was beautiful.

"A-all of them?" she murmured. "How . . . ?"

Joss took a ragged breath. There was no use prolonging the agony. "You were the sole survivor," he said. "I was returning home from London when the storm overtook me, and I came upon your carriage bogged down in the drifts. I frightened off a wild dog that had begun to . . ." He couldn't bear to give a detailed description.

"I prayed so for something to happen to spoil their plans. . . ." Her voice trailed off just as his had done. It was evident that she was thinking out loud. But what was this now? All lost, and not a tear? What sort of woman was this?

"The coachman told me the young gentleman was your betrothed . . . that you were on your way to Gretna Green to be wed. Is that so?"

Her incredible eyes, wreathed with dark lashes, honed in upon him cruelly. "What business is that of yours?" she said. "And where is the coachman? I would have a word with him."

"In time," said Joss. "I have given him lodgings in the servants' quarters until the storm subsides."

"You ought throw him back out in the snow!" she shrilled. "He left us—*left* us there to die!"

"To fetch help."

"Is that what he told you?"

"You haven't answered my question," Joss said. "Were you on your way to be wed?"

"I do not have to answer to you—or anyone anymore," she snapped.

Joss took another step toward her, his expression softened—he hoped. She was frightened. He had not caused her fright, and he was determined that she know he meant her no harm.

Like lightning, she seized the porcelain basin and menaced him with it. "Come one step closer and I will crown you again!" she warned.

Joss held up his hands in defeat. "I do not know what I must do to convince you that I mean you no harm," he said, "or what gave you the idea that you face some sort of threat from me. If I had not brought you here, you would be dead in that coach out there with the rest—"

"They are *still out there?*" she shrilled.

"It is impossible to retrieve the . . . bodies until the storm is over," Joss said. "You are welcome here as long as needs must. I do not know how long that might be. This storm is showing no signs of slacking anytime soon, and the roads are impassable. I shall certainly keep my distance, but we cannot hope to avoid each other altogether. If we are to have peace, a truce is in order, I think. Each time we meet need not end in bloodletting."

She let the basin slip from her fingers onto the counterpane beside her, but she did not replace it on the nightstand. Those incredible almond-shaped eyes were trained on his wounded forehead now. Was that remorse in her bluebell gaze? He wouldn't count upon it.

"You frightened me," she said, in a low murmur. How provocative her lips were when she pouted like that.

"Evidently," he said through a humorless chuckle.

"Well, you did," she returned haughtily, tossing her long mane. "I didn't expect to see someone lurking in the shadows out there."

"I was hardly lurking," Joss defended. "I could not trust Grace to stay awake, and I found your coachman standing over you in that bed when I came up to have her report and see how you were faring."

Cora gasped.

Joss nodded.

"I'm sorry for . . . eh . . ." she said, nodding toward his wounds. "But if you knew what . . . why . . ." She bit her lip and mercifully lowered those magnificent eyes.

"I am a good listener, Miss Applegate."

Cora shook her head wildly. "I hardly know you, sir."

Something I'd like to remedy, Joss thought. He gave a crisp bow instead. "As you wish," he said, "but since I sense something untoward here, I must insist that you not be left alone. You will accept Amy as your abigail while you are my guest. I shall have a cot brought up to your dressing room for her, and she will remain with you until you leave Whitebriar Abbey."

Cora gave a reluctant nod.

"Good! And I must insist that you keep your door locked at night—just as a precaution, until the coachman leaves the Abbey. He claimed that he was concerned for your well-being, and wanted to see for himself because he was responsible for your safe conduct. Well, like it or not, *I* am responsible for you now, since you are under my roof, and I must do my utmost to see that you come to no further harm. How are the cuts on your feet?"

"They are not deep, sir. Your housekeeper has tended them."

"And you have eaten?"

She nodded. "Very well."

He strode to the bellpull and yanked it. "Good," he said. "I've rung for Grace to carry out my wishes. Did you have baggage on that coach? I saw none."

"Two travel bags in the boot."

"I shall retrieve them once the storm is over. In the meantime, you may avail yourself of my mother's things. She and my father are . . . abroad. I'll have Grace bring a selection."

"You needn't go to all that trouble," she said. "I shan't be here long enough to wear them."

"I wouldn't count upon that. North Country storms are hangers on, and often others follow. It may be days—a sennight or longer—before I can dig the coach out of those drifts, and you cannot go about in your night rail, can you?"

"I . . . expect not," she said demurely, eyes lowered. How long and dark her lashes were against that creamy expanse of cheek, splotched now with red patches. His fingers itched to touch her.

"It is settled then."

She nodded. It was a reluctant nod, but a nod nonetheless, and at this point, he would take whatever he could get. There was more that needed to be addressed, however.

"Once your feet are sufficiently mended, I would like

you to join me downstairs for your meals. No, wait! I have valid reasons. It will give Grace and Amy a breather. This house is short staffed, Miss Applegate. My servants will do all in their power to accommodate you, but carrying food trays up and down stairs three times a day will be difficult. Grace is in her seventies, and she suffers from rheumatism. I would take it as a kindness if you would ease her burden. Breakfast and luncheon are served in the breakfast room. Dinner is served in the dining parlor." She made no reply, and he went on quickly. "I must insist that you not prowl the house unattended. The Abbey is old, and much of it is in need of repair. I would not want to see you do yourself a mischief." This, of course, was a half truth. His uneasiness in regard to the coachman and the strangeness that had begun to come over him were at the root of his warning. "There is one more thing," he said. "When you speak with the coachman, I will be present."

She was about to speak, when Grace appeared in the open doorway and made her presence known by clearing her throat.

"Evidently I did not make myself plain earlier, Grace," he said, "when I said Miss Applegate was not to be left unattended."

"I had ta take the tray down, sir," the woman defended.

"Yes, well, see that Jonathan brings a cot up to the dressing room for Amy. She will serve as Miss Applegate's abigail while she is in residence. And in the future, one of you must be at hand here *at all times*. I do not care if the trays pile up to the ceiling. Is that clear?"

"Y-yes, sir," said the housekeeper, her owlish eyes fixed upon his bloodied brow. It looked even worse now that the blood was drying.

"Good!" he responded, turning away. "I shall speak

with Amy. Carry on, and remember: either you or she must be in attendance in this suite at all times."

He quit the room without a backward glance, wondering what had made the Applegate girl so distrustful of men. It had to be something to do with the young knave in the coach on the moor—Clement was the name she had said. Why was there no remorse, no tears at his demise—or her father's either for that matter? Her scent threaded through his nostrils: lemon verbena and roses. It suited her. She was not unlike the rose, velvety soft and fragrant, inviting a man to touch if he dared brave the needle-sharp thorns that kept him at his distance.

There was no denying that Joss was attracted to her, and curious, and possessed of a fierce urge to protect her despite her obvious ability to take care of herself. That, he knew, was a brave front, and if it was the last thing he did, he was going to prove himself worthy of her trust.

CHAPTER FIVE

Puffing on a cheroot, Joss paced before the study hearth. Cora hadn't come down to nuncheon. He hadn't expected that she would; it was too soon. She was justified in being incredulous over one thing—disrespect of the dead. He might not be able to dig the coach out of the drifts in order to move it, but he could certainly fetch the bodies back to the Abbey, where at least they would be safe from desecration at the mercy of wild dogs. There was an old sledge in the stables. He couldn't recall the last time it was put to use. He would take Sikes with him. Aside from needing help with the bodies, he wasn't about to leave Cora Applegate and the coachman alone in the same house with naught but two feeble servants and a simple-minded maid-cum-abigail in attendance.

He yanked the bellpull to summon Bates. When the butler arrived, Joss closed the study door and faced him.

"Bates, have you kept an eye on the coachman as I asked?" he said.

"Aye, sir, I have. A mite talkative, but otherwise he's been no trouble."

"Good. I am taking him with me this afternoon to collect the bodies from the coach on the moor. It should have been done long ago. We need to fetch them before the wild dogs return. One of them is Miss Applegate's father."

"Beggin' your pardon, sir, but you're outta your head goin' way out there in this. It's a regular whiteout. You'll lose your way."

"Trust me not to do that," said Joss. "I'm taking the sledge. I cannot leave Sikes here—not after finding him prowling about the yellow suite right under Grace's nose. Besides, I will need help with the bodies. They will be frozen stiff by now, and likely buried under a mountain of snow in that coach. The door was flung wide. That's how the dog got in that I prevented from savaging her before."

The butler shook his head. "Who'll we send ta fetch you, when ya get bogged down yourself?" he said. "If your father was here—"

"Well, he isn't," Joss said, "and I shan't get lost. What I need from you in my absence is to look sharp, keep the doors bolted shut, and let no one in. *No one*, Bates . . . not even an animal, should one present itself on the doorstep."

The butler swayed as if he'd been struck, and his weathered skin turned as white as the snow frosting the study windows. He seemed to shudder visibly, and Joss took a step toward him.

"Are you unwell, Bates?" he said, reaching out toward the butler.

Bates swallowed audibly. "N-no, sir," he said.

"What then?"

" 'Tis only, what ya said just now, sir . . . Your good father said them same words ta me before he went off abroad before you was born. It gave me the creeps, it did, sir, is all. . . ."

"That reminds me," Joss said, scowling. "We need to talk when I return. I wanted Sikes out of the house before I broached the subject with you, but that may not be possible now. 'Tis about Father, and Mother, too, come down to it. About what happened to them, and what might be happening to me."

"S-sir?"

"Do not play the idiot with me, Bates," Joss warned. "You know exactly what I mean, and my very life could well depend upon it."

"A-aye, sir," the butler said. "I pray not, sir."

"As do I, Bates, as do I. But in their absence, I must have my answers from you."

"As you say, sir."

"Good! Now go and fetch Sikes. Where is he?"

"He's napping, sir."

"*Napping*, at this hour? Well, go and wake him. Tell him to dress warmly and meet me in the stables straightaway."

Bates loped off with a nod and a grunt, dragging his lame leg, clearly glad to escape, and within the hour the sledge was gliding over the snow with Joss at the reins and Sikes bundled head to toe beside him, scowling.

"I don't credit the press," the coachman growled from beneath his muffler. "The dead could stay as they lay until the thaw. They shall have to anyway. What matter if they do so here? It isn't as if we can bury them with all this snow."

"It will be up to Miss Applegate where they are to be buried. Meanwhile, we cannot leave them thus for the dogs to devour. I should have come back for them at once." The coachman passed a grunt, and burrowed down beneath the carriage robe, his eyes shuttered against the stinging snow.

"Bates tells me you were napping. Do you always nap after nuncheon?"

" 'Tis a habit of mine," Sikes drawled. "I'm not at my most powerful during the day—too many night runs."

"Well, I'm sorry to have roused you from your nice warm bed, but it couldn't be helped."

" 'Tis not fit out for man nor beast to rescue the living, let alone the dead," the coachman grumbled.

"I shall turn 'round and take you back, if you like, but you'll wait in the stables until I return." It was a gamble, but there was more than one purpose to this mission. Joss was looking for a reaction. By the look of the coachman's narrowed eyes—like two black obsidians trained upon him with what could only be described as venom—it was plain he was about to succeed.

"Why the stables?" Sikes said.

"Because I've given Bates instructions not to admit anyone in my absence—not *anyone*—'man nor beast,' as you say, unless they are with me."

"Why on earth would you give such a command? You let *me* in readily enough, when I darkened your door."

"So I did," Joss said, raising his voice above the wind. "But that was then and this is now, Sikes. What shall it be . . . do I turn 'round, or press on?" It *was* a dreadful day to be abroad on such a mission; the man's reaction thus far was normal enough, but still . . .

The coachman heaved a blustery sigh. "There's nothing for it now," he complained. "But I still don't see why you need me for this."

"To help me lift the bodies, man. They are surely frozen stiff." Joss urged the horses on with the buggy whip; their stamina had started to flag. "Who else had I to bring? Bates is far too old, and so is Otis, my stabler, and my footman is too frail. We are understaffed at Whitebriar Abbey at present. Besides, it is your coach after all; you should have a hand in its recovery."

The coachman shrugged. "I've written the coach off," he said. "By the time the elements have had their way with it, it shan't be fit for use again."

The drifting snow had changed the face of the landscape so severely Joss was hard pressed to stay on course. Mercifully, the coachman fell silent, though more than once Joss caught him staring at the gash on his brow. His beaver hat didn't quite cover the ragged wound the broken pitcher had made from his scalp to the middle of his forehead over his right eye. The brim of the hat rubbing against the wound had broken it open again, and fresh blood had begun to ooze. The air was so cold he hadn't felt it until the blood threatened his eyebrow.

"Is something amiss?" he asked the coachman, catching him staring.

"Perhaps it is I who should ask that of you, sir," Sikes replied, nodding toward the wound.

Joss wrinkled his brow and looked up, wincing. "Oh, this?" he said. "A piece of crockery fell from a shelf. I didn't step out of the way in time. It's nothing."

"Mmm," the coachman grunted. Burrowing his tall frame deeper in the fur robe, he closed his eyes and said no more.

Half an hour later, a large mound of snow rose up to meet them. The carriage was completely buried. Joss had nearly passed it by, thinking it a boulder. He reined the horses in, tied off the ribbons and nudged the coachman awake.

"We are here," he said, "and there isn't much time. The sun is descending. We will lose the light soon."

The coachman yawned and stretched awake. Joss lifted the shovels from the back of the sledge and thrust one toward Sikes. "Free the boot," he said, "Miss Applegate's traveling bags are inside. Then see if you can open the other door. The coach is filled with snow. It will go faster if we shovel from both sides."

The coachman nodded, and began shoveling snow from the back of the carriage, while Joss began shoveling out the inside of the coach through the wide-flung door. The latch on the boot was frozen shut, and it took several blows of the shovel to crack the ice, and more than one body slam to loosen the crust that had formed around the edge before it opened.

"Which are Miss Applegate's?" the coachman called over the howl of the wind.

Joss stopped shoveling and stared at the man. "You are asking *me*?" he said. "You loaded them, Sikes. How would I know?"

"Yes, yes, of course," the coachman said. "I load so many bags I tend not to notice anymore. They all look alike to me."

"Take them all, then," Joss charged. "Load them in the sledge, and start on that other door. The sun is setting!"

Thanking Divine Providence that he'd thought to bring a carriage lamp, Joss unhooked it from its bracket on the sledge, propped it in the snow nearby and began shoveling like a man possessed. The coachman's shovel thrusts on the other side grew sluggish, and the twilight was overtaking them. Joss called out to the man several times, but Sikes's mumblings grew fewer as time passed, and finally ceased altogether.

"Put your back into it, man!" Joss shouted. "We cannot both shovel from the same side."

"I'm doing my best," the coachman said.

Joss stopped asking. He heard no more shovel thrusts from the other side of the coach, though Sikes's grunts continued for a time. Joss scarcely noticed. He'd cleared the seats, but there were no bodies on them. *They must have fallen back on the floor,* he decided, directing his attention there. Shovelful after shovelful flew over his shoulder. He should be unearthing bodies now. Instead, his shovel scraped the carriage bottom. Frantically he scraped the snow away, exposing the bare wood planking. Tossing the shovel down, he snatched the lantern and thrust it inside. The squabs were still caked with snow, and some still remained in the corners, but the carriage was empty. The bodies were gone.

Joss staggered back from the coach, his eyes wide, the thin layer of remaining snow tinted pink with the blood of the victims that had lain there.

"Sikes!" he hollered. "Leave that and come here!"

Silence.

"Sikes? Damn it, man, wake up! Come and look at this!"

Silence.

Cursing the air blue, Joss plowed through the snow to the other side of the carriage, only to pull up short. Sikes's shovel lay discarded in the snow alongside a pile of clothing still warm from the coachman's body heat. Joss snaked Sikes's long red traveling scarf out of the mix, his head snapping in all directions in search of the coachman. There was no sign of him—not even a footprint. He took a closer look. Animal tracks! A dog? A long plaintive howl lingering on the wind corrected him. No, not a dog; a wolf. He ought to know: It was the same as his own wolf howl.

Cold chills that had nothing to do with the storm raced the length of Joss's spine. *Vampir.* The dreaded word too horrible to speak but in hushed whispers since he was a child—what his mother and father were, and what he feared he was becoming. Sikes was a vampire, and Joss had let him into the Abbey!

His mind reeled back to the night he'd found the coach, to the image of the dog that had savaged the passengers inside—all except Cora Applegate. Only, it wasn't a dog at all, it was a wolf. Could it have been Sikes, and he was still after her? Could that be why he'd been in her apartments?

He had to get back to the Abbey. Suppose Bates were to let Sikes back in? Staving through the drifts, Joss had nearly reached the sledge when a heavy mass of fur and flesh and sinew impacted him from behind, driving him down into a drift. Growling, snapping jaws were trying to get a grip upon his throat, and he rolled on his back in the snow, taking the animal with him in a snarling frenzy that ended with him nose to nose with the creature.

His gloved hands fisted in the wolf's shaggy ruff, holding the beast at arm's distance. But the animal was relentless, pinning him down, its lips curled back, jowls dripping, teeth clacking, clamping shut upon the snow-filled air. Anger roiled in Joss—anger at himself for being duped so easily; anger that he'd let a vampire in, the only way one could gain admittance to a private dwelling. Having sprung from the mating of two vampires turned vampire hunters, how could he have been so naïve? The answer to that was simple: He had never before had occasion to put his heritage to the test. Which harkened back to the fact that he needed answers, and quickly.

The sweaty-tooth wolf's foul breath puffing visibly from flared nostrils nauseated Joss. Steam rose from its drool as its saliva dripped onto his caped greatcoat. All at once he saw the animal through a wavy haze of red, as if the whole world had turned to blood. Then came the rapid heartbeat, the quickening breath, the heavy pressure above his canine teeth as the deadly fangs descended, long and sharp and hollow. There was no urge to feed, only to tear the wolf atop him to pieces.

Over and over they rolled in the snow. The wolf's guttural snarls rang in Joss's ears as if they were coming from an echo chamber. His own fangs were painful now, and he plunged them deep in the wolf's throat— once, twice—tearing fur and flesh and sinew, and drawing blood. The smell of it excited him, though it tasted vile. He spat it out, and plunged the fangs deep again, this time into the wolf's side. Yelping, the animal pulled back and bounded off into the darkness.

Rolling onto his belly, Joss pounded the bloodstained snow with both clenched fists, a frustrated howl leaking from him. It was a brief outburst. After a moment, his head shot up, flashing in all directions. Where had the wolf gone? Its bloody trail seemed to go in circles and then off toward the Abbey.

Sanity was returning. His deadly fangs had receded, and the winter world was white again, not bloodred. Joss scrabbled to his feet and staggered toward the sledge. Climbing the tor would not be half as easy as it had been descending. He had to reach the Abbey before the creature did. Leaping into the sledge, he cracked the whip

over the horse's heads and, thundering a command,
turned them toward home.

Though her feet really weren't damaged too severely to
prevent her, Cora hadn't gone down to the dining parlor for the evening meal; she took a tray in her room instead. It was just as well; she would have felt foolish
dining downstairs alone. Amy had told her Joss and the
coachman had gone off in the sledge to collect the bodies from the coach. That puzzled her. What use would
the coachman be on such a mission? Her host may just
as well have taken Bates.

She padded to the window. Sight of the snow swirling
down depressed her. Would it never cease? She was anxious to be on her way. But where would she go? Her
world, as she knew it, had been turned wrong-end-to
when that coach was bogged down in the snow. She
hadn't thought about it until then.

Pulling the draperies closed, she drew a ragged
breath and padded to the dressing room door. It was
ajar, as Joss had instructed. Amy had gone downstairs
with her dinner tray; Grace was feeling too poorly to
come and fetch it. The dampness had gotten into the
housekeeper's bones, so said Amy, and she couldn't
climb the stairs. Besides, there was some sort of fracas
going on below. The racket filtered up the stairs from
the Great Hall, and the silly chit would have the particulars. It was all right. Cora had bolted the door after her
when she left. She was mildly curious about the commo-
tion, but not enough to dress herself again in order to
find out. Amy had prepared her for bed in the thin
butter-colored nightdress. There was no wrapper, but
there was a paisley shawl, and she'd slipped that over
her shoulders for warmth. She certainly couldn't go

downstairs like this. *He* might have returned, and she hadn't forgotten how hungrily he stared at her in that nightdress before.

Prowling the length of the carpet, she stepped lightly so as not to dislodge the linen strips that bound her feet. The sounds below grew louder, and she crossed to the door and laid her ear against it. Her hand hovered over the door handle. Should she crack it open just a little? What would it hurt? She was just about to do so when a rapid knocking against the wood backed her up a pace. It was about time Amy returned. Now, at least she would find out what all the ruckus was about.

Without hesitation she unlocked the door, but it wasn't Amy who pushed past her, rushing over the threshold; it was a strange man dressed in coachman's garb. She recognized the uniform, the wide-skirted green coat with the large brass buttons, cord knee breeches, and painted top boots. His crimson scarf was sopping wet, as were the rest of his togs. But he wasn't her coachman. Had her strange host sent for another?

"W-who are you, sir?" she shrilled, backing away from him. "You aren't my coachman. Where is Mr. Sikes?"

The man made no reply, advancing. His eyes were like live coals burning into her, holding her gaze relentlessly. She couldn't tear her eyes away from the mesmerizing look. They were transporting her to a place far away—a dark place crimsoned with blood; he was covered with it. The room swam around her as he approached, and she groped for the foot of the sleigh bed for support. This didn't seem real, yet there was no question.

Whoever he was, his presence meant danger. The fine hairs on the back of her neck were standing on end. That feeling she could trust. It took all her strength to resist the man's stare, and even tearing her eyes away from his left her weak, her head spinning. Screaming at the top of her voice, she tore the yards of gauze curtain draped over the sleigh bed, and threw it over the advancing man. Then, screaming again in multiple spasms, she raced through the door she'd left flung wide—right into the cold, wet arms of Joss Hyde-White.

How safe she felt in those arms. That struck her at once, and it shocked her given the circumstances. Perhaps it was the suddenness of the impact that took her guard down. He was soaking wet, his fine woolen greatcoat spongy where she gripped it. He wore no hat, and his dark hair was scattered across his brow, combed by the wind. He smelled of the clean, fresh North Country air. She inhaled deeply, but the indulgence was short lived. Screams from below funneling up the staircase called her back to the urgency of the moment, and she strained against his grip.

"No!" he said, holding her at arm's distance. "Do not go down there. Do not move from this spot."

"The coachman!" she cried. "He . . ."

"I know," he returned, letting her go. "Get behind me, and do not move!"

His hands had scarcely fallen away, leaving her cold in their absence, when a shattering crash brought them both to the threshold of the yellow suite bedchamber door flung wide behind. They reached it in time to see a silvery streak of misplaced energy surge across the room and crash through the window. Glass shards and splintered wood flew in all directions, as the coachman's green coat hurtled through the broken windowpane. But it was something shriveled to a tiny splotch of black against the snow that soared off, sawing through the air to disappear in the snow-swept night.

"Who was that man?" Cora breathed. "What have I just seen?"

Joss's head snapped toward her, his eyes fastened to the blue-black lump on her brow. "Has that knock on the head muddled your memory?" he said. "That was your coachman."

Cora shook her head. "Not *my* coachman, sir," she said. "Mr. Sikes is a much older man, portly, spindly legged, and nearly bald."

Joss gave a start as if she'd struck him. "Then, who . . . ?"

"How would I know?" she said, bristling. "He is your guest, is he not? My coachman left us out in that blizzard to die. He said he was going for help, but no help ever came, and he never returned. He was saving himself. He never intended to return."

"I do not think so," Joss said absently.

"How would you know, sir?" she snapped at him. "Were you there?"

He seemed to snap out of some strange reverie, and took hold of her arm, turning her away from the window. "Come," he said, "you cannot stay here."

Cora wrenched free of his grasp. "Take your hands off my person, sir!" she said. "I mean to know what I just saw." She shuffled closer to the window, but he pulled her back from the shattered glass and debris, including the broken remains of the porcelain basin that had evidently caused the first crash, strewn over the bedchamber floor.

"Have a care!" he said. "You've a penchant for treading upon sharp objects, so it seems. Do you want more wounds to those pretty feet?"

Cora pried his fingers from her forearm. "Let me go!" she shrilled. "I'm not going anywhere until you answer me! Who was that man? Where has he gone? No one could survive such a fall from this height, the snow notwithstanding. What bird just flew out of here? I saw no bird before. Well? I am waiting."

"I do not know who he is," Joss said, raking his hair back from the gash on his brow. "He told me he was your coachman. That is why I let him in and extended my hospitality, giving him shelter from the storm. As to where he's gone, I do not know that either. And that was no bird. It was a bat."

Cora stared. "I do not understand," she said, nonplussed. "How could a man crash through that window and a bat fly off from it? I am not hallucinating, sir. I saw what I saw. Well?"

Screams from below were still traveling upward, and Joss scooped her up in his arms. "Do you hear that racket down there?" he said, stalking through the door and down the corridor. "I've no time to tell you. My butler lies dying below, and I must go to him."

Cora was in no mood to be manhandled. She kicked her feet and pummeled his head and chest with her fists. It stirred his scent, which wafted through her nostrils. The breath of fresh North Country air was now laced with citrus and spice, mysterious and evocative, spiked with his own distinct male essence, heightened from exertion.

"Here! Put me down!" she shrilled. "Where are you taking me?"

"Where you will be safe while I see to the press below. Now, kindly desist! You will come to no harm at my hand else you cause it yourself."

"Hah! Safe, you say, when you do not even know who prowls your halls, sir?"

He set her down inside a chamber whose walls were

painted in the design of a landscape in muted shades of amber on a cream background. Where had her paisley shawl gone? With nothing but the thin nightdress between her nakedness and his eyes, her arms flew in all directions in a vain attempt to hide herself from his view. Making matters worse, a strange elder gentleman shuffled in barefeet from an adjoining chamber. It was beyond endurance. Two pair of eyes were trained upon her: her host's gazing in blatant gawking admiration, the other man's in confused embarrassment. After a moment, the elder man started as if he'd been jabbed with a cattle prod, and pattered to the adjoining dressing room. He returned moments later bearing a silver-gray brocade dressing gown, and offered it. Cora snatched the gown and shrugged it on. It was a mile too large. Her hands disappeared inside the sleeves, and it all but dragged upon the floor. Still, she bore it regally, tugging it closed in front.

"These are my apartments, and this is Parker, my valet," Joss said. Then, to the slack-jawed elder; "Lock the door, and for God's sake keep her here till I return," he commanded. Spinning on his heel, he charged back out into the hall and disappeared.

CHAPTER SIX

Proprieties be damned! It was too late for preserving decorum now. Joss's feet scarcely touched the stairs as he raced below. So many raw emotions riddled him that he could barely walk straight; the arousal straining the seam in his breeches could have something to do with that. Twice now he had held that exquisite body in his arms—felt the softness of Cora's skin, smelled the sweetness of her breath puffing against his, felt the thumping of her heart, this time through the soggy woolen greatcoat. That garment weighed him down now, and he stripped it off and threw it over the banister at the bottom of the landing.

There hadn't been time to take Bates to the servants' quarters below; Joss was too anxious to get to Cora before the coachman could. Instead, they had carried the butler into the salon and made him comfortable on the chaise lounge there. Now Joss evicted Grace, Amy, and Rodgers the footman from their vigil, and bolted the door after them. Blinking back tears, he dropped down on one knee beside the chaise lounge, and tucked the afghan Grace had left there close around the butler's body.

"Why did you let him back in, Bates?" he moaned. "Why did you disobey me? He is *vampir*—an impostor. He is not the young lady's coachman. The real Sikes probably lies dead of exposure, naked in the snow . . . or has become a vampire. Those were his togs the impostor was wearing."

"Y-you left with him, sir," said the butler feebly. "He's been livin' below like one o' us. He said you was right behind him . . . and he was bleedin'."

"Were you . . . bitten? Did he bite you, Bates?" Joss said, his misty eyes flitting over the butler.

Bates shook his head. "No," he said, "I was looking past him . . . for some sign of you. He said you was coming on. When you didn't come . . . I stepped aside to let him enter, and he threw me down. I'm an old man, sir . . . seventy-seven come February . . . too old for sparring . . . too tired . . ."

Tears blurred his image from Joss's view. The beloved old butler had been his friend and protector for as long as he could remember. He couldn't be dying, and it couldn't be his fault. How could he bear it?

Joss's head was swimming with questions. Where were the bodies from the coach? How could he break the news to Cora that they had vanished? Who was the stranger posing as her coachman? Where had he gone? He was vampire, and a shape-shifter as well, with two animal incarnations—the wolf and the bat. How many other shapes did he command? Joss needed answers if he was to fight, and though he was loath to have them at the expense of his butler's last breath, he had no choice but to extract them.

"Is anything broken?" he asked, a close eye upon Bates's contorted features.

The butler shook his head. "Doesn't matter," he murmured. "He's done for me. My old heart's tired, sir. 'Tis my time ta go now."

"Not yet, old friend," Joss said, gripping the butler's shoulder. "Remember that talk we were supposed to have? We need to have it now if I am to fight this here." The butler stared through glazed eyes. "Who am I, Bates?" he said, his voice quavering. "*What* am I?"

The butler stared through rheumy eyes, his blue lips quivering. "Your good parents often wondered what you would be when grown, sir," he said.

"Do you know where they've gone?"

Bates shook his head. "Only . . . why," he said.

"Why, then?"

"They do not age, sir. Neither will you . . . if you are like them. They cannot stay long and watch while their friends and neighbors grow old and they remain the same. If you are like them . . . you will not age either, and one day, you, too, will need to leave your friends and loved ones behind. Talc in the hair, skill with arsenic and kohl—powder and paint can only disguise for a time."

"Is anyone else in the house aware—Grace . . . Parker?"

Again Bates shook his head. "No, sir, not to my knowledge. Only myself," he said. "They trusted me with their secret, your parents . . . and I have failed them."

"You have not failed, Bates. If I know what I am, I can face it, deal with it. It is the uncertainty that cripples me now. I have been able to take the shape of a wolf for as long as I can recall. We used to make a game of it, remember? Now, there is . . . something more. You say the coachman was bleeding." He thumped his chest. "*I* drew his blood with fangs that I could not control."

The butler's eyes slid closed, then came open again, staring vacantly. A thin trickle of blood seeped from the corner of the man's mouth, and he lay still, his glazed eyes staring off into nothingness.

"Bates?" Joss said, jogging the butler's shoulder. "*Bates!* My God, don't leave me now. Not *now.*"

Joss hadn't shed real tears since a child, but he shed them now, for Bates, and for himself left to fend on his own. But there were too many urgencies among the living to grieve long for the dead, and so he closed the butler's eyes. Staggering to his feet, he unbolted the salon door.

Grace entered. Inconsolable, she shuffled to her husband's side, leaning upon Amy's arm until Joss arrested the maid.

"Take her below as soon as you can and stay with her," Joss said. "Have Cook fix her an herbal tisane. She will want to prepare the body, but not until she is calmed." He turned to the footman. "Go out to the stables and fetch Otis," he said. "There's a broken window in the yellow suite that must be boarded up at once. Then one of you go 'round to the village and alert the undertaker."

"Yes, sir."

"Parker will take charge below for the time being," Joss went on, speaking to the footman. "You will have to take his duties now, Rodgers, when I am in need of him in his valet's capacity. We shall all have to wear more than one hat here now. We are understaffed to begin with, and I cannot hire more help until this odd business is resolved. Well, what are you waiting for? Run on and do as I've said."

Without a second glance, Joss stalked back into the hall and scaled the stairs two at a stride. It still remained to deal with Miss Cora Applegate. How much should he tell her? *Hah! How much will she believe? Certainly not the truth entire.* Joss scarcely believed it himself.

He reached his suite, squared his posture and entered to find Cora seated upon a rolled-arm lounge conversing with Parker, who was sitting on the edge of a wing chair opposite in a most awkward attitude, his spine ramrod rigid. "You have naught to fear from young master, miss," the valet was saying. "He is a gentleman of the first order."

"Yes, well, so I have been told of other gentlemen who turned out to be otherwise."

"Perhaps so, but I have served this house for over forty years, and in all that time, I cannot cite one instance in which young master or his father before him ever failed in that respect."

"Yes, well," Joss said, bringing them both to their feet, "you may as well save your breath, Parker. After tonight, the archbishop himself couldn't convince Miss Applegate of that, I fear. Dear lady, you are compromised, and there is nothing for it. My butler has died, and all the other servants are too occupied with the press of that to see to your needs. That duty has fallen to Parker . . . and me."

The valet gave a start, and Cora gasped. "What happened to him?" she said.

"He . . . took a fall," Joss said, choosing his words carefully. It would not be easy to dupe this little spitfire. "He was on in years, and well loved in this household.

He will be sorely missed." As straightforward as he was trying to be, he couldn't keep his voice from quavering.

"I'm . . . sorry," she murmured.

"As a result," Joss went on, "we are at sixes and sevens here now, and will be for some time. You, miss, are snowed in until the roads are passable. They are far from that at present, for which I can vouch, having just been out trying to find them under the snow. It was nearly impossible, even with the sledge. You are welcome, of course, to stay as long as needs must."

"How long do you expect that to be, sir?" Cora snapped.

The gel would benefit from a good spanking, Joss decided, though no trace of that sentiment came through in his speech. "Until Mother Nature permits, and not a second longer," he said. "You are *her* prisoner here, not mine, I assure you. This time of year, one storm often follows on the heels of another here in the North Country. That is what is happening now, I'm afraid. When such occurs, traveling the tor becomes impossible. We shall just have to bide our time."

"So, what is to be done?" she said. "Where is Amy? Am I not to have her now?"

"Amy is needed below," Joss said. "Grace is distraught and unwell besides. She needs Amy's care now else I have two bodies to bury when the snow melts. Amy will return to you once her duties permit. Until then, we must make do, commencing now." He turned to the valet. "Parker, you are needed in the yellow suite to help Otis and Rodgers board up a broken window. I shall remain here with Miss Applegate until you have done so. I will occupy that suite for the rest of her stay, and she will remain here . . . in mine. Proprieties will be observed whenever possible, but when needs must, like now, they will have to be waived. I am sorry, but there it is."

"I shall go at once, sir," said the valet, starting toward the door. He turned at the threshold. "Eh . . . where shall I go afterward, sir?" he said. "I was just about to retire. If young miss is to keep your apartments . . ."

"I have no idea," said Joss. "I shall meet with you in the yellow suite once I've spoken privately with Miss Applegate."

As the valet shuffled off through the wide-flung door, wagging his head, Joss faced Cora, arms akimbo. "Now then," he said, "What am I to do with you?"

"I beg your pardon?"

"I cannot leave you alone, and I cannot stay with you. That presents somewhat of a problem, since at the moment I have no suitable person to look after you properly."

"I am well able to take care of myself, sir," Cora said, tossing her long chestnut mane.

"Not . . . in this," said Joss. "I wasn't entirely truthful with Parker before. We have a serious problem here. I was going to keep it to myself so as not to distress you, but I can see by your very demeanor that it's best that you are made aware. Please sit. There is no need to brace yourself for battle, at least not with me. You look as if you think I have arranged all this just to compromise you, which couldn't be farther from the truth." He swept his arm toward the wing chair. "Please."

Cora sank into the chair, spine rigid, her tiny hands folded in her lap. How beautiful she was, even now, lost in yards of sumptuous brocade, her hands having disappeared inside his dressing gown sleeves in the manner of a Chinese potentate. She presented such a comical image he would have chuckled if the situation weren't so grave. Instead, he went on quickly, while her hands were out of sight and disinclined to hurl some inanimate object at his head again, at least for the moment.

"My butler has not merely died. That coachman has killed him," Joss said.

Cora gasped.

He nodded. "The bounder threw him down on the hard terrazzo floor downstairs. He was an old man, and he died of his injuries. That criminal seems to have his sights set upon you for some reason. Twice now he has gained access to your apartments, and I have no doubt that he will try again. Now do you begin to see the necessity of taking precautions and realize the dilemma I find myself in? I dare not leave you alone, and I have none to tend you. It is personal only in the regard that I have never permitted—nor will I ever permit—a lady to come to harm in my presence, much less my keeping."

"Who was that man?" Cora demanded, "And what does he want with me?"

"That is what I am hoping you can tell me."

"How me? I have never set eyes upon that object before this very night, sir."

"Then I need to know what went on in that coach before it bogged down in the snow . . . and after. I know recalling will be painful, but I beg you to indulge me. Lives could well depend upon the conversation that takes place in these apartments tonight—yours and mine among them."

Cora hesitated, moistening her lips. How he wished she hadn't done that. Since he'd first set eyes upon her he'd been fantasizing about what those pouty lips would feel like beneath his own. The image of his fangs killed that air dream, but not the arousal it caused. He was hard against the seam.

"The painful memory goes back beyond that dreadful day," she said absently, "but you need not be privy to that. . . ."

"As you wish," Joss said. "Whatever you are inclined to impart will be met with the utmost appreciation. I am trying to discover when it was that this man entered your entourage. Are you certain you had not seen him somewhere before—at a coaching inn perhaps, or a changing station?"

Cora hesitated. "My father was most anxious to reach Gretna Green before the snow. We stopped but twice to change horses, trying to outrun the storm. I only left the coach once. No, I don't recall seeing the man."

"The young man in the carriage was your intended, then?"

She nodded.

"And the other gentleman?"

"Clive Clement, Albert's father."

"Both fathers in attendance?" Joss prompted. "Is that usual?"

"No, it is not usual, sir," Cora snapped. "Suffice it to say that they were giving us . . . safe conduct."

"That's rather ironic given the outcome, don't you think?"

"The outcome would have been an answer to prayer, if it had not ended in death, sir."

"I see."

She did not soften. "You do not 'see,' sir, but you do not need to see. It has no bearing upon the situation at hand, and it is personal—something private, the painful details of which I do not choose to share with a virtual stranger. However, if I have come to this pass from observing proprieties, whatever next, alone with you here without them? It seems I have a genuine penchant for being compromised." She surged to her feet. "Oh, pish-posh!" she said. "You may as well have it. I am a ruined woman, sir, through no fault of my own, and proprieties no longer signify except in my mind—though in that quarter I am as pure as the driven snow outside, and mean to stay so. You would do well to take that to heart. I may be only twenty summers, but life has singled me out for knowledge far beyond my years, and taught me how to use it, I assure you, so beware."

Joss's eyebrow inched up a notch. So, it was to be a forced union at Gretna Green? He had surmised such was the case when she'd shown no remorse at news of her betrothed's demise. Was it merely that she had been compromised for the lack of a proper chaperon, or was it something more? He longed to ask: *How ruined?* but thought better of it, recalling his all too recent bout with a certain porcelain pitcher. Instead, he offered a deep, respectful bow, and changed the subject.

"How did you become bogged down in the snow?" he said, aiming for neutral ground.

"The storm worsened," she said, "and I tried to per-suade Father and the others to stop at an inn until it passed over, but they would have none of it, not when we were so close to the border. The drifts grew too deep for the carriage to pass through. The horses were labor-ing, and Mr. Sikes, the real coachman, couldn't see a foot ahead for the blowing snow. Finally, the wheels slowed, then stopped turning altogether. Mr. Sikes was getting the worst of it. He looked like a snowman, and there wasn't room for him to take shelter in the car-riage. Then he saw lights and went off to bring help—so he said. We tried to convince him to unhitch the horses and ride for help, but he said it would be too much trouble to hitch them up again in such a blizzard, and he set out afoot, insisting it was but a short distance. He never returned."

"Who opened the carriage door?"

"Albert did. He had a terror of close confinement. He feared the snow would bury us and prevent the door from opening; only one would open as it was."

"His phobia cost him and the others their lives. That is how the wolf that savaged them got in."

"Wolf, sir? There are no wolves in England any longer. A dog, surely."

Joss hesitated. He hadn't meant to say wolf. Should he throw caution to the winds and tell the whole truth? Not quite yet. It was too soon for that, and with any luck there wouldn't be a need.

"That is what the animal looked like," he said. "The same beast tried to savage me out there just now. How long were you waiting for Sikes to return?"

"Hours, I think. I can't remember. I must have passed out, it's all so vague."

"When I found you, you were at the bottom of a mountain of bodies. I do believe that is what saved you. The press of those bodies kept you from freezing. Those bruises there on your temple . . . and your cheek, are they related to what happened in that carriage?"

Cora shook her head. It was clear that she was becoming uncomfortable. This could be dangerous ground. She looked so forlorn all of a sudden, he wished he could take her in his arms. It was a pleasant fantasy, but not a very practical one.

"You can think of no reason why this man would go to such lengths to gain access to you?" he said, amazed by his composure.

"It makes no sense," she replied. "And you haven't explained what happened in my suite earlier. What I saw was impossible, sir. How do you explain it?"

Joss hesitated. "You will not believe the truth, Miss Applegate, which is why I choose to spare you from it."

He folded his arms across his chest, arresting the hands that itched to reach out and touch her. He was near enough to smell the rosewater drifting from her hair, to see the rise and fall of her breast beneath the silver gray brocade dressing gown. Her scent would be on it when it was returned to him. He could scarcely wait to wrap himself in her essence. What dreams would sleeping naked in that garment bring? He could not remember when a woman had affected him thus.

"I would have it nonetheless, sir," she pressed. "What happened in that room?"

"Very well," he said with a deep nod. "Since you insist, what you saw was a vampire shape-shifting into the form of a bat while crashing through your bedchamber window—a rather strong vampire, since he is able to change clothed and unclothed, a thing that I am given to understand is common only among the very powerful undead." Cora stared. She didn't even blink. All color seemed to roll off her face as though some unseen hand lowered a white shade upon it. It was as if she had turned to stone, and he went on quickly, "Last night, I entered the yellow suite to inquire of your progress from Grace, and I caught Sikes bending over you in your bed while she slouched snoring in the chair. He had mesmerized her. I feared so then but I am certain of it now. If I had not come when I did, he would have taken your blood and made you his consort . . . or worse. I have no doubt in my mind."

"A-are you telling me—"

"I am telling you that it *was* a wolf that savaged your companions. I know, because tonight the imposter shed his clothes, transformed into that very wolf and tried to savage me out on the fells. I fought him off and drove back here like a madman, but I was not in time to save poor Bates. I was in time to save you, but he will return. This entity is relentless."

"I have heard of such," she murmured. "Every now and then there are rumors in Town . . . but I have always thought them tales to frighten children. When Mother was alive, she used to caution me never to go down 'round the docks or enter Whitechapel unescorted for fear of being *taken*, as she put it, but I never took the warnings seriously. It never entered my mind that the threat could be real."

"Well, you can now," said Joss. "I believe this creature attacked your Mr. Sikes, and in wolf form attacked your companions. Then he took your coachman's clothes and came here to finish the job. Unless I miss my guess, when the snow melts Sikes will be found dead in the fells, so do not judge him too harshly for not returning."

"W-where have you put the . . . bodies?" she asked. "They cannot be buried until the snow melts."

Again Joss hesitated. "I do not have the bodies," he said at last. "When we reached the coach, they were gone."

Cora groaned and swayed. She was in his arms before he knew what had happened. This time, though she stiffened, she did not struggle, and he folded her closer, soothing her with gentle hands. Her hair felt like spun silk sifting through his fingers. There was no way to avoid it; it was everywhere, long and thick and fragrant, falling from a middle part like a curtain to her waist. A thrumming in his sex caused alarm bells to go off in his brain. Still he held her, stroking her hair that until now he had only been able to stroke with his eyes. Excruciating ecstasy, until her posture clenched again, so severely she'd begun to tremble.

"You have been hurt," he murmured in her ear. "That is evident, but I am not the one who hurt you. Nor will I ever. There is a very real danger among us, Miss Applegate. I seek only to protect you from it."

"I-if what you say is true, and he could exit so easily, can he not enter as easily, also?"

"Rumor has it that a vampire must first be invited before it can enter, except in the case of a public place. Unfortunately, I did invite him once—in ignorance, as Bates did just now as well. I do not know if that is all that is required, and I dare not take that chance; that bat could have flown back down any vacant chimney in the Abbey."

Cora shuddered again, and Joss swept her up in his arms and carried her through the sitting room door into the adjoining bedchamber. He set her down on the mahogany four-poster bed. Parting from her was physically painful. His sex was on fire—a throbbing, aching threat to his reason. It challenged the seam in his breeches for the second time since he'd returned, despite the stress that would render another impotent, and the teeth-chattering chills his wet togs brought to bear. Overexertion and exhaustion always heightened his libido, but *this* . . . this was beyond bearing. Nonetheless, he tucked the counterpane around her and stepped back, his spine arrow straight. A pity his cutaway frock coat did not cover the obvious; her eyes were drawn there, and there was genuine fright in them.

"If all the servants are occupied elsewhere, perhaps I can be of help also. I could—"

"Ohhh, no," he interrupted. "I want you where I know you are safe. The others have no inkling of what I have just told you, what I fear we are facing. If they were to discover the truth there would be pandemonium here, so I must ask you to keep my confidence."

"But I would be safe with the others, would I not? Otherwise, who is there to stay with me? Wouldn't it be better if . . ."

"*I* will stay with you," Joss said. "I will not let you out of my sight. The others have no inkling that a vampire moves among us. Even if Amy were not needed below, how could I trust you to her care in such a situation? I am the only one who knows the seriousness of what we are dealing with, the only one equipped to deal with it. Now, given that, do you finally see the uselessness of social proprieties?"

Whether she did or she didn't, she made no reply, and he went on quickly, fearful that she might. "What matters here now is hardly the dictates of society," he said, "but rather that we view the impossible as possible for the sake of survival. Given that, we may just have an edge. The power of such creatures lies in our disbelief; it makes us vulnerable. If we could begin with that— regardless if you believe or not—we may just get through what it is we're facing here."

CHAPTER SEVEN

Joss sat, with his head in his hands, upon Parker's cot in the dressing room adjoining his bedchamber. He had told Cora the truth, but not the truth entire. She had taken it well—almost too well. Did she believe? And how well would she take the reality that he himself might well be a vampire, too? He dearly hoped he would never have to find out.

Was she just patronizing him, or had her previous ordeal been so terrible that even the threat of the undead paled before it? Joss might never know. He didn't like the way she had trembled in his arms, as if she were enduring a terrible hardship just to allow him to touch her. Now she was sound asleep on the other side of the tall, gilded dressing room door he'd left ajar between them, exciting his sex even at that distance.

He'd locked her in that dressing room while he went below to check on Grace and instruct Parker, who was now residing in the yellow suite. She'd made no objection. He'd toyed with the idea of confiding in Parker, but decided against it; the valet didn't have a superstitious bone in his body and would surely have thought him mad. As it was, in the valet's eyes his actions were likely suspect, though Joss was certain Parker viewed them as having carnal motivations and chose not to question them. All in all, the situation had come to a satisfactory pass for the present. He had even managed to change his wet togs for a clean shirt, buckskins and hose, with a dry pair of top boots at the ready just in case.

He was exhausted. One last glance through the gap in the door showed him that Cora was sleeping peacefully. No candles or lamps were lit. The only light issued from the blazing hearths in all the master suite rooms, which he had given instructions be kept burning day and night. *No bat is going to fly down these chimneys, by god!*

Finally giving in, he stretched out full length on the valet's cot, and groaned. How did the man sleep on such an inhospitable piece of furniture? Making a mental note to see that the valet had a more comfortable bed to rest his brittle old bones upon in the future, at last Joss fell asleep.

Cora tossed in bed. It was happening again, the dream that wouldn't cease haunting her. She was running through the maze at Clement Hall in Manchester. That wasn't where or how it had really happened, but that was the way of dreams. Some things were just too terrible to remember exactly as they occurred, but her situation was the same and the fear was palpable. She was fleeing from someone in stark terror.

Her rapid heartbeat rose in her throat until she feared her heart would burst from her breast. She was running as fast as she could, but her knees were trembling and he was gaining on her. His breath was fouled with liquor. He'd been drinking, but he was not in his cups. If only he were, she might have escaped him. But there was no escape from the hands that used her cruelly now, from the body that weighted her down . . . from the pain like firebrands searing into her, from the cruel mouth that forced hers open beneath. Again the screams rose in her throat, cut short by the sharp blows to her cheek and temple. Dazed, she gasped then found her voice and screamed again and again—

All at once, strong hands lifted her into stronger arms, pulling her to the edge of consciousness. This wasn't a dream; the nightmare was real! Only, this time her hands were free. She balled them into fists and used them, pummeling her attacker about the head and face and shoulders.

He shook her awake. Through her tears an image took shape. It wasn't the assailant of her nightmare she was attacking, it was Joss Hyde-White. He was sitting on the edge of the bed, attempting to comfort her. She had dropped her guard—let down her defenses, albeit unconsciously—and let him glimpse her vulnerable side, something she'd sworn never to show another man ever.

She slapped his arms away. "What do you think you're doing?" she snapped at him. "Take you hands off me, you clod!"

"You were having a nightmare," Joss defended. "I was trying to wake you without frightening you before you roused the whole house. Everyone's nerves are on edge under this roof now."

She slapped his arms again. "Well, I am awake now, and the nightmare was far less irksome than waking to find you pawing at me, sir. This will not do!"

His hands fell away, and Cora shuddered; a cold fugitive draft rushed at her in their absence. That only made her angrier. There was no denying that his touch comforted her, that it caused strange, frightening sensations both wonderful and terrible, that flagged danger at her very core. This was more terrifying than anything else, and she fought against it with all her strength, both physical and mental. All that had been spoiled for her.

She kicked her feet beneath the counterpane, striking his behind a heavy blow, and he rose with a heaved sigh and tossed several fresh logs into the hearth. Stalking to the window, he parted the portieres. From her vantage, Cora could see that the wind had died off somewhat, though snow still hissed against the panes. The sky had begun to lighten, gray and cheerless. Another sigh escaped him as he turned back to face her, his dilated pupils catching red glints from the fire.

"I must go below," he said. "When I pass through that door, you must bolt it after me, and let none in except those who are familiar to you. Stay here. Do not go prowling about unescorted. That bat could well have come back in through any cold chimney, and we are too few and far away to come to your aid if needs must. Can I trust you not to scream the house down, telling all and sundry that which I confided in you last night?"

"Who would believe it?"

"The women in this household are a superstitious lot. They are distraught already. The last thing needed here now is panic over vampire tales. Can I trust you? Will you at least give me that? I could have left you in that carriage with the rest. I brought you here to save your life, but you don't know a whit about gratitude. If I had meant you harm, it would have happened already. I do not know what demons plague you, miss. I would gladly try to exorcise them if you would let me. Barring that, will you at the least recognize me as your friend, and cease the battery?"

Cora suppressed a giggle of hysteria. What a sight this man was, standing before her in his stocking feet, head bruised and bloodied, fists on his hips, moving stiffly for the "battery," indeed. She was almost ready to melt—until her eyes slid lower, picking out the conspicuous bulge his togs couldn't hide straining the seam of his buckskins. *All men are alike,* she thought dourly. That he made no move to act upon his urges meant nothing. Cora wasn't ready to wrestle with her emotions in that regard, despite that he had aroused her also; she doubted she ever would be.

"Just go," she snapped.

Joss sketched a stiff bow. "I shall get my boots," he said, rubbing his back as he disappeared through the dressing room door.

Tears misted Cora's eyes. She had never felt so alone. She longed for the comfort of those very arms that she had driven away. He had been naught but kind. It was she who had aggressed him, and he had borne it gallantly. Had she happened upon a true gentleman? It didn't matter. Her wounds were still too fresh.

Striding out and toward the bedchamber door, his buckskins tucked inside his boots, Joss turned to her. "Lock this after me," he said.

Cora hesitated. The silvery brocade dressing gown was draped over the arm of the chaise lounge across the way, out of her reach. She wasn't about to get out of bed in that nightgown, inviting his eyes to feast upon her through the thin voile gauze again. Instead, she hugged the counterpane closer, alarmed at the rapid rhythm of her racing heart.

"I could disable the bolt and lock you in myself, you know," he said. "I would rather not, because I want you to feel safe in my care, but I will if needs must in order to ensure that safety."

"Hand me that dressing gown, then," she said, "and kindly avert your eyes."

He did as she bade him, then crossed the threshold, and she didn't hear the clacking of his boot heels receding along the corridor until she'd slid the bolt shut.

Obstinate little spitfire! he thought, jogging down the stairs. Parker met him halfway.

"Sir . . . oh, sir, Vicar Emmerson's come. I put him in the study. I know you told us not to admit anyone, but the vicar? How could we bar him from the house—especially now, with Bates lying dead in the parlor."

Joss raked his hair back roughly. "I suppose it's all right, Parker, but next time come and fetch me first." There was nothing for it. He was going to have to take Parker into his confidence before the valet let the Devil himself into the house. "What brings him to the Abbey at such an hour?" he said. "He couldn't know that Bates has left us."

They had reached the bottom landing, and Parker slowed his pace. "He's come to bring the young lady's abigail, sir. 'Tis a miracle! She's alive! And she's sorely needed here now."

Joss froze in his tracks, spine rigid. Gooseflesh drew his scalp back. "What?" he breathed. "What are you on about? Are you addled? Miss Applegate's abigail is *dead*, Parker. She died in that carriage with the others. I saw her corpse myself!"

"You must have been mistaken, sir, begging your pardon," the valet said. "She's very much alive. Come and see for yourself."

"The study, you say?"

The valet nodded.

"See that a breakfast tray is brought up to Miss Applegate," Joss said, moving past the valet. "Then make yourself available. Wait for me in the yellow suite. We need to talk directly."

The valet sketched a bow and shuffled off, while Joss woodenly descended to the lower landing, trying to envision the abigail's face. Whoever this was that the vicar had brought had to be an imposter, and Parker had let her in.

Joss thought a moment. He couldn't have been mistaken, could he? Slowly the woman's image took shape in his mind. She was a homely sort, slender and dark-haired. He'd seen the stray wisps peeking out from beneath her bonnet, and that unsightly mole sprouting dark hairs above her upper lip. Bursting into the study expecting to expose an imposter, he pulled up short before the very image in his mind. There was no mistake, and cold chills riveted him to the spot.

The vicar and the abigail surged to their feet from the lounge and the wing chair respectively. "Joss," the vicar said, "this is Lyda Bartholomew. Lyda, your host, Joselyn Hyde-White."

The woman curtsied to Joss's bow.

"I've had her at the vicarage," the vicar said. "I'm given to understand that you have her charge here . . . a Miss Cora Applegate. Had I known, I'd have brought her on sooner, before the storm worsened. It was all I could do to coax the sleigh horses up the tor. 'Tis like a sheet of glass out there."

Joss nodded toward the woman, indicating that she sit, and she sank back down in the wing chair from which she'd sprung. "How could you know Miss Applegate was here?" he said, addressing neither directly.

"Your footman made mention of it," said the vicar. "I was at the undertaker's when he came about Bates—dreadfully sorry to hear that he's gone. He will be sorely missed."

Joss slapped his forehead, having forgotten his wound, and winced. Of course! He had totally forgotten sending Rodgers to the village. The whole event, for it was all related, had nearly addled his brain.

"Where have you got him?" the vicar went on seamlessly. "I've brought unction. I can give him a conditional anointing."

"He's laid out on the lounge in the salon until the undertaker brings the coffin and we can set up a proper bier," said Joss absently. He was taking the abigail's measure. Yes, it was she; there was no question. But how could that be? He could have sworn she was dead in that coach.

"Surely you can't be thinking to bury him in *this*?" the vicar said. "The snow is four feet deep if it's an inch, not counting the drifts! The sexton won't put spade to ground in such as this, no matter what I pay him. That's a blizzard out there!"

"No," said Joss. "Once the staff has paid their respects, I shall bring him down and put him in the Hyde-White crypt until we can give him a proper burial."

"Very well, then, while you two become acquainted, I shall see to Bates," the vicar wheezed, shuffling toward the door. He wasn't a young man. Past middle age, and rotund besides, he huffed and puffed when he walked, which was more of a waddle.

"That can wait," Joss said. "Take a seat, Vicar Emmerson. I would hear more of how Miss Bartholomew here came to be at the vicarage, of all places, in this blizzard, as you say."

"Lyda, if ya please, sir," said the abigail. "Bartholomew just takes too long ta say."

Joss nodded. "As you wish," he said. "When I came upon the carriage, there were five passengers. Miss Applegate was the only one still living—or so I thought. I chased off a . . . wild dog that was attacking the bodies. Were you . . . bitten, Lyda?"

"Oh, she was," the vicar interrupted before she could answer. "The missus tended her."

The abigail rubbed her shoulder through her torn cloak. "That she did," she said, " 'Tis healin' right fine, too."

"How did you reach the kirk in such a storm?" Joss said, a close eye upon the abigail's expression. She seemed composed—too composed for his liking. He couldn't credit that he'd been mistaken and left the poor woman to die in that carriage. She'd been dead! How could this be? And yet it was.

Since the strangeness began in him, he had gleaned what knowledge he could on the topic of vampirism. Mulling over that information in his mind now, he tried to remember everything he'd read, and what tidbits his parents had shared over time. It all came flooding back: those bitten by vampires became vampires themselves in varying degrees, depending upon the severity of the "infection." Some were repelled by all things holy. Many could not stand the light of day, while others, though lethargic, like the coachman, could go about during daylight hours, but they could only exercise their greater powers at night. His own parents were such as these. He didn't know the whole of it, only that they had been spared the bloodlust that drives all vampires by a mysterious blood moon ritual they'd learned of through another like them, and fellow vampire hunter, the equally mysterious Gypsy, Milosh, whom they had met in Moldovia. At best, his information was contradictory. There had to be a way to tell for sure. Thus far this woman had passed two critical points. She was able to be abroad in daylight, and she had been staying on holy ground. But still . . .

It was a moment before he realized the woman was answering his question. "Then, when I came to," she was saying, "I heard the dogs howlin'. I was all alone, sir, and I was scared o' them dogs. One o' them had bit me already. I couldn't stay there, so I started to walk toward the lights I saw at the foot o' this hill, and finally come upon the kirk. The good vicar and his wife took me in and tended me. Then they told me young miss was here. Is she safe, sir? Can I see her, please?"

"What happened to the others?" Joss said, avoiding the question. He wasn't prepared to answer it yet. "There were three men in that carriage besides you and your charge when I found it."

" 'Tweren't nobody in it but me when I woke, sir," she said. "They musta wandered off lookin' for help, too— and good riddance, if ya ask me, leavin' me there like that, to say nothin' o' the rest o' their mischief! Bad hats, the lot o' 'em—the poor lass's father, too, God forgive me, 'cause 'twas him what's been payin' my wages, but that don't make him an upstandin' gentleman. Please . . . can I see her, sir, the young miss? I ain't goin' ta rest until I do."

Joss grunted, unconvinced. "In due course, Lyda," he said, turning to the vicar. "Was she seen by the surgeon?" he asked.

The vicar took his arm and led him off toward the corner of the room, out of Lyda's hearing, and spoke in a low whisper. "I had Dr. Everett in," he said. "She ran a high fever. The missus couldn't bring it down. We thought it could be due to exposure, her coming so far in such a storm ill clad for such a trek. We feared pneumonia. Dr. Everett was afraid it might be something . . . more. He fears the dog may have been rabid, but we have no way to be certain without the dog. Others have sighted dogs since the storm as well—big, shaggy, wild-looking animals—and the word has gone out to shoot on sight any four-legged creature that cannot be accounted for among the villagers." Joss started to move away, but the vicar held him back. "As you well know," he went on, "old Everett tends our livestock as well, and he says the animal's bite more closely resembles the bite of a wolf, though there hasn't been a wolf in England for centuries. He has books on such. Could be a cross-breed, something that came over on a vessel from the east. Who is to say? She will have to be watched."

"Have no fear of that," said Joss. He wasn't about to let the woman out of his sight until he was certain she wasn't what he feared she might be. For if she were *vampir*, albeit through no fault of her own, she would have to be dealt with. He knew enough about his sorry predicament to be certain of that. Why hadn't his parents prepared him for such as this? He knew the answer. When the years rolled by and the only manifestation of his level of infection was his ability to shapeshift into the dire wolf, they had evidently decided he knew all he needed to know.

Joss spewed a string of expletives in a low mutter. The vicar heard, and raised his eyebrow. Joss ignored him. The poor man had no knowledge of the situation—that at least two of his parishioners were vampires, and that he very likely stood before a fledgling vampire at that very moment; two, if his suspicions in regard to the abigail were correct. It was just as well he'd brought the woman to the Abbey. Emmerson being a man of the cloth was at the greater risk, since the undead dearly loved to corrupt God's anointed. This Joss knew firsthand, since his father had been ordained to the clergy just before his own nightmare began.

"Is there more?" he asked the vicar, leading him out of earshot. "I need to have it all if there is. We may be dealing with something far more dangerous than rabies here."

The vicar's nonplussed expression told him he had no inkling of what that might mean. Vampire scares had popped up in the village from time to time over the years; this due to the handiwork of a creature called Sebastian Valentin, who'd begun the corruption before Joss was born. It was Sebastian who had infected his parents, who had begun recruitment amongst the *unfortunates* plying their trade around Whitechapel and the docks. His minions and consorts had traveled to the four corners of the country, spreading their disease that came and went in spurts as time passed; all very hush, hush. None dared say the word *vampire* aloud for fear of being rushed off to Bedlam. It had been years since there was an epidemic, and even then it was called by other names: consumption, the bleeding sickness, anything that remotely involved blood. There hadn't been an outbreak since Vicar Emmerson took over the parish. But still the sickness existed: *vampirism.*

As a child at his mother's knee, Joss heard the tales of how she and his brave father had destroyed Sebastian. It was almost a desperate hope, their telling the tale—that saying it would make it so, for after the final confrontation in the Carpathian Mountains, though Sebastian was not seen again, the vampire's bones were never found.

"Nothing more that I can think of," said the vicar, low-voiced. "Look here, you don't seem overly enthusiastic to have the woman join you, after all my trouble carting her up the tor. I should think you would be glad to have her in this understaffed mausoleum. Who is tending Miss Applegate now? Your footman tells me poor old Grace has been taken with a fit of apoplexy since her husband passed, and she's likely to be the next to go. Why, he said—"

"My footman is a blabbermouth," Joss interrupted. So was the vicar, and the last thing he needed was wagging tongues in the village. "He gossips like a woman," he went on. "We are managing splendidly, all things considered, at this difficult time."

"Hmmm," the vicar growled. "Very well then, I'll have that moment with poor Bates and be on my way before this tempest grows worse. The winds died down a bit earlier, but they are worsening again."

Joss watched him waddle off. He yanked the bellpull, his lips twisted in a sardonic grin. *Managing splendidly, indeed!* He almost laughed aloud. Who would come that wouldn't make a liar of him? Amy was tending Grace, Cook had never answered the bells in her life, Parker was awaiting him in the yellow suite . . . which left Rodgers, the footman, whom in that moment Joss would love to strangle for carrying tales. He was glad the vicar had left the study. While he waited, he turned to Lyda.

"So!" he said, folding his arms across his chest. "We are to have you join our household until the roads are passable. Tell me, where will you go when it's fit to travel?"

"Why, to Applegate Manor, in Yorkshire, sir—young miss's home. Our home," she said. "And just so's ya know, I ain't sure what it was bit the others, but 'twas a *dog* what bit me, no wolf. There was more than one four-legged animal roamin' around out there that night. All I want is ta take young miss home so's I can care for her proper."

"I see," said Joss. "Well, that is days off, if not weeks, I'm afraid. Aside from the weather, we must first attempt to find your *dog* and be certain it isn't rabid. In the meanwhile, I will see that your needs and comforts are met at Whitebriar Abbey. I have rung for . . . one of my staff to take you below to freshen up and take nourishment, while I prepare your charge for your arrival. She believes you dead. I would not shock her unnecessarily by having you suddenly appear without first breaking the news gently."

"Yes, sir," she said, visibly disappointed.

"You have no idea what has become of the others in that coach?"

"N-no sir, like I said, they was gone when I come to."

"You were on your way to Gretna Green?"

"Y-yes, sir."

"In such a storm?"

"It wasn't stormin' so when we left the manor, sir," said the abigail.

"Hmmm. What was the press?"

"Oh, I couldn't carry tales, sir," she said, spine stiffening until the wing chair creaked beneath her. "The particulars would be up to young miss ta tell."

"I wish my servants were so disciplined. I did not mean to pry. If I was mistaken about you, I might also have been mistaken about your traveling companions. I do not like surprises, Lyda. If such is the case, and they, too, turn up on my doorstep, I need to know something of the situation, since I do not believe your charge was at all comfortable with it."

"Still, you'll have to have it from young miss, sir," said Lyda unequivocally. "It isn't my place to carry tales. Besides . . . if I did, and they do come, I would have ta answer for it, wouldn't I."

She was afraid. That was obvious. Joss wouldn't press her. He had too many other situations to deal with at present. One of them, Rodgers, the footman, appeared in the study doorway.

"This is Lyda, Rodgers," Joss said. "Take her below, introduce her to the others, and see that she is refreshed and fed and that accommodations are made ready for her." He turned to the abigail. "Cook is a gifted herbalist," he said. "She will make preparations for your wound, but I must insist that you tend it yourself . . . in case of infection, since she handles the food. Now then, you are dismissed. Run on with Rodgers here, and stay below stairs until I summon you."

Lyda sketched a curtsy, but Joss's voice boomed through the study, arresting the footman before she reached the threshold. "Not you, Rodgers, he called out. "I would speak with you here in half an hour. Do be punctual. Carry on."

Three urgent interviews ahead and the morning was wearing on. It was going to be a long day.

CHAPTER EIGHT

Parker was busy hanging some of Joss's things in the armoire when Joss entered the yellow suite; the man was never lazing idle. The valet left the chore, shuffled into the sitting room and took a seat on the lounge as Joss directed. Would that all his servants behaved with such obedience.

"Parker, now that Bates has left us, I'm going to have to . . . expand your duties, at least until I can hire another butler."

"Yes, sir."

Joss cleared his voice and began to pace, his hands clasped behind him. "Not just your physical duties, old boy," he went on. "Bates was privy to certain . . . situations that no one else had knowledge of, situations that I find I must now entrust to you."

"Yes, sir."

"First of all, I have to swear you to secrecy," Joss said. "What I am about to tell you must not go beyond these rooms or we will have a panic. It is not a new situation. It has existed since the year before I was born, so you may rest assured that you are in no danger. If you were going to come to harm from it, you would have done long since. That is not to say that there is no danger, which is why I must make you aware. If you know what we are facing, there will be less chance of you blundering into what could well be a life-threatening situation—just as poor Bates has done, and he *was* aware."

"I beg your pardon, sir," said the valet, "but I believe I already know much of what you wish to confide . . . concerning your good parents . . . and yourself, sir. About the affliction."

Joss stopped in his tracks and stared at Parker, slack jawed. "Bates *told* you?" He was incredulous.

Parker smiled and shook his head. "No, sir, he did not," he said. "And he never knew that I was aware. The servants in a house oftentimes know more of what goes on in it than the master and mistress. Things . . . happen in a house that couldn't happen without the servants. Sometimes, they see or hear things, and sometimes they just *know*."

"Are the others aware as well?" said Joss.

Again the valet shook his head. "The women are too busy—too frivolous to notice, and Rodgers is too jingle-brained. I am not untouched by the . . . infected myself. Not personally, of course, but one killed my grandniece in London fifteen years ago. I am well able to part wheat from chaff, if you take my meaning. If I thought there would be danger, I would have left long ago. Your secret is quite safe with me, sir."

"Well, that you have an understanding of the situation is a load off my mind, at least, Parker, but there is more that I must confide of an immediate nature. Please bear with me. It is not easy, this."

"Yes, sir."

"Knowing as you do, I am surprised at you for going against my orders in regard to admitting folk to the Abbey."

"But the vicar, sir! How could I not admit *him* in such a storm?"

"The vicar has brought with him someone whom I am all but certain has been . . . infected. It is my father's word, that, for lack of a better one, for it is a disease—we have always considered it so."

"Sir?"

"I would be willing to wager my entire inheritance that Lyda Bartholomew has been infected, and you have let her in. Reputedly the only way a vampire may enter a residence is by invitation."

The valet stared.

"That is right," said Joss, answering Parker's shocked silence. "She is now anxious to see her charge—too anxious—and I do not believe Miss Applegate will be safe in her care."

"Oh, sir, I am so dreadfully sorry! H-how can you be sure?"

"I cannot be sure, Parker; that is the problem. It may take a disaster, as if we can bear more, to be sure. Do you begin to see why we are having this interview?"

"Y-yes, sir . . . but what makes you think it . . . that she is a . . . a . . . *vampire?*" He whispered the last.

"Every occupant of that coach except for Miss Applegate was dead, when I reached it. I would stake my life upon it. A wild dog was feeding upon them. I chased it off, only it wasn't a dog, it was a wolf. The coachman you had below stairs was *vampir,* there is no question. He tried twice to attack Miss Applegate, and I watched him shapeshift into the form of a wolf that attacked me when we went to collect the bodies. I believe it was the same wolf that savaged the others."

"He didn't bite you, sir? Please say not!"

"No, he did not, but it was he who crashed through that window you have just boarded up yonder, then shifted into the form of a bat. He could be in this house, or anywhere. Believe me, he is alive."

"Oh, sir, I had no idea. . . ."

"Well, you needs must look sharp now," said Joss. "Miss Applegate was safe while I was standing guard. Once I admit Lyda to her rooms . . . Well, I think you take my meaning."

"Will you make the young miss aware, sir?"

"Yes, but the young miss does not trust me, Parker. I am going now to put the fear of God into Rodgers about his wagging tongue, then I will speak with her. What I need from you is absolute confidence . . . and looking after when I am in my other incarnation, if you take my meaning."

"Yes, sir, I do, and you have my word. If I may be so bold, sir . . . your other incarnation. Is that the extent of your infection?"

"I do not know, Parker. That is why I went to London. I just do not know."

Joss dragged himself back up the staircase after his interview with the next servant on his list, Rodgers. Had his talk with the loose-tongued footman done a whit of good? He had no inkling. It was like conversing with the air. He had never thought the footman simpleminded, but those views were changing. Had he gotten through to the man? Doubtful. He should have sacked him—would have, if he had dared hire another. That he couldn't do—not now, as things were, though he had threatened to do just that if any more tales were carried. Things would just have to stay as they were for now. The most dreaded interview still lay before him, and he was anything but ready for it.

Raking his hair back, he squared his posture, shrugged his shirt into place and ordered his buckskins, then rapped on the door of his suite and waited.

"It is I, Miss Applegate," he said. No answer came. He was just about to knock again, when the sound of the bolt being thrown open on the other side shot him through with an unexpected thrill. He was as giddy as a schoolboy in this woman's presence, as malleable as putty in her hands. The trick was not to let her know it.

The sight of her took his breath away. He'd forgotten that he'd brought her traveling bags back from the coach in the sledge. She had dressed in a wool crepe frock of cornflower blue that precisely matched her eyes. It lacked whatever underpinning ladies employed to make their skirts bloom around them; that had been consigned to the fire with the rest of the things she'd arrived in, but its loss posed no hardship. He'd always believed those who dictated fashion had designed the hoop and such to the sole purpose of keeping men at their distance. The fashions of the day screamed "keep away," as opposed to the soft, slender welcoming flutters of muslin and silk he recalled his mother floating about in so gracefully. No, the lack of underpinnings was no hardship. Cora was exquisite, with her long chestnut hair falling like a curtain about her in silken waves and tendrils. The hairbrush in her hand as she stepped aside to admit him suggested that she was attempting to order it when he knocked. He was glad he had interrupted her toilette. She was breathtaking as she was, like something feral and wild; a nymph of the forest.

He crossed the threshold and closed the door behind him, keeping a close eye upon the potential weapon in her hand.

"Is something amiss?" she said.

"Amiss?"

"You are staring, sir."

"Ahhh! Forgive me," he gushed. "I'd forgotten I brought your bags back from the carriage. That color blue becomes you."

"Have you come to let me out of prison?"

"You are no prisoner here, Miss Applegate," he said dejectedly. "Won't you sit down? There is something we need to discuss, something you'd best be seated to hear."

"I shall have it on my feet, if you please," she said. "Do I appear the shrinking violet to you, sir?"

"Hardly." He frowned. Doing so puckered his scalp, where the wound was still too new to risk taxing, and he winced. "But this is something that stopped me in *my* tracks, and I believe it will affect you more severely."

"Try me."

How gorgeous she was with her eyes snapping like that, flashing blue fire. And where did roses come from in the snow? He breathed her in deeply. Of course it was impossible. What had he to offer her as he was—neither man nor beast?

He gave a deep nod, a close eye again upon the silver hairbrush in her tiny fist. "Do you remember my telling you that your traveling companions were all dead when I found the coach?"

"I do. What of it?"

"And do you also remember that when I returned to fetch the bodies, they were gone?"

"What? Have you found them now? You were afraid I'd swoon at that?"

"Not . . . exactly."

"Well, what then?"

Joss swallowed hard. "The vicar has come," he said. "He has brought your abigail, Lyda Bartholomew, and she is very much alive."

"*Lyda* . . . ali—?" She swayed as if he'd struck her. It was as if her knees had given way. Reaching for her was spontaneous, but when Joss took her in his arms, she raised the hairbrush and began to strike him with it.

"Enough!" he thundered, wresting the brush from her hand. Scooping her up in his arms, he carried her to the bed and sat down upon it. Flipping her over his knees, he raised the brush and paddled her behind. "In my opinion, miss, this is much overdue," he said. "Obstreperous children need correction. Since you put this ugly dent in my head and marked me for life, I have been of the opinion that a sound spanking would benefit you immensely. Hold still, or it will take longer. I like this no better than you do, but believe me it is for your own good! We have a serious situation here that could be life threatening. We need to be allies here now, not enemies. How else am I to make you see it? I have tried kindness, reason, and respect and gotten naught for my pains but battle scars. You have brought this down upon your own head, miss!"

"Stop! Please . . . *stop*," she sobbed.

He gave her one final spank and let her go. He hadn't hurt her body, just her pride, though she scrambled off his lap, tears streaming down her red-splotched cheeks, and backed away from him, rubbing her behind through the blue wool frock. In that moment, despite his exasperation, she was the loveliest creature he had ever seen, and he threw down the brush, surged to his feet and took her in his arms.

This time she did not pummel him with her tiny fists, or drub his shins, or reach for some inanimate object to crown him with. She sobbed her heart dry, her tears soaking his Egyptian cotton shirtfront. His hands soothed her gently, lost in the fragrant fall of hair tumbling over them, which only served to wrench more sobs from her. Perhaps this was just what she needed to exorcise whatever demons she was battling.

After a moment of this heaven, one of her tiny hands came to rest over his thumping heart, and he was undone. Trembling fingers lifted her chin, and he swooped down and took her lips in a hungry kiss, tasting her honey sweetness deeply. As their tongues entwined, he groaned. A similar sound escaped from her throat, more a gasp than a groan that set off a firestorm in his loins. Was he dreaming? No, he tasted the salt of her tears, and his heart leapt as his own eyes misted. What terrible ordeal had she suffered to bring her to such a state? She had aroused him—again! What was she, a sorceress? That notwithstanding, what she needed more than anything was comfort.

To his horror, pressure above his canine teeth began. The fangs! Though he had no desire to use them, they were descending, and he drew his lips away from hers and held her head against his chest, diverting her eyes while he strained, not even knowing how to force the deadly fangs back before she saw them. What if he couldn't? That thought was too terrible to think, and he drove it back. Mercifully, the fangs went with it. Dared he kiss her again? He longed to, but he couldn't chance it. What was he playing at? What could he be thinking? It was hopeless, he'd just proven that, but oh, how he wanted to taste those velvet petal lips again, to feel the soft, malleable pressure of her perfect body molded to his muscled hardness, and the gentle flutter of her heart against his like the wings of a butterfly.

All at once, she strained against his grip and he let her go. A cold draft replaced her body heat, attacking his wet shirt where her tears had soaked it, and he shuddered with her warmth taken from him.

Zeus, what an awkward situation! Should he apologize, or carry on as if it hadn't happened? But it had. There was no getting around it. He had kissed her intimately, and she had let him. Had the brief interlude in the battle they were waging served to bring her out of her shell? He hoped so, because considering what had just happened to him in her arms, he wasn't likely to get another chance to do so. He dared not risk her discovering his terrible secret in such a horrific way.

He walked his fingers through his hair with painstaking control, and cleared his throat. "Miss Applegate, I—"

"No," she interrupted, holding up one hand while slapping what remained of her tears away with the other. "The fault is mine," she murmured. "Please . . . let us just forget it, shall we? Pretend it never happened. I am not myself . . . it is too soon."

"Sometimes . . . when one speaks of a troublesome thing, brings it into the open and faces it, it doesn't seem so terrible. As I've said, I am a good listener, should you ever—"

"Thank you, but no," she said, shaking her head unequivocally. "Please say what you've come to say and leave me in peace, if such a thing can be in this accursed place."

Joss had nearly forgotten what he had come to say; she had so thoroughly bewitched him. In that one wonderful, terrible moment, he wished with all his soul that he hadn't come upon the carriage, that someone else had rescued her. Yet in the same heartbeat, he was jealous of whatever phantom that might have been—a nameless, faceless figment of his imagination! What was happening to him?

He drew a ragged breath. "Your Lyda is below stairs refreshing herself and becoming acquainted with the staff," he said. "I thought that a better plan than presenting her to you without preparing you first. Considering your reaction to the news, I evidently decided rightly."

"It was a shock, is all, after grieving for her among the dead," she murmured. "Other than that, why should such news upset me, sir? Is it not a reason to rejoice?"

"Under ordinary circumstances, it would be, yes," he said. "But these are no ordinary circumstances. She was *dead*, Miss Applegate. I have searched my conscience and my memory, and there is no question. There was no pulse, and she had been bitten by the wolf, which I am certain was the coachman who gained entrance to this house. She is *vampir*. I'd stake my life upon it."

Cora stared. *"Vampir,"* she echoed, clearly doubting all he had told her.

Joss threw wild arms in the air. "Would you wait until she drains your blood for proof?" he said. "That is how you shall have it if I let her enter these apartments. Forgive me, but I did not save you thrice from vampires just to turn you over to one on a silver salver. Do you not see the predicament I'm in?"

"*You* let them in?"

He wagged his head wearily. "My valet did," he said. "I have had to take him into my confidence about my suspicions. He shan't make that mistake again. He is the only one I told, but rest assured, I put the fear of God into the rest, and no one else will enter here, I promise you."

All at once Cora went as white as the snow frosting the windowpane, and Joss gave a lurch. Were they about to have it all over again? He resisted the urge to take her in his arms.

"My God, what is it?" he said. "The snow has more color than you do."

"If . . . if what you say is true . . . if it is, then what of the others? Suppose they turn up on your doorstep as well. Will you admit them? You will! Oh, you will!"

She backed away from him, her hands clamped over her mouth. Her eyes were wild, tear glazed and trembling. She looked for all the world like a frightened doe sighting death down the barrel of a hunter's musket.

She continued: "Even if it isn't true, even if you were mistaken and they weren't dead . . . You are no surgeon; you could have been wrong. If such is the case, they will surely come. Folk in the village know I'm here now." She shook her head wildly, her enchanting blue eyes darkened with raw, palpable fear.

Joss took a step nearer, despite his better judgment.

"Don't you come near me!" she cried. Again, her eyes oscillated about the room—in search of some weapon to prevent him, he had no doubt. "How do you know so much about vampires?" she hurled at him. "Why should I trust you?"

He raised his hands in a gesture of defeat. "Vampires

exist. Remember what you saw, the coachmen! I know the topic is forbidden, not spoken of in polite society, excused away as any number of ailments and afflictions to disguise its true nature—but that does not mean it doesn't exist. My valet's own grandniece was savaged by a vampire fifteen years ago, and my parents . . . are celebrated vampire hunters. They are abroad about the business of that now. *That* is why you should trust me. Pretending that a thing does not exist does not make it so, Miss Applegate. What alarms me is that whether your companions are or aren't infected does not seem to matter to you; you are *that* terrified. Your own father numbers among them. What have they done to you to cause"—he gestured toward her—"this?"

"I do not have to explain myself to you," she snapped, tossing her long chestnut mane. How like a proud thoroughbred she seemed to him then, glazed eyes flashing, ready to rear and strike. He thrilled at the sight. "I insist that you hire a coach for me at once. I have the price of one." She darted toward the vanity and took up a beaded chatelaine purse. Drawing out a fistful of notes, she waved them at him. "See?"

He nodded. "But you could offer the coffers of Croesus and no coachman would venture out in this. No coach can climb the tor."

"Your vicar managed."

"In his sleigh, miss—and beat a path back to his kirk, coattails flying."

"You have a sledge," she persisted. "Take me to the village in that, then, and let me find my own way. You have no right to keep me here! If you do not let me go, I shall go on my own! You say that I am not your prisoner here—prove it!"

Joss's shoulders slouched in defeat. "You are frightened, and you are talking nonsense. Look out that window—look!" he said, steering her toward it. Outside, the wind howled about the pilasters and snow hissed against the panes as though some unseen hand was flinging it. All the world was blinding white, in swirling, wind-driven motion. "I wouldn't turn a dog out in such as this, but there *are* wolves abroad in it—one at least, and it is *vampir*. Do you honestly think I would let you risk yourself?"

"I am not your concern."

"Ohhh, to the contrary, miss," he said. "I did not save your life only to have you throw it away. Like it or not, you are my guest until the tor is navigable and the coaches are running again, so we shall just have to make the best of it. I have my butler's corpse to be respected in the salon, his poor wife, my housekeeper, is on the verge of madness at the loss, and physically ill besides. My help has already admitted one vampire to the Abbey, and I fear they have just let in another. I have quite enough to deal with without your irrational desire to flee. Besides, where would you go? Back to Yorkshire? That would be the first place they'd look."

"That does not concern you," she spat.

"It certainly *does* concern me," he argued. "In saving you, I seem to have opened myself to a vampire invasion. That means everyone under my roof is at risk now because of you."

"Please, I beg you . . . do not let them in!"

"You do not comprehend the graver ill—what am I to do with the one we *already* have let in?" he said. "If my suspicions are correct, her powers will be useless during the day. She will be lethargic, to the point of weakness, unable to infect you. But once the sun sets, she will gain strength. If I leave her in these rooms with you, you will be at risk from dusk to dawn, Miss Applegate."

"Not from Lyda," she sobbed. "She would never harm me. Why, she watched beside my bed for days on end when I was taken with the scarlet fever. Without her tending, I would have died."

He sighed. "A vampire cannot help itself once the bloodlust comes upon it. The craving for blood will overpower any other emotion."

"Well, I am warned," Cora said, her haughtiness returning. It was likely she'd dismissed all he'd told her. "Send her to me and I shall see. I think I have known her long enough to make an assessment. Since you have no proof, I do not see that you have a choice. Besides, you have no one else to see to my needs."

Joss stared long and hard at her. How could he refuse? Though his gut instinct was to evict the abigail—storm or no—suppose he *had* been mistaken? It had been bitter cold with blowing snow, and dark as sin when he came upon that coach. Numb fingers and poor vision in the blowing snow could have deceived him. He did not have proof of her vampirism like he did of Sikes's; that was why he could not act.

After a moment he nodded. "Very well," he said, "but on your own head be it." Stalking to the door, he turned. "Do not touch her wound," he said. "Dr. Everett in the village found it suspect. He thinks the animal may have been rabid. As you know, I believe it to be something far worse. Either way, you mustn't touch the wound. It could infect you." She nodded, and he went on quickly. "Look for signs of lethargy during the day and increased energy after sunset. We already know she can tread upon holy ground, as she has been recuperating at the vicarage. If you have any religious articles, leave them about and see how she reacts to them . . . just in case. Watch for fangs. They will appear over her canine teeth, her eyes will glaze over with a green iridescence and glow red when she is at her most powerful. If this occurs, run as far and as fast as you can. I am right down the hall in the yellow suite. Come to me at once."

Cora nodded, averting her eyes, and turned away from him. Would she take his advice, heed his warning? Only one thing was certain: The interview was over. He stepped into the corridor and closed the door behind him.

CHAPTER NINE

Cora reeled away from the window at the sound of the door clicking shut. She flew to the vanity. Lyda mustn't see her like this, with her face all tear streaked and blotched with red, and her eyes nearly swollen shut. She flitted back to the window and opened it enough to snatch a handful of snow from the sill, then shut it again. It took all her strength to budge it, and even through the tiny opening great clouds of blowing snow blasted the room.

Applying the snow to her swollen eyes, she left it until it melted. It was so cold it actually hurt and did little to reduce the swelling, but there wasn't time for another application. Talc was needed. Thanking the stars that her toiletries were amongst the things her host had brought back from the carriage, Cora lavished the powder on and smoothed her hair back behind her shoulders with a quick sprinkle of rosewater, all save the obstinate tendrils that always wreathed her face. She had no sooner finished when a knock came at the door.

"C-come," she said, her eyes riveted to the door as she

spun. She held her breath as it opened, and Joss handed Lyda over the threshold. Yes, it was Lyda! Her quick intake of breath at sight of the abigail caused a narrowing of Joss's eyes that Cora couldn't miss. Nor did she miss the thrill those quicksilver eyes delivered straight to her core, just as they had when dilated with desire earlier, passion turning them a smoky shade of gunmetal gray. Now they were sending another message altogether, and it stood the fine hairs on end at the nape of her neck and sent cold shivers unrelated to the chill she'd taken opening that window walking up and down her spine. He really did believe he was delivering her into the hands of a vampire. She almost pitied him. Their gazes locked for one heart-stopping moment before he broke eye contact and bowed out, closing the door behind him. That click reverberated through her, undermining her balance as she ran into the abigail's outstretched arms, fresh tears streaming down her carefully powdered cheeks. But it didn't matter anymore; the new tear tracks would cover the earlier ones. Lyda would never know.

"I thought you were dead!" she sobbed, holding the abigail at arm's distance to take her measure. She gasped. "My God, you look dreadful! Are you sure you're all right?"

"I don't think I'm ever goin' ta be warm again," Lyda said. "I don't blame the master o' this fine place thinkin' I was dead. I musta been near frozen stiff out in all that cold. I still don't know how I ever made it ta the village, unless it was sheer fright o' them howlin' dogs. Somethin' just come over me, and I done it."

"The others . . . ?" Cora asked. "What of them?"

Lyda shook her head. "I never seen 'em," she said. "I was all alone when I come to. Good riddance to 'em, that's what I say, leavin' me ta fend all on my own like that." She spat in punctuation. "*That* ta them! Are ya sure you're all right? A dog bit me. Are ya sure ya wasn't bit, too?"

Cora gestured that she hadn't been. "I'm sure," she said. "Come and sit down, Lyda. You look worn to a raveling. There's a cot in the dressing room, and I have your traveling bag. Mr. Hyde-White brought all my luggage from the coach, yours included. You'll have to make up the cot yourself, though. The butler's died, and the house is in sixes and sevens."

"So I gathered," said the abigail. "I've met the staff below. They seem a fine lot, but it's you it does my poor heart good ta see." She embraced Cora again. "I'll do up the cot and all once I've rested. I'm plumb tuckered, Miss Cora, and that's a fact."

Joss lumbered along the corridor to the yellow suite, growing more apprehensive with every heavy step that put distance between him and Cora Applegate. Every instinct in him screamed: *Go back! Don't leave her with that woman! She was dead. Dead! Dead! Dead!*

The only saving grace came in the form of a vision of Cora wielding a porcelain pitcher and a silver hairbrush. Woe betide and heaven help the fool who tangled with Miss Cora Applegate in one of those moods. She was a cheeky little spitfire. That was enough to defend her against him, but was it enough for her to hold her own against a vampire? At least she hadn't wholly denied the possibility of such creatures. She wasn't like so many shallow, self-serving females he'd met, who accredited the affliction as symptoms of other ailments, as if acceptance of the existence of vampires tainted them somehow. There was much to be admired in Miss Cora

Applegate. Still, he dared not get too close. It was one thing for her to accept the possibility of vampires; it was quite something else for her to want to make love with someone who possibly was one.

Joss knew what he needed. If his suspicions were correct about Lyda, Cora would be safe enough now, during the day. Blizzard be damned, nothing but a long-legged run on the fells—in the body of a sleek, fleet-footed dire wolf, with the cold wind cooling the fever in his blood—would put things to rights for him. He burst into the yellow suite where Parker was brushing his greatcoat.

"Leave that," he said, and the valet stopped brushing midstroke. "You're about to have your initiation as my confidant. I need a run on the fells."

"In this?" the valet breathed, incredulous, the greatcoat dragging on the floor as his posture collapsed. "There's a blizzard out there!"

Joss smiled. "You sound just like Bates," he said. "He never could understand that a dire wolf doesn't feel the cold the way a human does."

"What must I do, sir?"

"Not much. I cannot shapeshift clothed . . . well, not conveniently. I will leave my togs where I can find them when I return. There is an entrance below that I have always used for such outings. Bates was aware and saw to it that it was unlocked for my return. Do you know of it?"

"No, sir," said the valet. "Only that you always returned from below stairs."

"A wonder that you never sought it out."

"Oh, I did, sir, but I was never able to find it."

Amused by the valet's guilelessness, Joss threw his head back in the first spurt of real laughter he'd indulged in since returning home. It felt good, but was short-lived. The day was slipping by, and if he was to be back before dark, he had to make haste.

"I thank you for your honesty, old chap," he said, "and for keeping my secret all these years."

"Oh, it wasn't my place to do otherwise, sir."

"Just the same, it is appreciated, and I would have it continue. That is vital. Now, if you will follow me . . ."

Taking up a candle branch, he led the valet down the back stairs, through an archway, along a narrow corridor that ran parallel to the servants' quarters, where the walls and floor were thick with cobwebs and dust. Chambers there, once used for storage, were empty now.

"Back in my great-grandfather's day," he said, "this portion of the Abbey was elegantly furnished and reserved for the servants of guests attending hunting parties here. All that was before your time, Parker—and mine, of course. It's gone to ruin now. I doubt it could ever be refurbished, by the look of it."

"But there is no door, sir," the valet said. "This corridor ends in a solid wall. I know. I've seen it."

"Watch," said Joss. They had nearly reached that point, and he stopped before the last door on the west side of the corridor. Glancing behind to be sure Parker was watching, he depressed a carved circle motif in the center panel. A click was heard, and when he pushed gently on the right side of the door it swiveled open.

Parker gasped.

"Come," Joss said, entering the chamber. It was barren of furniture but for an old four-poster bed, nightstand and chair draped with Holland covers, and an antique candle stand. A large hearth dominated the room, and Joss strode to it. He handed the candle branch to Parker. "Hold it down here," he said, squatting on his haunches inside the vacant hearth. Swiveling a decorated bar at the bottom of the fire wall, he freed the metal back panel and swiveled it as he had the door to the chamber. Parker gasped again as a tunnel was revealed that gradually inclined upward. It was small, too shallow for a man to stand upright in, but just right for a wolf.

"The tunnel rises to the height of the second floor of the Abbey," he explained. "No drifts have ever reached that height, nor are they ever likely to, so there is no need of shoveling."

"But the height, sir—to exit at the second floor!" the valet said. "Is not such a jump dangerous?"

Joss smiled. "My father built this run for me," he said. "He used it also on occasion. It is quite safe. In wolf form I can jump great distances. At the end, there is a leather flap that swings both ways. From the outside it looks like part of the architecture. I have been exiting and entering this way since I was thirteen years old."

"What is my function?" Parker queried.

"As I said, to see that the door to this chamber is not locked when I return," said Joss. "Depressing that circlet will lock as well as unlock it. Also, be sure the exit in this fire wall is not barred when I am out of the house. I will leave my clothes in this chamber when I go, and dress again when I return. I will lock the fire wall and the chamber door before I reenter the house proper, so if you ever find it open, you know that I am still out of the house. And, of course, you needs must simply be aware . . . in case anything untoward should occur."

"Untoward, sir?" said Parker, going white of a sudden.

"My father was once shot in his wolf form," Joss said. "That occurred before this tunnel was built, and, I have

no doubt, was one of the reasons for it. If I am behind-
hand returning, someone needs to know where to look.
That someone, Parker, is now you."

"Y-yes, sir."

"It really entails naught but my announcing to you that
I am to have a run. You do not even need to come down
here . . . unless, well, you know. That you are made aware
is just a precaution. So! You may go back to your duties."

"W-when should I expect you to return, sir?"

"Before dark, ideally," Joss said, "in time for a nice
hot bath before dinner at eight, at the very least."

"Yes, sir."

Joss waved Parker off then, watching from the chamber doorway as the valet shuffled back along the corridor whence they had come, puffed with pride at his new
situation. Content that the man would guard the secret
with his life, Joss turned back, tugged off his boots,
stripped naked, and surged into wolf form.

A quick lunge with his great front paws and a nudge
with his shoulder put him through the fire wall. His extraordinary vision let him see through the velvet blackness as he loped up the tunnel, his nostrils flared with
the scent of mildew, dust and general neglect. Having
reached the leather flap, he forced air through his
snout to clear it of the acrid stench, and burst out onto
the snow-covered ledge. He inhaled the cold, clean air.
It crackled in his nostrils, and tasted spicy-sweet from
the pines hemming the westernmost ridge of the tor.

He scarcely thought about the drop as he leapt from
the ledge and sailed through the air. The snowdrifts
were heaped so high that it wasn't as far a distance as
past runs. Plowing through them, he hit level ground
running on all fours, streaked through the pines beard-
ing the ridge, and bounded down the tor.

The snow was falling softly now. Flakes as big as shillings sifted down on a gentler breeze instead of the bitter wind that had been assailing the Abbey since he'd come home; a sign that the current storm would soon end. The sun made no appearance, but if it could be seen, it would be somewhere midway between zenith and horizon. There wasn't much time. Dusk would too soon swallow the light, and it would grow colder, if such a thing could be.

Running on, Joss scarcely noticed the temperature. But for the visible puffs of white breath coming from his flared nostrils, he would hardly have been aware of it at all. He, like his father before him, loved his wolf incarnation—loved the freedom of streaking through the wood in winter, through the woad field beyond the kirk in spring and summer, and through the black heather on the moors in autumn, when the wind set the stalks clacking and spread the last sweet scent of the dying blooms through air already heady with the aroma of bonfire smoke. It was good to be alive—good to be in tune with nature, to be welcomed by the elements in such a tactile way.

Stopping below at the edge of the moor, he raised his head and howled toward the heavens. It was a deep, guttural exclamation of pure feral maleness, a chest-beating declaration of virility—or would have been if he'd had fists to beat with. The howl lost nothing for lack of them.

Prancing now, he walked out upon the fell, only to stop in his tracks, listening. Another howl answered. An echo? The acoustics were right for it. His ears pricked and, scarcely breathing, he strained for sight or sound of the author. After a moment, the other howl came again, and the hackles shot up along the ridge of Joss's backbone, feathering the great silver ruff about his neck and standing the short hairs on end upon his head. *That was no echo.* It came yet again, and his lips curled back exposing fangs dripping with drool. The howler was not a dog, it was a wolf, and the only wolves he knew of in this domain were *vampir.*

Snarling, Joss followed the sound, slinking into the open. His great paws scarcely made a sound. His keen eyes, trained in the direction of the last howl, were sensitive to the slightest movement, monitoring every swaying tree branch and whorl of snow that turned blue-white as twilight approached. He snarled again. What had been meant to release him from the cares that strung him as tight as a fiddle bow had turned into another stress, its severity twofold. He had to face it, and there was precious little time to do so if he were to return to look after Cora before sunset.

His snarls were involuntary spasms now, rage expanding his barrel chest. All at once he was seeing the landscape before him as if a curtain of blood hung before his eyes. To the south, a tributary of the river Eden snaked lazily through the snowbanks at the edge of a denser forest. It was narrow at this pass, and frozen. He tested it. It probably wouldn't have been firm enough to support the weight of a man, but it seemed solid enough for a wolf, and he trod gingerly, his sharp claws clacking on the ice.

The howl came again, closer now, and he stopped in his tracks. It was an odd feeling, standing upon the frozen stream. The water in motion beneath the groaning ice reverberated through his paw pads like blood pumping through veins. At first he thought his ears deceived him, but the howl came again and there was no question—it wasn't the same wolf! There were two of them, and they were nearly upon him, one approaching from the west, the other from the east. Joss's head snapped back and forth between the sounds. The light was almost gone. There was no time for this.

He'd just crouched to spring onto the far bank of the stream when a hulking mass of muscle, fur, and sinew impacted him hard, driving him down through the ice crust, which gave with the impact. He fell through into frigid water that siphoned off his breath and turned his howl to a screeching whine.

He struggled to throw off the wolf on his back and at the same time scramble up onto the snowdrift that edged the stream. The water wasn't deep enough to drown him. He was a strong swimmer, but the weight of the other wolf on his back made exiting the stream awkward until he rolled over in the water, forcing the hanger-on to lose its grip. Reaching the edge of the bank, he turned like lightning and lunged, sinking his fangs into the attacking wolf's throat.

For a moment, Joss thought he had the edge. The other wolf's moves were awkward at best. They had wrestled out of the water and up the bank, and thus far he had managed to prevent the attacking animal from biting him. His gray fur was frosted with ice, though his blood was boiling with rage. Which one was this: the coachman or one of the others? Fury moved him now. But in losing his concentration, he also lost his balance, and negotiating a deceiving pocket of snow he slipped and went down hard upon his side.

A third wolf appeared, advancing from the west. It seemed to have come out of nowhere, but to Joss's surprise it did not attack him, but rather his aggressor. Leaping through the air, the great white wolf with a silvery streak down its back slammed into both of them, taking down the other wolf.

Gore splashed and spurted in all directions, peppering the twilit snow with blood that looked black in the fading light. Through the racket of snarls, a voice rang in Joss's ears saying: *Get up, young whelp! This is not the only danger in these woods.*

Taken aback, Joss blinked. What was this, a wolf speaking in his mind? *Who are you?* was all he could make his mind reply.

You would like to solve that mystery, eh? said the other. *Well, you'd best help me, then.*

How do I know that you will not turn on me afterward? Joss persisted. *I do not know you.*

Ahhhh, but I know you, young whelp. I knew you before you were born. Hah! I knew your good mother carried you in her womb before she knew it herself!

There is only one who knew that, Joss said, *and you could not be he. He is on the other side of the world.*

Ships sail around the world, young whelp, said the wolf. *But no matter, your parents will vouch for me. Now, let us finish this so we can be about that, hmm?*

Joss joined the foray against his better judgment, and the first wolf soon fell back in the bloodied snow. He and the white wolf stood facing each other, their chests heaving.

The white wolf shook his entire body, ruffling his thick fur, tinted blue in the darkness. *Come,* he said, *It is not safe here.*

I am not going anywhere with you, Joss said. *Besides, I need to see who this is that we have killed.*

Oh, he is not dead, the other said. *He needs staking and decapitating for that, and you cannot do that in wolf form. I would if there were time, but there is not. Now, come!*

Joss cocked his head, studying the other. It was beginning to sink in. How often his parents had spoken of Milosh, the Gypsy who had saved them and who shapeshifted into the form of a snowy-white wolf. Could it really be . . . ?

And why not, young whelp?

Milosh is a vampire-turned-vampire-hunter from Moldovia at the foot of the Austrian Carpathians. What would he be doing here?

The other wolf growled, backing Joss up a pace. *Just like your father,* he said, *a skeptic till the end.*

It was awkward conversing with his mind. Joss had never done it before, and it both thrilled and frightened him. Could the strange wolf be telling the truth?

You will never find out standing here, the other said.

Another howl broke the silence that had fallen over the thicket. Neither Joss nor the other answered, though both their hackles raised at the sound.

That is why I cannot leave until I see who lies here, Joss said of the blood-chilling howl. *There is no time to tell you now, but lives depend upon that knowledge. I have left one that I care about in the hands of someone I believe to be* vampir. *See? He changes!*

And indeed he did. At their feet the savaged wolf began to take human form, and Joss's heart sank like lead in his breast. It was one of the passengers in the carriage lying naked in the snow, one of the older, portly members of Cora's party. If he was infected, chances were better that Lyda was also. His heart nearly stopped at that realization. What he had was five vampires running loose—counting the one at his feet that there was neither time nor means to kill—not to mention the strange white creature standing beside him.

There was no time to lose. He spun on his heels and bounded back toward the Abbey, without a thought of anything but Cora.

CHAPTER TEN

The white wolf growled behind him. *Just like your father! Where are you off to?*

The Abbey, said Joss.

Good! said the other. *Your parents will vouch for me.*

Joss inclined his head toward the tor as they forded the stream. *It is—*

The other interrupted his thoughts. *Oh, I know the way. Your father spoke so often of this place, I've needed no map.*

Well, you won't find my parents in, Joss informed him. *And knowing where the Abbey is isn't a great feat. Any of the locals could have told you.*

The other let loose a strange-sounding titter. *Like this?* he said. *I think not, young whelp.*

Where are your togs? Joss wondered.

On the ship.

Joss stopped in his tracks and faced his strange companion. *You disembarked like that?* He was incredulous.

The wolf snorted. *Let us say that I was in rather a hurry.*

They had just begun to pick up speed again, when shots rang out behind, followed by angry voices, then more shots, and a yelp. Joss spun around. The white wolf had fallen on his knees, high-pitched whines testifying to his pain. It was a shoulder wound that would leave a trail of blood.

Damn and blast! Joss seethed. All at once he remembered the Vicar Emmerson's warning, and he cursed again. *Bloody hell!* His father had made the same mistake before Joss was born. He, too, had been brought down by a hunter's musket. Wherever the hunters were, they had both wolves in their sights, and Joss would surely be next. Then what would become of Cora? It wasn't until that moment that he realized he'd been thinking of her as Cora instead of Miss Applegate. He shook himself. So what? He could think of her however he liked.

Go on without me. The white wolf growled, its voice somewhere between that of man and wolf. *I will only slow you down.*

But Joss was undecided. If this strange wolf was Milosh, as he claimed, Joss needed him now. Of course, if he was just a vampire glamour and he admitted him to the Abbey, he would be letting death itself cross his threshold.

Another wolf howled in the distance, and again the white wolf snorted. *The hunters will not be long diverted by that. If you must risk both our lives deciding, ask me something only Milosh would know.*

Joss thought for a moment and then said, *My mother's animal incarnation . . . what is it?*

The white wolf snorted. *Well done, young whelp. Your lovely mother's first incarnation was a tiny kitten. It evolved twice more from cat to cub before becoming what I assume it still is to this day—a sleek black panther.*

Joss checked his instinct to howl into the night. *Forgive me for doubting,* he said. *It is just that—*

That you are a Hyde-White through and through, Milosh concluded for him.

Are you badly hurt? asked Joss.

A shoulder wound—just a graze, I think. Believe me, I have suffered worse.

Joss scanned their surroundings. The stream was the safest choice, considering Milosh's wound. Joss had also made a mess of the ice crust by fighting with the other animal earlier, and much of the layer had fallen away. *Follow me,* he said. *Stay in the stream until we reach those trees ahead. Our tracks will be less noticeable once inside the wood. When we are close enough, we will make a break for the tor. If the snow keeps falling it will hopefully cover our tracks and the trail of blood you're leaving, but we haven't much time. The storm is soon over.*

Milosh didn't answer. Whether it was the wound or that he felt no more need to talk now that his identity was proven, Joss had no idea. The great white wolf followed silently along the stream, over the bank, and through the wood.

The hunters' shouts grew distant, but Joss took no comfort in that. He wouldn't draw an easy breath until they were back inside Whitebriar Abbey. Glancing behind, he took Milosh's measure. *My father said you taught him how to jump,* he said. *Are you able as you are?*

I will try, came the white wolf's response.

Very well, Joss said. *I would like to say 'rest,' but we dare not, for more than one reason. Stay close, and do as I do.*

Leading the way, Joss bounded over the remaining drifts, streaking through the darkness, depending upon his extraordinary vision as he hoped Milosh was doing. The distant howl of wolves rode the wind that had picked up again, and now and then a gunshot echoed also. The falling snow had ceased by the time they'd climbed the tor. Joss wasted no time leaping up to the second-story ledge and accessing the tunnel. Milosh moved somewhat awkwardly because of his wound, but followed him through the chimney fire wall to the chamber where Joss had left his clothes. Surging to his full height, Joss dressed himself like a man possessed, then turned to Milosh, still in wolf form, lying on his side on the dusty parquetry, chest heaving.

What have they named you, young whelp? Milosh said.

Joselyn, though I prefer Joss, after my paternal grandfather.

They have named you well. It suits you.

Joss strode toward the door. *Wrap yourself in the Holland cover on that bed,* he said. *I will send Parker, my valet, to tend you. He will prepare rooms for you close to mine, and once you're settled, we will talk. Forgive me for running on, but unless I miss my guess, there's a vampire in the house.*

"Make up the fire in the toile suite across the hall," Joss charged Parker. He tossed a suit of clothes on the bed from the selection the valet had transferred to the yellow suite from the master apartment. "Then take those below to the chamber I showed you earlier, and tend my guest that you will find there. He has been shot. I do not think it is serious, but you will be the better judge. The villagers are hunting rabid dogs that do not exist, and maiming the populace." Parker's eyes were wide as saucers, so Joss went on quickly. "Once you've dressed his wound and clothed him, show him to his rooms then wait for me here, and I'll explain."

"Y-yes, sir," Parker stammered, his Adam's apple leaping. "W-will you be wanting a bath before dinner, sir?"

"God knows, Parker. I do not even know if I will be having dinner. Just carry on."

Joss stalked out and went straight to the master suite.

His knees were shaking when he rapped at the door, his heart in his throat when it came open in Lyda's hand. She was beaming as she sketched a curtsy.

"I would have a word with your mistress," he said.

The abigail curtsied again as she stepped aside to let him enter. Cora floated across the threshold from the adjoining bedchamber. She was exquisite in a plum-colored frock with an oval neck edged with lace at the décolleté, her waist-length chestnut hair swept up in a graceful cluster of curls cascading down her back. Tendrils framed her face, and there was color in her cheeks. She took his breath away, and Joss worked his hands in and out of white-knuckled fists against his thighs for want of seizing her in his arms from sheer relief that she was unharmed.

"I would like you to join me in the dining parlor at eight for dinner this evening," he said.

She raked him from head to foot with skeptical eyes. "What has happened to you?" she asked, aghast.

Joss glanced down. He'd dressed so hurriedly that his buckskins were twisted around his legs. They were mushrooming haphazardly from his top boots, and his Egyptian cotton shirt was buttoned askew. He raked wet hair back from his brow and cleared his voice.

"Ahhh, we have another houseguest," he said. "A friend of my parents. There was a difficulty climbing the tor, and my help was required. I got quite drenched, and I dressed hurriedly in order to extend this invitation before you made other arrangements."

"Well, you are too late," Cora said. "It is already arranged that I have dinner on a tray in my rooms, sir."

"What? All dressed up so prettily to dine alone in these dreary old rooms?"

"Oh, she won't be dinin' alone, beggin' your pardon, sir," Lyda put in. "She'll be suppin' with me."

Incredulous, Joss stared at the abigail. "I think not," he said frostily. "Miss Applegate will dine in my rooms with me, and you shall dine below in the servants' hall with the staff. I need a word alone with your charge."

Lyda gasped. "Oh, but that would be highly improper, sir," she said. "I couldn't leave her alone with ya unchaperoned. 'Tisn't done, as I'm sure ya know."

"And how do you suppose we conducted ourselves before you joined us, Lyda?" Joss said, out of patience. "It's far too late to stand on ceremony over proprieties. She was compromised the minute we met, and you, miss, must remember your place."

"Y-yes, sir," Lyda said, her eyes downcast. But it was no demure demeanor; she was angry.

Joss's eyebrow lifted, and he studied her. "Very well, then," he said, yanking the bellpull for the footman. "When Rodgers arrives, have him clear the sideboard in the sitting room for the food, and set up the drop leaf table before the fire with the Chippendale chairs. There will be no 'trays.' We shall dine as we would in the dining parlor . . . only more intimately." Cora's eyes flashed like blue fire, and her lovely lips pursed in an unattractive crimp. "When Rodgers leaves, you are to go with him, Lyda, and remain below stairs until you are summoned. I may have a chore for you later." Then to Cora he added, "I will return once I have managed a more appropriate toilette."

Affecting a heel-clicking bow, he left, not giving them a chance to protest, and poked his head into the toile suite. The fire was blazing in the hearth, but the rooms were empty; Parker and Milosh were apparently still below.

He went to his own camp across the hall to find that Parker had set a steaming tub before the hearth in his dressing room. *Bless the man!* Stripping off his togs, Joss sank into the water fragranced with crushed rosemary and pine tar soap. He inhaled deeply and sank down to the neck, a rapturous moan escaping him, and shut his eyes.

What was he thinking? An intimate dinner for two in his—well, what used to be his—suite, with a wounded vampire-turned-vampire-hunter across the hall, a dead butler laid out in the salon, a housekeeper stricken with a fit of apoplexy, and God only knew how many more vampires taken refuge under his roof, himself included? Madness! He tried to excuse his dinner arrangements as a ploy to keep Lyda away from Cora, but what would he do when the intimate dinner ended and Lyda returned to her charge? This was to be a long night.

On top of it all, the girl was again hostile. He was likely to come away wearing more food than he'd eaten.

He wouldn't examine his motives too closely. Until a determination was made as to whether Lyda Bartholomew was infected or not, he could salve his conscience in that he was protecting Cora from harm. That would justify anything . . . well, almost anything. That her closeness turned his legs to jelly, made him sweat, stammer like a schoolboy, and caused his sex to betray him had nothing to do with the issue at hand . . . or so he told himself. What did matter was the dark legacy with which he was wrestling—a legacy he scarcely believed and didn't understand. Milosh couldn't have come at a better time; perhaps he could shed some light on the subject.

Joss was pondering this when Parker entered. The valet's face was ghost gray, a haggard look about him, from the fringe of his thin silver hair fanned out on end like a slipped halo, to the way he moved with jerky steps, half shuffling, half staggering. Joss's jaw dropped at sight of his valet, and he surged upright in the tub.

"Good God, Parker, what is it?" he said. "Has he died?"

"N-no, sir," the valet replied, taking up a towel from the bureau in anticipation of Joss's rising. That was what made him such a prized servant: he always seemed to anticipate Joss's needs before Joss did. It had been that way when he tended Joss father, too.

The water having grown cold around him, Joss stood and let the old man wrap the towel around him. The valet continued, " 'Tis just a flesh wound, little more than a graze, but a real bleeder. He needs the surgeon, sir . . . but I do not suppose . . ."

"No," Joss said. "We cannot have the surgeon tend him. We shall have to make do with Cook's herbals."

"I thought as much," said the valet. "H-he told me his name, sir . . . and that he was an . . . acquaintance of your good parents. There couldn't be more than one Milosh among them, could there?"

Joss smiled in spite of himself. "So, you've heard the tales, too, have you?"

"I never eavesdropped!" the valet defended. "It is just . . . well, sometimes the master of a house tends to forget that a servant has ears just like everyone else. We are oftentimes mistaken for furniture, sir."

"I see," Joss said. "And you want reassurance, is that it?"

"Is he . . . that is to say, has he been . . ."

"He is as Mother and Father are, Parker," said Joss,

sparing the valet from putting his thoughts into words. "A vampire hunter."

"Then we haven't let in another . . . ?"

"Not one who will cause us harm, Parker," said Joss. "He's one who will help us. I haven't time to go into detail now, but my suspicions are founded. The others in that carriage have been infected—all but Miss Cora, who would have been if I hadn't come on when I did; I am certain of it. Let no one new into the Abbey now. Fetch me at once if someone comes, and see that the others do so as well, but do not tell them why."

"O-of course, sir."

"When your duties are done and you've taken supper, return here and wait for me. I will explain then."

"Very good, sir. Where do you go now? In case someone comes and I need to fetch you."

"To have a word with Milosh," Joss told him. "Then I will dine with Miss Applegate in the master suite. Do not tell the others anything except that a friend of the family from abroad has come calling, and was injured accessing the tor. That is all they need know. Now, then! Help me dress. Oh, and keep a close eye upon Lyda below stairs. I will want your evaluation of her later."

"A-are we going to die, sir?" the valet whispered, helping Joss into his dressing gown.

"Not if I can help it, old boy," Joss said. "Not if I can help it."

CHAPTER ELEVEN

Milosh was seated in a tall wing chair before the fire when Joss entered the toile suite. The enigmatic Gypsy seemed quite at home in the pastoral setting. French country figures and scenes in shades of blue papered the walls, and similar themes threaded through the upholstery. This had been his mother's chamber. At sight of him, Milosh attempted to rise, but Joss motioned him back, taking note of his color, which was pale despite his olive complexion. Sharp, dark eyes took his measure as well. Joss assessed the man to be in his early forties, or thereabouts, ruggedly handsome, with angular features collecting shadows in the firelight, his hair touched with silver at the temples. Joss distinctly recalled his father telling him Milosh sported a handsome mustache. That was the only contradiction; the Gypsy was clean shaven now. Who would have guessed that the man was indeed centuries old? Joss longed to hear his story, but that would have to wait; there was scarcely time to tell his own.

"My valet tells me your wound will soon mend. You

were fortunate. Parker is the next best thing to a surgeon, and we couldn't coax one to come up here from the village in this blizzard."

The Gypsy nodded, his misted obsidian eyes raking Joss from head to toe, seeming to plumb the depths of his very soul. It triggered gooseflesh up and down Joss's spine.

"Is something wrong?" Joss asked, meeting the Gypsy's hypnotic gaze.

"You are so like your father it is . . . disarming," said Milosh. "I could be looking at him, you are that alike."

"Oh," Joss gushed. "I fear you are not at all what I expected. I cut my teeth on tales of your escapades. Somehow, I believed the famous Milosh would be much older."

The Gypsy smiled. "I *am* older," he said. "You see me at the age I was when I was infected. It is the same with your esteemed mother and father as well."

"And . . . me?" Joss asked.

The Gypsy studied him again, and when he spoke, an audible breath delivered the words. "We have to talk, Joss Hyde-White," he said. "In depth."

"Indeed, but not just yet," Joss responded. "I hate to burden you in these circumstances, but your visit could not have come at a better time. I am facing a dilemma that I am not qualified to assess. I'm in hopes that you can help me sort it out. As I told you, lives could well depend upon it, and there is hardly time for me to tell all."

"Speak your piece," said the Gypsy.

Joss briefly told about Cora and the coach, about all that had occurred before they met on the fells. "The wolf we took down out there just now was in fact one of the passengers in that coach," he concluded. "So was

Miss Applegate's abigail, who arrived on my doorstep earlier today. According to her tale, she made her way to the kirk in the valley, where the vicar and his wife have been tending her. She insists it was a dog that bit her. You were shot because the townsfolk have taken up arms believing the animal may be rabid. I believe that to be preposterous. A wolf later disguised as the coachman savaged the others, and that was no mere dog I tangled with in the stream. The abigail was dead when I first saw her in that coach; I'd stake my life upon it. My question is, would you be able to tell me for certain if she is infected? It's true, Miss Applegate needs her. We are short staffed here, but until I'm certain she poses no danger to Miss Applegate I fear to leave them alone together—and that is what will happen if I cannot show just cause to the contrary."

"Is Miss Applegate alone with her now?"

"Yes, but my footman is in and out of my suite also, preparing dinner arrangements. I took the liberty of having a tray brought here for you. I thought that best considering your injury and until I can join you in the dining parlor. Lyda will dine in the servants' hall with the others. Afterward, if I brought her here, could you evaluate the situation before I leave Miss Applegate in her hands?"

The Gypsy thought a moment, his dark eyes narrowed. The look in them was fearsome. "Has she showed any symptoms as yet?"

"Lethargy during the day," said Joss. "But that could be from the ordeal."

Milosh grunted. "You say you are short staffed? Bring her here to me after your meal and let her change the dressing on my wound. Let us see how she reacts to fresh blood."

"Yes!" Joss cried. How was it that he hadn't thought of it? He was about to speak when a knock at the door turned him toward it. "Come!" he said, expecting some new disaster. He was acutely aware of Milosh's eyes studying him, though he didn't look into them directly. There was something powerful in that all-seeing gaze—almost too powerful to bear. The door came open in Rodgers's hand, the footman balancing a dinner tray with the other.

"Ah, Rodgers," he said. "Set it on the trestle table."

The footman obeyed, and Milosh's eyebrow lifted. The covers were raised on the serving dishes, revealing puree of grouse and a healthy serving of hot braised mixed-game pie, braised fennel, and apple compote.

"I hope it's to your taste," said Joss. "This time of year, our gamekeeper provides most of our fare." He cast a warning glance meant to signal the Gypsy to take care what was said in the footman's presence, and Milosh's slow blink replied.

"You spoil me," he said. "I do not know when I've eaten as well."

"Good!" Joss said. "My parents would wish that you had the best I could offer."

"They are well, your parents?"

"They are. I just do not know where they are. Abroad, I expect. I was returning home from the townhouse in London when all this began. I had just missed them there." He nodded toward the food. "You'd best eat that while it's hot."

"Will you not join me?" the Gypsy asked.

"Forgive me," Joss replied, "but I am dining with Miss Applegate. It was arranged before you joined us." He turned to the footman. "Is everything prepared in the master suite?" he asked.

"Yes, sir," Rodgers said.

"Good. Where is Lyda?"

"In the servants' hall, sir."

"Run on then, and keep her there until I ring for her."

The footman bowed out, and Joss turned to the Gypsy. "It's best that nothing is said in the servants' hearing," he said. "Parker is the only one who knows who you are. He knows more than I ever suspected, and never spoke a word of it to anyone in this house in all these years. But still, caution is the watchword."

"Of course."

"I shall spread the word that you are an old friend of my mother and father, come for a visit while you are in England on holiday. It's truth enough, else we have a panic here." He hesitated. "It's good that you've come. As soon as Lyda is dealt with, we need to talk further. There was a reason that I went to London in search of my parents. Barring them, you are the only living soul that might be able to help me."

Cora stared at the virtual banquet the footman had laid out on the sideboard. The delicious smells wafting toward her from the food caused her mouth to water. In spite of herself, she was ravenous. Why hadn't she consented to go down for dinner in the dining parlor? At least that would have been neutral ground. What was her enigmatic host planning? Candlelight gleamed off the wine goblets and silver chafing dishes. The table linens were dazzling, reminding her of the snow outside, and she crossed to the window and peeked through the portieres. All the land as far as the eye could see was draped in pristine white. The snow had stopped falling, and the sickle-shaped moon peeking through dark-rimmed clouds cast an aura of sugary frost over the tor. It looked like a land enchanted. It was hard to believe that violence and death lurked in that innocent winter wonderland, that unspeakable bloodthirsty creatures roamed it. At least that's what Joss Hyde-White would have her believe. Were those tracks in the snow? She leaned closer to the windowpane for a better look, narrowing her eyes against the cold puffs of wind seeping in through the casings, but a knock at the door turned her back around, and she hesitated before pulling the portieres closed and answering.

As she expected, Joss stood on the threshold. He'd changed into an elegant toilette for dinner. How handsome he was in his black cutaway coat and trousers, and his white brocade waistcoat. His dark hair gleamed with rich mahogany lights in the candle glow, and his eyes shone like mercury. He smiled, and dawn broke over her soul.

"I hope you're up for game pie," he said, his voice deep and sensuous. "It's one of Cook's specialties." How was it that this man could say "game pie" as if it were a seduction? Well, it wasn't going to work. It was going to take more than game pie and a dashing toilette to tear down her defenses; her psyche was too bruised.

"You shouldn't have gone to all this trouble," she said, "I'm really not that hungry." The latter was a lie, but she didn't want to appear too eager for his company.

"Nonsense. No one can resist Cook's fare." He held out a chair and invited her to sit. "I shall serve you tonight," he said. "I thought it best that we be alone. I do not want the servants privy to what I'm about to say."

Cora took her seat and waited while he filled her soup plate, and the rich, piquant aroma of puree of grouse teased her nostrils. He then filled his own plate and took his seat across the table.

"Before we begin," he said. "I need your evaluation of Lyda."

Cora shrugged. "Aside from being a bit lethargic, I saw no change in her," she said. "Considering all she has been through, I found that not surprising."

"And . . . when twilight fell?

"Well, she slept most of the day," Cora said. "It would stand to reason that she wake refreshed."

Joss grunted around a swallow of soup. "We shall see. Was there anything else—anything at all? The slightest variance. It may not seem important to you, but believe me, the Devil could well be in the details here."

"Nothing that I could see, except . . ."

"Yes?" he prompted.

"Being so long exposed to the elements must have taken a toll upon her physiognomy. She has lost her color so severely I can actually see the veins beneath her skin."

Joss stared at her, his soup spoon suspended. "You never noticed that about her before?" he said.

"No, never. She is usually ruddy complexioned."

"That is one of the symptoms, Cora."

She set her soup spoon down none too gently. "Pish-posh!" she said. "She was nearly frozen to death out there, and bitten besides. You do not think such an ordeal could alter one?"

"Of course it could," he responded. "But what I am looking for here are specific symptoms, and what you've just described is one of them. So is the lethargy. I shan't depend upon my own opinions, however. We have another houseguest, an old friend of my parents from Moldovia, where such things are commonplace. His name is Milosh, and he is a celebrated vampire hunter. I will have him assess the situation before I commit you to her care."

"I believe you are quite mad, sir," she breathed. "I am not even ready to concede that there is such a thing as a vampire. Oh, I let you go on about it, just to see how far you would take this preposterous farce. And now this intimate dinner? It is easy enough to see where you mean to take this." She surged to her feet and tossed down her serviette. "I will have no part of it, sir."

Joss rose also. "Sit back down in that chair and do me the courtesy to hear me out," he said, his voice like a whip. "I am not going to pretend that I am not attracted to you. I am not even going to pretend that this intimate little dinner wasn't intended to improve our relationship—"

"We have no relationship," she interrupted, tossing her curls in defiance.

"Please let me finish," he persisted. "I am not attempting to seduce you. Someone has hurt you very badly, and you are angry; you have every right to be, but for some reason, you have transferred that anger to me, when all I have done is see to your safety and comfort. I wish to rectify that, because it cannot continue. There is a serious situation playing out, and we need to be allies, not enemies."

Cora gave it thought. She had been hard on him, but that was a defense mechanism. It would be easy to become attracted to Joss Hyde-White. Truth be told, that had already happened. Which presented a whole new spectrum of problems that she wasn't ready to face.

"I fail to see—"

"I had wanted to spare you," Joss cut in. "At least until I was certain exactly what we are facing here. But I see that isn't possible. My other houseguest was in difficulty trying to navigate the tor in the storm, and I went out to help him. A wolf attacked us. All vampires shapeshift. This wolf was not the same wolf that attacked me at the carriage. If they are killed in their animal incarnation, they return to human form. That is what occurred, and it wasn't the coachman that tried to attack you; it was one of the passengers in your coach. We had to leave him there. The village folk are bearing arms. They think rabid dogs are prowling the countryside because of Lyda. Milosh was hit by one of their bullets—"

Cora's gasp interrupted him.

"That's right," Joss said. "Thank God it wasn't serious—a flesh wound. Parker has tended him. There's more, but I shall spare you the details. My point here is that if one of your fellow travelers has been infected, it is very likely that all the others have been also. That includes your Lyda. *Now* do you see why I hesitate to leave you alone with her?"

"The m-man that was killed . . . w-what did he look like?"

"He was an older, gray-haired man, portly and balding. Was that your father, Miss Applegate?"

She shook her head. "No, my father is portly, but he is not balding, and his hair is dark . . . like mine, only slightly silvered at the temples. Clive Clement fits your description."

"Your intended's father?"

Cora nodded. "He was killed, you say?'

"If he were human and hadn't been infected, he would be dead. Unfortunately, he will rise again. He is *vampir* now, and cannot be killed except by driving a stake through his heart followed by decapitation. We had neither the means nor the time to do either out there in that storm, not with armed villagers on the prowl."

Cora stared. He was serious. "And you say that Father, and . . . and . . ." She couldn't put her fear into words.

"Do you finally begin to accept what we are facing here?" Joss asked, nodding. "Can you put your hatred of me aside and spend your energy on the real danger?"

Cora bit her lower lip. He was easily read: he wanted her to say she did not hate him. Of course she didn't, but she wouldn't give him the satisfaction of admitting it. That would only encourage him, which was the last thing she wanted to do. It was best that he think she did hate him. There could be nothing between them, ever. She was ruined. She had nothing to offer a man like Joss Hyde-White.

"What will we do?" she murmured. The soup had grown cold in her plate, and her throat had closed over the prospect of game pie. Joss cleared the soup plates and she called out to him before he could address the pie. "No, none for me. I couldn't eat anything more. I've quite lost my appetite."

"I'm sorry," Joss said. "Cook will be disappointed. This is her favorite company meal. She has never had anyone refuse it before." He laughed. "She won't be fit to live with."

"Oh, well, in that case I suppose I could taste just a little," she conceded, rolling her eyes. He was just too slick for her. She had no argument with Cook, after all.

As if he hadn't heard, he heaped a generous portion of the entrée on her plate and delivered it with a flourish.

"You haven't said what we will do," she reminded him as he set the plate before her and poured wine in her goblet.

Joss filled his own plate and joined her. "You need only keep your eyes open. When we are finished here, Milosh and I will give your abigail a little test. If she passes it, I will return her to you. If she does not . . . well, you need not concern yourself with that. You must trust us to know what's best, Miss Applegate. Trust me when I say that you were extremely fortunate that you were not bitten . . . that I came upon you in time to chase the creature that savaged the others away before it attacked you as well."

Tears welled up in Cora's eyes. She blinked them back furiously. Of course he had saved her life. He must think her a total ingrate. Too many unfamiliar feelings were tugging at her. She relived the comforting warmth of his strong arms around her—longed to feel them again. All at once she could taste the sweetness of his kiss, the gentle pressure of the skilled lips that had all but stopped her heart when they closed over hers—those same lips that now glistened provocatively with wine in the candlelight. The scorching fingers of a blush crept over her cheeks. She didn't need a mirror to know that she had flushed crimson. Her face was on fire.

"More wine?" he asked, holding the bottle above her goblet.

Having already had enough to make her dizzy, Cora shot her hand out to cover the glass before he could pour, and their hands touched briefly, but it was enough to send shock waves coursing through her sex. She drew her hand back as though she'd touched live coals.

"No more for me," she said. "Spirits make me giddy."

Joss laughed. How white and straight his teeth were! He was a handsome devil in his elegant attire, with the candles picking out all the angles and planes in his clean-shaven face. And those quicksilver eyes!

"You can hardly call this excellent wine 'spirits'—too mild," he said.

"Just the same, I shan't indulge," she replied. "If I am to stay awake while you conduct your little test, I need my wits about me."

"More pie . . . some compote?"

"I couldn't eat another bite," said Cora, "And you may tell your cook that I have never tasted game pie as delicious." When he nodded, stalked to the bellpull and tugged it, she said, "Oh, but do not deprive yourself on my account. Please . . . finish your meal."

"If I am to be truthful, I am anxious to get on with the test," he said. "You are tired, I see, and Milosh is surely wanting to rest after being shot."

He didn't return to the table, but went to the window. Frowning, he gazed down at the snow-covered tor, and did as Cora had done before, leaning closer, squinting toward what had to be animal tracks in the courtyard below. What must he be thinking? Were there more wolves afoot?

"Is something amiss?" Cora asked, rising from the table.

"I do not know," he mused. "There are tracks down there. They could be deer tracks, though deer usually leave a more delicate imprint. No matter," he said, closing the portieres again. "I've given orders that none be admitted unless I interview them first."

Cora took a seat on the rolled-arm lounge beside the fire, and tried to draw an easy breath, but her heart was hammering so severely that she feared it would jump from her breast. Could he see it? Could he *hear* it? That pulse echoed in her ears like thunder, and glancing down she watched her bosom heave to the erratic rhythm.

In two strides Joss reached her, took her hands in his and raised her to her feet. If he were to let her go then, she was certain her knees would fail her—and if he didn't let her go at once . . .

"We will sort this out," he murmured. "You have my word."

"This . . . test," Cora said. "What will you do exactly?"

"Vampires cannot resist the lure of fresh blood," he remarked. "We mean to have her change the dressing upon Milosh's wound. If she has been infected, he will know."

"You won't . . . hurt her?"

"One thing you should know of vampires," he said, avoiding the question. "When one is killed—really killed—its soul is saved from damnation. If needs must, you may rest assured that there is peace at the end of what must be done."

Cora swallowed. Her throat felt parched, too parched to speak. Joss hadn't let go of her hands. Instead, he drew her closer, gazing down into her eyes with a smoldering intensity that drove hers away. The blood was racing through her veins. Surely it was the wine. She tensed and was just about to break the spell, when the footman's knock at the door caused them both to lurch.

Joss let her go. "Come!" he said, raking his hair back roughly.

Rodgers entered and stood at attention.

Joss strode to the door. "Where is Lyda?" he asked.

"In the servants' hall havin' her supper, sir."

"Good," said Joss. "Clear all this away, then go below. When she has finished, send her to the toile suite, and have her bring bandage linen and antiseptic."

"Yes, sir," the footman said, stacking the dishes on the silver tray on the sideboard.

Joss turned to Cora from the threshold. "Bear up," he said. "We shall soon know what needs must be done."

She opened her mouth to reply, but he was gone. He had melted into the shadows of the corridor.

CHAPTER TWELVE

Milosh was seated in a wing chair beside the hearth when Joss entered the toile suite. The enigmatic Gypsy's black eyes flashed toward him and cold chills raced along his spine. He could scarcely believe that he was in the company of the legendary Milosh.

The Gypsy was handsome still, for all the horrors he'd endured. Joss had cut his teeth on the tales of Milosh's travels through the ages. He'd thrilled at the jousts with death, the narrow escapes, the unbelievable lore and daring feats of the strange, shapeshifting Gypsy. It was Milosh who had helped his parents through the mysterious blood moon ritual that brought an end to their bloodlust, though they were still *vampir;* nothing could change that. Joss knew the Gypsy would know what he was, how much had been passed on to him in the womb. He was almost afraid to ask.

"Lyda will be here directly," he said. "What must I do?"

The Gypsy studied him. "Observe," he said, "and do not interfere . . . no matter what occurs."

Joss nodded. "What brought you here?" he said. They

hadn't really taken much opportunity to talk, and there were many questions banging about in his brain.

"As you know from your parents, we who are infected do not age. We can only remain in one place for so long before it becomes noticeable, for others age as we do not. Then, we must move on. It was my time to do so."

"And so you came to England?"

Milosh nodded.

Joss gave a chuckle. "You could have picked a kinder season to visit our shores," he said. "North Country winters can be brutal."

Milosh smiled. "Winter in the Carpathians is no better," he observed. "And they know me too well at home now. It will be awhile before I can return . . . though I will one day. All I have ever loved is there."

He had a wistful, faraway look in his hooded Gypsy eyes, and it seemed too sacred to probe. This was a lonely man condemned to live out his eternity as a shadow, wandering on the periphery of life and death, hunted by both man and monster alike, clinging to life yet waiting for the hour that one or the other would put him out of his misery.

"Well, you are welcome to stay as long as you wish," Joss said, breaking the awkward silence. "I'm just sorry my parents aren't here to receive you."

"You do not know where they've gone?"

"No," Joss said. "It could well be as you say, that they have stayed as long as they dare, and have moved on just as you have done. They will send word, then. They may have already done. Surely no mail coaches can get through until the roads are cleared. Of course, they will be devastated to have missed you."

The Gypsy smiled again, wistfully this time. "You are so like your father," he said yet again, "it is as if he is here with us." He laughed outright. "And it is just as well that your mother is absent. I was quite smitten with her, you know. Oh, she never knew, nor did your father. I am quite the professional martyr. But I was as enamored as a schoolboy. She was the most beautiful creature I had seen in centuries. Alas, she had eyes only for your father."

Joss didn't know how to respond. "I went to London seeking answers to my own . . . situation," he said, shifting the subject. "Father and Mother thought my being able to take the form of a wolf was the extent of my infection, as it were. But there is more. Milosh, I need to find myself in all this. I cannot get on with my life until I do. Perhaps you can help me sort it all out—not now, of course . . . one coil at a time, eh?"

Milosh frowned. "You say there is more?" he said. "How so?"

Joss opened his mouth to reply, but a knock at the door turned him toward it instead, and he strode to answer.

Lyda appeared on the threshold, bearing a tray laden with a length of bandage linen, a bottle of antiseptic, and a basin of warm water. Joss took it from her and set it on the gateleg table near Milosh's wing chair. *Not a minute too soon by the look of her,* he decided, taking in her incredulous gaze oscillating between them. She had almost dropped the tray as it was.

"I thought 'twas you what needed doctorin', sir," she said. "I didn't know you had another guest."

"This is Milosh," Joss said. "A very dear friend of the family, come for a visit. He was injured climbing the tor. Parker tended him when he arrived earlier, but the dressing wants changing. The wound isn't deep, but there is much blood."

"Y-yes, sir," said Lyda.

Milosh stood, opened his shirt and stripped it off. His braces were already hanging down, since positioning them would have grieved the wound. Resuming his seat, he settled back, a close eye upon the abigail.

Joss was watching her closely as well. She was trembling as she unbound the dressing; fresh blood had stained the linen, and her eyes were riveted to it.

"Do not say you will faint at the sight of blood," Joss said, aiming for levity.

Lyda seemed not to hear, and he used the time to study her complexion. It was as Cora had said. Her skin was milk white, the blue veins showing through in a crazed network of spiderweb-like traceries. Cold chills gripped him, watching Milosh as Lyda discarded the bandage, hovering over the oozing wound beneath. Without taking her eyes from the blood, she reached for the bottle of antiseptic, and it crashed to the floor, its contents bleeding in a slow ragged circle toward the hearthstone.

"Noooo," Lyda wailed. "I'm sorry, sir, I . . . I can't. 'Tis like ya said, the sight o' blood has always made me queasy since I was a little girl. I'm goin' ta faint!" She covered her mouth with her hands, uttered a strangled sound and fled the room, leaving the door flung wide behind her.

Joss streaked after her in time to see the abigail disappear through the servants' door on the landing, her wails living after her.

He went back and closed the door after him. "What do you make of that?" he asked the Gypsy.

"I will need more proof," Milosh said. "It could be as she says, that she cannot stand the sight of blood. Many suffer from this. It could also be that she is newly infected and confused. She certainly has the coloring. I have been doing this for a long time. My gut instinct? She is *vampir*. She may not know it yet. We shall have to watch her closely in the coming days. Where has she gone?"

"Below stairs, to the servants' quarters."

Milosh took up his shirt and began to shrug it on.

"Wait," Joss said, taking up the bandage linen. "Let me bind that." Tearing off a length, he wound it around the wound, secured it in place, and helped the Gypsy ease his shirt back on.

Milosh sank back in his chair and lowered his eyes, pressing his thumb and forefinger against the bridge of his nose. Joss took his measure. Were those tears seeping from beneath his fingers? *Yes.* The Gypsy's jaw muscles had begun to tick, and his lips had formed a thin, crimped line. When he glanced up, the stricken look in his misted eyes was so devastated that Joss sank down on the edge of the lounge.

"What is it?" he asked, almost afraid of the answer.

"We haven't had a chance to talk about your . . . situation yet," Milosh said, clearly striving for composure. "I haven't only been watching Lyda. I was also watching you. Whatever your concerns, young whelp, you are *not undead*—at least not yet. Not *vampir* in the conventional sense. If you'd had the bloodlust, you would not have been able to dress my wound as you just did without reacting. I do not know what I would have done if you were. You see, my wife and unborn child were infected centuries ago, though it hardly seems that long. I believe that is because I am so haunted by the memory that it was I who had to kill them in order to save their souls."

"You had to . . . ?"

The Gypsy stayed him with a gesture. "My friendship with your parents extends to you because I knew you before you were born. I was able to save them with the blood moon ritual. That is a rare occurrence, only possible in special circumstances. It called for willingness and blind trust, which they did possess, and we—all three—nearly died! Had we not succeeded, I would have had to do to them what I did to my own flesh. I am a vampire hunter, after all. If I were faced with a similar decision regarding you . . . I do not know if I could have borne it. I am getting old, young whelp."

Joss gulped. "You may yet be faced with that decision," he said. "As I said, my condition is changing, and I neither know why nor how."

"Explain."

"I know my parents' situation. They never kept it from me. Up until recently, the only power I possessed was the ability to shapeshift into the wolf."

"When did that begin?"

"When I reached puberty," Joss said. "My father taught me the way of it so that I could do so safely. We often roamed the fells together. We did so enjoy it."

Milosh smiled. "Your father loved his wolf incarnation—the freedom of it. It was the only aspect of his condition that he did love. I am not surprised that he has taught you to love it also."

"When nothing else manifested," Joss went on, while he had the courage, "they thought that was the only symptom I had inherited. So did I . . . until just recently, when the fangs appeared."

"But there has been no bloodlust—no feeding frenzy?" the Gypsy interrupted. He seemed desperate that there be none, which rattled Joss's confidence.

"N-no. None," Joss returned. "The fangs appear when I have need of weapons, just as they did tonight. They also appear when I am . . . aroused. It is a very uncomfortable thing."

"But you do not drink the blood," Milosh said, answering his own question, again as though he needed reassurance.

"No." Joss hedged. The rest was too personal, and he hesitated to speak it to this virtual stranger, but it was, perhaps, the most important thing of all, and this was Milosh—the legendary Milosh, the mysterious, larger-than-life hero he'd heard tales of since his first conscious memory. If he could not discuss it with him, who then? "There is no bloodlust," he said, "but the sight and smell of blood sometimes . . . arouses me," he admitted. He wouldn't confess, however, that it was especially *Cora's* blood that had such an effect upon him. "What does it mean? And why has it taken until now to surface? Am I becoming as my parents are? I am their son, after all. How much of their infection was transmitted to me in the womb?"

The Gypsy gave it thought. "This is what troubled your mother when she first realized she was carrying you, and she asked me the same question that you ask now. I do not know the answer, though I have a theory."

"Tell it then!" Joss cut in. "Anything that might shed even a glimmer of light upon the situation."

"You were conceived of two infected vampires after, or very possibly during, the blood moon ritual," Milosh said. "It may well be that the ritual extended itself to you in the womb, and thus, while it couldn't spare you vampirism, it has spared you what it has spared your parents—the bloodlust. A potent herbal draught was drunk beneath the blood moon to bring it about. It is an ancient rite taught me in Persia centuries ago. I an Romany, and the eastern lands hold many mysteries known only to my people, who originated there."

"So you think I am tainted, but . . . exempt from the worst of it?"

"I *know* you are tainted," Milosh corrected him. "We both do. It remains to be seen how severely."

"Why has it taken until now to manifest itself?"

"You are the age your father was when he was infected. I presume that is why. Your mother was younger when it happened to her, and she was bitten less severely. I can come up with no other explanation offhand. Vampirism is not an exact science, and much is contradictory. Believe me, I know. I've had nearly four hundred years of experience in the field. I must confess, however, in all my years I have never witnessed such a situation where a child experienced the effects of the blood moon ritual from the womb."

"When will we know?" asked Joss.

"The ritual must be renewed at intervals. This your parents must do, or they will revert back to the bloodlust. Even I must do it. Having taken your infection from the womb—and the blood moon antidote as well—you may be exempt. If not, we will learn of it. We can address it then. Perhaps the fangs are nothing more sinister than a child's second teeth appearing, and you can be taught to control them. Time will tell."

"But how *much* time?" he pressed.

"Patience, young whelp," the Gypsy replied. "Believe me. Unless I miss my guess, we will know very soon indeed."

Chapter Thirteen

Cora yanked the bellpull and waited, pacing the carpet. It was late—too late for what she had in mind, but that didn't matter. She was overexhausted. If she were to sleep at all, a nice warm bath was necessary. Neither Joss nor Lyda had returned. She could manage the bath herself, but she needed someone to carry the water up. It was Rodgers who answered her summons.

"I want a bath," she said, with as much authority as she could muster. Judging from the footman's expression, it was enough. "I wish the tub in the dressing room filled, if you please. Have Parker help if needs must."

"Yes, miss," the footman said. "Will you be wantin' your abigail?"

"Where is she?"

"Below in the servants' hall with the others, miss," he said. "The coffin's come. The master's goin' ta take the butler's body down to the kirk in the sledge tomorrow, and they're makin' it ready."

"Don't disturb her in that case," Cora said. "I can manage on my own."

"Very good, miss."

He bowed and left then, and Cora went to the window. The glass was etched with frost like delicate lace framing the panes. Somewhere, a dog or a wolf howled at the absent moon. The voice of another joined it, echoing in the distance, and cold chills inched along her spine. She was grateful that the new sickle moon had slipped behind the clouds again; she didn't need to see the paw prints in the snow to know that wolves were closing in upon Whitebriar Abbey.

She would never sleep without it, but all at once she began to have second thoughts about the bath. Suppose Joss returned. No, he would not come now, not at this hour surely. But what of Lyda? Had she passed the test? Why hadn't Joss come to tell her? Cora had given over trying to sort out the motives of her strange host. *If it were anything serious, he would have come by now,* she reasoned. So she would have the bath and go to bed. Tomorrow would be time enough to sort it all out.

By the time she had brushed out her hair, Parker and Rodgers had filled the tub beside the fire in her dressing room. Once they'd gone, she stripped off her frock, thankful that her corset had been burned with the rest of the clothes she'd arrived in, otherwise she would never have been able to undress without help. Exchanging the frock for a fine voile wrapper as thin as a cobweb, she sprinkled the steaming tub with rosewater and eased herself into it. She always bathed thus: demurely robed, as her mother had taught her. It was a point of modesty, though the gossamer gauze of the bathing wrapper hid nothing.

The fire in the hearth provided the only light, though it did little to chase the drafts that snaked their way over the floorboards, teasing the flames in the grate. The wind outside seemed to have a voice of its own, moaning about the ledges and crevices and pilasters of the manor's ancient architecture like a woman wailing her sorrows in the night. Combined with the distant howls of whatever animals roamed the frosty darkness, the effect was bone-chilling despite the warm fragrant water she'd submerged in to the neck. Rose-scented steam ghosted through her nostrils, lulling her to sleep, and she had nearly drifted off when the sound of a door gently closing and being latched vaulted her upright in the freestanding tub, sloshing water over the side onto the parquetry. For a moment she held her breath, her heart hammering so violently in her breast that ripples formed on the surface of the water.

"W-who's there?" she said, chilled by her own voice breaking the awful silence: she hardly recognized it. Despite Joss's warning, she'd left the door unlatched for Lyda, but when no answer came, there was a heart-stopping moment of raw fright before the patter of familiar feet accompanied a reply.

" 'Tis only me, miss," the abigail said, skittering over the threshold. She gave a quick glance about the room. "How are ya ever managin' a bath all on your own?"

"Quite well, actually," Cora said, easing back in the tub. "Where have you been?"

"Making a fool of myself," Lyda said dourly. "The master has another houseguest. He's been injured, and he wanted me ta change the man's dressing. I all but fainted at the sight o' the blood. It's done that ta me since I was a wee one. I ran outa the yellow suite like hellhounds was after me. Then, down below, they're gettin' ready ta take the butler's body 'round ta the kirk in the mornin', and I lent a hand ta that chore. Here, bend your head back. Let me towel dry your hair, 'tis drippin'. . . ."

Cora lifted her wet hair over the back of the tub, and did as the abigail bade her. She shut her eyes, languishing in the pleasure of the soft, thick towels Lyda was using on her long hair. The abigail urged her head back farther still, taking up another towel and continuing to rub more briskly, babbling all the while.

"Ya have such pretty hair, miss, so long and thick," Lyda said. "Hold now, while I get your brush, so's I can stroke it till it gleams. Thick as it is, 'tis goin' ta dry right quick in front o' the fire."

Cora uttered a soft moan as the abigail began to brush her hair. She was utterly relaxed for the first time since she'd entered Whitebriar Abbey. Lyda chattered on, her soothing voice nudging Cora closer and closer toward sleep. Then the abigail fell silent, and supposing that she had tired, Cora was just about to speak when Lyda wound her hair around her fist and jerked her head back sharply over the back of the tub.

Unprepared, Cora cried out. "Here! What are you doing?" she shrilled, trying to pry the abigail's fingers free. "You are hurting me! Have you gone mad?" Twisting her body, Cora kicked her feet and thrashed until the painted tin tub began to wobble, but the abigail's fist only tugged tighter on her hair, tethering her closer. From her vantage, Cora caught a glimpse of Lyda's face, and her heart gave a lurch. She gasped. Lyda was bending over her, mouth open and revealing long, sharp fangs oozing drool.

"*Lyda!*" she screamed. "What has come over you? Let . . . me . . . go . . . !"

Cora struggled with all her might, clawing at the abigail's hands and arms, but she was no match for Lyda's strength, which had become almost superhuman. The fangs inched lower. They were aimed at Cora's arched throat. *Joss was right!* she realized too late, and she screamed at the top of her voice again and again as she thrashed and twisted and floundered in the water.

Suddenly, a sound! She was making such a din herself she scarcely recognized her name being shouted, or the thunderous hammering on the master suite door. Again and again it came, and she answered it, shrieking at the top of her voice.

"He cannot help ya. I've barred the door," the abigail gloated. "Don't struggle so. 'Tis for the best, this. . . ."

But Cora only struggled all the more as the hammering at the door gave way to shattering blows, which she took to be Joss's body slamming against it. Once— twice—three times before he came crashing through, setting the door off its hinges judging by the sound it made. Cora heard the rasp of metal and groan of splintered wood as it crashed against the foyer wall, heard the string of expletives he uttered as he charged through and into the dressing room.

Lyda tipped the tub—Cora and all—into his path, them skittered past him and out of the suite. The tub struck him in the legs, undermining his balance, and he slipped on the slick, soapy residue and fell hard in the midst of the spilled bathwater. But he didn't stay down long. As he lifted the tub off Cora—it had pinned her to the floor—their eyes met for a brief moment, quicksilver jousting with shimmering blue. She may as well have been naked for the way the thin wrapper revealed her charms. His eyes were devouring her.

"Did she . . . ? Were you . . . ?" he panted, raising her to her feet.

Cora couldn't speak. Her breath was coming in involuntary spasms. All she could manage was to shake her head.

Snatching an afghan from the dressing chest, he wrapped it around her and set her on the lounge. "Stay where you are!" he charged. "I'm going to lock you in this room where you'll be safe until I've settled this. I will be back directly."

Cora scarcely heard. Her head was swimming. She pulled her feet up on the lounge, out of the spreading puddle of rose-scented water. The last thing she saw was his tall, dark silhouette—no more than a blur—streaking through the dressing room door. The last thing she heard was a drawer opening, then the jingle of keys and one finally turning in the lock. Vertigo blackened her vision but for the tiny white pinpoints of glaring light behind her hooded eyes. The wail of the wind gobbled up the shouts and snarls that lived on the edge of consciousness. *Snarls?* They were coming from somewhere close by. Then, nothing.

Joss hated leaving Cora in such a state, but his angst was short-lived. Apologies could wait; she was safe and unharmed. He dared not lose sight of Lyda.

Bursting through the corridor, he was just in time to see a huge white wolf backing the abigail into the toile suite.

Fetch a blade—a cleaver, Milosh spoke to his mind. *Quickly!*

Two crossed swords and a halberd graced the landing at the far end of the hall. Joss raced back and snatched one of the blades from its wall bracket. By the time he reached the toile suite, the abigail's screams had ceased. The wolf had torn her throat out.

Sever her head, Milosh said, padding into his dressing room. *Do it quickly, else she rise again,* he added from a distance.

Joss stared down at the abigail's inert body, hesitating. Twice he raised and lowered the sword before Milosh returned, in human form, tucking his shirt inside his trousers.

"Your father would not have hesitated," the Gypsy said.

"I have never—"

"You were correct," Milosh said. "She was dead when you found her, and has risen *vampir.* There is no way to save her. She serves the master who created her. She must be destroyed, now *raise that sword and strike!*"

"I do not know if I can," Joss murmured, hovering over the inert abigail. By all accounts she was dead already. "There was none of this ever," he mused, thinking of his parents. "I was never a part of their mission to seek out and destroy the undead. I had heard the legends, the bloodthirsty tales . . . but I was never along on their forays."

"Evidently I am here to remedy that," Milosh said. "They were wrong to shelter you, though surely they did so thinking there was no need to share the details." He nodded toward the savaged abigail. "There are at least four others like her roaming the tor—possibly five, if you count the creature that made them its slave. I do not believe that creature was the coachman you spoke of. He was, unless I miss my guess, and I rarely do, just another victim. There is much evil here. You are either one of them or their enemy. There is no time to lose. Decide. *Now!* It will be harder if you wait."

Joss bent closer to the abigail. It wasn't just the concept that made him hesitate. He was too rooted in his moral and cultural background, and could not conscience murdering a woman. His fingers clenched and unclenched on the hilt of the blade, grown clammy in his hand.

"Now!" Milosh demanded. "It must be now—before she rises."

The abigail's eyes snapped open, and she bared her fangs. Joss jumped back, raised the sword and in one hack severed the creature's head. It happened so quickly, he scarcely realized what he'd done. Staggering back from the body, he dropped the sword.

"Watch," the Gypsy said.

Joss's eyes misted with tears. He blinked them back. He couldn't take them from the decapitated corpse at his feet. What had he done? But, what would have happened to Cora if he hadn't come when he had?

A foul-smelling smoke began to rise from the body, which began to change shape. Flesh and blood shriveled until all that lay inside the abigail's clothes was a pile of smoking bones, which Milosh quickly scooped up and heaved into the fire in the hearth. The Gypsy then turned toward him, his fisted hands upon his hips.

"So!" he said. "Congratulations. You have killed your first vampire. Welcome to the Brotherhood! Your revered parents would be proud."

Joss barely made it to the chamber pot on its stand behind the folding screen in the corner before he retched. Staggering back, he sank down upon the lounge at the edge of the carpet and raked his hair back from his brow. He had been right all along: Lyda was dead in that carriage when he found it, which meant all of the others were vampires as well. He had surmised as much, but this was different; now he *knew*.

"What did you mean before, that the coachman wasn't their maker?" he asked.

"This is not just a social call, Joss Hyde-White. I have been tracking an age-old nemesis. My quest has brought me here. I am relieved that your parents are not in residence, actually. I believe it is they that he hunts, and he has come full circle. He first came to England the year before you were born, to London, and here to your North Country . . . to the doorstep of this very Abbey. He is no stranger here. It was he who infected your father and your mother. If he cannot corrupt them, he will settle for you; I'm certain of it."

"*Sebastian Valentin?*" Joss murmured, incredulous. "How can that be? They destroyed him in Moldovia. I have heard the tale many times over the years, how you and they—"

"Proof that he exists no more was never found," Milosh interrupted. "We assumed it was so because he made no more appearances, and because we wished it so, but in these matters one must never assume. He lives still. You can take my word for that. He is an evil that I have fought for centuries. I followed him aboard the ship that brought me here. He is the reason I disembarked in wolf form, so I could track him well hidden. He knows my human incarnation well.

"As a wolf, in England?" Joss repeated. "Wolves are extinct here."

"So your father once told me. But I needed speed as well as stealth, and I had to hope that Sebastian would not know this. It was a gamble, and it has been an . . . eventful journey, but that is a tale for another time. We need to deal with the present. Your Cora will need consoling now."

"Judas priest!" Joss cried, vaulting to his feet. "Cora! I left her locked in my dressing room."

"You had best see to her. I have work to do."

"What work?"

"The wolves are gathering. I will make use of your tunnel to prowl about and see what we are facing."

"The villagers," Joss reminded him. "They have already shot you once, Milosh."

"I will be more careful now that danger is revealed. Besides, it is rather late for hunters at this hour. Do not worry over me. I have not come all this long way to fail, young whelp."

"What good to go alone and hurt?" Joss asked, thinking out loud. "Would it not be wiser to wait until your wound has healed and we can go together? How will you dispose of a vampire once you take it down, with no stake for its heart and no blade to sever its head?"

Milosh smiled. "I can count upon one hand the times over the centuries that I have been fortunate enough to work with a companion," he said. "I work alone, and the white wolf's jaws are more than capable of severing a vampire's head. I should have done so earlier when we met, but time was of the essence, and I did not want to greet you in that fashion. That was my mistake. Now I must remedy it. No, do not fear for me. We each have our own coil to unwind and we'd best be about it."

CHAPTER FOURTEEN

Cora sat on the edge of the cot, cocooned in the afghan Joss had wrapped around her. Despite the blazing fire in the hearth, she was shivering with teeth-chattering chills. She had removed her wet bathing dress, and would have changed back into her frock if it hadn't been soaked when the tub tipped over. Now she waited. Would Joss never come and let her out of the dressing room?

Presently, voices echoed through the suite, and she heard hammering. Vaulting off the cot, she padded to the door and pounded upon it with both hands fisted in the afghan.

"Let me out of here! Let me *out!*" she cried.

The shuffling of feet replied to that, then a voice so close to her ear on the other side of the wood that she backed up a pace.

"I will have you out of there in a moment," Joss said. "Parker and I are repairing the door first. All is well. You must trust me to ensure your safety, Miss Applegate."

His voice soothed her like balm; there was much comfort in it. She opened her mouth to ask after Lyda, but closed it again hearing his heavy footfalls recede. He had returned to the chore at hand, and so she padded back to the cot, her feet slapping on the wet floor. But she soon grew restless. She couldn't just sit still and calmly wait while her world as she knew it crumbled around her. Lyda, the trusted abigail who had served her selflessly since she was twelve years old, had died a horrible death along with the others in the coach on the fells. She had been savaged by a vampire and become one herself. All the denials by society that such a monster even existed, all her own protests and disbelief, now faded in the face of the absolute truth. Cora had been cast in the midst of resident evil. That she had escaped it thus far was miraculous. She could still scarcely believe it. It hurt her heart to even consider.

The mournful howl of wolves called her to the window. Drawing back the portieres, she wiped the condensation from a pane and gazed below. *A wolf.* It was standing in the snow, its proud head raised to the starlit vault above. It was a white wolf, as white as the snow. Cora blinked and it was gone, though its tracks remained alongside the tracks of another. She shuddered in wonder at the dreamlike appearance of the animal. What did it all mean?

The rasp of a key in the lock spun her around to face Joss on the threshold. Dark shadows wreathed his eyes. His lips were like chalk, his hair disheveled. His whole attitude was that of a man just come from battle. He reached her in three great strides and took her in his arms.

"You are certain you weren't bitten?" he murmured, searching her face in the firelight.

"I was not," she said. "Lyda . . . ?"

"That was not the Lyda you knew," he said. "That

Lyda died in the coach. What replaced her was a fiend, a fiend that has been destroyed."

Cora dropped her head against his shoulder. The muscles there flexed at her touch. His clean, woodsy scent laced with citrus and charged with the musk of exertion threaded through her nostrils. She drank him in deeply. No. There was no use to deny it; she was attracted to this man. As improbable as it was after what she'd been through, her body responded to his closeness, to his maleness. Their hearts beat to the same rhythm. His anxiety flowed into her as if through some inexplicable cord that linked them. That the only thing between him and her nakedness was a frayed afghan heightened the strange waves of silken fire coursing through her very depths. A man had held her thus before, but there were no such delicious feelings upon that occasion, only terror and pain. If this was what one was supposed to feel, she was a virgin still, despite that she had been robbed of her virtue.

"You are trembling," he said, tilting her chin until their gazes met. "This afghan is sopping wet. Lying about in wet clothes in such drafts you'll likely take pneumonia. But wait . . . I know just the thing." He let her go, and strode back into the bedroom. Minutes later, he returned with the silver gray brocade dressing gown he'd lent her when she first arrived. "Here," he said, turning his back. "Slip into this. I will have my maid come up and dress you properly when the day begins. Her chores will be lightened now, as my butler's body is to be taken below in the morning. Once his physical presence is removed, things will go quite back to normal in this house." He righted the upturned tub and set it before the fire. Cora didn't take her eyes off it.

"How did she ever turn that over?" she said. "She was so . . . strong. I couldn't free myself."

Joss slipped his arm around her again and led her toward the door. "Come," he said. "I'll have Parker clear all this away. Put it out of your mind." As Cora reacted to that, her posture clenching against him, and he added, "No . . . I know how impossible that sounds, but you must not dwell upon what happened here. At least now you know I was telling the truth."

"How do you know so much about vampires when no one will even admit there are such things?" asked Cora.

Joss hesitated. "As I once told you, my parents are vampire hunters," he said, stopping her in her tracks. "I have *always* known there were such things, but I was never faced with destroying one until your carriage brought them to my very doorstep. You don't remember anything untoward occurring before the coach bogged down in the snow? I'm confused about the coachman. Something doesn't ring true. You said there wasn't room for him in the coach, so he set out to find help. There should have been room for him—three to a seat. There were only five passengers."

"N-no!" Cora cried, suddenly remembering. How had she forgotten? "There was another. We took on a passenger at the Cumberland border—a gentleman, meticulously attired, though his clothes fit him poorly. He spoke with an accent . . . German, I think."

"There was no such person in the coach when I reached it. There, by God, was our vampire. I would stake my life upon it."

Cora stared. Joss seemed far away suddenly, and his detached air frightened her. "What is it?" she murmured, almost afraid of the answer.

"Nothing," he replied, seeming to shake free from whatever dark thoughts had gripped him. He ushered her into the bedchamber and eased her down upon the bed. "I want you to rest. You're exhausted," he said. "I will stand guard outside your door until dawn. The hinge needs replacing. We have managed a temporary mend, but my stabler will have to forge a new one tomorrow before I will trust it."

Cora surged to her feet and took a step toward him. "Thank you," she murmured. "If you hadn't come . . ."

He slipped his arm around her waist. His hand was warm through the cold satiny brocade. She wanted to lean into the firm, comforting pressure, but she stiffened instead, and lurched again when his free hand reached to slide her long hair back behind her shoulder and cup her face. Would it always be thus? Would she ever be able to bear a man's touch again? What she felt in this man's arms was scandalous, but she wanted more in spite of herself. Did she dare find out what her violent loss of innocence had robbed her of so cruelly? Did she dare reclaim it? Was she brave enough to trust herself in the hands of this enigmatic savior who had ignited a spark she'd once thought extinguished for good and all? Was she courageous enough to even try?

He took her lips before she could decide, and a white-hot surge of scalding fire ripped through her loins so suddenly that she swayed in his arms—and instinctively resisted, pulling back as he deepened the kiss.

"Please, sir . . . don't . . ." she murmured. She should have struck him, as she'd done with the pitcher, but she couldn't. She should reach back and lower the flat of her hand across his handsome face, but she couldn't do that either. She was weary of fighting.

"You want me," he murmured. "I can see it—I can *feel* it in your trembling, in your quickened breathing, in the pounding of your heart."

"What you feel is my fear," she said.

"Fear of what? Of me? Have I ever done one thing to cause you to fear me? To distrust my honor?"

"Not fear of you," she moaned. "I fear myself . . . I fear the very feelings you describe."

"Who hurt you so that you cannot bear a man's touch?" he asked.

"That, sir, is none of your affair." She snapped at him: that tack was better—much better. If only she could cling to hostility.

"It *is* my affair," he shot back, "because you have transferred whatever it is that has harmed you to me, and I am enough of a cavalier to resent it. And to want to prove myself to you."

"There is no reason for you to prove yourself to me," she said, "and I have transferred . . . nothing, sir. I have nothing to offer you. As I have already said, I am a ruined woman. That does not give you license to expect favors, however, which is how I see your advances."

"You are far too young and beautiful to martyr yourself in such a way," Joss said, soothing her with gentle hands. The heat of them through the silk brocade made her heart skip its rhythm. His hooded gaze alone was a seduction, without the honey-sweet intimacy of his murmured words and his warm breath puffing on her cheek. "Who was it . . . the young gentleman in the carriage? Is that why you were in such a rush to reach Gretna Green?"

"No," she said, low-voiced.

"Who, then?"

Cora hesitated. Perhaps if she told him it would be enough of a deterrent to keep him at his distance. She hadn't spoken a word of it since it happened, and only then to her father. Perhaps now was the time.

"My father arranged a marriage between Albert Clement and myself for monetary gain," she began. "And to avoid a scandal, I was later to learn."

"A scandal? What sort of scandal?"

"Albert was in danger of being brought up on charges for . . . an illegal association with another man. I knew nothing of this when I attended a house party on the Clements' estate to announce my betrothal to Albert. It was to last the weekend, and Albert's . . . lover was also in attendance. I happened upon them in a . . . compromising situation. I spoke privately with Albert. He no more wanted the forced betrothal than I did. We saw my discovery as a way out of our predicament. I would be spared a loveless marriage, and he would be free to go abroad with his lover, somewhere safe from the threat of imprisonment. The betrothal was preventing him from doing that, you see. It would have only caused more of a scandal were he to have left me in the lurch, so to speak, but if *I* were the one to break it off . . . Well, I went to Father straightaway, but he would not hear of canceling the betrothal. Albert's father, Clive Clement, was holding something over Father's head as well. I never did find out what it was."

"In this day and age?" Joss asked. She had his attention now, but he wasn't repulsed as she'd thought he'd be; he held her tighter.

Cora nodded. "To make short of it, they must have drugged Lyda in some way, because her chamber adjoined mine, and she never woke or heard my screams. . . ." She swallowed dry. Maybe telling was the right thing. Maybe it would exorcise the demons that had haunted her ever since. "It was the father, not the son, who assaulted me," she went on. "Clive Clement, who had a wife still living. He made it plain that he would 'service' me, leaving his son free to carry on his affair, and if I were to become enceinte, all the better for his son's image, should it ever be in question. That was when I found out Albert was sterile from a childhood malady, and rumors had spread that he could father no children."

"But how—"

"Clive Clement attacked me while I was sleeping," Cora said quickly, while she possessed the courage. "For all I know I may have been drugged, also. I fought him to a fare-thee-well, but I was no match for his strength. When I told Father the next morning and begged again to be released from the betrothal . . . he refused. Whatever Clement was holding over his head was more important than I, so I ran away. They found me, of course, and brought me back. Hence the mad race to Gretna Green in such weather, else I attempt it again. The rest you know."

"From your description, it was Clive Clement that we killed below in wolf form," Joss said. "When he rises, he must be killed in his human form and his head severed from his body to free his spirit, otherwise he will keep returning in one form or another."

"I care naught for his 'spirit,' sir," Cora said frostily. "But, what of my father? If it is as you say, then he, too, is *vampir*. Please God, I beg you. Do not let any of them in!"

"I shan't," Joss said, folding her closer in his strong arms. This time, she made no resistance. Tears blurred her vision, and she leaned into the embrace. Her arms slipped around him as if they had a will of their own, her hands fisted in the back of his shirt. Whatever alchemy it was at work that tethered them would no longer be denied. This time when he took her lips, she gave them willingly.

He deepened the kiss, and Cora moaned. He tasted of raw maleness and the wine he'd drunk at dinner, honey sweet and sultry. She drank him in and could not get her fill. All at once, she was lifted in those strong, warm arms that were such a comfort. When he laid her on the bed and stood stripping off his clothes, she scarcely breathed. Her heartbeat was hammering in her ears, the blood thrumming in her veins. It was like watching a graceful dancer move exquisitely to music that he alone heard. It drew her in totally, and when he slid into the bed beside her and untied the sash on the gray brocade dressing gown she was wrapped in, her breath caught, and caught again.

For all that she had been ravaged in the night, and her virtue taken not given, she had never seen a naked man before. Joss Hyde-White knelt above her in all his magnificent glory, his sex turgid with arousal, and something pinged deep inside her—something hot and involuntary, like ripples spreading from a stone dropped in still water. It was magical.

"You may have lost your innocence," Joss murmured, "but not your virtue. You are still a virgin in every sense save one . . . and even that is virgin still. You have never been reverenced. You have never been adored, never *loved*."

Cora swallowed the lump in her throat but couldn't speak. There was no need. Joss gathered her into his arms and took her lips in a kiss that was both tender and passionate. He deepened it, sliding his silken tongue between her teeth, coaxing hers to reciprocate, and the stirring in her sex as she tasted him deeply took her breath away. She lay in pleasant oblivion then, as if she were outside herself looking on, feeling strange sensations at her very core, which indeed was still virgin territory.

He hadn't shaved recently, and the tactile ghost of fresh stubble against her soft skin thrilled her. It quickened her heart, which nearly stopped its beating when his mouth left her lips and blazed a fiery trail along her arched neck to her breast beneath, capturing one tall, hard nipple. Her whole body throbbed like a pulse beat. It was as if she had been transported outside herself, looking down as he did indeed reverence her with a tender strength that left her breathless yet again.

As if it possessed a will of its own, her body reached for him as his hand splayed across her belly and ignited a riptide of searing hot sensations coursing through the swollen mystery that was her sex. Cora stiffened as that hand slid lower, caressing the soft mound between her thighs; and his hooded eyes, dilated with desire, looked into hers.

"I mean to show you what *should* be between a man and a woman," he whispered. "There will be no pain. If I fail, a word will stop me."

Cora dared not reply. She dared not break the spell. She could not bring herself to quench the achy fire that had spread through her body from the inside out until every nerve, every pore in her skin, was charged as if she had been lightning struck. But then it began; the cruel memory flashes, recollections of the moment that had begun her nightmare, the moment when, groggy with sleep, she lay helpless, pinned beneath another body in the deep dark. Could she have been drugged, too? She

YES! ☐

Sign me up for the **Historical Romance Book Club** and send my TWO FREE BOOKS! If I choose to stay in the club, I will pay only $8.50* each month, a savings of $5.48!

YES! ☐

Sign me up for the **Love Spell Book Club** and send my TWO FREE BOOKS! If I choose to stay in the club, I will pay only $8.50* each month, a savings of $5.48!

NAME: _____

ADDRESS: _____

_____

TELEPHONE: _____

E-MAIL: _____

☐ **I WANT TO PAY BY CREDIT CARD.**

☐ VISA   ☐ MasterCard   ☐ DISCOVER

ACCOUNT #: _____

EXPIRATION DATE: _____

SIGNATURE: _____

Send this card along with $2.00 shipping & handling for each club you wish to join, to:

Romance Book Clubs
1 Mechanic Street
Norwalk, CT 06850-3431

Or fax (must include credit card information!) to: 610.995.9274. You can also sign up online at www.dorchesterpub.com.

*Plus $2.00 for shipping. Offer open to residents of the U.S. and Canada only. Canadian residents please call 1.800.481.9191 for pricing information.

If under 18, a parent or guardian must sign. Terms, prices and conditions subject to change. Subscription subject to acceptance. Dorchester Publishing reserves the right to reject any order or cancel any subscription.

must have been; that would account for the haze that cloaked her memory of that night.

The hands that explored her body now were skilled and gentle, not cruel and demanding, though she felt those cruel hands still. The breath that puffed against her skin was sweet, not fouled with sour onions, strong drink and stale tobacco, but she smelled the fetid breath just the same. No fist came crashing down upon her face—once, twice, she could not recall how many times. A gentle hand caressed it now, and lightly traced her breast, her narrow waist, the curve of her hips that rose to meet those probing fingers. Her heart began to pound. Both ecstasy and terror were doing battle in her then. She wanted Joss. . . . Oh, how she wanted him, but other hands were groping her in her mind, other lips were bruising her in rampant flashes. Clive Clement's lips, hot and cruel, his tongue forcing—choking her. Would it always be thus? Would she relive the nightmare each time a man touched her?

Joss's lips were warm and soft, edged with just enough stubble to ignite her as a match bursts into flame when struck. The sensation crippled her reason. She could not help but arch her body toward him. That involuntary thrust seemed to ignite him as well, for he murmured her name and spread her legs, but he did not enter her; instead, he wrapped her trembling hand around his hot, hard member, lifted her nearer and paused, his broad chest heaving.

"I am . . . in your hands, Cora," he panted. "Do with me what you will."

Cora stared. His thick, veined sex was throbbing in her hand. His eyes were so dilated with desire, they shone like two jet beads gleaming in the firelight. This was the last thing she would have expected. All at once,

the memory of hard thrusts and tearing flesh spread
gooseflesh across her skin. She relived clawing at that
other member which gave her no choice, relived her
failure and the pain, the tearing searing pain that followed, relived the dizzying blows to her head and
cheekbone. A soft sob escaped her lips. It was too
soon . . . or rather *too late* for her. Mixed into the whole
were propriety, modesty and decorum. It seemed ludi-
crous after what she had been through, but there it was.
She had no control over what had happened before,
but she did have control of what was happening now;
Joss had just given it to her. She may have lost her vir-
ginity, but she hadn't lost her values.

Yet, would she ever be able to indulge in the pleasures of the flesh? How could she bear it if she couldn't
now, after he'd given her a taste of ecstasy, and when
she so needed the comfort he offered—when she
longed for the promise of his gentle strength, his fiery
passion?

Cora literally held the future in her hand. Joss had
put her in total command, and she loved him for it. But
it was too soon. The wounds were too new. The flesh
had healed, but her spirit had not.

The pulse—the very life in his member—was pumping to the rhythm of his blood. It was beating as his
heart beat: in rapid, thudding shudders. It was on fire
in her hand, the veins distended—thrumming with life,
ready to ravish her, to fill her, to bring her to the brink
of rapture and beyond. But it was too soon.

Tears welled in her eyes. She could not stop them.
They came in a great flood as her hand fell away from
his sex, and she groaned, covering her face instead.

"I . . . I can't." she sobbed.

Joss swooped down and gathered her into his arms. The tenderness of that embrace only served to bring on more tears, and he soothed her gently.

"Shhhh," he murmured. "I am yours to command, no? Not all men are savages, Cora. I mean to prove that . . . in time."

He took her lips gently, in a slow, tantalizing kiss that left her weak and trembling for more when he drew away. Her body betrayed her. Part of her wanted to repel his advances while another part hungered for the very pleasure she feared. It was not a comfortable thing. He had to notice her quaking. It was as though both facets of her psyche—the memory that stained it and the passion that Joss had awakened in her—were warring inside, rending her in two.

The memory won. Cora pushed against his chest and tore her lips from his. "Please," she murmured.

Joss rose from the bed and covered her with the counterpane. "I told you," he said, "I am in your hands. You mustn't judge all men by the measure of one reprehensible whoreson." He gathered his clothes from the floor and strode toward the dressing room adjoining. How finely he was made! How narrow his waist, how taut his buttocks. How striking his corded thighs lit in the fire glow. "Get some sleep," he said. "It is still several hours before dawn. I shan't leave you entirely. I shall nap in the dressing room as I did before. You needn't fear. I shan't disturb you. But I shan't leave you unattended either, especially now that you know what we are facing. I am a light sleeper, Cora. You have only to cry out and I will be at your side."

He didn't wait for a reply, but strode through the door and closed it all but a crack. Cora lay very still, lis-

tening to his movements. His ragged sigh echoing
through the stillness moved her. Her pulse was racing,
her heartbeat pounding in her ears. Hot blood was
coursing through the distended veins in her neck,
pumping through the arteries, thrumming through her
very core. She was on fire for him, her sex swollen with
arousal, moist and tingling. Why had she let him go?
Why? She lay awake for a long time thinking.

There was no sound coming from the dressing room
now. Had he fallen asleep? If he had, she would wake
him. He had proven his stamp. She would go to him,
embrace him, find comfort in those warm, strong arms.
She would quench the fire surging through her loins—
the fire he had kindled despite her fears, which he had
assuaged.

Cora scrambled to her feet, slipped the silvery brocade dressing gown back about her shoulders, and took
up the candle branch on the nightstand. Padding to the
dressing room door, she pushed it open with a finger
and peered inside. His togs were lying on the boot chair
in the corner, his turned-down boots on the water-
soaked floor beside. But for a sheet draped over his
waist, he was lying naked on his back on the cot, his face
turned to the wall, his breast heaving with the peaceful
rhythm of sleep. Cora tiptoed closer. How handsome he
was, and how vulnerable. Should she wake him?

Yes.

Reaching her hand toward his broad, moist shoulder
glossed with sweat, she froze in place as there came a
hitch in his deep, tremulous breathing. Her own breath
caught as he snorted and turned his head toward her.
His eyes were still closed, his long, dark lashes sweeping
against his skin. She was just about to gentle him awake,
when he drew a deeper breath. His lips parted, and she

stifled a cry, her teeth biting into her lower lip until they drew blood. Her hand flew to her open mouth to hold in the cry. There, beneath the candle branch, two long, sharp fangs gleamed in the firelight, protruding below that sensuous upper lip.

Cora's body clenched. It was as if a fist had gripped her heart, or a dagger had pierced it. Cold chills crashed over her, body and soul. She blinked to clear her vision. No, she hadn't been mistaken. Fangs! He was a vampire. No wonder he knew so much about them.

Horrified, her head reeling, she backed away from the cot and fled.

Chapter Fifteen

One thing and one thing only moved Cora then; she must leave Whitebriar Abbey. She had nearly succumbed to the lure of a vampire's kiss. As improbable as it was, she was falling in love with Joss Hyde-White. She would have given herself to him if she hadn't seen those fangs. Was this attraction a result of his hypnotic charm? She had heard of such amongst vampires. Or was this feeling genuine—was it inevitable that she would melt in the arms of the right man after what she had been through in the clutches of the wrong one? She could not stay long enough to find out. Either way, the outcome would be the same if she stayed: sooner or later, he would break down her resistance.

No, there was nothing for it but to go. She gave no thought to where, only that she must put as much distance between herself and Joss Hyde-White as was humanly possible. It would be light soon. They would take the coffin below to the kirk, and she would be on that sledge, even if she had to climb into the coffin with the dead butler to do so.

Cora dressed as warmly as her wardrobe would allow, in a gunmetal-gray wool frock, her sturdiest pair of ankle boots and her chinchilla-lined and hooded mantle that the servants had set to rights below stairs. That would have to do. She would have to leave the rest of her things behind. She shrugged. What did it matter? What use were her pretty frocks if she were doomed to pass the rest of her days among the undead? It all seemed like a terrible nightmare. It couldn't be real—any of it! Her ruination, this trip, these monsters . . . She would wake soon, and laugh at such a stupid dream. But she did not wake. The nightmare was real, and tears stung her eyes as she slipped out of the master bedchamber and crept through the shadows that clung stubbornly to the old halls as dawn approached.

She had no trouble finding the salon; Grace's mournful wails echoing along the empty corridors led her straight to it. Cora had never met the woman, yet sorrow welled in her as she came nearer. Other voices ringing from the rafters joined the din, driving her deeper into the shadows. She backed into a recessed alcove where a small, rounded door was almost obscured by a tapestry. Without giving it a second thought, she turned the knob and entered a small vacant chamber.

Dawn hadn't yet broken. There were no draperies on the room's only window, and she backed toward it as the voices outside grew louder. Glancing through the frost-painted glass, she searched the frozen breast of the tor for some sign of life. It wouldn't do to be discovered leaving. There was no sign of anyone, though a sledge waited directly below. Cora held her breath. From the scuffling outside and the wails and sobs and hushed whispers, she could tell that they were carrying the coffin below. Three men. She distinctly heard the difference in the pitch of their voices. Rodgers was one of them. She knew his voice well, and Parker's. The third voice was that of an older man—the stabler? It must be. She breathed a sigh of relief that it wasn't Joss. The minute he woke to find her missing, pandemonium would surely break loose. She had to be away before that.

The women did not follow; their voices still echoed along the corridor from a distance. Cora could scarcely hear them over the pounding of her heart. Below, the men were sliding the coffin into the sledge. She watched them toss a tarpaulin over it, but they did not tie the tarpaulin down. There was no need. The wind had died, and seemed unlikely to rise again. They evidently planned to be away soon. Joss would not be going with them by the look of things.

Cracking the door open, Cora poked her head into the hall and looked both ways. She was just about to chance flight when voices drove her back inside. The men were coming back. What luck! She waited until they passed and their voices faded before slipping out into the corridor and racing silently in the opposite direction. Now, if she could only find the way out and climb beneath that tarpaulin before whoever was going to drive the sledge returned, she would be away with no one the wiser.

A cold draft funneling up the stairwell whipped along the hallway, ruffling the hem of her wool frock. Could they have left the door open? Yes, it was ajar, and she slipped through to find herself before the sledge, its horses prancing in place, their nervous cries riding a gentle wind that had suddenly risen, as though the dawn were sighing awake. But neither the animals' complaints nor restless pawing and prancing were due to her sudden appearance. The snow, like sugary frost, was pockmarked with wolf prints, and she pulled up short at the sight.

Nothing met her eyes as she first approached the sledge. What had spooked the horses? She dared not take the time to sort it out; the racket they were making would surely bring the driver. Scrambling up beside the coffin, she pulled the tarpaulin over her.

No sooner had she done so when a mournful howl pierced the predawn silence, and she peeked from beneath the canvas to see a magnificent wolf, as white as the driven snow, a few yards from the door through which she'd exited. Her breath caught in a gasp, for the animal seemed to be watching her, its silver-gray eyes rimmed with red. They had an iridescent glow about them that shot her through with gooseflesh; they almost looked human, and they definitely were trained upon her. What if the beast were to attack? It started toward her.

It couldn't attack her inside the coffin, and so she lifted the lid and climbed inside atop the butler's corpse—not a moment too soon. The wolf had jumped up in the sledge atop the tarpaulin, upon the coffin beneath. Its heavy footpads tramping back and forth served to tamp the lid of the coffin down. There was precious little room left for her atop the butler's rigid corpse.

Cora bit into her lower lip until it bled to keep from screaming. The cadaverous bulk beneath her had an otherworldly feel that made her blood run cold. She had never seen a corpse, much less touched one. Now she was forced to lie atop one, its cold, corrupted flesh giving off a sickening-sweet stench of death and decay. Overhead, the lid of the coffin groaned with the wolf's weight, and the beast had begun to claw at the wood and gnaw with its long, curved fangs. Where was the driver? In one way, she wished he would come. In another, she wished he wouldn't, for fear he would find her if he did. Suppose it was Joss! Suppose that was why the men had gone back—to wake Joss. Perhaps he was to drive the sledge after all.

Bloodcurdling snarls and high-pitched whines began filtering through the coffin lid. The wolf had scratched the tarpaulin off and was running back and forth overhead. It was *vampir;* there were no wolves in England, so it had to be. Which one was it that was trying to get at her through the seasoned ash? Was it her father, or the coachman that had stalked her—or the strange passenger they had taken on just before the coach bogged down? Was it the real coachman . . . or Albert Clement, or was it Clive Clement, his lascivious father, who had begun all her woes? Or was it *Joss?* Her mind was reeling with the possibilities, and she was alone against any or all of them. There was no way to tell, but whichever the monster was, it was digging and scratching so fiercely at the coffin lid that she feared it would work it free.

All at once a shout broke the stillness, and the coffin groaned as the weight of the wolf lifted. Cora heard its four feet touch the ground, felt the vibration as it bounded off into the predawn darkness. The horses reared, and Cora's heart leapt as the sledge jumped forward. There was no one at the reins! The stabler's voice pierced her like the edge of a sword. His heavy footfalls crunching in the snow, following, nearly stopped her heart. She was trapped in a coffin in a runaway sledge that was plunging down the steep incline of the tor toward the valley below. Soon traveling at breakneck speed, the swoosh and scrape of the sledge runners drowned out all but the distant cry of a wolf.

The old stabler would never catch up afoot. And by the time he ran back to the stable for a horse, the sledge would be halfway to the village. It was rocking from side to side, skimming the frosty ground. Her angle was such that Cora felt as if she were standing on her head as it picked up speed and raced crazily down the grade. The unsavory event that there was a dead body beneath her scarcely mattered now in this new press, despite its flaccid bulk and the foul smell as the jostling forced gasses from the cadaver. Not being able to see was the worst, and she pounded upon the coffin lid in a desperate attempt to raise it, but the huge wolf's heavy feet had tamped it down too securely for her to budge.

Cora screamed, even though she knew there was no one to hear. Shouts echoed in the distance—more than one raised voice—and unless she was mistaken there was more than one wolf howling, too. She screamed again, but it was cut short. It was so close inside the coffin that she could barely breathe. Light-headed for lack of air, she had nearly lost consciousness when the horses' shrieking and jingling tack struck terror in her heart. The sledge gave a violent lurch, rolled over and over, finally striking some immovable object that ejected the coffin, sprung the lid and sent her tumbling down the last of the grade in a cloud of displaced snow.

Dazed, the last thing she saw was the staved-in sledge on its side against the rowan tree that had stopped it, and the horses running off dragging broken bits of wood and iron. The last thing she heard was one wolf answering another wolf's call before blackness swallowed first light.

* * *

Joss woke to a jostling. Parker was shaking his shoulder none too gently. "Wake up, sir!" he was saying. His voice seemed to be coming from an echo chamber. "Sir, you must wake! There is a grave press. Sir, *please.*"

Joss groaned. His eyes slowly opened to the valet's frowning face hovering over him. His mouth was dry. Running his tongue over his teeth, he found to his dismay that his fangs were still extended, and he groaned again.

"What is it, Parker?" he grumbled, trying to grit his teeth and force the fangs back to no avail.

"The young miss is not in her room, sir," said Parker. "We have searched everywhere."

Joss bolted upright on the cot. "What do you mean, she is not here?" he demanded. "Of course she's here. I just left her next door."

"That was hours ago, sir," the valet said. "Dawn has broken, and she is gone, I tell you. Her mantle is missing."

"Fetch my clothes!" Joss said, slinging his feet to the floor. His head was reeling. The fangs were finally beginning to recede. Could she have seen them? *My God, she must have done! What else would have made her leave the Abbey with so many dangers lurking outside?*

Joss surged to his feet as Parker shuffled back laden with his clothes, and he let the valet hurriedly dress him.

"That's not the whole of it," Parker said, helping him shrug his waistcoat on.

Joss stopped midshrug. "What else?" he snapped. "Come, come—out with it, man!"

"Bates's body, sir," the valet stammered. "A wolf spooked the horses and they ran off with the sledge, coffin and all. Otis is out looking for it now, but it's started snowing again."

Joss's scalp drew back, tingling with chills. "A . . . a wolf, you say?" he murmured.

"Aye, 'twas a great white wolf in that sledge when Otis got there," the valet said. "It had torn the tarpaulin off the sledge, and it was tramping back and forth on the lid of Bates's coffin till it saw Otis, then it ran off howling loud enough to wake the dead. There was more than one animal, come to that. Others answered its call, and—"

"Where is Milosh?" Joss interrupted.

"Why, in his rooms, I expect, sir. I haven't seen him."

"Enough!" Joss seethed, rejecting the frock coat the valet was attempting to help him into. He grabbed his greatcoat instead. "Do the others know?" he asked.

"Just Otis and Rodgers . . . and me, sir."

"For God's sake don't tell Grace," said Joss, "or we'll have another coffin to fetch. Bloody hell! How could Otis be so careless?"

"We came back in for the key to your father's vault in the kirkyard, so Otis and Rodgers could put the coffin in there till the thaw, like you said, and that wolf must have spooked the horses while we were about it. The others think it was a wild dog, but I know it wasn't, sir. It was a wolf all right. I've never seen the like."

Joss dragged his fingers through his hair as if he thought the motion would keep his brain from bursting. "Continue to search for Miss Applegate," he said. "I shall lend Otis a hand. If you find her, keep her here and stay with her until I return."

He didn't wait for a reply. Streaking through the master apartments he went first to the toile suite, though he knew he wouldn't find Milosh there. It was the Gypsy in wolf form in that sledge; he would stake all upon it.

That being the case, the man must have had a reason, so his search for the enigmatic vampire hunter stopped there. He wouldn't find him in those rooms, or in the secret tunnel below, or anywhere in the Abbey proper, come to that.

Tearing down the back stairs like a madman, Joss burst out into the fresh falling snow and narrowed his eyes, scanning the tor in all directions. Dawn had broken, but one would scarcely know it for the dark, brooding clouds, as dusky as smoke, hugging the horizon, and spewing out fresh snow. He could barely see the tracks the sledge runners had made, or the footprints and wolf prints all around, though the whole of it smacked of calamity and made his blood run cold. Could Cora's footprints be among them? There weren't any other footprints anywhere else in sight.

There was no time to lose. It was impossible on foot, and he trudged off into the wind toward the stable to saddle a horse. If she was in that sledge . . . *No!* He wouldn't think about that. He had to find her, and as mad as it was, explain something that he had no understanding of himself.

He had nearly finished saddling Titus when Otis rode in leading the two spent sledge horses, their sleek, snow-dusted hides rippling, their broad chests heaving.

"Where is the sledge?" Joss hollered over the animals' complaints.

"I dunno, sir," said the stabler, winded himself. "I had ta chase these two beasts clear ta Carlisle, they was that afeared. I didn't see no sign o' the sledge. I'm goin' back out soon as I settle these two down. Poor old Bates is probably lyin' in a ditch somewhere. If we don't find him quick, he'll be a snowdrift till the spring thaw."

"Did you see any wolv—dogs in your travels? There are wild ones about."

"No, sir, I did not, but I heard them plain enough, and gunshots, too. The only animal I seen was the big white one with a silver stripe down its back, and a big bushy tail, what was runnin' around in that sledge when I come out with the key to the vault. It was passing strange, sir, that's what it was. It was almost as if it was tryin' ta get inta that coffin, the way it was whinin' and scratchin' and digging at that coffin lid."

Joss swung himself up in the saddle. "They obviously broke free of the sledge," he said. "You didn't see the point where that occurred?"

"I seen a few dents in the smooth snow halfway down the tor, but the new snowfall was fast coverin' 'em." He shrugged. "I decided ta go after the horses first, since I could still see their tracks. Bates is dead after all, he ain't goin' nowhere. I'm a stabler, sir. Live horseflesh comes above cadavers in my book. I figured I'd best catch up ta these two before they run themselves ta death."

"Did you see . . . anyone walking about?"

"In *this,* sir? I should say not! They'd be daft!"

"My . . . houseguest, Miss Cora Applegate has gone missing," Joss said, halfway through the stable toward the doors Otis had left flung wide. "The only footprints—jumbled though they were—led to that sledge," he called over his shoulder. "Are you sure you didn't see anything?"

The stabler froze slack jawed in his tracks. "I wasn't lookin' fer a lady," he said. "My eyes was on that animal. It had the tarp all twisted off the coffin, and I—"

"See to those horses and continue your search," Joss

shouted, riding out into the snow. "If you find Miss Applegate, have her back to the Abbey at once and see that Parker attends her until I return."

The stabler said something more, but Joss didn't hear. He could make better time in wolf form, but distant gunshots scotched that idea. Besides, if he found Cora, he could hardly carry her back to the Abbey stark naked and afoot. Relentlessly driving the horse beneath him through impossible drifts, he leaned his hatless head into the wind, for he'd left in too great a hurry to fetch his beaver, and pressed on, following what remained of the trail the sledge runners had carved in the snow.

CHAPTER SIXTEEN

Cora awoke to the sensation of being dragged. Her eyes fluttered open, narrowed against the fresh snow falling into them, and saw the image of the great white wolf of earlier now backing her up the tor. Its great teeth were sunken into the hem of her chinchilla-trimmed wrapper. Its iridescent, red-rimmed eyes were trained upon her, their hypnotic stare both calming and frightening as it hauled her along up the steep grade. White breath was puffing from its flared nostrils, and it made a guttural complaint neither threatening nor trustworthy, but rather something more akin to evidence of its labor. Somehow, she didn't fear the beast anymore, though it had to be the same creature that had danced on the coffin earlier and nearly torn the lid off.

How strong it was! The cords in its sturdy legs stood out, and its barrel chest was flexing steadily. All at once, the hackles on the ridge of its silver-tipped back and great white neck ruff stood on end. It dropped her mantle and raised its snout, sniffing the snow-filled air. Why did that motion freeze her stock-still? It was like a dream. It must be a vision conjured from her ordeal with the wolf in the sledge—or so she thought until the animal's silent snarl became a bared-fang growl that hit her like cannon fire. It turned in time to be broadsided hard by another wolf that took it down, and the two began rolling, connected tooth and jowl in the snow.

Free of the white wolf's hypnotic glare, as though a tether had been severed, Cora scrambled to her feet and ran back down the tor, slip-sliding in her haste on the icy crust beneath the deceptive new blanket. Glancing behind, she glimpsed the white wolf streaked with blood, snapping the neck of the other wolf which now hung limp as a rag in its great jaws. She screamed as it continued to chomp. Was it trying to sever the creature's head? It was! She screamed again as it shook the limp, dead carcass, whipping it back and forth, severing sinew, bone, and flesh until it succeeded.

The beast seemed to have forgotten her, and she bounded on, helter-skelter, scrambling over the drifts, falling and struggling upright, running blind through the snow until a portly figure rose up in her path and seized her arms, shaking her to a standstill.

A troop of screams spilled from her throat as recognition set in. It was her father—but if what Joss had said was true, he was *vampir*, and she fought with all her strength to break free of his grasp.

Her strength was flagging so severely that she could not break his hold, which wrenched yet another scream from her dry throat. This was not the father she knew. His eyes were glazed in the same iridescent, red-rimmed manner as the wolves' eyes were, and his breath stank—not befouled with brandy and stale tobacco as it usually was. Now, it was fetid with the metallic stench of state blood, recalling the smell of the butcher's stall at the end of a hot day in the public market. Cora gagged at the recollection.

"Here you are, daughter," he said, his voice clipped and monotone. "You must come with me now. The others await. We must continue our journey."

Cora stared at him, at the vacant eyes, the pale skin veined with blue like tributaries on a map, and at the lethargy. He seemed almost to slur his words like a man in his cups, and when he walked he dragged his feet. She broke free of his hold, and she did so none too gently.

"I am not going anywhere with you!" she snapped.

Shoving him aside, she ran, glancing back over her shoulder at the sound of guttural growling. To her horror, the white wolf, whose fur was slimed with blood, had impacted her father and taken him down in the snow, just as it had the other wolf minutes before. Screaming at the top of her voice, Cora found her eyes riveted to the nightmare taking place before her. She failed to see the horse and rider coming on at breakneck speed, the horse's hooves flinging clouds of snow in all directions, until the thunder of its approach moved the earth beneath her feet, reverberating through the soles of her morocco leather ankle boots.

The rider's thunderous command rode the wind. "Not in front of her!" he shouted.

Was he speaking to the wolf? There was no one else about, and the animal responded, freezing in place, though it did not let its quarry go. Its huge paw pads were planted in the center of her father's chest, bared fangs dripping blood inches from his throat.

Cora gasped, and gasped again. The rider was Joss, and he scooped her up kicking and screaming, turned his mount, and plunged through the drifts back toward the Abbey, with her flung on her belly in front of his saddle.

He hadn't hurt her, just knocked the wind out of her. She was afraid to struggle in her precarious position for fear of falling off the horse's rippling back. It was already complaining over the added burden. Unfortunately, her vantage gave her a clear view of the bloodied snow, and of what once was the gray wolf that had attacked the white as they passed by. She blinked to clear her vision. She could scarcely believe her eyes. The wolf was gone, and in its place lay a naked man. It was the imposter coachman who had twice tried to corrupt her. His head was severed.

Veils of snow churned up by the horse's hooves rose to meet her, stinging her face, narrowing her eyes. Who was that screaming? It couldn't be her, though her mouth was open. Then the light was snuffed out by glaring white pinpoints starring her narrowed vision, and she saw no more.

Forgive me. Milosh's voice whispered in Joss's mind as the white wolf padded along beside him through the empty corridors. *I am so accustomed to doing . . . what I do, it has become second nature to me.*

Joss heaved a sigh and spoke as Milosh had done, in mind-speak. *I couldn't let you destroy it before her very eyes. She still views it as her father. I am hoping that before the sun sets upon this day we can convince her we are her best hope for survival.*

They had reached the yellow suite, and Joss stepped inside and tore a sheet off the bed.

What do you do? Milosh queried.

What is needed here are drastic measures, Joss said. *Humor me awhile. Unless I miss my guess, she saw my fangs and that is what made her run. If that is so, she will never take my word for anything now. I am hoping she will take yours.*

The wolf leaked a piercing whine that smacked of skepticism, and they began walking again.

High-pitched voices filtering along the hallway met their ears long before the master suite came into view. Joss squared his posture, and snapped the sheet in his hand. *Steady on,* he said. *Just humor me.*

"You cannot keep me here against my will!" Cora was screaming. "I will only run again."

"The master would skin me alive if I allowed you to go back out in that," came Parker's thin voice. It was plain he had grown hoarse from arguing with her. "Please, miss, you will bring the others, and we don't want to cause poor Grace any more upsetment."

"Poor Grace, eh?" Cora shouted. Joss winced, as some object shattered noisily. The girl had a penchant for breakage. He could only hope she had been kinder on Parker than she had been to him. Judging from the racket within, it didn't bode well.

Again, the wolf's whine captured Joss's attention. *I'm hoping your appearing will give pause enough for us to carry out our little demonstration,* he said to the wolf, as he gripped the master chamber door handle.

Our demonstration, is it? Milosh responded mentally. *This is your idea, young whelp. You are your father's son, I'll give you that. Do not fault me when it backfires in that handsome face of yours.*

Joss threw the door wide to find Cora, a porcelain tray above her head, the shattered remains of the wash basin it was about to join at her feet. The sight of the blood-streaked white wolf at his side froze her momentarily, just long enough for Joss to dismiss the valet, who had gone paste white.

"Leave us, Parker," he said.

"Y-y-yes, sir," said the valet, whose popping eyes were

also trained upon the wolf. Giving it a wide berth, he skittered past, bumping into the woodwork in his haste to flee. Joss shut the door and faced Cora.

"Keep that beast away from me!" she cried. "What? Have you brought it here to savage me the way it savaged my father? You—"

"Your father is dead, Cora," Joss said. "He died in the coach with the others. This noble animal killed the vampire your father became after death—the vampire that would have made you into one as soon as look at you."

"That is preposterous!"

"Have you forgotten Lyda so soon?"

"No! Come no closer," she cried. "Keep that animal back, or I will crown it with this priceless antique!" She brandished the tray.

Milosh growled. *This one would benefit from a proper spanking,* he said.

I have tried that, Joss returned. *It will take something more, believe me.* He unfurled the sheet and threw it over the wolf's back. *Quickly, man—change! Her aim is faultless. I have the scars to prove it.*

On your own head be it, Milosh said. Surging forward in a silver streak of displaced energy, he expanded to his full height, quickly draping the sheet like a toga about his nakedness.

Cora screamed, backpedaled toward the bed and sank down on the edge, clutching her porcelain tray as if it were a lifeline. Joss would have laughed at the slack-jawed expression on her beautiful face if the situation weren't so grave.

"W-w-what have I just seen here?" she stammered.

"You have seen more proof that what I say is truth," said Joss, turning to the Gypsy. "Milosh, may I present Miss Cora Applegate. Cora, this is Milosh, my other houseguest, and a living legend from Moldovia. He is *vampir* turned vampire hunter . . . as my mother and father are. It was he who saved them from the bloodlust with an ancient Persian ritual of the blood moon, which has also spared him from the feeding frenzy."

Milosh offered a heel-clicking bow that was somewhat less than effective executed barefoot in a makeshift toga, and Joss smiled in spite of himself.

"May I?" the Gypsy said, sweeping his arm toward the dressing room. "I make a better ambassador clothed."

Joss nodded. "Help yourself," he said. "Take whatever you fancy from the wardrobe."

Milosh bowed again and left them.

"Y-your parents are . . . *vampires* . . . ?" Cora murmured.

Joss nodded. He dared not tell her more just yet. That would have to wait, as she looked as if she were about to faint. "It is a long story," he said, "which I will save for another time."

"W-where is the wolf?" Cora murmured.

"Many vampires are shapeshifters," Joss said. "The white wolf is Milosh's creature. He is centuries old, Cora. Believe me, we can trust his judgment and assistance. In fact, we require it."

"He killed Father . . . and that impostor coachman."

Joss nodded. "He killed them, yes. He had to. But they were already dead. He freed their souls and gave them peace. Destruction is the only way to free a made vampire, which is what they were. An ancient entity infected them, we suspect. Sebastian Valentin, the very same that infected my parents before I was born."

"And you also," she snapped.

Joss hesitated, his posture deflating. "I do not know," he said. "That is something I am hoping Milosh will help me sort out."

"I saw your fangs," she said. "You would have in-fected me!"

"No," he returned. "You must believe me. The fangs exist, yes, but there is no feeding frenzy. They come upon me when I need to defend myself—and when I am aroused."

"How . . . if you are not a vampire?" Cora demanded.

"I do not know exactly, but Milosh and I have a theory."

"Tell it, then."

Joss cleared his voice and began to pace before the blazing hearth. "I was conceived after my parents em-braced the blood moon rite," he began. "I believe that when they drank the herbal draught necessary to the ritual—that is, when my mother drank it—some of its properties were passed on to me in the womb."

"It cured their infection, then?"

"No. There is no cure. They are still *vampir*—but the rite makes it possible for them to live without the blood-lust. Like myself, their fangs appear when they have need of weapons." Should he tell her that he, too, since he was thirteen, could shapeshift into wolf form when-ever he willed? No, she was not ready for that truth. He wondered that she ever would be.

"I have only just begun to experience the fangs," he said instead. "That is why I recently went to London, to our townhouse there seeking answers, but my parents had gone. I thought they might have come back here for the winter. It was while returning to the Abbey that I came upon your coach and this nightmare began."

"And the Gypsy?"

"His arrival was unexpected, but welcome, consider-ing. He could not have chosen a better time to pay his visit. I am hoping he will be able to sort my problem out for me."

Milosh stepped back over the threshold, neatly dressed in buckskins and an Egyptian cotton shirt, and Cora gasped. Fresh blood was seeping through the fabric, where exertion had stressed his wound.

"He speaks the truth," the Gypsy said. "You are infested here. Three have been so far released from their damnation and gone to their eternal peace: the abigail, Lyda; he who pretended to be your coachman; and your father. I am sorry. How many more have we to deal with, miss? How many more were in that coach?"

Cora had gone as white as the snow frosting the windowpane, and Joss took a step toward her, fearing she might swoon, but she stiffened and recoiled as he approached, so he kept his distance.

"The man I was to marry . . . and his father," she stammered. "And the real coachman."

"No others?"

"The passenger we picked up along the way who I'm told seems to fit the description of your . . . Sebastian. But none of this can be real! There are no such things as vampires! They are legend—*myth*!"

"Here in England, perhaps," said Milosh, "but believe me, little lady, there are places in this world where people know how real they are, and you have just seen yourself proof positive of what I say."

"No. I have seen some clever sleight of hand—some magic trick. I know there are those who can cloud the minds of others. . . ."

Milosh smiled. It did not reach his eyes. "Yes, I am such a one," he said, "but not with someone as hostile as you, a true skeptic." He began unbuttoning his shirt. "I could change back if that would help convince you," he said. "I much prefer my wolf incarnation of late in any case."

Joss suppressed a smile. It was plain Milosh was in earnest, and Cora's slack-jawed expression was priceless.

"No!" Cora shrilled. "Don't you dare!"

"Well, then," Milosh said. "Are you prepared to admit that the undead walk among us?"

Cora gave a hesitant nod. Her lower lip had begun to tremble, and her eyes—those incredible, shimmering blue eyes—were awash with tears. How Joss longed to enfold her in his arms and soothe away the terror and the anger he saw. Instead, he held his peace and kept his distance. Milosh was in charge now, and he would bow to a higher authority. Nothing he could possibly offer would sway Cora's thinking, and he was wise enough not to test it. Perhaps in time she would soften toward him, but in this moment it didn't seem likely, and he heaved a sigh.

"You are in no danger from me, little lady," Milosh went on. "I would have spared you much of this ordeal if only I had been able to scratch the lid off that coffin in the sledge and tether you until Joss arrived."

"Hah! And what of *him?*" she snapped, injecting as much venom in her tone as she could muster judging from her up-tilted chin, and the tight-lipped mouth that delivered the words. How exquisite she was when anger blushed her skin and flashed in her bluebell blue eyes darkening them to a smoky hue. Nonetheless, as hard as it was to tear his eyes away from that beautiful face, they flashed toward Milosh.

The Gypsy studied him, hesitating. "I would stake my life on it that you are in no danger from him," he said.

"It took you long enough to say so," Cora noted.

Again, the Gypsy smiled. "He is his father's son, young lady," he returned. "His father suffered agonies you could not possibly imagine to keep his lady safe before the blood moon ritual freed him from the feeding frenzy."

"I am not his lady," Cora snapped.

Joss winced in spite of himself. Those words stung.

Milosh blinked, then went on. "You are in grave danger, miss, but not from Joss Hyde-White," he said. "I smell Sebastian Valentin. Believe me, he is near, and he is relentless. He has a grudge against this family, and he will stop at nothing to wreak his vengeance. What troubles me is the coachman I have just killed. I am told he was not your coachman, and he was not one of your party. Unless I miss my guess, he was Sebastian's creature—one of the minions brought along to aid in this plot to bring low the house of Hyde-White. So!" he said with a flourish. "You can either trust us to protect you until we destroy the evil come among us, or strike out on your own. What shall it be?"

"How have I a choice, held captive here?" She asked.

"You are not a prisoner, Cora," Joss interrupted. "You tried to set off on your own. How well did you fare? But for Milosh here, you would be one of them by now. And the whoreson that . . . attacked you is still out there, still lusting after you—only now his menace is a thousand times greater. He is undead! His bloodlust is unstoppable. You have no idea of the strength he has gained now that he has become *vampir.*"

"I saw his fangs," she said, nodding toward Joss and shivering. "I *saw* them."

"And you will likely see them again," Milosh replied. "But there has been no bloodlust. Has he hurt you? No. He was conceived *after* his mother embraced the blood moon ritual, and while I cannot be certain yet, I believe as he does that the blood moon has spared him becoming what they were before the rite. If we are correct, it has affected him in the manner of an antidote . . . or a preventative. It has done for him what it did for them . . . and for myself. The fangs will appear only when he is emotionally charged or in need of a weapon, but there will be *no* feeding frenzy—no bloodlust to drink from the veins of a living creature."

"And if you are not 'correct'?" asked Cora.

Milosh was silent moment. "We shall address that issue if and when it presents itself."

CHAPTER SEVENTEEN

"Do you think we've convinced her to trust us?" Joss asked, padding down the back stairs with the Gypsy at his side. It still remained to find Bates's body before the new falling snow buried it, and to see it below to the kirkyard before dark; then the real danger would begin.

"We have given her pause for thought," Milosh said. "For now, it is enough. I doubt she will run again—at least not today, though I would be more at ease if there were someone with her at all times."

"I do not know how to thank you for your efforts," Joss said.

"There is no need." Milosh waved him off with a hand gesture. "What is her connection to the others in that coach . . . the ones still at large? I sense something other than the threat of vampires is distressing her."

Joss heaved a sigh. "Her father arranged a marriage between her and the young man in the carriage, but it was the young man's father who took her innocence after drugging her and her abigail. They were on their way to Gretna Green in Scotland, where marriages are performed no questions asked, when their coach became bogged down in the snow. Not all the animals hereabouts walk upon four feet, Milosh," he added sadly.

The Gypsy growled. The feral sound raised the short hairs at the back of Joss's neck and riddled him with gooseflesh. After centuries of shapeshifting, Milosh had evidently become more wolf than man—even in the way he moved, which brought another concern to the fore. As he'd noted before, Milosh was more than three and a half centuries old and yet looked not a day past a striking, virile forty, youthful and darkly handsome still. Joss couldn't help but wonder how it would be with him. Would he stop aging, too? But there were too many pressing concerns to address that now, though it remained under the surface like a splinter, just painful enough to annoy.

"They were planning to *share* her?" Milosh asked.

"No," Joss returned. "It was hardly a love match. Cora wasn't in love with young Clement, and his affections lay . . . elsewhere. The marriage was a cover-up, to take suspicion off the son while the father took his pleasures whenever he wished. He planned to get an heir on her and pretend it was a legitimate successor. The son—Albert was his name—was rumored to be sterile since a childhood illness. The old man meant to cancel those suspicions." There was no need to go into further detail, and he did not.

Again, the Gypsy growled. "And these are aristocrats?" he said.

Joss nodded. "But they are hardly exemplary of the British aristocracy. There are lowlifes in every class—a different sort of vampire, eh? But vampire nonetheless, bleeding the innocence of young maidens."

"What sort of father—?"

"A desperate one," Joss interrupted. "Either he stood to gain a staggering sum for the sacrifice, or the bounder had something on him. Not even Cora knows for certain, and it hardly matters now. What does matter is finding the rest of the creatures among us, and destroying them before more harm is done."

When they burst through the rear door into the snow, falling softly now, at last showing signs of stopping, Titus was still standing as Joss had left him. He jerked the reins free of the bracken he'd tethered the animal to and stroked its muscular neck. He was just about to lead Titus toward the stables to saddle another mount for Milosh when Otis appeared on the crest of the tor leading a limping horse.

Joss left Titus and ran toward the stabler. Milosh sprinted alongside. What was the man made of that he could be so athletic come so soon from suffering a bullet wound?

"I've found . . . poor Bates," Otis panted. Bending at the waist, he gripped his knees and gulped air into his lungs. "He's lyin' below . . . not far from the old rowan tree. I drug him back inta his coffin and I righted the sledge, with old Gideon's help here, though I fear I've maimed the poor beast doin' it, but . . . I couldn't get the coffin inta the sledge on my own."

"We'll do it," said Joss, taking hold of the stabler's arm to steady him. "Go on and rest. You're worn to a raveling." Still gulping air, the stabler glanced at the Gypsy, and Joss rose to the occasion. "I'm sorry," he said. "This is Mother and Father's friend, Milosh from Romania, come for a visit. Milosh, this is my stable master, Otis McFee."

The Gypsy sketched a respectful bow.

"You'll want ta get old Bates below before dark," said

Otis. "Them wild dogs have started howlin' again. I'm goin' ta fetch my pistol. They're comin' closer to the Abbey."

"I hope you will exercise discretion before you fire," Milosh said. "I have brought my . . . own dog along, and I would not like him peppered with lead."

"What does he look like?" Otis said.

"He is large and wolflike—white, with a streak of silver-tipped fur down his back. I believe you met him earlier."

Otis gave a start. "The animal in the sledge?" he cried.

"The very same," the Gypsy said. "He can be quite precocious at times, I'm afraid."

"Well, I'm sure glad ya told me," Otis replied, " 'cause I was set to give him a taste o' lead. I never seen a dog do what he was doin' in all my life. It was like he was tryin' to open that coffin!"

"I shall do my best to keep him in control in the future," Milosh said. "But at least now you know which dog not to shoot, hm?"

"Aye," said the stabler, glancing between them. "Are ya sure ya don't need me?"

"You've done enough," said Joss. "Go and rest. We can ill afford any more casualties here now."

"Thank ya', then," Otis said with a nod, trudging on toward the stables.

Joss stared at Milosh, slack jawed. "Why did you confess to that?" he said. "I've taken great pains all these years to keep my wolf a secret—only venturing out at night for the most part, keeping to the wood, to the shadows—and you dare so much. Why?" He was incredulous.

"Folks haven't been so keen on gunning down animals 'all these years,' I'll wager," Milosh said. "I've already been shot once. I'd rather not take any more lead if I can avoid it. It may be necessary for me to go about in wolf form more than I do on two legs, Joss. At least now Otis won't be gunning for me—but *you* will need to be more careful than ever. Your silver wolf with its dark-masked face looks nothing like mine."

"My wolf has a mask'?"

Milosh nodded. "A handsome one, like dark smoke about the eyes and face, just like your father's. It has a smoky saddle, too. As you resemble Jon in human form, so you resemble him in your wolf incarnation. Side by side, it would be nearly impossible to tell you apart."

They said no more, leading Titus and slip-sliding halfway down the tor to the naked rowan tree, standing like a petrified sentinel, its twisted arms pointing toward the kirkyard at the bottom. Between them, they hefted the coffin into the sledge. The old conveyance was badly damaged on one side, but the seat was intact, and they tied the coffin in place and fashioned a makeshift hookup to hitch Titus to what remained of the framework. The horse shied and complained at first, but finally gave in and let Joss attempt to climb up in the seat.

"Will it hold the two of us, do you think?" Milosh queried, eyeing the awkward repair skeptically.

"I hope so, but you needn't come. I can manage on my own. The sexton will lend a hand once I have it below."

"Oh, but I must," Milosh said. "Listen."

Joss raised his head. Titus had finally stopped complaining, and in the absence of the wind, he heard the wolves clearly, howling in the distance. It was an eerie sound that riddled him with chills.

"It will soon be dark," Milosh observed. "We go together. Sebastian is somewhere in that number. He bides his time and waits. You have no inkling of his power. If your father, your mother, and I together could not bring him down, how can you hope to do so alone? If your parents knew I was here and let you come to harm, how could I live with myself? I have eternities to live through, young whelp, and I will not suffer them with you upon my conscience. Move over."

Cora rested her head against the velvet draperies at her bedchamber window, inhaling the faint musty odor that lingered about the thick burgundy fabric. She'd watched Otis trudge toward the stables, and followed Joss and the enigmatic Gypsy, Milosh, with her eyes until they disappeared beyond the slope of the tor. She couldn't see them now, nor hear the mixed vibrations of their speech through the snow-frosted pane. Then she heard the wolves howling out of rhythm—one . . . two . . . three distinct feral voices, plaintive and sad—and she backed away from the window. Soon it would be dark. Joss and the Gypsy would never return in time.

Oddly, she took some comfort in the fact that Milosh was with Joss. Madness! There, in the lonely confines of the master bedchamber—*his* chamber—staring absently toward the bed—*his* bed; the bed she'd nearly made love with Joss in but hours before—she could no longer deny her heart. Vampire or not, she was worried about him. His Gypsy friend was also concerned.

The fire was dwindling in the hearth. *Mustn't let it go out. A bat won't fly down a lit chimney. . . . But what about all the other chimneys in this house?* The vampires that had gained access were dead. But did the invitation extend to the rest, since they were evidently all this vampire named Sebastian's creatures? That thought was too terrible to think, and Cora shrugged it off and tossed several small logs—the last of the wood—into the hearth. Watching sparks rush up the chimney, she stirred the fire back to life with the poker. When the knock came at the door, she lurched so violently that the poker slipped from her hand and crashed to the hearthstone with a clang.

"W-who is it?" she said.

"It is Parker, miss," came the valet's hoarse voice from the other side. "I've brought more logs for the fire."

Cora threw the bolt and let the valet in. He was carrying fresh wood in a leather sling, which he set down with a grunt and began stacking in a container beside the hearth.

Cora went again to the window. The snow had stopped falling, and the light was fading. Where could they be? Had Joss and Milosh found the sledge and the butler's body and driven it below to the kirkyard?

"Did the master say when he would be returning?" she asked Parker, who rose from his chore.

"We spoke only briefly," the valet said. "He wanted to be back before dark."

"It is nearly that now," she said. "And listen. Do you hear that dreadful howling? Those animals are abroad, and the villagers will be hunting them. Suppose . . ." She couldn't finish the thought, wouldn't give it substance with words.

"You mustn't worry, miss," the valet said. "Young master is in good hands with Mr. Milosh. He is a good and loyal friend to this house, and his deeds are legend. He will let no harm come to young master." He lit the lamps and shuffled toward the open doorway. "It was young master's wish that you join him in the dining parlor for the evening meal. I will come and fetch you when 'tis time."

As he turned to go, Cora called him back. "Parker, wait." She turned him around on the threshold. "Please forgive my behavior earlier."

He waved her off with a hand gesture. "There is nothing to forgive, miss," he said.

"No, there is," she argued. "I was . . . distraught. I had no right to take it out on you."

"Think no more about it, miss," said the valet. "Will you require anything else?"

Cora opened her mouth to answer, but the hollow banging of the brass knocker funneling up from the main door below froze them both in place.

"Joss wouldn't knock . . . would he, Parker?"

"No, miss. I will see to it. Please remain here."

"You won't let anyone in?" Cora panicked.

"Trust me not to do that, miss. No one will cross the threshold unless young master brings them himself, I promise you."

The knock came again, three steady bangs ringing from the rafters that riddled Cora with gooseflesh. Sketching a bow, Parker shuffled off without a backward glance. She hadn't missed his complexion turn gray of a sudden, or his silver eyes darken beneath their wrinkled lids and, almost without thinking, she tiptoed after him at a discreet distance.

Exhaustion was telling on the valet, and she pattered down the stairs before he had traveled the length of the Great Hall, and slipped beneath the staircase, where she could observe without being seen. Holding her breath, she swallowed her rapid heartbeat as Parker opened the door to find . . . Clive Clement!

"Yes?" said the valet—rather staunchly, Cora thought,

given his frail appearance. There was evidently more to the aging valet than met the eye. He had barred the entrance with his body, one hand gripping the door handle, the other clutching the jamb, and brought himself up to his full height. *Impressive, indeed,* she thought, though she still trembled with raw fear toward Clement, nearly toe-to-toe with him.

"Clive Clement, my man," said the other. "I'm come for my son's intended, now that the storm has stopped. He awaits her in the village. May I come in and warm myself while she readies herself for travel?"

Cora glimpsed two horses prancing in the drive through the open doorway. A frigid blast of wind funneling down the corridor swirled about her ankles. It ruffled the hem of her gown, riddling her with legitimate chills, and she gripped the burled wood staircase support. *No . . . please, no! Don't let him in!* her mind pleaded.

"I'm sorry, sir," the valet said. "The master isn't in, and—"

"I haven't come to see the master," Clement interrupted. "I've come to take my son's betrothed off his hands. Now, if you will kindly stand aside . . ."

Parker adjusted his posture, barring the way. "I'm sorry, sir," he said. "I've strict orders not to admit anyone in the master's absence."

"Preposterous!" Clement barked, his white breath puffing against the twilight. "Stand aside! I am half-frozen, man. Is this the sort of hospitality you North Country folk extend to wayfarers?"

"I am sorry, sir," Parker repeated with a grunt, attempting to close the door, but the other's hand planted firmly on it prevented him. "I cannot go against the master."

"I have never heard the like!" said Clement. "Do I have to fetch the constable's men, or whatever you call them here in the north? I will, you'd best believe, if you do not let me in at once or fetch Miss Cora Applegate to me posthaste. I know she is here. The vicar in the village confirmed it."

Parker held his ground. "Fetch whomever you like," he said. "There is no law against barring strangers from one's door. You will have to wait until the master returns to be admitted here. I haven't the authority. He is expected shortly. You may wait in the stable if needs must, out of the weather, or come back another time. I have my orders, and I must obey them. Good evening, sir."

It clearly took all the valet's strength to shut the door in Clement's face. Afterward, he threw the bolt and sagged against the ancient wood, only to lurch away from it as a methodical banging began at his back.

Cora rushed to his side from the shadows. "Thank you," she sobbed, and then realized: "The rear entrance—is it barred as well?"

Parker gave a lurch. "I shall see to it," he said. "Go back to your rooms and lock the doors. You shouldn't have come down. Have no fear, miss, he shan't get in, I promise you."

"If they are right, he is *vampir*," Cora said.

"Yes, miss," Parker returned. "There was never danger of his entering without an invitation. I will check below, though . . . just to be sure."

Cora held him back one more time as he shuffled past. "Parker," she said, "Forgive me, but . . . are you . . . ?"

The valet offered a crimped-lip smile. "No, miss," he said. "That I am not, and I have no desire to become one. Now then, please go back to your rooms, lock yourself in, and let me see to house business until young master returns. Knowing you are safe will make my job all the easier."

He shuffled off then and disappeared below stairs. Cora stared after him until she could no longer hear the patter of his feet on the back stairs before returning to her suite. Slipping inside, she locked the door and went to her bedroom window, hoping for some sign of the sledge returning. There was none. All was still and dark. The snow had stopped falling, but the clouds had not yet yielded to the moon, and the only glimmer of light was the glow of a lantern in the stable throwing dappled puddles of golden sheen on the drifting snow. The howl of a wolf cut through the silence. It seemed closer somehow. Another, more distant howl answered the first wolf's call. Cora shuddered at the sound.

Drawing the draperies against the pending darkness, she sank down on the edge of the bed and dropped her head in her hands. She wouldn't light the lamps. The firelight was all she needed while she waited for Joss's familiar knock at her door.

Joss locked the crypt and climbed back into the sledge. "We'll never make it back by full dark," he said, snapping the reins. "Walk on!" he called to the horse, guiding him out through the graveyard gate. The howl of wolves, some near, some distant, made his blood run cold. "Listen to that," he said. "What do you make of it?"

"They have been following us since we left the Abbey," said Milosh. "We are being watched."

"Sebastian?" Joss had heard blood-chilling tales of the

notorious vampire since he was old enough to comprehend them. Milosh was right. If he and his parents—all three—couldn't destroy the creature, what hope had Joss of succeeding? It didn't bode well.

The Gypsy hesitated. "He is near," he said at last. "I have his scent. It is like no other, but the wolf is not his preferred creature. He usually shifts into the shape of a bat, and it is sure, swift and deadly. I have seen it tear men's throats out. Keep your head down, and tighten that muffler. Protect your neck. It is no ordinary bat. We're probably safe enough for now. Sebastian likes to toy with his victims, to torment them and break them down. He is ever confident of his powers, and well he should be. They have served him admirably enough for centuries. This is no mere vampire in the general sense. He is a ruthless, evil, undefeated creature, a former high official in the Romanian Church before he was infected. He—unlike your noble father, who was also a man of the cloth—succumbed to the lure of his maker and fell into the realm of outer darkness. He lusted after your father, and still does, since men of the cloth are a vampire's greatest prize. Another might have succumbed, but your father resisted. And since he cannot have Jon Hyde-White, whom it is obvious that he has come here seeking, Sebastian has set his sights upon you. Our contest—Sebastian's and mine—goes back over three-and-a-half centuries, and will continue until one of us is victorious. It is a bleak prospect . . . for all of us."

Joss hesitated. The only sounds were the mournful howling of near and distant wolves, and the swish of the sledge runner slicing through the new-fallen snow. "So, what you're saying is that there isn't much hope I shall be victorious. Is that it?"

"I am saying that it is little reflection upon you if you aren't," the Gypsy said. "Your noble father nearly died in the attempt . . . and your brave mother. Hundreds have tried and failed in my homeland. I do not care to count and recount the times that I have failed to bring Sebastian low. One day someone will. With age comes complacence. Eventually that will be his downfall. All I ask is that I be there when it happens. Right now, needs must that we concentrate upon coaxing this poor beast up that tor. I am not liking the voices of the wolves. One cannot walk half one's life in the body of *canis dirus* and not become that creature to some extent—think with its mind, understand the speech of its brethren. They make mock of us. That is not a good sign. Can you not hear it, young whelp? You, too, now belong to the Brotherhood of the Vampire Wolf, the only society that embraces *vampir* of all persuasions, all resistors whose creature is the wolf. Listen closely and look sharp." He raised his hand as Joss opened his mouth to speak. "No—*listen*," he said. "The power to discern may someday save your life. Beheading the abigail was your first accomplishment, but this is your first lesson."

Joss had had no idea until that moment that he was under the legendary Gypsy's tutelage. The realization thrilled and frightened him all at once. He did as Milosh bade. Scarcely breathing, he listened to the howling wolves, his ears pricked for any inflection, any pitch in the mournful sounds that might speak to him.

"What do you hear?" asked Milosh.

"We are surrounded," Joss said. "They twitter like children."

"Can you urge the horse to climb any faster?"

"Titus is not a carriage horse," Joss said. "It pains me to use him thus, but I will try."

Snapping the whip over the horse's head did little to coerce the animal to pick up its pace on the steep, slippery upgrade. What it did provoke was a bevy of shrill complaints from the thoroughbred, which only served to agitate the wolves. Nonetheless, Titus finally reached the summit, dragging the wounded sledge to level ground.

Nearing the stables, Joss called out to Otis. Meanwhile, both he and Milosh climbed down from the crooked seat, which shuddered and groaned with their lifted weight. Trudging through the drifted snow, Joss had nearly reached the open stable doors when a huge gray wolf charged through, all but knocking him down. Its thick, hackle-raised fur was matted with blood, its eyes blazed red like two live coals. Taken by surprise, Joss backpedaled, lost his balance and fell, splayed out in a drift beside the stable doors as the animal streaked past so closely he could smell the strong metallic odor of the blood that decorated it, and the feral musk of its exertion.

Milosh quickly hauled him to his feet, but Joss shrugged free and ran into the stable calling Otis at the top of his voice. No answer came; neither did the horses greet him with their familiar complaints, sensing something untoward in him as they always seemed to do. That chilling reminder harkened him back to the reason any of this was happening: his thirst for the knowledge of who—of *what*—he truly was. But now was still not the time to theorize. The stabler's name froze half-spoken on his lips, his eyes focused through the bleak lantern light inside. Only two of the six horses stabled there were standing, and the straw-strewn floor was running with blood.

Joss's eyes flashed toward the loft. No lantern was lit there. All was in darkness in Otis's quarters. With Milosh at his heels, Joss ventured farther in, unable to keep his knees from shaking. Hope still moved him, though he knew what he would find as he stumbled past the savaged horses' stalls. Otis lay beyond in the hay-mow, his throat torn out and his body sprawled in the blood-fouled hay.

Groaning, Joss sank down on his knees beside the stabler. His eyes misty with tears, he reached to close Otis's eyes, and gave a lurch as Milosh gripped his shoulder with a firm hand.

"You know what you must do," said the Gypsy.

Joss stared at him through glazed eyes as if he were a stranger.

"He will rise undead," Milosh reminded him.

"And the horses?" Joss murmured.

Milosh nodded. "They will rise to serve their new masters. We must prevent this. That is your second lesson." A sickle hung on the stable wall alongside the tack room. He strode over and seized it. "Here," he said, extending it. "Your stabler first. Do it now while he lies thus. It will be harder once he wakes. I see your anguish. I know how difficult this is for you. Remember, I had to do the very same to my beloved wife, who was increasing with my child. It was to save them. Take this! Do not let your trusted servant rise undead to hunt you like the others!"

Just then the howl of a nearby wolf pierced the stillness, and Joss staggered to his feet. He shoved the Gypsy's outstretched arm away. "It isn't over. Cora!" he gritted through clenched teeth, in a vain attempt to hold his fangs at bay. Then, bolting out of the stable with a crashing disregard for Milosh or Titus in his path, he ran slip-sliding through the snowdrifts toward the Abbey.

CHAPTER EIGHTEEN

Cora yanked the draperies back, releasing a shower of dust motes, her eyes trained upon the stable below. She could hear the terrible snarls, and the screams—a man's screams—high-pitched and desperate, even at her distance through the frozen windowpane. Frantically she yanked the bellpull, meanwhile pacing before the window. Tears welled in her eyes. Those horrible screams had all but stopped her heart, and she covered her ears to shut out the sound, but she heard it still. Something unspeakable was happening in that stable. Had Joss returned? Was that him screaming? She yanked the bellpull again. Why didn't someone answer?

With all her strength, she tore at the window latch, but it was frozen shut and wouldn't budge. Straining her eyes toward the stable below, she saw the sledge heave to a stop beside the doors, saw Joss's tall, muscular form silhouetted against the snow as he leapt out with Milosh close behind. It wasn't him that she had heard screaming after all. Her heart gave a tumble of relief in her breast, and her breath released audibly. Yet while the dreadful screams had stopped, whatever had caused them was still inside that stable, and now she screamed herself, at the top of her voice, pounding on the glass with both her tiny fists.

"No! Don't go in there!" she cried. "I beg you, don't . . . !" Why wouldn't they look up? Why didn't they hear her?

All at once a huge streak of gray fur and muscle sailed through the open stable doors. It came so close to Joss that he lost his balance and fell on his back in the snow. Cora screamed again. She could bear no more. She couldn't stand here helpless and do nothing. She'd darted toward the door just as a knock came upon it, and she threw it open to find Parker on the threshold. The look of him wrenched yet another scream from her throat. He was as white as chalk, and what little hair he had was fanned out about him in wild disarray. From the lurch he gave, she knew she'd frightened him more than he had frightened her.

"Steady on, miss," he said, heaving to catch his breath. "Young master has just now come. All will be well."

"All will be well, is it?" she shrilled. "Someone has just died down there! I heard his death screams. I saw the wolf!" Snorting in exasperation, she shoved him aside and ran out into the corridor. Flying over the landing, she raced down the back stairs and out into the now moonlit snow, the valet's cries behind falling upon deaf ears.

She hadn't taken her wrapper, and the cold hit her hard, taking her breath away. Gripping chills all but crippled her, racing along her spine. Her footing was anything but sure as she tried to negotiate the drifts that had piled up beside the rear door, but she didn't have to struggle far. She had scarcely taken three steps when Joss seized her, crushing her against him in trembling arms.

"Thank God," he murmured. "What are you doing out here? Where is Parker?"

"H-here, sir," the valet said from the doorway. "I-I couldn't hold her, sir."

"I saw you fall," Cora sobbed. "That wolf! I thought . . . I was afraid you . . ."

Parker started to trudge toward the stable, but Joss's quick hand arrested him. "No, stay away," he said. "Go back inside. Milosh is seeing to it."

"Seeing to what?" Cora asked. "I heard screams. What's happened?"

Joss swept her up in his arms and rushed her through the back door. "Close that," he charged Parker, "but leave it unlatched for Milosh."

"Is it Otis?" the valet queried, his voice thin.

Joss nodded. "And all but two of my horses," he said. "Are the others all right?"

"Grace is abed. She grieves still," Parker said. "Amy is tending her, and Rodgers is helping Cook in her absence."

"Good!" said Joss, having reached the landing. "Do not leave the Abbey for *any* reason. Pass the word to the others. We are surrounded. They will lose their strength at dawn, those that can bear the light of day. Let neither man nor beast into the Abbey day or night. The undead take many forms."

"Y-yes, sir."

"We need to talk, Parker," Joss said from the second-floor landing. "Later . . . make yourself available."

He didn't wait for an answer. Cora tightened her grip about his neck as he carried her to the master suite. His heartbeat was thumping beneath the heavy-caped greatcoat. He smelled clean, of citrus and musk, and of the cold north wind. She inhaled deeply, nuzzling closer.

Entering the master apartments, Joss kicked the door shut behind them, carried her into the bedroom and set her on her feet. Cora scarcely breathed. His eyes were wild, feral things boring into her, searching her face, her body, raking her from head to toe, memorizing every contour, every line of her face and body.

His hands were trembling as he unwound the muffler from his neck and discarded his multicaped greatcoat. Then she was in his arms again. Neither spoke. There was no need. He reached out and removed the combs that held her hair in place, and it fell in a cascade to her waist. His fingers threaded through it, smoothing it over her shoulders, then cupped her face. His hands were cold, so cold, but that wasn't what caused the icy-hot chills that turned her spine to jelly and molded her body to his, and it didn't prevent what felt like molten fire from coursing through her loins. Such feelings should flag danger, but they didn't. The look in his quicksilver eyes so dilated with desire riveted her unmercifully. He had the power to seduce her with a glance, to possess with a smile. This time, she let him.

He murmured her name in that husky baritone that set her afire from the inside out. It crackled with longing. Her breath caught as his lips descended, before they ever touched hers. Partly because she remembered the fangs she'd seen spoiling that handsome mouth, but mostly because of the thrum at her very core. Whatever these feelings were, they would be denied no longer, as they'd been all tangled up in the horror she'd felt when she feared for his life. She wanted him in a way that she never thought she could ever want any man, considering what had gone before. There was a palpable facet of desperation in their embrace, as if his very life depended upon it. It was contagious. There was no stopping now. Whoever he was, whatever he was, didn't matter anymore; he had bewitched her.

They scarcely parted long enough for him to tear his boots off and discard his clothes. When her frock and petticoats joined the pile at their feet, she scarcely knew. They stood naked together, the hard shaft of his arousal between them. Gripping her hand, he curled her fingers around it.

"I am still in your hands, Cora," he gritted out through clenched teeth. Clearly, he was making a valiant attempt to hold back his fangs. "I will never hurt you. I hope I have already proven that."

Cora gazed into the moist onyx depths that desire had made of his eyes. How the firelight gleamed in them! He was clearly torn between raw passion and grief for the faithful servant who had been savaged to death in the stable below; she could see it. She herself had never felt like this, as if a raging fire were burning inside, a fire that would only be quenched by yielding to the same desire that drove him . . . and by comforting him. No, she had never felt like this before. Her past ordeal paled before all that was now happening. He had *not* hurt her. Somehow, she knew she could take him at his word that he never would, the fangs he tried so to hide notwithstanding. Though deep down she feared those fangs, the fiery ache coursing through her sex would not be denied, and she threw her arms around his neck, and stood on tiptoe to reach his lips.

Joss groaned as her fingers combed through his hair.

"You are sure?" he murmured, forcing their mouths apart. Cora thrilled at his obvious struggle to spare her the sight, the feel of those deadly fangs.

"I'm sure," she whispered, and gasped at the suddenness of his response as he lifted her hips, guided her legs to encircle his waist, and entered her in one slow, tantalizing thrust.

Cora gasped again, and tears filled her eyes. There was no pain. She had steeled herself against the kind of pain she'd felt in the cruel, sweaty arms of the bounder who had taken her virtue. Instead, the warm, silken pressure of his life throbbing within her—filling her, paralyzing her senses of all save him—set loose a firestorm inside unlike anything she had ever dreamed possible. It was as if her very bones were melting.

The ache that tightened her moist sex was almost beyond bearing. The strength of him! And yet it was a gentle strength that defied description; Cora had never experienced the like. He was beyond stopping, and as volatile as their coupling was, she did not fear it; neither did she resist. To her complete surprise, she leaned into his embrace as he backed her against the wall and pushed deeper into her—into what was indeed virgin territory. Realizing that, she sobbed, and he stiffened against her.

"Have I hurt you?" he murmured, his hands roaming up and down the contours of her sides, along the indentation of her waist, over her breasts, his thumbs grazing her nipples as he caressed her.

Cora couldn't speak. Clinging to him, she buried her face in his shoulder and shook her head wildly that he had not.

"What, then?" he said.

She felt the urgency of the member filling her, felt it pulsate, though he stood stock-still as his hands—those strong, skilled hands—cupped her buttocks again, moving her body in a circular motion in rhythm with the pulse beat of his sex, so strong inside her.

"Do you want me . . . to stop?" he whispered hoarsely. His hot breath puffing against her ear riddled her with gooseflesh. His lips were touching her throat—those *fangs* were touching her throat—grazing it ever so slightly, and yet she still did not pull away. He seemed to have no inclination to use those teeth, though in that wonderful terrible moment, as startling as the realization was, if it had been his intent to sink those deadly fangs into her flesh, she would have let him; she was that captivated by his ardor and his passion. The thrill riveted her from head to toe.

Still she dared not speak, but her body spoke for her. Joss was clearly avoiding her lips with those fangs, and she tightened her grip around his neck and searched his arched throat for the source of the pulsating rhythm beating in his blood when she kissed him there. Joss cried aloud at the touch of her lips on the corded muscles and distended veins, causing her to grip him tighter still. His pelvis jerked forward, and he plunged deeper into her, groaning as her body tightened around his member in an unexpected reflex that forced a cry from her lips.

Moving in mindless oblivion, Cora matched the rhythm of his thrusts, riding the slick, moist dew of an unexpected climax, matching his pleasure sounds moan for moan as if they spoke with one voice until all the breath left her lungs in one guttural groan. She shuddered in his arms, every cell of her body engulfed in icy-hot waves of silken fire that took her breath away. He had frozen inside her, his breath coming short; but the moment he moved, she gripped him with her sex as orgasmic contractions riddled her again, and she milked him dry as he erupted inside her, filling her with the lava-hot rush of his seed.

Cora burst into tears. So *this* was what it was supposed to be, this achy ecstasy, this all-consuming fire that left her barely conscious and completely whole, sated, pleasantly flushed—limp in the powerful arms that crushed her so close their hearts beat as one. His broad chest heaving, Joss withdrew himself and gathered her into his arms. Carrying her to the bed, he laid her down, climbed in beside her, and gathered her against him beneath the downy counterpane.

Brushing her tears away, he searched her face in the hearth light. "I *have* hurt you," he said, his voice like gravel.

"N-no," she said, low-voiced. "It is just that . . . that . . ."

"That what, Cora?"

"Is it always supposed to be like . . . like *this*?"

"You didn't enjoy it?"

"I never dreamed . . . I never imagined it to be anything like . . . like this!"

His moist eyes were smiling as he took her lips in a gentle kiss. There were no fangs now; they had vanished. His mouth was soft and warm, his skilled tongue searching. But it was short-lived. Cora knew why. His sex had begun to tremble to life again against her thigh. He dared not risk the fangs returning. If only she knew what it meant. It was clear that he didn't know the answer himself, only that he must fight against it. She would not mention it. Not now. Not while she still glowed from his passion. Not while her whole body still tingled from his love. She clung to him as if for dear life, and said no more.

CHAPTER NINETEEN

Joss was a man with a mission, and he was proud of his accomplishments thus far if he did say so himself. He had broken through Cora's defenses and showed her what it meant to be loved by a man. True, it was not exactly as he'd pictured, and he still worried that he might have hurt her, though she said not, but he knew she had finally lived in his arms. He had felt her wetness, like liquid silk sheathing his sex. He had thrilled to the tug of her contractions again and again until she drained him dry. Right and wrong, sensibility and propriety did not enter into it; the only thing that mattered was proving to Cora that all men were not like the savage sort that had taken her virtue. Yes, he was proud of himself. It was a start, and despite the worst possible circumstances.

That she had even let him near her after running the way she had was a miracle. He still had the deadly fangs that had driven her away. What had turned her? It was an entirely different Cora who'd run from the Abbey into his arms through the drifting snow with no cloak or mantle and clung to him as if her very life depended upon that embrace. That was what had encouraged him. Whatever it was, he would not question it. He was grateful.

It was early. Soon it would be time for dinner. Raised up on one elbow gazing down at her so peacefully asleep beside him, he didn't have the heart to wake her. She needed sleep more than she needed food; that could come later. Toying with a handful of her long, lustrous hair, he raised it to his nose and closed his eyes, breathing deeply. Roses. A soft moan escaped him as he caressed the locks, but it was a luxury he could ill afford. He'd lingered too long already. Guilt pangs gripped him of a sudden. He'd left Milosh to deal with Otis. He needed to find the Gypsy and set it to rights. Yes, this was supposed to have been his chore, his lesson, and he'd failed before he'd begun. Was the Gypsy trying to make a vampire hunter of him? Why? His own parents had never attempted that. If Milosh was, there was a reason. Joss didn't want to speculate as to what it might be.

He heaved a ragged sigh and left the bed with a sinuous motion. He didn't want to wake Cora. He didn't want to leave her either, but that he must do. Outside, the wolves were gathering. Their howls rode the wind. Their nagging menace filtered through the frozen windowpane and thick velvet portieres shutting out the night, but not their bestial voices. He would have Parker keep watch outside the master bedchamber door . . . just in case. A close eye upon Cora, he dressed himself, looped his greatcoat over his arm and tiptoed out into the corridor. It was going to be a long night.

Parker was already stationed outside the master suite, where he could stand guard and hear the door if anyone came. The faithful valet retained a penchant for anticipation—the mark of a valuable servant.

With the burden of one worry lifted, Joss went first to the toile suite, but Milosh wasn't there. Shrugging on his coat, he wound his muffler around his neck—not for warmth but for protection. He hadn't forgotten what Milosh had told him about Sebastian, though he hadn't seen a bat since the nightmare began.

The rear door was still unlatched. Just as he'd thought, the Gypsy was still outside; Milosh would have locked it if he'd reentered the Abbey. All at once fear gripped Joss like an iron fist in the pit of his stomach. Milosh should have finished by now. The wounded sledge was still standing where they'd left it, though Titus had been unhitched. There was still a faint glimmer of light coming from the stable, and Joss bounded over the drifts past the paddock and burst inside. It took a moment for his eyes to become accustomed to the light. The stable still stank of the carnage that had taken place there earlier. The straw beneath his feet was fouled with blood. He followed the slick trail back out into the snow. All the savaged horses save one, and the beheaded stabler, had been dragged outside behind the paddock and piled in a heap that was slated to become a pyre by the look of it. Milosh was nowhere in sight.

Chills riddled Joss, and he shuddered visibly. Bracing himself against the wind, he trudged back inside the stables. His heart began to pound, and the fine hairs on the back of his neck stood on end. His hackles were raised. That never happened in his human incarnation without good cause. Something was not as it should be. It seemed as if Milosh had been interrupted before he could finish his chore. And what sort of strength did the Gypsy possess that he could haul horse carcasses on his own? Joss couldn't imagine.

Feet crunching straw spun him around, but there was

no one there, though he saw the straw tamp down where a man's boots were leaving footprints. They were carrying toward him. Whatever invisible creature stalked him had a distinct odor, sickening sweet, like mold, dead funeral flowers, and rotting meat. It rose up in his nostrils and choked him.

Sebastian?

Another wave of chills crawled along Joss's spine. His lips parted, making way for the fangs that had begun to descend. Disembodied laughter echoed from the exposed beam ceiling. It rang in the darkened loft, where last night at this time Otis had been climbing into his pallet bed at the end of the day. That bed was empty now. It would no longer receive the faithful stabler.

The footprints were coming closer. Joss backed away. He could hardly fight what he couldn't see. Besides, he had no weapons against the undead at hand. His parents kept holy water in the study. How could he have come here without it?

You cannot fight this entity all on your own, Milosh's voice echoed in his mind. *With or without holy water.*

Milosh? Thank God! Joss's mind replied. *I thought—*

Clear your mind, Milosh interrupted. *Your enemy is soon close enough to read your thoughts.*

Emboldened now that he knew Milosh was safe, Joss glanced about, looking for somewhere to retreat. There were plenty of empty stalls now, but one would box him in and he backed out toward the open doors, hesitating on the threshold. All at once the stable filled with blood-chilling laughter, and from the footsteps there appeared a towering creature surging to fill the span—half man, half bat, whose ugly head scraped the exposed beams above. Long fangs dripping blood gleamed in the lantern light, and its wingspread stretched from wall to tack-hung wall. The foul stench it gave off filled Joss's mouth with bile.

The laughter came again, and with it the thunder of hoofbeats as the savaged horse that had lain dead minutes earlier rose up and galloped out into the bitter night. Another burst of laughter filled the span, and the creature before Joss shriveled from its gargantuan form to an ordinary bat, soaring past and away after the horse, but not before sinking its sharp talons into Joss's muffler and carrying it off like a trophy. The last thing Joss saw as the phantom horse galloped off into deep, starless dark, was the bat sawing through the midnight sky above it, the muffler still caught in its talons, flapping in the wind like a standard on the field of battle.

Joss turned back, searching the stable for some sign of Milosh. His mind called the Gypsy's name. He dared not speak aloud then; it wasn't over. *Where are you?*

There was no answer, though outside the wolves' voices echoed from all directions. Joss spun toward the snow-swept tor, his eyes narrowed. The wind was growing stronger now, whistling past him, seeming to mock his frustration.

A rustling from behind turned him around to face the portly form of a man emerging from the shadows at the back of the stable. Joss froze. It was Clive Clement.

"How did you get in here?" Joss snarled. "I gave you no leave to enter!"

"No," Clement replied, "your man did. He barred me from the Abbey in your absence, but said that I might wait here in the stables for you to return. It was a costly invitation, that, and a foolish one. Had he admitted me to the house proper, I would have collected my son's betrothed and been on my way. You have him to thank for your stabler's untimely demise."

Joss wasted no words upon the creature. Like lightning he leapt through the air—unprepared for his own strength and the distance of his leap, nearly twice that from the secret tunnel to the ground. It was the first time he had used a greater maneuver, and he hadn't been aware that he had the power until he tapped it. Fangs extended, he collided with the vampire and took it down. He should have finished the job when he first felled the creature out on the moor. He had not known then what he knew now, that Clement was the bounder who'd taken Cora's virtue, and so his rage was twofold.

Brute force ruled Joss. Seeing through a bloodred haze that always accompanied such passion, he rolled over and over on the fouled straw that carpeted the stable, grappling with the creature, his fully extended fangs poised to rip out the vampire's throat; but so were the creature's fangs extended toward him, just inches from his jugular. He failed to see the great white wolf poised above in the loft until it sailed through the air and slammed into them both. The impact broke Clement's hold, and the vampire scrambled to his feet and out of the stable, the wolf's snarls ringing in Joss's ears. It padded to the stable doorway and stood its ground until Clement was out of sight.

Joss leaked an exasperated groan and pounded the straw beneath him. "Why the devil did you do that?" he thundered. "I had him!"

Again the wolf growled. *Had him, did you?* Milosh said. *You think with your heart instead of your head, young whelp, and it would have bested you. You must learn to think with the instinct, mind and soul of the hunter, Joss Hyde-White, or you will become the hunted.*

Joss did not like the sound of that. "What?" he murmured, one eye upon the vacant tor, the other on the white wolf surging back into the loft in a silvery streak of displaced energy that spewed the Gypsy into the shadows naked.

"I am saying that when your heart rules your head you are vulnerable to error and bad judgment. Never surrender your acumen to your passion. You were about to prove me right. In your haste to avenge your lady's honor, you would not have tapped the powers that would have given you the edge. You would have been bitten, and I likely would have had to kill you. I had to stop you before it came to that."

"But you let him get away!"

"He won't go far. He wants the girl. The night is young, my impetuous young friend, and it is going to be a long one."

Joss was silent apace. "What do you mean . . . 'powers'?" he asked at last.

Milosh sauntered to the edge of the loft. He'd tugged on his trousers and top boots, and was shrugging on his shirt. " 'Gifts,' if the term better sits," he said. Snatching up his greatcoat, he leapt down with no apparent effort and faced Joss, meanwhile whirling the garment about him with flourish. "There is one gift you've just discovered, eh? I saw the astonishment on that handsome face of yours when you bridged the span between yourself and that creature in one stride."

All this nattering was proving something Joss did not want proven, and he hung his head. Powers, gifts—it didn't matter what he called them; they were more evidence that he was something he did not want to be: *vampir.*

"Come!" the Gypsy said, clapping him on the shoulder. He stooped, picking up an oil can. "Bring the lantern. I must finish what I started earlier, and light the bonfire.

The flames will keep the vampires at bay for the moment, but not for long. Afterward we need to talk—in the hidden room by the wolf tunnel, where you took me when I first arrived, I think. What I have to say should not be spoken within the hearing of others."

Joss nodded and said no more. Doggedly, he followed the Gypsy and helped light the bonfire. He was well aware that Milosh was studying him. It didn't matter. This was too big a disappointment to hide. He had been hoping . . . Well, it didn't matter anymore. A very real danger was threatening Whitebriar Abbey and all its inmates. That was the task at hand, and he would rise to the occasion.

A gentle wind fanned the flames, and Joss's nostrils flared as the musky, sickening sweet stench of burnt flesh—horse and human—filled them. Somewhere beneath the pile Otis lay beheaded, and tears not entirely brought on by the acrid smoke welled in Joss's eyes. *Good-bye, old friend,* he murmured in his mind. *Poor devil didn't even see it coming. Good God! Could I have prevented it?*

"There is no time for nursing regrets," Milosh said. Joss gave a start. Would he ever get used to the Gypsy answering his very thoughts? No, probably not, but there were times in the past when that talent had saved him—and his father before him—and he had no doubt such a moment would come again.

They didn't access the secret room by way of the tunnel. The rear door was closer, and the howling of the wolves seemed louder now despite the fire that should have kept them distant. Joss threw the bolt on the door behind them, and they made their way below stairs to the all but forgotten room at the end of the hall.

It was cold inside without a fire on such a bitter night, but Joss scarcely noticed the chill after coming in from the windswept snow. His mind was upon the conversation he was about to have with the legendary Milosh, and what it meant for his future—if he even had a future. He had begun to doubt it.

He set down the lantern he'd carried from the stable, and took his seat in an ancient straight-back chair. Milosh remained standing, resting his elbow on the mantel of the vacant hearth. Wind from the tunnel beyond the false back behind the grate made a mournful, wailing sound. It rattled the sliding panel and ruffled the hem of Milosh's greatcoat. It echoed the howl of the wolves, and sent cold chills racing along Joss's spine. When the Gypsy broke the awful silence Joss stiffened, and the chair beneath him creaked.

"You are not undead," the Gypsy said, "I told you that already. You are not a vampire in the conventional sense either, though you are *vampir*—you know that already as well. What else could you be, the offspring of two infected with the corruption?"

"Then, what use this conversation?"

"Let me finish," said the Gypsy. "You've known this all along. How else do you account for your extraordinary senses of smell and hearing, your ability to communicate with your mind? How else do you account for being able to shapeshift into a wolf since puberty?"

Joss relaxed somewhat, and the Gypsy went on. "I came here fearing what I might find. I put it off for years, afraid that . . . Well, no matter, I fault your parents for not preparing you more thoroughly for what may come. But that is neither here nor there at this point. So far, you've experienced the fangs but not the bloodlust that goes with them. It is still thus . . . yes?"

Joss nodded. "But how long before I do?" he said.

Milosh hesitated, smiling the half smile that didn't reach his eyes. "I still cannot give you a definitive answer," he said. "I have seen many things in my more than three-and-a-half centuries. Now I must discern between that which I want to be the case, and that which is. It is much harder in this, because I have allowed myself to become closer to the Hyde-Whites than any of the other hunters I have mentored. If my first assessment was correct, your fangs will simply be your weapons, and your 'gifts' the side effects of the condition—including the heightened sexual intensity you were afraid to tell me about."

Joss gave a start. Was the legendary Gypsy clairvoyant as well? "And if you are wrong?" he said.

"Then the bloodlust will eventually come upon you, and you will be as your parents and myself, needing to renew the ritual in order to keep the feeding frenzy at bay."

"When will we know?"

"I would like to offer an opinion," said Milosh, "but I cannot. I have never seen this before. I have never seen nor heard of such a case."

"There has to be some way to tell—a test, something to try?"

"My answer," Milosh said, "you won't like. The only test is time, and you are not a patient entity, Joss Hyde-White."

"There are reasons for that."

"The girl?"

"What can I offer her, Milosh . . . like this? She has been cruelly used, and now me—and *this*." He flicked his teeth with his thumb. "I'd sooner die than cause her harm."

"She accepted you, fangs and all, did she not?"

Joss nodded. He wasn't going to question how the enigmatic Gypsy knew. He didn't have to; Milosh knew his innermost thoughts. Hadn't he proven it again and again?

"Yes, you have that gift as well," said the Gypsy, answering Joss's next thought almost before it crossed his mind.

"You see, that is what frightens me, Milosh," Joss defended. "These 'powers,' these 'gifts' my inheritance has bestowed upon me. I fear they come at a price."

"All worthwhile things come at a price," said the Gypsy. "But let me tell you what I told your father: Do not question the gifts, *use* them for the good. Use them to fight that which you abhor—that which through no fault of your own you have become: the *vampir*. It is a noble calling for such as we, the resistors the Brotherhood—more wolf than man or vampire, we have embraced the blood moon, and we are committed to hunt and destroy the evil that has marked us."

"Werewolves?" Joss breathed. "Is that what we are? What you have become—what you want *me* to become? Is that possible?"

The Gypsy smiled his humorless smile. "No, Joss, not werewolves," he said. "Are you a werewolf when you shapeshift? No. It is simply that so much of the work of the Brotherhood is done in the form of a wolf that we tend to take on the traits of that noble creature."

Joss's brows knitted in a frown, and the Gypsy went on quickly. "When you shapeshift, do you not think like a wolf? Do you not move and hunt and kill with the instincts of a wolf? When humans lose one sense, another grows stronger. If we lose our sight, our hearing improves. If we lose our hearing, our sense of smell improves. This is a simplistic explanation, but it illustrates my point. When we lose the bloodlust and take on the mantle of the wolf in our mission to seek out and destroy the vampire, our wolf incarnation becomes stronger. And we cannot exist as the wolf over time and *not* become one with it, Joss."

"I have always been one with it," Joss said. "Since I was breeched, I've run in the body of the wolf. We are as one. The wolf is an extension of myself—of my being— able to do things I cannot do in human form, to take me places I cannot otherwise go."

"It was the same with your father," Milosh reflected, a faraway look come to his deep-set Gypsy eyes. "As I am sure it still is. And your mother also, though she is one with the panther."

"I wish they were here . . . ," Joss said.

"If they were, they would not be able to help you. I do not even know for certain if *I* can."

Joss hung his head. "I've fallen in love with Cora, Milosh," he murmured. "I was attracted to her the minute I set eyes upon her. Then, when I learned that Clement robbed her of her virtue, I set out to prove that all men were not of his ilk. It was a cavalier undertaking—at least at first, but now it's become something more, something I have no right to hope for. Oh, I've had women, but there was never any danger of my heart becoming involved, if you take my meaning. But this. I *want* this, Milosh."

"Then take it," said the Gypsy. "If she accepted you, fangs and all, you can face whatever may come together."

"I would have to tell her all of it."

"Then do it! Love transcends all things. If she has already accepted the worst, you have naught to fear. There is a more important question to face. May I welcome you to the Brotherhood? You have been a member since the womb, Joss Hyde-White, though you did not know.

What I need to know before we enter into battle is, will you embrace it now that you are aware?"

Joss got to his feet and looked the Gypsy in the eyes. "Yes," he said. "I will."

CHAPTER TWENTY

Cora yawned and stretched awake, alone beneath the counterpane. No, she hadn't dreamed it; the imprint of Joss's dynamic body was clearly defined in the feather bed beside her. What time was it? She threw back the quilts and swung her feet to the floor, which was cold despite the thick Persian carpet underfoot so far from the fire's reach.

She stretched again. A dull ache grieved her body; but what a pleasant ache, evidence of the intimacies she had shared with Joss. A soft moan escaped her lips remembering his embrace, and she slid her hands the length of her body where his hands had been, where his lips had been, and moaned again.

Splashing water from the pitcher into the basin on the dry sink, she refreshed herself. Joss had draped her frock and underthings over the rolled-arm lounge. She padded over and struggled into them, proud of the way she was managing without an abigail. Slipping on her shoes, she went to the window and opened the portieres, hoping to determine the time. Unprepared for the sight that met her eyes, Cora gasped, and gasped again. The ink blue night sky, vacant of stars, was sullied with great belching plumes of smoke rising from a fire raging between stable and paddock. Hungry tongues of crimson flame licked the sky, spewing showers of sparks upward into the starless vault. The deadly crackle and roar of the inferno rushed at her ears through the frozen windowpane.

"Joss!" she cried.

Spinning on her heel, she snatched her hooded mantle from the armoire, flung it over her shoulders and ran from the room. The corridor was vacant, and she raced along it to the yellow suite, but no one answered her knock, and she poked her head in but neither Joss nor Parker was there. Their absence flagged danger, and Cora wasted no more time in her search. Racing down the back stairs, she burst through the rear door and bounded through the drifts toward the fire, her heart hammering in her breast for fear of what she would find.

Why hadn't he wakened her? That something untoward was afoot there was no question. That there was precious little she could do never entered her mind. She could not sit idly by and let the stars alone knew what danger Joss was facing go unchallenged. Whatever it was, they would face it together.

Cora's morocco leather slippers were bulging with snow by the time she reached the stable. She scarcely felt the cold. She was numb to all but raw fear that she was too late—for what exactly, she neither knew nor cared; her mind would not process what her fears tried to plant there. The deadly fangs she'd seen—felt against her lips, her tongue—told all too well Joss's dark secret.

It was true that he had not harmed her with them. Yet, even if there was danger that one day he might, she had taken him inside her. To her, he was the first because she had given herself freely, and he had awakened her to mysteries of the flesh she never dreamed existed. She had accepted him wherever it may lead. Right now, that was toward a blazing bonfire, the heat of which narrowed her eyes even from this distance.

Sickening-sweet corruption threaded through her nostrils. *Burning flesh!* There was no mistaking the smell of charred musk, rot, hair and decay. Was Joss among those towering flames? She had come as near as she dared. The scorching heat was driving her back. It had melted the snow in her slippers, and snatched her breath away; her nostrils burned from it. She called out Joss's name over the roar of the inferno, but it was siphoned off on the wind, and no answer came except the roar and hiss and crackle of the flames licking— what was it, horses? So intent upon the fire that was driving her back further still, she failed to hear the hoofbeats approaching. She failed to see the portly caped figure mounted bareback upon a wild-eyed stallion until snorts of white breath from flared nostrils spun her around. Her heart leapt in relief, expecting Joss's handsome figure at her back when she turned, but the hands that hauled her up onto the phantom horse's back were pinching and cruel, and she screamed at the top of her voice, but the sound was carried off on the wind.

To her horror, it was Clive Clement, and she was trapped in his arms with the breath knocked out of her. He spun the glowing-eyed animal beneath them toward the descent from the tor to the valley below.

"So, I have you at last!" he triumphed. He shook her roughly. "Do not struggle," he warned. "You cannot escape me, miss. Now then, hold fast! Your bridegroom awaits, and there isn't a moment to lose."

"I shall tell her at once," Joss said, stopping beside the toile suite with Milosh. "I should have long ago, but I feared she would do something foolish—run screaming from the house and put herself in harm's way among the vampires stalking this Abbey."

"If you need me to back you up . . ."

"Believe me, I shall not hesitate if I do."

The Gypsy nodded, and slipped inside his apartments.

Joss took a deep breath and continued along the corridor. He had to act now, while he still possessed the courage. Thinking about how he would begin to tell her all that he knew of his situation, it took a moment to notice that the bench outside the master suite was vacant. Where was Parker? It wasn't like him to vacate his post.

Reaching the door, he rapped upon it gently, deciding the valet must have been summoned inside. When no answer came, he threw the door open to empty apartments, and adrenaline surged through him. He streaked through the sitting room, bedroom and dressing room, calling Cora's name, all the while knowing she wouldn't answer. Where could she have gone, and why, when she was safe here? Striding back through the bedroom, he pulled up short before Parker on the threshold, a missive in his hand.

"Bloody hell, man, where the devil have you been?" he barked.

All color left the valet's face. He looked like a cadaver standing there. "Th-the door . . ." he stammered. "I went to answer the door. 'Twas a messenger from the village with this, sir." He extended the missive. "I was gone but a moment."

"Miss Applegate is not in her rooms," said Joss, snatching the sealed parchment. "You were away long enough for her to disappear. Where could she have gone? Do you hear that howling? We are under siege here!"

"What was I to do, sir? You told me to admit no one. I went at once when I heard the knock, for fear one of the others would let someone in. They have their orders, but they have no understanding of the danger—especially Rodgers. I couldn't take the chance."

Joss broke the seal on the missive, whipped it open, and read:

> *Joss,*
> *It has become necessary for us to leave England for awhile. You knew this would come. We are needed abroad. The weather prevented us saying our good-byes in person. The Abbey is in your hands until we return. Look for us in the spring, when it is . . . safe. Until we meet again,*
>
> > *Your loving father and mother.*

"Is it bad news, sir?" the valet asked anxiously.

"Hm?" Joss grunted, his brows knitted in a frown. "It is encrypted. See here, it's dated nearly a fortnight ago. They sent it well before I went to London seeking them, before they left in great haste. They didn't even tell the townhouse servants where they were going."

"But what does it mean, sir?"

"It means, Parker, that my praying they'd come home and lend a hand in this is to no avail. They will be gone until they can return without their youthful appearances damning them, and that when they do return, it will be in the spring—a generation from now at least. We had discussed this. It isn't wholly unexpected. But someone must have questioned their appearance for them to have left so abruptly." He jammed the missive into his pocket. It had shown another thorn on the rose he longed to pluck: Would he stay youthful as the years passed, as his parents had done, or age like a normal man? "No matter now," he said, beating that thought back. "They know what they're about. When it is safe to do so, they will contact me again. Right now, we have a greater press. What has become of Miss Applegate?"

He strode to the window and took another chill that crippled him so he nearly lost his footing. He hadn't noticed until that moment that the draperies had been drawn back. He was almost afraid to look below. That vantage gave a clear view of the stables and the raging bonfire, which hadn't even begun to die down. He could have sworn his heart stopped. There, in the drifted snow, he picked out Cora's footprints in the weak slice of moonlight finally breaking through the clouds. The trail carried toward the stable, and there were no footprints returning.

Spinning from the window, Joss strode to the armoire and rummaged through Cora's things. Her fur-lined wrapper was not among them. "Bloody hell!" he seethed. "She's out of the house. Make sure the tunnel room remains unlocked. I can make better time in wolf form than I can on two feet." Crashing through the door with little regard for his valet, he called out: "I'm taking Milosh with me. Search the Abbey in any case, and the old rule stands . . . admit *no one*. Look sharp, and pray that we find her before our enemies do!"

Milosh threw the door to the toile suite open almost

before Joss's knuckles addressed the ancient wood. "What is it?" he said, stepping into the corridor.

"Cora's left the house," Joss panted. "She must have seen the bonfire and gone to investigate. I saw her footprints from the master suite bedchamber window. There isn't a moment to lose."

The last was spoken unnecessarily; Milosh was sprinting along beside him as they ran down the back stairs and burst through the rear door into the snow. Beyond the stable, the eerie red glow of the bonfire cast a blood-red haze over the indigo sky. Sparks rose, fanned by the wind that spread the stench of burning horse and human flesh to where they stood. The sickening sweetness threatened to make Joss retch. Eyes narrowed upon the trail at their feet, the pair trudged on, taking great care not to sully the tracks picked out by the moon.

Reaching the stable, Joss called out Cora's name. It echoed back to him, ringing from the empty stalls, rousing the horses, whose complaints funneled down the long length of the building to meet them; but there was no human sound, and Joss's heart began to hammer against his ribs. There was no sign of Cora.

"This way," Milosh said, pointing to the place where her footprints passed the stable. They hadn't taken two steps when he seized Joss's arm. "Stop!" he gritted. "Look here."

Joss squatted down over hoofprints. Glancing further west, he saw signs of a struggle. The horse had pranced in circles. Cora's tracks led there then stopped altogether, and the hoofprints led off down the tor.

"They've got her!" he seethed, surging to his feet. "The tracks are fresh. We haven't a moment to spare. Choose your mount; I'll saddle Titus."

"Wait," Milosh said, crouching down to examine the

prints. "No horse will catch that beast, not even your Titus. It's the phantom, and infected. It won't sprout fangs, but it would tear your throat out with its teeth right enough, and it now has extraordinary powers. It will do the bidding of its master."

Joss blinked the mist from his eyes. "Sentinel," he murmured. "It was Sentinel . . . the mildest gelding in my stables. I cannot imagine him as you describe."

"He is a killer now, Joss. This wants the Brotherhood. You will never catch it otherwise. Infected animals are the nastiest. One never knows what they might do, and it will take more than one wolf in a confrontation with it; it will have the strength of ten horses, I promise you. Come. We are wasting time."

The two men left their clothes in the stable and, minutes later, a pair of wolves—one white, one darkly masked and saddled silver-gray—loped down the tor to follow the phantom horse's tracks in the moonlit snow.

CHAPTER TWENTY-ONE

It was no use to struggle. Sooner or later Clement would relax his grip upon her—he would have to—and she would run. The kirk came to mind as a likely place; she would seek refuge there. It was a reckless plan, but something to cling to as her captor's high-stepping horse pranced down the tor.

Joss would have discovered her missing by now. He would surely come, but she dared not wait for that. As soon as an opportunity to escape arose, she would take it. One thing was certain: never again would Clement— or anyone else for that matter—touch her in the vile manner he had when he took her virtue. Of course, this was not Clive Clement. This creature using Clement's shell of a body was *vampir*, and what it could do to her was far worse than what she had already endured, or could possibly imagine.

Now and then the phantom horse tossed its mane, curled back its lips, and jerked its head around, as if it had in mind to bite her with its great teeth. Its eyes were glowing red, even though that they'd left the fire behind, and long strings of drool dripped from its mouth. Her instinct should have been to shrink away, but that would mean leaning into Clement's embrace, and that she would not do even if the hideous beast chomped her head off with those great horse teeth. There came a guttural chuckle from Clement, but it was short-lived. They had nearly reached the bottom of the tor, and a blood-chilling flapping sound drew Cora's eyes toward a large bat hovering over the phantom horse's head. Its presence seemed to strike terror into the animal, breaking its stride and causing it to cower. It did not slow its pace, though, Cora had never seen the like.

In a blink, Clement was plucked from the horse's back in a silvery swirl of displaced energy and flung without ceremony into the snow. She had scarcely blinked again when the bat surged to human height. Its wings became a black mantle that covered its emaciated body as it took Clement's place behind her and urged the horse into a gallop, leaving the man behind.

The new vampire drove the horse relentlessly onto the fells. No ordinary horse could have possibly traveled at such a speed through the tall mounds of drifted snow. The creature's cold, foul breath puffed against Cora's hair and sent gooseflesh racing along her spine, and she shuddered visibly, wrenching a lascivious chuckle from the vampire behind her. Was this Sebastian? It must be. If it was, there was no hope of outwitting him—not if neither Joss, nor his parents, nor the legendary Milosh had been able to conquer him in almost four hundred years. Still, she must try something, if only to escape, and she began by taking the lay of the land around her.

The creature chuckled again. "You cannot escape

me," he said, "though it amuses me that you will try. I do so love the games you mortals play. Your time is not yet, unless you anger me. I have another plan to set in motion before I make you my consort, and you must be as you are to bait the trap, so it will serve you well to obey me in the meanwhile, hm?"

He could read her thoughts! She must guard against that to put her plan into motion. With that decided, Cora tried to clear her mind of all save trivial thoughts, but it was impossible. The howling of wolves chilled her blood. How many voices—three, four, five? Cora had lost count. It seemed like more. The vampires had had plenty of time to attack others in the village, and it would stand to reason that at least some of them would have changed by now. But she mustn't think about that. Sebastian was too close, and he was listening.

They passed the kirk by, and the kirkyard, with its crooked headstones listing this way and that. Legend had it that crooked stones were a sign of *revenant*; ghouls that rose from their graves after death to wander the earth and prey upon the living. In the old days, such graves were dug up and their occupants beheaded just in case. Sebastian gave the place a wide berth, and Cora marked its location in her memory. If he feared it, she would be safe there.

It was difficult to tell, what with the snow, but they passed what seemed like a large field where some crop or other would be planted in the spring, judging from a few dead stalks in ordered rows poking through the drifts. Next they entered a deep, dark forest to the south. Sebastian seemed to know the way, as if he'd been there before. Here Cora was at a distinct disadvantage, having no knowledge of the terrain.

The scent of pine rushed up her nose and she greedily drank it in. It had a calming power, which was what she needed now. It was darker than dark in the forest, an eerie sort of green darkness that enveloped them and caused the horse to shy as if some unseen entity lived in the viridian shadows. It was peaceful among the trees for a time, until they began to thin and a brake appeared at the edge of a thicket farther south. Wild and overgrown with all manner of bracken and thorn, it seemed a place where a cottage once stood. That suspicion was confirmed when Cora spotted a wedge-shaped silhouette protruding from a heavy windswept patch of gorse so deeply buried that the moonlight scarcely picked it out.

"Astute of you," the vampire said, answering her thoughts again. "The tract of land we passed is a woad field, and a cottage used to stand here. It burned down thirty years ago. I am no stranger to your England, lady. I know it well. I have many haunts, like this one that I used to frequent before first light." He laughed. The sound nearly stopped her heart. "Your lover's father always wondered where I'd gone to escape the dawn. My refuge was right under his nose all the while. He was a fool." Fisting his hand in her long loose hair, he leapt to the ground and yanked her down alongside.

"Do you hear that?" he said. Until then, Cora had blocked out the blood-chilling howls of the wolves. She heard them clearly now, close by. "They are my creatures," he said. "Do not think you can escape. They will rip your pretty throat out."

Still tethering her by the hair, Sebastian dragged her across the snow-crusted ground to the wedge-shaped structure rising above the snow. Reaching down, he swept the snow away from an iron ring and yanked it, forcing the door he'd unearthed to creak open.

"Go down," he said, giving her a shove that undermined her balance and sent her sprawling inside. "I won't be long," he drawled. "Do not worry, you shan't be lonely." Then, the door came crashing down, shutting out the light and causing loose snow to sift down through cracks between the boards that had formed over time.

Cora cried out, scrambling to her feet. She was standing on the earthen floor of what obviously had once been a root cellar. Only thin slivers of moonlight seeped in through the rotting wood in the door overhead, enough to catch a glimpse of movement outside. The earth shook with the vampire's heavy footfalls. He hadn't gone.

She hastened to climb the crude wooden steps beneath the door, but the decayed boards gave out and she tumbled back down to the cold, frozen earth. "Let me out of here!" she sobbed, rubbing her behind, for she had landed hard. "Let me *out*, I say!"

Sebastian laughed. "In due time, my dear, all in due time," he said. "Though I wouldn't be in such a hurry for that, if I were you."

The scuffling of his feet in the snow was the only sound then, until something heavy slammed upon the door overhead, causing the wood to shudder and more loose snow to sift through the cracks. Cora cried out, but this time there was no reply, only the sound of Sebastian's top boots carrying him away.

Cora groped through the dark until she found the steps. There were four, and it was the third step that had broken, sending her sprawling. Testing the others, she began to climb again. The old wood creaked and splintered at her weight, slight as it was, but she managed to make it to the top and began pushing her hands against the overhead door with all her strength. Again and again, she heaved against it. From what she could see through the gaps in the wood, a large flat stone covered the door. What if more snow came and buried the root cellar, she wondered; it wouldn't take much. Suppose Sebastian never came back? She would die a slow, horrible death down there in the bitter cold. That thought drove her relentlessly, and it took some time, but she finally raised the door a crack—just enough to see what lay beyond. She froze with the door suspended. Two poison-green iridescent eyes wreathed in red stared back at her from the head of a massive wolf, its foul and visible breath puffing in her face, its hackles raised from the shaggy gray ruff about its neck to the razor-straight ridge along its spine. Its mouth hung open, its lips curled back over yellow fangs dripping foam. For a long moment Cora's eyes met the creature's boldly, before the animal snarled and lunged. The sound of its great teeth striking the wood ran her through like a javelin as she backpedaled, half falling, half scrambling down the steps to the hard dirt floor, the creature's guttural growls ringing in her ears. She covered them with her hands to shut out the sound, and the noise the beast's claws were making as it dug and scratched at the wood overhead. But she heard it still, and she pulled on the fur-edged hood of her mantle and held it against her ears with her tiny hands balled into fists.

His creatures, she reflected. Of course they all were, and this was one standing guard. Praying that the dawn would break before Sebastian returned, and that Joss wouldn't have to face that wolf, she resigned herself to the only thing she could do: wait.

* * *

The two wolves bounded down the tor—one gray, one white—following the trail of the phantom horse that had carried Cora away. They had her scent and that of the animal; that was the easy part. Time was their enemy. Whatever entity had her now, Joss prayed it would lose its power with the dawn. The object was to find Cora before the creature acted.

Sebastian, Milosh growled, speaking with his mind. *I would know his foul stench anywhere.*

Joss snorted. *He will kill her! He will make her his concubine.*

Again Milosh growled. *That is not his objective here. He uses her to bait you, young whelp. I have seen it before. He did the same to your mother to trap your father. As I told you, in Jon's absence, it appears that Sebastian will settle for you.*

Joss raised his wolfish head and sniffed the air. *Listen,* he said. *They are near.*

Milosh bobbed his head and leaked a low, guttural snarl. There was no need of mind speech as they cautiously prowled down the tor; the trail was easy enough to follow. The horse was traveling the snow-covered descent as if it had wings. They had nearly come abreast of the kirkyard when Joss broke the eerie silence.

How many are there, do you think? he said.

Milosh sniffed the air. *More than what was in your lady's coach. They have been busy.*

The lumbering bulk of a shaggy black wolf suddenly slammed into them, breaking both Joss's and Milosh's strides. Its breath was foul. Its yellow-green eyes were rimmed with red, and its bared fangs were dripping blood-tinged foam. Its growl ferocious, it lunged first at Joss, then at Milosh, lips curled back and ravening.

Milosh dove for the black wolf's sensitive hind legs,

biting first one and then the other. As it turned to counter, Joss sank his wolfish fangs deep into the creature's neck.

Well done! Milosh said. *You are learning, young whelp. Finish him!*

Me? But—

Finish him!

But it was not all that easily accomplished. Joss had scarcely sunken his fangs into their assailant's neck when another wolf sailed through the air and impacted him, driving Joss's fangs into the throat of the wolf he'd been battling, severing the creature's jugular. Blood spewed onto the snow in a heavy stream. The mortally wounded wolf leaked a garbled growl, convulsed and fell back in the snow.

Milosh took on the new animal, another black wolf. Joss stood in amazement as the white wolf chomped the newcomer's neck in one viselike bite, whipping it through the air until the sound of its neck breaking ran Joss through with shudders.

I hope you have been paying attention, Milosh said. *Watch closely now. Remember what we have just done here is not enough to kill a vampire. Remember that its head must be severed from its body to destroy it, elsewise it will only rise again. When you are in human form, you will have instruments for this, and you must keep them close at hand. When you are in wolf form, you must rely upon your animal incarnation's . . . natural weapons— ergo those magnificent fangs of yours. Now finish your kill, while I finish mine. We waste much time.*

Joss didn't need the lesson. He'd watched in horror and disbelief as Milosh severed his quarry's head, without ceremony, and now he did the same. It wasn't something he was likely to forget. But Milosh was right; there was no time to lose.

A snort of approval leaked from the great white wolf.
A little sloppy, but well enough for a beginner, Milosh said.

What now? Joss queried.

We wait. They will revert to human form long enough for us to identify them, then either stay as they lie or melt away like the snow as if they have never been, depending upon the severity of their infection.

It didn't take long before the shaggy, blood-soaked fur of the two felled wolves receded and they took on human form—two men of middle age; one fair, one dark-haired.

Do you know these? Milosh said.

No, Joss returned. *These were not in the carriage.*

Milosh growled. *Like I said, they have been busy. Come.*

If there had been a test, Joss had evidently passed. Blood was dripping from his fangs. It splattered on the blue-tinged snow, appearing black in the fractured moonlight. Joss plunged his wolfish snout into a drift, filling his mouth with the snow. He abhorred the taste of the blood, though the accompanying euphoria riddled him mercilessly. Again he routed in the snow, but it was no use. He could still taste it. Why hadn't his parents prepared him for this?

They had nearly reached the end of the graveyard gate, when loud howling pulled them both up short. There, among the tilted gravestones, three gray wolves were milling about in the snow, their acid green eyes wreathed with red, moisture running from their flared nostrils, their drool sullying the pristine snow.

Joss's gray wolf growled. *Shall we separate?*

Those in the Brotherhood do not separate in a situation such as this, Milosh replied. *Besides, you are in training. These are dangerous because they are of the type that can trod upon sacred ground. Look sharp, and do as I do, and above all take care not to get bitten!*

All Joss saw, in the blink of an eye, was a silvery streak of displaced energy as the white wolf soared through the air, over the spiked iron kirkyard fence and slammed into the wolves he'd caught off guard, fangs bared to sever arteries.

Now! Milosh said unequivocally.

Joss howled into the night. Could he do *that*? He'd never tried. It was nearly twice the distance he had jumped in the stable. Suppose he missed and impaled himself upon that deadly spiked fence, or miscalculated and landed on one of those tilted headstones? There was no time to worry over it. He took a deep breath and in one swift, silvery motion joined the snarling, growling ball of hackle-raised fur rolling over the kirkyard.

His impact separated the others. Two fled yelping, and the third went down wedged between two headstones, where Joss pinned it, while Milosh killed it.

Well? Milosh said, backing away from the beheaded wolf. It was changing into a portly, older man before their very eyes.

Joss snorted. *No,* he said. *I do not know him either.*

Come, young whelp, those that have scattered will soon return.

The words were scarcely out when a swarm of bats took flight, sawing through the air from a stand of pines that hemmed the kirk to the north. Almost simultaneously the vicarage door swung open, a lemon-colored shaft of lamplight spilling out around the spindly silhouette of the vicar in his nightshirt, an antiquated blunderbuss in hand. The weapon was leveled at them. The vicar had taken dead aim, and Milosh lunged, striking Joss a blow to the shoulder.

Make haste! he said. *Do not stand there gaping. A moving target is harder to hit. Run!*

The crack and boom as the gun fired set Joss in motion, and not a moment too soon. Hot lead parted the hair on his hackle-raised back. Another half inch and it would have drawn blood.

They were quickly out of range, and they kept up their pace. Joss's intuition cried danger. More shots rang out behind. The other wolves must have returned. And then there were the bats.

Sebastian often takes the form of a swarm of bats, Milosh whispered across his mind. Joss gave a start. Would he ever get used to the Gypsy answering his thoughts?

You mean, he separates into many?

He does. He takes many forms. Once in Moldovia, when your father and I approached his castle stronghold, he took the shadow form of more than a dozen wolves that blocked our path. On that occasion I taught your father how to leap . . . a gift he did not know he possessed. You have that gift also, Joss Hyde-White, and you must perfect it. One day it may save your life.

They reached a field at the edge of the wood. Behind, more gunshots echoed through the quiet, but the shooter was not shooting at them, and Milosh slowed his pace. Eyes flashing in all directions, Joss slowed with him. The trail led into the wood. It would be harder to track them there, where the great skirted pines shut out the light of the misshapen moon. They would have to rely upon their extraordinary senses of vision and smell with their normal sight impaired.

Look sharp, Milosh said. *Sebastian is near. I feel it in my bones. Do not underestimate the creature he has become. He is almost undefeatable. I have been hunting him long enough to attest to that, young whelp. Oh, I have come close but not close enough, not even with your noble father at my side.*

And I am not the man my father is—is that it, Milosh? Is that why you keep reminding me?

Only in that you lack practice. I have great hopes for you, Joss Hyde-White.

Silently they padded through the forest, weaving this way and that among the trees, keeping the trail in sight whenever the moon showed the phantom horse's tracks; following their instincts, extraordinary senses, and the scent of horse and riders when it did not. But Joss was puzzled. If it was Sebastian that had carried Cora off, how could it have been him in the grove behind the kirkyard taking the form of a flock of bats? How could he be in two places at once?

Milosh gave a low growl that flagged danger. *He cannot,* he said in reply to Joss's unspoken question. *He has hidden her somewhere to lure us to our death. Now, focus. He has been with us since we set out. Clear your mind. He, too, can read your thoughts, and it is a long while yet before the dawn is our ally.*

Picking their way among the thinning trees, they reached the thicket and saw the brake beyond, overspread with all manner of undergrowth poking through the snow. They were just about to cross the span when the swarm of bats they'd seen take flight earlier converged upon them. Before their eyes, the many merged into the entity Joss had seen in the stable: a creature of towering height—half man, half bat, with a wingspan as broad as the sails of a ship and a head that scraped the midnight sky. Its eyes glowed red, pulsating like two live coals, and though they seemed all-seeing, they appeared dead, like a poppet's eyes. The effect was jarring—and mesmerizing, Joss realized, quickly looking away.

Its grotesque legs resembled those of a man, except for the talons on its feet, while from the waist up its head—sporting long, daggerlike fangs—and barrel-chested torso were those of a bat. The mold-colored skin stretched over its bones looked shriveled and dead, and gave off a putrid stench that flared Joss's nostrils and backed him up a pace. Milosh, on the other hand, stood his ground, feet apart, head down, white ruff and hackles raised. There was no mistaking the enmity between the two. It took Joss's breath away.

Another apprentice, Milosh? the creature said. *The Brotherhood alive and well, eh?* Though it spoke to the Gypsy, Joss heard as well. Should he let on? While deciding, he inched around the vampire, taking its measure from all perspectives, looking for a likely place to attack. It was far too tall to go for the throat—or the wings either for that matter, unless he exercised his newly acquired gift of leaping great distances. He was contemplating just that when Milosh broke his silence.

Watch your back! he said. *Quickly! Behind you!*

Joss spun on all fours, and leapt aside as another wolf soared through the air. It would have landed on his back if he hadn't dodged out of its way. The animal struck Sebastian instead, too quickly to prevent its fangs from sinking into one of the huge creature's wings and disabling it.

A screech unlike anything Joss had ever heard escaped Sebastian. Blood leaked from the crippled wing, and the creature shriveled and disappeared before their eyes. Joss quickly felled the wolf that had inadvertently attacked its master.

There's justice in that, crowed Milosh. *Taken out by one of his own! Do I dare to dream? It would be so sweet after all that has gone before.*

Do you think?

Milosh ground out the closest thing to a laugh Joss had ever heard a wolf utter. *I only wish,* the Gypsy said. *But no. He will lick his wounds and regroup. Look sharp now, young whelp. The one thing that beast cannot abide is humili-*

ation. He will strike back, believe me—and do not grieve over that wolf there you have just brought down. If you had not, Sebastian would have. If I know naught else, I know this entity. Remember, I knew him when he was a holy man of God, a bishop of the Holy Church. As pious as they come was Sebastian Valentin, and as arrogant. Some things he has carried with him into deep darkness.

Joss trotted toward the fallen wolf he'd flung a distance away into the thicket, to finish the kill.

Wait! Milosh said, padding toward him. *I will do that. You have earned a reprieve. We must continue our search while Sebastian is removed. The dawn will not do our work for us. You saw those wolves in the kirkyard. There is no time to lose.*

CHAPTER TWENTY-TWO

Horrified, Cora stared through the cracks between the boards. She couldn't see much from her vantage, teetering on the shaky top step. If the root cellar hadn't been wedge shaped and slanted, she wouldn't have been able to see anything. As it was, what she did see was in brief glimpses through the gorse and bracken in what scant light the moon begrudged through fast-moving clouds rolling in from the north. *Another storm?* If fresh snow were to fall, it would bury her alive. She had to get out of this cellar.

The wolf was no longer guarding her, and the terrible creature she'd seen rise up out of the thicket had vanished. All she could see now was a moving streak of white against white. *The white wolf! Milosh? Could it be?* Every hair in its thick coat was burnished into her memory, from the dense ruff about its neck to the silvery streak down its spine. It *was*, and there was another wolf with it. They were prowling straight for the root cellar, noses to the ground. Of course! They were following the phantom horse's tracks. Should she make her presence known? Suppose she was wrong. Suppose that wasn't Milosh at all . . . or suppose it was, and he wasn't what he'd once seemed to be. She had to take the chance. She drew a deep breath, braced her tiny hands on the slanted door overhead and pushed with all her might.

There! Joss said. *Something is moving in that bed of bracken.* He prowled closer, his ears pricked toward the muffled sound coming from the groundcover ahead.

Milosh sniffed the air, regal white head raised, his thick fur spangled with the first flakes of new-falling snow in the fractured rays of moonlight. Joss could not help but be in awe of his mentor, just as his father had been before him. The legendary Gypsy was more wolf than vampire now, after so many centuries under the protection of the blood moon ritual. Would Joss be as well? If only he knew. If only he could be sure; but he could not, and what worried him most was that Milosh evidently wasn't sure either.

"Let me out!" a voice cried—Cora's voice!

Joss leaked a high-pitched whine.

Milosh snorted. *It is she!* he said. *We've found her. Hurry!*

Joss didn't wait to reply. Bounding over the snow-crusted clumps of bracken and gorse, he reached the root cellar and leapt up upon it. Cora had only lifted the door a crack, and his weight pushed it closed again. Ignoring her scream, he began clawing at the large, flat stone that weighted down the door of the dilapidated underground structure. By the time Milosh reached him, his paws were bleeding from clawing at the stone.

Milosh jumped up alongside and butted Joss's shoulder with his head. *You cannot budge that boulder in wolf form; give over!* he said.

What? And leave her like this? Joss returned. *Help me here. Together we can free her.*

The stone is too great, even if we pool our strength. Look at your claws. You are bleeding. You must change back to lift that boulder. She needs to see this, young whelp. She needs to know.

But not like this, Joss said. *I have no clothes. I . . .*

The white wolf's low titter, more laugh than growl, cut Joss off. It was Milosh laughing. Of course. Would he ever get used to the Gypsy being privy to his thoughts— to the deepest secrets of his soul? The intimate details of his lovemaking with Cora were foremost in his mind, and nothing was sacred to those who possessed the gift of thought transference and thought invasion.

Whatever put her in there will return, Milosh said. *Hurry and change. You do not have a choice. Do it quickly. Our foes grow nearer.*

Joss heard the howling. He needed no reminder. Sebastian had been driven off, but he would not stay away for long. Milosh was right yet again; Joss had to act quickly. Fully aware that Cora could see him through the cracks between the boards, he surged to his full human height in a silvery, bone-crunching streak, tossed the boulder off the slanted root cellar door and gripped the iron ring to raise it.

Below, Cora staggered back from the opening at sight of him silhouetted naked against the snow, though she didn't swoon as he'd expected. She did sway, however, and Joss leapt down and seized her in his arms. That extracted another raw scream from her throat. She trembled from head to toe, every inch of her body quivering as he crushed her to him.

"Do not scream," he cautioned her. "You are safe. It is me."

"What did I just see?" Cora demanded, straining against his embrace. "Where is the gray wolf that just clawed on that door? And that other there, the white one. Is that . . . ?"

"Milosh, yes," Joss said. "We were looking for you."

"I do not understand what just happened here," Cora repeated.

"I know," Joss murmured against her brow. "I didn't mean for you to find out this way, but circumstances necessitated it. A wolf could not raise the stone, but a man could. Never mind that now. Who brought you here, Cora? And what were you doing out of the Abbey in the first place?"

"Never mind?" Cora cried. "I have just seen you emerge from the body of a wolf! Who are you, Joss Hyde-White? *What* are you?"

Joss winced. Her words wounded him to the core, but there was no time to address it. He was standing naked with the woman he loved in his arms, but no matter what he said, she would not be ready to hear it.

"I will explain, Cora," he said, "but not here. Not now. How did you put yourself in such a position? I need to know *now* . . . before those wolves come any nearer. What ever possessed you to leave the Abbey?"

"I . . . I saw the fire. I thought you were in danger."

"And just what did you think you could have done if I was?"

"I . . . I don't know. Come to your aid, I suppose. I . . . I couldn't just stand there imagining you trapped in the midst of that fire. But that doesn't matter now. Don't change the subject. What did I just see here, Joss? Where are your clothes? It is freezing. Are you mad?"

Joss hesitated, pulling her closer in his arms, inhaling the scent of roses in her hair, drifting from her skin. Despite his anger that she had put herself at risk, he was on fire for her, as castaway by her closeness as a lord in his cups.

Quickly, young whelp, Milosh's stern voice ghosted across Joss's mind. *Danger comes, we must away.*

Joss ignored them both. "Was it Sebastian who brought you here?" he demanded, shaking her gently. "I must know, Cora. We have driven him off, but he will soon return, and we are at a disadvantage with you in the middle of this. What did he look like?"

"Clive Clement seized me first," she said. "Then . . . a dreadful creature drove him off. They rode a vicious horse. It . . . the animal, it tried to bite me!"

"It didn't, did it, Cora?" he urged, shaking her again. "Tell me you haven't been bitten!"

She shook her head that she had not, but the terror in her eyes was clear. "What did it look like, this creature?"

"He was tall and bald headed," she began. "He wore ill-fitting clothes that hung on his frame, and his skin was chalk white. It had a greenish cast. It looked and smelled like mold, and I could see the blood running in his veins through it." She shuddered in Joss's arms, and he pulled her closer, fully aware of his hard sex pressing against her belly. "His eyes," she went on. "They glowed red and they were sunken in deep shadows— ugly, dark circles for sockets. He was hideous, Joss, and his *fangs.*"

Milosh growled from the ledge above. *Sebastian.*

"I . . . I don't understand any of this," Cora sobbed.

Joss swooped down, buried his hands in her long, fragrant hair, and took her lips with all of his pent-up passion. Her mouth felt like hot silk as his tongue explored it, stroking hers, drawing it into his mouth. She tasted honey sweet, with a touch of rose milk like that which his mother used to make of cow's milk and rose hips, distilled to create an elixir for the bath.

Young whelp! Milosh's sharp voice speared Joss's mind. It was all Joss could do to tear his lips from Cora's, all he could do to restrain himself from laying her down on the root cellar floor and ravishing her then and there. His breathing was painful and shallow, his heart racing so he feared it would leap from his breast. His manhood grew and throbbed until he was certain it would burst, and sweat beaded on his brow despite the bitter wind puffing against his naked skin.

Joss lifted his lips from Cora's and crushed her close against his heaving chest, sparing her the sight of his fangs. Their infernal appearance brought bitter tears to his eyes. He would spare her that sight as well.

"The creature you saw here earlier," he murmured, struggling to control his rapid breathing, "was Sebastian Valentin in his true form—what the centuries have made of him." Ignoring her gasp, he went on quickly. "As I said before, he infected my mother and my father, though he did not complete their 'making.' He is obsessed with finishing what he started . . . and in their absence, he is settling for me. One good thing has come of it. He has used you to bring me to him, and so you have his obsession with the Hyde-Whites to thank that you are still untouched. Now, then! The rest we will speak of after I have you safely back to the Abbey. Where is Sentinel, the horse that brought you here?"

"I . . . I don't know," Cora despaired. "And it doesn't matter. It was evil, I tell you. I shan't go near it again."

"Ahhh, but that horse was mine before it was bitten. I

raised it myself, as I did most of the others that had to be consigned to the flames back at the Abbey." He couldn't help but desire the beast's redemption—or destruction, if it came to that.

"I will walk before I climb upon that creature's back again," Cora announced unequivocally.

There is no time for this! Milosh reminded Joss. *We must go. Now. Give over thoughts of the horse; it is yours no longer. Sebastian commands it now. Change back and let Cora ride you. She cannot walk; it is too far. She will be frostbitten before we ever reach the kirkyard in those thin clothes and shoes. It is that, or we stay here until dawn and see how many can bear the light of day.*

Joss gave it thought. His dire wolf form was certainly large enough to accommodate her, and she petite enough to ride upon his back with ease. But the last thing he wanted was a repeat performance of his transformation. Though he had managed to calm her, she'd been anything but sanguine. He needed to explain—as much as he could explain—but not here, not now. He took her face in both his hands and gazed into her eyes.

"Will you bear with me just a little longer before your explanation, Cora?" he murmured.

She hesitated, then nodded that she would.

"Good!" Joss gushed. "I must do again what I did before. You cannot walk the distance returning; it is too far. I must become the wolf again and carry you to the Abbey on my back. It is a dire wolf—more than large enough to accommodate your weight. Do not be frightened. Once I change, I shall leap out of this hole. You must then climb up and mount me. We must away at once. Do you hear the howling? It grows nearer. Our enemies will be upon us soon, and I do not mean to frighten you, but the last two we came upon tonight were *not* your companions in that coach. Sebastian and his minions have infected half the village, I'll wager. Once we reach the Abbey, I will try and explain these mysteries to your satisfaction, but right now what I need from you is blind faith . . . or at the very least, your tolerance until I get us out of here. Do I have it?"

Cora stared slack jawed at Joss. He wanted so much, and she was terrified, but more of the entire circumstance than of him. Somehow she knew he would not harm her. But still . . .

"Stand back," he charged. "There is no time to take your silence as anything but consent. I shall just have to let my actions speak for me."

He pushed her gently from him, and while she watched in mute amazement, a silver whirlwind rose around him, blazed, then shrank and blazed again. Before her wide-flung eyes, the man who had just clasped her to his naked body leapt from the root cellar in the form of a great silver-gray wolf with a smoky mask, and joined the white wolf on the brink above.

Cora could not keep the gasp within her cold-parched throat. Both wolves stared down at her in silence, but it wasn't those two but the not-too-distant howls of other wolves that set her in motion. Scarcely believing what she was doing, she scrambled out of the root cellar, climbed upon the gray wolf's back, fisted her tiny hands in his thick, black-tipped ruff, and held on for dear life. It leapt off through the deep, drifted snow. As bizarre as it was, Milosh's white wolf presence loping alongside was a comfort.

They passed through the brake and the thicket without incident. Soft, silent snow was fluttering down. The wind had died, and the air was so still that Cora could hear the gentle sound the tiny snowflakes made falling all around. This seemed an otherworldly wonderland, sparkling with sugary frost. In any other circumstance, it would have been a breathtaking experience she and Joss were sharing. Instead, it was a nightmarish journey, fraught with the howling of predatory wolves, and the stars alone knew what else they would face before they reached the Abbey.

Entering the eerie green darkness of the forest, they found the atmosphere suddenly changed. The snowflakes did not penetrate the thick, interlaced treetops that shut out the night sky above, and the only light came from that which was reflected back from the drifted snow. The only sound was that of the two wolves' feet crunching through the snow and ice-crusted leaves, padding along at a steady pace, weaving in and out among the trees' black trunks. The howling seemed stronger now, though Cora saw no sign of the howlers. She kept a close eye upon Milosh's white wolf—upon the way he seemed to scan the terrain in all directions without breaking his stride. She didn't need to see the expression on the gray wolf's face to read its demeanor. Every sinew in its body was stretched to its limit. Its hackles were raised, and the ruff Cora clutched as it sped through the forest was standing on end. Try as she would, she could not join man to beast. Though she'd seen Joss become the creature beneath her with her own eyes, she could not join them in her mind. They were two separate entities—they had to be, or she would lose her mind.

All at once, the white wolf growled, jarring Cora's train of thought. She glanced about. The wolf beneath her must have felt her tense, because he stiffened, the fine hairs along the back of his spine standing on end. Adrenaline surged through her body, and she found herself searching among the trees, not even knowing what she was searching for. It wasn't long before she realized what had captured their attention. Shadow shapes were weaving in and out among the trees; shadow shapes with iridescent, red-rimmed, acid-green eyes. They were closing in from all sides; some animal, some human. The only consolation was that they were moving slowly, almost mindlessly.

The wolf beneath her picked up speed, as did Milosh, running so close alongside that it almost seemed joined to the gray. Cora no longer felt secure on the gray wolf's back, and she threw her arms around his thick neck and clung with all her strength, her face buried in the thick mane of black-tipped silver fur. It smelled clean, of the crisp, cold North Country air . . . and of *him*—of Joss. They *were* one and the same. How could she bear it?

Cora didn't look behind; she didn't have to. The gray wolf's speed told her the others were still in pursuit. They sped over the fells, past the kirkyard and the rowan tree at the bottom of the tor, its skeletal branches, like outstretched arms, clacking in the wind that had again risen. It wasn't until they started to climb toward the top of the tor that the full impact of what they were facing loomed before them. Lazy plumes of smoke still drifted upward, though the bonfire had died to embers. No red glow tinged the night sky, though the air was heavy with the stench of char and burnt flesh. It impacted Cora's nostrils, threatening to make her retch. They started to climb, but it wasn't until they'd nearly reached the summit that what they were truly facing came into view. Strange two- and four-legged creatures prowled what was the courtyard buried beneath the snow. Whitebriar Abbey was surrounded, and it was still hours until dawn.

Chapter Twenty-three

Joss skittered to a halt in lee of an ancient crag. *Now what do we do?* he asked Milosh. *The dawn is still awhile off.*

The white wolf snorted. *That matters not. There is no telling how many of that number will still be abroad in the light of day.*

We are hopelessly outnumbered, Joss grieved, *and I cannot communicate with Cora as you and I do. We must get her back inside the Abbey, where she will be safe.*

Will the rear door be open?

Parker would never lock the door while I'm out of the house, Joss assured him.

And the front entrance?

Joss snorted and shook himself. *It's locked,* he said. *Parker will answer, but it will take awhile. He would be asleep at this hour.*

The rear entrance, then, Milosh said. *I will distract them, while you reach it.*

You can't mean to take that number on single-handed. Joss was incredulous.

The white wolf bristled. *Much of that number is Sebast-*

ian himself, Milosh said. *He challenges us—makes mock of us. I have seen this many times before. He has the power to divide into an army. And besides the wolves you see there prowling on all fours, other wolves will soon join them, walking upright depending upon the level of their infection.*

Then we are doomed, Joss said.

Not doomed, young whelp, Milosh said. *We are in need of reinforcements. We are a brotherhood, remember. Now, make straight for the rear door and see your lady safely inside!*

Joss started to make an objection, but the white wolf darted out into the open and streaked up the tor toward the front of the Abbey. There was nothing for it but to follow Milosh's direction, and he bolted from behind the crag and rushed up the incline toward the rear door.

He had almost forgotten that Cora was mounted upon his back, and she nearly slipped off as he raced up the grade. Her two tiny hands fisted in his wolfish ruff, and though they pinched, they put him at ease and he snorted, hoping she would understand the sound as praise for her quick thinking.

They reached the rear door without incident, Milosh having diverted attention away toward the front of the Abbey. Skittering to a halt, Joss shook himself in an attempt to shed Cora, but she only held tighter. Joss shook himself again, and when she still clung tenaciously, stood on his hind legs and slammed his front paws against the door.

"I won't leave you!" she cried. "You cannot fight that out there—not even with Milosh at your side. No!"

There was no time for argument. Joss sprang through the air, bones, fur and sinew stretching in a silver streak, a strenuous motion that used to be a painful experience. Now he scarcely felt the pain of transition. Cora cried out as she was dumped unceremoniously in the snowdrift beside the rear door. Joss reached her in two strides and lifted her up none too gently. Things had been much simpler when he was dodging porcelain pitchers.

"I am sorry, Cora, but you must do as I say. *Now.*" He threw the door open and handed her over the threshold. "You must go inside and *stay* inside."

"What is happening?" she shrilled, resisting.

How much should he tell her? He had to tell her something, but the truth was too hard to believe, and a lie would not suffice—not now, when he stood before her stark naked and having just transformed from wolf to man before her very eyes again.

"We must ride this out until dawn," he said. "Then we will know how much of what you see and hear out there is real, and how much is vampire glamour. If all those wolves are truly *vampir*—creatures Sebastian has infected—it is one thing. Milosh believes they are Sebastian himself, as Sebastian has the power to divide into legions. Either way, we are surrounded. You must leave it to Milosh and me, Cora. I have no time to explain more, but I will once the sun rises. Then we will know—*I* will know . . . how and what we will do. You must trust me in this. Stay in the Abbey. Do not interfere. You have too little fear of the danger we are facing here. Milosh diverted their attention so I could see you safely inside. I cannot leave him alone out there with that."

Aroused, he seized her and crushed her close in a smothering embrace. His kiss was savage, his passion feral. He tried to hold back his fangs, but he was on the verge of shapeshifting back into the wolf and he could not. Cora melted against him. He tasted her deeply, hungering for her honey sweetness. It was like balm on the frayed edge of his reason and, as if they had a will of their own, his trembling hands roamed her body, committing every curve, every soft malleable contour to memory. He was like a man possessed, but this was a luxury he could ill afford, and he tore his lips away and put her from him, searching her moist eyes. He couldn't speak—wouldn't speak. There was no need. He spun away, leapt back across the threshold, hit the ground running on the huge, thick pads of the sleek gray dire wolf, and disappeared in the darkness.

Stunned, Cora swayed on the threshold. She staggered back into the dimness of the lower corridor, staring long after Joss disappeared in the predawn darkness. She closed the Abbey's rear door. There had been a chilling finality in Joss's parting embrace, in the savage kiss that drained her senses and left her weak and trembling. It almost seemed a good-bye. No! She would not credit that.

So many emotions riddled her, she could hardly mount the stairs. When had she fallen in love with Joss? She hardly knew. But there it was. Her knees were trembling for fear she'd lose him. At the same time, anger fisted her hands and she pounded on the banister. Why hadn't he confided all this to her before? What was really happening? That kiss . . . that desperate, feral, soul-wrenching kiss . . . No! She wouldn't believe it was good-bye. Providence had brought them together, and Providence was not so cruel as to separate them now. Not now. Not after all she'd been through.

Cora unclenched her fists when she reached the first-

floor landing and pushed the hood of her mantle back.
It was wet with snow, the weight of it wearing her down.
She had just begun to climb toward the second floor,
when something slammed against the front doors of the
Abbey. The sound funneled down the Great Hall and
echoed through the corridors, freezing her in her
tracks. The slow, methodical rapping came again before
the shuffling of weary feet met her ears, and she backed
into the shadows watching. Parker labored along the
dimly lit corridor toward the racket in his nightshirt
and wrapper.

"All right, all right. I'm coming!" the valet growled.
The sound came again. It was a softer sound than the
rasping metallic racket the door knocker made, and
Cora held her breath as Parker threw the bolt and
opened the door a crack, and then a little wider to admit a great gray wolf with a smoky mask. It bounded
past him, disappearing along the servants' wing hallway.
The valet poked his head out for a moment, then closed
the door with a wag of his head.

Though there was no sign of Milosh, Cora sagged in
relief. Joss was safe inside the Abbey at least. The charis-
matic Gypsy certainly must know what he was about after four centuries of vampire hunting. She was just
about to continue her climb, when another knock came
at the door. Was this Milosh? She stopped in her tracks
again, watching Parker turn back, muttering what could
only be expletives under his breath.

"What now?" the valet grumbled, opening the door a
crack.

"Let us in," said a small voice. "It's cold . . . so cold . . ."

The sound ran Cora through. Not even knowing why,
she bolted from the shadows, ran down the stairs, raced
along the corridor, through the Great Hall and, wrest-

ing the door from the slack-jawed valet's hands, slammed it shut upon what appeared to be a gathering of refugees from the storm, many mere children.

"Here, miss!" Parker cried. "What ails you?"

Cora threw the bolt and sagged against the door, only to dance away from it as the methodical knocking came again, reverberating through her body from the old, scarred wood. She shuddered and leaked a startled cry.

"They are *undead*," she moaned. "I know little of this . . . situation, but enough to be certain you must not even open the door—not even a crack—to such creatures. They take it as an invitation to enter, and we are outnumbered!"

"I would not have let them in, miss," the startled valet said.

"Hear how they knock?" Cora cried. "Like a drummer banging his drum in a funeral dirge."

The sound came again: *thump . . . thump . . . thump.* Cora covered her ears with her hands. "I cannot bear it! Will the dawn never come?"

"Now, now, miss, don't take on so," the valet soothed. "Young master is safe inside, and Mr. Milosh knows what he's about. There is none finer in such situations . . . so I'm told."

The footman Rodgers came running, his wig askew and his hose twisted. The valet stayed him with a raised hand. "It's nothing, Rodgers, go back to bed."

"Who can sleep with that bangin' goin' on?" the footman said. "Who is it, then?"

"Just beggars from the village," said Parker, "A . . . a band of Gypsy folk—tinkers. I've attended to it. Run on and leave it to me."

"Don't sound as if you've 'attended to it' to me," the footman said as another round of knocks shook the seasoned wood of the door. "It's bad luck to send a Gypsy off without a coin. You'd best give them a tribute, or they'll never quit that bangin'."

"I need not remind you that young master left strict orders that *no one* be admitted here," Parker said, sour voiced. "Especially Gypsies. Now, remember yourself! You know better than to argue with me. You are not to open the doors to anyone hereafter. Not so much as a crack," he added, casting a sideling glance at Cora, standing with her hand over her mouth as the thumping continued. "Ask who it is from now on through the closed doors," Parker went on, in what Cora believed must be his most authoritative voice, "and admit only young master and Mr. Milosh. Is that clear?"

"As a bell, sir," the footman said, though it was obvious that it was anything but.

"Never mind," Parker said, bristling. "I rescind that. You are not to answer the door—either door—*at all* until further notice, should Gypsies pound upon it till doomsday. And pass the word below. Ignore the door. I shall be responsible for it solely; no one else. That should settle the matter. Now, run on!"

Shaking his head, the footman shuffled off mumbling, and Cora's jaw dropped as her hand fell away from her mouth.

"He doesn't know, does he?" she murmured, stupid with astonishment.

The valet shook his head. "No one does, miss," he said, "No one save Bates, rest his soul, and me. And I only know from what curiosity earned me over time."

Cora gasped. "Is that wise?"

"It is necessary, miss," said the valet. "Why, if the others knew, they'd run screaming from the Abbey. They are a superstitious lot—especially the women."

"Are you telling me no one knew that Joss's parents . . . that *he* . . . ?" She couldn't put her thought into words. "How could that be possible all these years?"

"They showed no symptoms, miss, and took great care to conceal it. I can say no more. It isn't my place to carry tales. You must ask young master these things. I'm sorry, Miss Applegate. Come away now. Pay no mind to that racket. None will get in." He turned her away from the door, and guided her along the corridor to the first-floor landing. "Go on up," he said. "I will have Rodgers fill the tub in your dressing room, and see if Amy can be spared to tend you. You are sopping wet. You must be chilled to the bone. You're courting pneumonia in those wet clothes in this drafty old mausoleum."

"You needn't trouble Amy. I can bathe myself, Parker."

"Very well, miss," said the valet. Sketching a bow, he disappeared toward the servants' wing.

Cora started to climb. Every muscle in her body ached. She hadn't noticed until now how sore she was from head to toe, as she began dragging herself up that staircase weighted down with her cold, wet frock and mantle. She had scarcely reached the master suite when Rodgers and Parker appeared with water for the tub. She was almost sorry she had cried off having Amy assist her. She had done so hoping that Joss would come to her, and she was weary and would have welcomed the girl's assistance. Still, the bath was heavenly, silkened with attar of roses and lavender oil, and she lingered in it until it had nearly grown cold around her, before wrapping herself in one of the thick soft towels the valet had provided and padding to the window.

Outside, the first gray traces of the dreary, snow-swept dawn had come stealing over the fells. It was an eerie, ghost-gray landscape as far as the eye could see. Cora shuddered, despite the freshly stoked fire and the luxurious towel. Though she saw no wolves, nor any living creature, man or beast, she heard their mournful howls, some close, some near. Suddenly, above the rest, there came a howl like none other. It seemed to be coming from above—the voice of a lone wolf at first, then two wolves' voices almost in perfect harmony drifted off on the wind.

Swirling snow hissed against the windowpane. No sound had ever seemed so lonely. The glaring brightness of the morning hurt Cora's eyes and she narrowed them. She hadn't slept, and they wanted to close. She longed to stay awake to welcome Joss. He would come to her soon. They needed to talk, but the bed seemed so inviting, its eiderdown featherbeds waiting to receive her weary body.

She shed the towel and took up Joss's silvery dressing gown. Despite that she'd worn it for days, it still held his scent, and she wrapped herself in it and climbed beneath the counterpane to wait.

As dawn broke, events outside took another turn.

The dawn comes quickly, Milosh said, his wolfish head raised to the heavens. He and Joss had paused beneath a spreading holly tree to catch their breath. All around, the snowcapped tor was strewn with the evidence of their night's labor. The snow was crimsoned with the blood of dead vampires both man and animal. Their thick fur coats were likewise streaked and spattered with blood, which looked black in the darkness. *Is there a way up to those turrets . . . a way that wolves can climb?*

Joss snorted. *Through the tunnel,* he said, shaking the snow from his thick gray coat. *We can climb the old tower stairs from there. I did it many times as a boy. Why?*

You will see, Milosh said. *Show me quickly. First light comes any moment.*

Together they leapt up to the second-floor tunnel and raced along its narrow confines to the secret room, but they did not stop then to dress. Joss led the white wolf up the rear stairs, along a narrow, roughly hewn passage so thick with mildew and dust their foot pads slipped and nearly sent them tumbling down to the bottom several times before they reached the Abbey roof and padded out onto the narrow, snow-clad ledge that wreathed the span between turrets.

Milosh sniffed the cold dawn breeze, faced south, opened his throat and howled into the predawn darkness. It was a different sound than Joss had heard him make before, and it rocked him to the core. Spinning, the white wolf howled to the north, west, and east before facing him.

Look! Milosh said, nodding toward the fells, where a swarm of bats sawed through the air just as the sky began to lighten. *Sebastian.*

Is it over? Joss said.

The white wolf leaked a throaty snarl. *Over?* he said. *It has only just begun. He takes shelter from the light of day. He will return at dusk for the final battle. No, take no comfort from his momentary weakness, or from the others who flee first light. Those who take refuge from the dawn shall grow stronger . . . and more dangerous for the respite. Come! Do as I do. Raise your voice with mine.*

To show our strength? Joss queried.

No, young whelp, to bring reinforcements. We are the Brotherhood, remember?

CHAPTER TWENTY-FOUR

Cora hovered on the edge of consciousness. That she shouldn't be sleeping the day away bothered her conscience marginally; she was never one to nap in the daytime, but the bed was so warm and comfortable, the fire so soothing to sore muscles, Joss's silver-gray brocade dressing gown releasing his evocative scent. It seemed stronger somehow than she remembered it earlier, and she moaned softly, stretching beneath the counterpane. The satiny fabric slid over her naked body beneath with the motion. It felt cool against her hot skin, and she ran her hands over her breasts, along her waist, the curve of her hips, and back up again, lingering on her belly before sliding over the hardened buds of her nipples poking through the brocade.

What a delicious dream. Joss had been with her—holding her—igniting her senses. How else could she smell his scent, feel his presence, his thigh leaning against her, the featherbed beneath her sagging with his weight until she rolled down the incline made by his body right into him.

Cora's eyes flashed open.

"Was I in your dream?" Joss murmured. He was seated on the edge of the bed beside her, one arm across her body, his other raised, his hand smoothing her hair out on the pillow.

Cora vaulted upright, her eyes still glazed with sleep. No wonder his scent was so strong! "W-what time is it?" she stammered.

"You've slept half the day away," he said. "I hated to wake you, you were so exhausted . . . but I had to. We need to talk, Cora, before the sun sets."

Cora's breath left her body in a ragged sigh. She needed to know many things—wanted to know, but dreaded the answers to her questions. What had begun as hostility toward her mysterious host had somehow blossomed into love. The attraction had always been there. That was the reason for her first hostility toward Joss. She hadn't admitted that to herself until now, as his soothing hands caressed her, and his hypnotic eyes, shuttered with desire, gazed longingly into hers. If she knew what was good for the both of them, she would snatch the new pitcher from its basin on the nightstand and crown him with it as she had before. She would cloak her true feelings and run for her life . . . and his. Joss Hyde-White deserved a whole woman, not a tarnished one. If she truly loved him, what *she* wanted didn't matter. Albeit through no fault of her own, Cora had lost the privilege of expecting a happily-ever-after.

Tears closed her throat and pooled in her eyes. Better that she steel herself against what he was about to tell her. Better for them both.

"You deserve an explanation," he said, raising her hands to his lips. "Once, I told you there was more to my parents' story . . . and mine. It's time I told it."

He hesitated. From the look of him, he seemed about to change his mind, so Cora spoke up quickly. "Go on," she said.

"I can only tell you what I know," he said. "When I was a lad, I discovered that I could shapeshift into the body of a wolf. My father possessed the same power and mentored me, taught me how to exit the house without anyone knowing—anyone except Bates, of course. These things can never be done without the help of a servant."

"And Bates wasn't . . . afraid?"

"No; he knew my parents' condition well, as he was here when it all began."

"When they became . . . v-vampires?"

Joss nodded. "They were betrothed when Sebastian Valentin infected them. My father, being the second son of an earl, chose the church as his vocation. There is no greater reward for a vampire than corrupting a man of the cloth. Sebastian was one himself before he was turned; he was a bishop in Moldovia centuries ago. To hear Milosh tell, Sebastian was taken with ambition and easily turned. He became the exact opposite of what he'd been when he first set out in his vocation, as evil as his original instincts were good. Such men are the most dangerous of all when they become *vampir*. Jealousy drives them to corrupt others like them, others of the cloth. They obsess over it, which is why Sebastian is so driven to corrupt my father."

Cora gasped, and Joss gently soothed her. "Sebastian was interrupted on both occasions, so my parents' 'making' was incomplete. But he has dogged them to this day. The blood never forgets, Cora. Sebastian has tasted theirs, and he will not rest until he has killed my father and taken my mother as his concubine. In their absence, he evidently has decided to settle for me . . . for now."

"Your parents did not become Sebastian's creatures," she remarked.

"My parents resisted. They married and traveled to Romania to find help from the clergy there, where such things are commonplace. It was there, in Moldovia, in the Romanian Carpathians, that they met Milosh. If he has a surname, I have never heard it. He is a Gypsy, and a vampire himself, as I've already told you. He, too, resisted, and became the fearsome vampire hunter you see today."

"How can he be a vampire and a vampire hunter at the same time?" Cora said.

"It seems odd, I'll grant, but that is what my parents are as well—thanks to Milosh. Centuries ago, in Persia, he learned of a ritual that, when performed under the blood moon, would spare a vampire from the bloodlust, the feeding frenzy that causes him to crave the blood of animals and humans."

"But they are still vampires?" Cora interrupted.

"Yes, they are. However, as long as they continue to repeat the ritual at intervals, aside from not aging they will appear as normal as you are, and harm no one, Cora . . . except the vampires they hunt down and destroy."

Cora hesitated; what she must ask next could change their lives forever. "And . . . you?" she murmured. Had her voice really cracked?

Something moved him. His hands slipped away and he rose to his feet. Crossing to the hearth, he picked up the poker and began stirring the embers to life.

Cora followed him with her eyes, suddenly cold in his absence—how bitterly cold and lonely. She longed to reach out to him, to take him in her arms and soothe away the pain of what he was about to tell her. Whatever it was must be too dreadful to bear, much less put into words. His demeanor damned him, and she threw back the counterpane and slid her feet to the floor. Waiting.

"I was conceived after my parents experienced the blood moon ritual, possibly that very night," he began, avoiding her gaze. "Conceived of two infected vampires, what could I be but one myself?"

Cora almost winced. Her instinct was to rush to his side. *Steady on, old girl,* she told herself. She must remain indifferent if she were going to end this, for both their sakes.

"Go on, Joss," she murmured. Thank Providence his concentration upon what he was saying was so intense he didn't notice how she struggled for composure.

"An herbal draught is drunk, and Milosh believes that the effects of that draught in the blood moon ritual transferred to me at conception, giving me the benefits of the rite to some degree. It's just that we don't know how much of a degree."

"What do you mean?"

Joss heaved a mammoth sigh and tossed down the poker he'd been toying with. "Until just recently, the only symptom I've had was shapeshifting into the wolf. I didn't mind that. I actually enjoy it—the freedom of running in the wolf's body. I know that sounds mad, but it's true, Cora. I know that you've seen the fangs that appear when I am aroused, angry, or threatened. That has just begun, and so far there is no bloodlust when they do appear. Things are changing in me. It's the reason I went to London in search of my parents. I was hoping that they could shed some light upon the situation, but I was too late. They'd already gone abroad. But for that trip, I would never have come upon your carriage bogged down in the snow, and you would either have died or been infected like the others."

Tears welled in Cora's eyes. Yes, she loved Joss; there was no denying it. Her heart was breaking for him. All her noble resolve to spare him the tarnished offering of herself dissolved in those bitter tears. How could she leave him? How could she bear it?

She vaulted off the bed and rushed into his arms, but he stiffened and put her gently but firmly from him. "No," he murmured. "Let me finish, Cora. You are in grave danger here. I have no right to subject you to this nightmare . . . *my* nightmare. I love you too much to ask you to share it." She took a step closer. "No! Come no nearer," he cried, spinning away from her advance. "Let me finish this while I still have the courage."

"Finish what, Joss?"

"What I've started. Don't you see? I don't know what I am—what I might become—when I might change into a creature like the fiends laying siege to this Abbey. How long will it be before the bloodlust begins? Milosh as much as said I am probably immune to the blood moon ritual."

"Why? What does he say?" Cora pressed.

"It's what he doesn't say that worries me," Joss said. "What if one night the feeding frenzy comes upon me and I infect you? Do you think I could live with that? No! It must end here and now . . . while we still can end it. It never should have begun. I wanted to show you that all men weren't like that whoreson Clement. I wanted you to experience what it would be like to be cherished . . . I have done so. I did it out of love, which is how I do this . . . it is the only way, Cora."

His image swam before her eyes. There was no stopping the tears that blinded her. Here she had made the decision to leave him, then couldn't go through with it, and now *he* was ending it? This was the last thing she would have expected, and it rocked her back on her heels. He stood before her, clearly aroused by her nearness, the thick bulk of his sex straining against the seam of his buckskins, gritting his teeth to hold back the fangs that had already begun to change the shape of his handsome mouth. She suddenly realized what she was wearing—his dressing gown. It always had this effect upon him when she wore it.

No! She wouldn't accept this. He was serious. He would never make love to her again. She would never again feel the ecstasy of him filling her, setting fire to her blood, to her body, to her sex. Her flesh was on fire now, throbbing like a pulse beat.

"You don't mean this!" she sobbed. "How could you mean this, Joss . . . after all we've been through?"

"I've saddled two horses," he went on, his voice like a whip, his jaw muscle ticking. He could not or would not meet her eyes. "I want you to get dressed and collect your things. I shall escort you to the kirk in the valley, where I shall arrange for a sledge to see you safely south before nightfall. The roads are now passable, and you can hire a coach for home."

"Alone?" she shrilled. "That is out of the question. You must be mad!"

"Cora, we are besieged here! Before another dawn breaks, there will be a reckoning. We are surrounded by Sebastian and his ilk. You've heard the wolves howling—"

"Oh, yes, I have," she cut in, waving her arms. "And you would send me out alone in that? You don't love me, Joss. You must hate me to consider such a thing!"

"It is what must be . . . for the both of us. We are hopelessly outnumbered here. Milosh has summoned the Brotherhood. If all goes well they will arrive before dark. You cannot be here for the battle that will come."

"Brotherhood? What *Brotherhood?*" she snapped at him.

"He calls it the *Brotherhood of the Vampire Wolf*—vampires like us, who have embraced the blood moon ritual—resisted the lure of the undead, and become hunters of the very thing we are—*vampir*. What we had together was beautiful, Cora . . . beautiful and fine, but it must end here and now, while we still can end it. I have nothing to offer you. I do not even know who—or *what* I am; neither does Milosh. Now that I know that, I could not burden you with such an existence."

"And what if I do not look upon it as a burden?"

"It is not your decision to make, Cora. You are not the one afflicted. It is over."

"When did you come to this decision—while you held me naked in your arms in that bed? Or was it when you seized me like a madman before you went back out into that . . . that madness earlier? Is that why you came bounding back through that front door down there in your wolf's body nearly knocking poor Parker off his feet, just to shapeshift back and dress and saddle two horses?"

Joss's eyes flashed toward her, quicksilver jousting with shimmering blue. He reached her in one giant stride and seized her upper arms, shaking her gently, though the motion jarred her welled-up tears loose and they streamed down over her hot cheeks.

"What are you talking about?" he said through clenched teeth. "Answer me, Cora! When? What happened?"

"Don't you remember what you do in wolf form?" Cora snapped. "You had just left me. I was on my way up to my suite when there came a sound at the door. I watched from the shadows. Parker opened the door a crack, spoke to you, opened the door wider and you bounded past him and disappeared toward the servants' wing. You nearly knocked the poor man down. Were you in so much of a hurry to evict me from your life?"

Joss's scalp drew back. His eyes bored into her; wild, feral lights danced in them, catching red glints from the resurrected fire in the hearth. "That was not me!" he pronounced. All at once he let her go and streaked toward the door.

"What do you mean it wasn't you?" Cora cried, rushing after him. "I saw you with my own eyes!"

"You saw a gray wolf with your own eyes, but not *my* gray wolf. I was with Milosh until dawn, killing vampires, Cora. Lock this door and open it to no one but me—not anyone, is that clear? I'll be back as soon as I get to the bottom of this."

"Joss, what is it?"

"Don't you understand?" he snapped, prying her

hand off his arm. "It wasn't me! If Parker let a wolf into the Abbey, he's let in a vampire, and that vampire can now invite others to enter. If what you say is true, we are under siege inside and out. Now, lock this damned door and pray you dreamed that wolf!"

CHAPTER TWENTY-FIVE

Joss stepped into the hallway, his hands fisted by his head as if he meant to keep his brain from bursting. He started first in one direction, jerked to a halt and started in the other. He raked his hair back ruthlessly and leaked an agonized groan, then bellowed at the top of his voice: *"Par . . . ker!"*

At his back, the sound of a bolt being thrown, and a bitter sob shot him through like cannon fire. He had hurt her, but at least now she would do as he told her. Finally she knew what she was facing under his roof. It was done, and he would stick to his decision. He could offer her nothing but danger and heartache. He had to let her go.

He shouted for the valet again, and the servants' wing door snapped open. So did the door to the toile suite. Milosh burst into the corridor and swaggered toward him at the same instant the valet shuffled toward him from below leaking a string of expletives under his breath, his sparse gray hair fanned out like a misshapen halo that had slipped down over his ears.

"There are bellpulls in the chambers, sir," the valet

grumbled. "You needn't shout the house down. You're making enough noise to raise the dead!"

"You'd best pray not, old man," Joss snapped.

Milosh reached him. "What's happened?" he asked, his dark eyes as black as onyx.

"They're in the house, thanks to Parker here!" Joss railed.

The valet gave a start and backed up a pace. "Never!" he blurted. "The only thing I let inside this Abbey was you yourself, sir, when you came barging in before! You nearly knocked me down."

"That wasn't me," Joss pronounced, his voice dangerously calm.

The valet's jaw dropped. What little color he had left his face. "It was!" he cried. "It had to be—that great gray wolf with the mask about its face. Why, I'd know it anywhere. Young miss saw it, too."

"Have you any idea how many masked gray wolves we have slain out there?" Joss said. "They are a common variety."

The valet's posture sagged, and he sank down on the settle beside the master suite door. He couldn't speak. Though he opened his mouth to do so, no words came, and Milosh placed a hand on the poor man's shoulder and looked him in the eyes.

"There's no use lamenting it now," he said. He nodded toward the master suite door. "Come away," he said, raising Parker up. "The walls have ears now, and we do not want to frighten young miss."

"Go below, Parker," Joss said, his voice strained, "and assemble the others in the servants' hall. Tell them only that I wish to meet with them collectively. We will join you directly."

Then, turning Milosh toward the front stairs, Joss

sprinted along the corridor, over the landing and into the study. He threw open the liquor cabinet, took down a silver decanter and stalked back out into the corridor. The Gypsy followed at his heels.

"What do you do?" Milosh asked.

"Holy water," Joss explained, exhibiting the decanter. "There is nothing for it. The others have to know now— not all of it, of course. Not about you and me or my parents. They know only that we are vampire hunters, not that we ourselves are infected. No one would work here if that were the case."

"Is it wise, telling them anything?"

"It is *necessary*, Milosh. They are in danger. I should have warned them earlier and now I have no choice. The creatures are in the house! Whatever creature it was that Parker admitted will invite the rest. We have to find and destroy it, and even then . . . We don't know how many it has already let in. Pray God it is not the sort that can go about in daylight."

"Take care, young whelp. You don't want to start a panic."

"I don't want any more dead or infected servants on my conscience either," Joss snapped. "Don't worry. I know what I'm about."

Joss tried to ignore Milosh's sidelong glances as they made their way below. The Gypsy might have more experience in the field of vampire hunting, but Joss knew how to handle his motley crew of excitable servants. If Grace was still abed grieving for poor Bates, with any luck she could remain in ignorance as long as she was watched. That would have to be up to Amy. But then, what to do about Cora? That decision had to be made in great haste, while they still had daylight, when the vampires who could bear it were drained of their powers.

It was with relief that he found as he entered the servants' hall that at least one of his hopes had been fulfilled; Grace Bates was not among the gathering. But that made his task no less formidable. He still had to deal with Cook, Rodgers, Amy and the despairing Parker, the picture of contrition.

"Well done," Joss said to the valet. "Is Grace not well enough to join us, then?"

"No, not, sir," said Parker. "Cook has just dosed her with an herbal draught, and I thought it imprudent to wake her for this. But if you wish—"

Joss raised his hands in a staying gesture. "No, no, let her stay as she lies," he said. "I am not encouraged with her progress, and as soon as things are settled here I shall have the doctor in." He glanced toward Cook, twisting the corner of her apron in obvious dread of this unprecedented visit below stairs; something that just wasn't done. They all looked awestruck, come down to it. He refused to let that daunt him. "Continue your herbals until I can have Dr. Edwards in," he said to her. The woman nodded and sketched a graceful curtsy despite her age and girth.

Joss cleared his voice. "Very well then," he began, ". . . we have a situation here that you must be made aware of before nightfall. You all know my parents vocation . . . and mine, for I have joined them in it; we are vampire hunters. You know such things exist. Some of you—even Parker here—has had someone harmed by these creatures." He glanced around the gathering. Rodgers, Cook and Amy had sunk into chairs at the table. Parker was the only one standing. Joss had their rapt attention, and he turned toward the Gypsy at his side and went on quickly.

"You have all met my houseguest, Milosh," he said. "He, too, is a vampire hunter—one of great renown. He is our family friend from Romania, where such things are commonplace, and he couldn't have arrived at a better time."

A dark murmur rumbled through the group, and Joss cleared his throat above it. "Yes," he repeated, "his visit is a timely one, because there has been an outbreak of vampirism hereabout. When I came upon Miss Applegate's carriage bogged down in the snow, she was the only occupant that wasn't infected. I reached her just in time. Some of those others have been destroyed, but not all, and those who survived have infected many in the village."

As if on cue, howling began, audible even there, in the lower regions of the Abbey. "Do you hear that?" he said. "I must be honest, there are many outside. But you will be quite safe as long as you remain calm and keep your wits about you. Milosh and I will deal with these, though we cannot do so without your cooperation. That is why I've given strict instructions that no one but Parker answer the door. No one must be admitted—not even an animal."

Their gasps and murmurings grew louder, and Joss slapped the silver holy water decanter down on the table, silencing them. If they panicked over what he'd told them thus far, he didn't want to imagine how they would react to the news that one or more vampires might already be in the house. He chose his words carefully.

"We have been very diligent," Joss went on, "but despite our efforts there is a possibility that one of these creatures may have gotten past our defenses and entered the Abbey—"

An uproar responded to that, and all three servants seated at the table vaulted out of their chairs.

Joss picked up the decanter and set it down before

Cook. "Holy water," he said. "Use your herbal vials, and divide this equally—one for each of us. It will not destroy a vampire, but it should chase one off long enough to keep you from harm. Carry it with you always. If you should need more, come to me." That was enough to tell them. They needed hope. With luck they would never have to learn that some *vampir* were immune to holy water.

"Beggin' your pardon, sir," said Amy. "You're sure there's one o' them creatures in here?"

"It is a distinct possibility," Joss said. "You will need to see that Grace is guarded, since she cannot protect herself in her present state."

"Y-yes, sir," Amy mewed, passing an audible gulp.

"Look around you," Joss went on, addressing the group. "With the exception of Grace and Miss Applegate, the only people that belong inside this Abbey are here in this room right now. Should you see anyone else—human or animal—you are to come to me straightaway. Do *not* approach any stranger on your own. If you encounter anyone—*any thing* out of the ordinary, come for me or Milosh at once. You are to take his orders just as you take mine. Is that clear?"

Another murmur broke the silence, accompanied by reluctant heads bobbing. It would have to do, and Joss took a ragged breath—the first time he'd filled his lungs completely since he began his address.

"Good!" he said. "My previous order still stands. Ignore the door; Parker will be the only one to answer if anyone knocks. Go about your business as usual. Keep your holy water at hand, and come to me with anything untoward that might occur. Milosh and I aren't alone. Others are coming to our aid. Meanwhile, stay inside the Abbey until I give you leave to go abroad, and carry on as usual. You are dismissed." He turned to go, then turned back. "Not you, Parker," he said. "Come with us."

The trio had scarcely left the servants' hall when Parker sketched a bow. "I cannot thank you enough for allowing me to man the door still . . . after . . . after what I've done, sir," he said.

"I'm confident that you won't make that mistake again," Joss replied as they climbed to the first-floor landing. "I called you aside because I do not wish that the others know any more than I've just told them. It's important, Parker. If they knew what you know, they would likely flee and the creatures lying in wait outside would have their way with them. I won't have that on my conscience. If that were to occur . . . well, death would be a kindness. Am I making myself plain?"

"Y-yes, sir, perfectly plain," the valet stammered, his Adam's apple bobbing.

"Good."

"They all knew something was afoot, sir," Parker said. "They saw the bonfire. I'm glad you told them what you did, because they also know I am privy to more than they, and I was hard put to appease them with explanations."

"I shan't deceive you, Parker," Joss said, "we are under siege here. You needs must look sharp. Milosh and I will search the Abbey now, before dark, for the creature you let in. It's still here; I'd stake my life upon it. It will stay where it can invite others in once the sun sets. Let us hope it hasn't done so already."

"I am so dreadfully sorry, sir. I thought—"

"There's no time here for that," Joss interrupted. "Go about your business as usual, and try to keep the others calm. With any luck, when the sun rises again this night-mare will be over."

The valet shuffled off, and Milosh turned to Joss. "I'm

glad you didn't mention your stabler," he said. "That lot would never take the way he passed in stride."

"It would be best if they think he's run off—at least for now, while the danger still exists. Everyone loved poor Otis. He was a loyal servant . . . and a good friend, poor blighter."

"Where shall we begin the search?"

"Brotherhood or no, we need to split up. The Abbey is far too large to search together. We shall never be done by dark."

"What about the young miss?"

"Bloody hell!" Joss erupted, slapping his forehead with the heel of his hand. "How could I have forgotten her?"

"You do not really want her to go," Milosh answered bluntly.

"It doesn't matter what I want, Milosh. I have no right to keep her here. *You* don't even know what I am . . . or what I will become. Given that, what can I possibly offer her? Suppose my symptoms continue to worsen with no hope of preventing the bloodlust. She would be at gravest risk. I would not be able to control my urges. I couldn't subject her to the remotest possibility of that."

"She loves you."

"Yes, *and I love her.* That is why I cannot keep her. Don't you see?"

"So . . . what will you do?"

"What I planned earlier. Take her out of here—now, before dark. I'll take her to the kirk—to the vicar. She'll be safe there while we deal with this. Afterward, if I can I'll see her safely south, on her way to her estate and away from all this. It's all I can do."

"You're sure?"

"I've saddled two horses already," Joss said. "It's still a good two hours before twilight. I won't be long. Can

you begin the search without me? Parker said the wolf
went below stairs."

The Gypsy nodded, though there was a troubled look
in his eyes. He didn't approve. Well, it couldn't be
helped. Joss couldn't concentrate upon the task at hand
while Cora was in danger.

They parted at the landing, Milosh disappearing into
the servants' quarters while Joss bounded up the staircase toward the master suite, and Cora. The urgency of
seeing her to safety gave his feet wings. If he hurried, he
could have her safely to the vicarage and return before
dark. Thinking of nothing else, he took the stairs two at
a stride.

Cora paced the Aubusson carpet in the master suite
bedroom. Just hours ago, she'd been resolved to make
an end to what was happening between herself and
Joss. Now she knew too late that she could never, ever
leave him.

The last thing she'd expected was that *he* would end
it. But while she'd lain cocooned in the down feather
beds where they had made love, wrapped in his silvery
brocade dressing gown that smelled of citrus, musk
and *him*, dreaming of his embrace, he'd been saddling
horses to send her away. Well, he couldn't send her if he
couldn't find her, and so she tugged on her frock,
tossed a shawl over her shoulders, for the corridors
would be cold, and peeked out into the hall. It was de-
serted. All was still. It should be fairly easy to find a hiding place without being seen in such an understaffed
house. Determined to do just that, she slipped out into
the hall on feet that made no sound, and closed the
door behind her.

It stood to reason that their search for the vampire would begin in the lower regions of the servants' wing, since that was where the creature first disappeared; she'd seen it herself. Given that, she began to climb upward. When she reached the third-floor landing, the halls were in darkness. Of course they would be, with no lit candles in the sconces. None of the rooms on the third floor were in use. The only light was coming from the oriels at each end of the east and west wings, and that was fading. The day was almost done. Soon she would need a candle to light her way . . . but not yet. It might show below.

There would be no fires lit on the third floor, or in the attic either. Since that part of the Abbey wasn't in use, the flues were capped off. She was glad she'd brought her shawl. It was thick, woolen and black. Not only would it keep her warm, it would blend well with the shadows. When the siege was over, somehow she would convince Joss that they belonged together. She knew he loved her. He'd told her so, but he hadn't needed to; she'd felt it in his arms, in the tender strength of his embrace. She'd seen it in his haunting, quicksilver eyes, tasted it in the deepness of his kiss. No, she wouldn't be cold prowling the unlit hearths of the third-floor recesses with just her frock and shawl; her whole being was on fire with the sultry memory of his love.

Which area would they search first here? They would probably do just as she was doing, begin with the third-floor bedrooms, and then the attic, whose access was a narrow flight of stairs recessed beside the east wing oriel. There were no draperies at either window—east or west—and already the alcove was steeped in shadow. Any moment it would be black as tar in that hallway, and those stairs would be invisible. Without a candle, she would be groping blind in the dark. Maybe she should explore the attic now, while there was still enough light to do so.

Cora had to keep reminding herself that somewhere a vampire was hiding in the Abbey, biding its time until darkness fell, when it would regain all its strength robbed by the dawn. Her ears pricked to detect any sound, she inched along the corridor on tiptoe, her heart hammering in her breast, echoing in her ears, the ragged beat of it rising in her throat. She tried to swallow her fear down, but it wouldn't budge, and she began to tremble. She always trusted her instincts. They had never betrayed her in the past, and they were screaming danger now.

Between the storm and the hour, the light was almost gone. She had nearly reached the attic stairs when a darker shadow alongside the alcove loomed up before her, the shadowy silhouette of a man. Her heart nearly stopped. Chills raced up and down her spine, dousing the fire her memory of Joss's embrace had ignited. Why didn't the person move? She backed down the corridor a few yards. Why didn't he follow? Cautiously, she crept nearer the alcove again. Still the figure made no advance. He was holding something in his hand. A broom? No . . . a halberd! She reached out, pulled her hand back, then reached out again and touched it. Cold metal met her fingers. It chilled her to the marrow. As if she were touching live coals, she patted the chest of the specter and nearly laughed aloud. A rush of relief left her lungs instead. This was a suit of armor, not a man at all, and she gripped the halberd and leaned against it, calling back her composure.

Her breathing had just begun to even when suddenly there was a sound. She jerked around to face another figure. This one wasn't armor-clad; it was tall and portly and real, emerging from behind the attic stairs. Cora opened her mouth to scream, but a thick, foul-smelling hand clamped over her mouth, and another encircled her waist to pull her against his bulk. Frantically she struggled to free the halberd for use, but her trembling fingers failed her and it crashed to the floor, grazing her ankle as it landed. Its sharp edge sliced into her flesh, drawing blood, and she bit down on her trembling lower lip and the pain along with it.

The figure jerked her closer. "You had best pray that no one heard that," he growled in her ear. She had her back to him, but she didn't need to see his face for recognition. It was Clive Clement, and the last remnants of daylight had just given way to night.

Joss didn't bother to knock; bursting into the master suite, he stormed through the rooms calling Cora at the top of his voice, but she didn't answer. Denying the obvious, he stalked through the rooms again, then sank down on the edge of the bed, raking both hands through his hair as if to order his runaway brain. A surge of déjà vu washed over him. She was gone *again*. Would the woman never stay put? Now there were more than vampires to search for; Cora was abroad in a house full of unspeakable dangers. It was going to be a long night.

The impression of her exquisite body remained in the feather bed. Joss ran his hand over it absently. His silver-gray brocade dressing gown lay in a heap at his feet. He snatched it up and held it to his nose, inhaling the delicate scent of roses and lemon verbena—her scent, heady and evocative. Tossing it down, he surged to his feet and went to the window. The draperies hadn't been drawn, and he gazed out onto the snow-covered tor. The howls of near and distant wolves rode the wind. Above the noise, one lone wolf's howl drowned out the rest: Milosh, calling the Brotherhood from the rooftop, just as he'd done the night before. They were gathering. It was begun.

Joss quit the chamber without a backward glance and went in search of the Gypsy. He found Milosh locking all access to the second-floor tunnel, something he himself should have thought of straightaway, and would have done if his brain wasn't so hopelessly fogged with love.

"Cora is gone," he blurted, breathless from the climb. "We must find her before whatever Parker let in does."

"I have the scent of the intruder," Milosh said. "It is not Sebastian. That hellish creature's stench is embedded in my nostrils and my memory since time out of mind. Believe me, I would know if he were lurking nearby. Which leaves one of the passengers in the coach or someone he has corrupted in the village. Either way, whatever it is in this house is his creature, you can count upon it. We must find and destroy it."

"Where have you searched already? There is no use going over the same spaces twice."

"I went to the rooftop to call to the others, then came here straightaway to make the tunnel secure."

"How many others can we expect?"

"Many, Joss," said the Gypsy. "The Brotherhood thrives everywhere now, after the success of your parents embracing the blood moon ritual. I have been busy these past thirty years. Any and all who are within the sound of my voice will come to our aid. It ends tonight, this siege."

Joss nodded. "We'd best be about it then," he said. "Since you've begun here, I'll take the third floor." He crossed to a chest alongside the vacant hearth, and opened it. Inside were lengths of rope, hatchets and blades, wooden stakes, mallets, vials of holy water—all manner of tools for destroying vampires.

Milosh took up a rope mesh net, his eyebrow raised in admiration. "Your father's work, I take it?"

Joss nodded. "He has such chests throughout the Abbey. Take what you need. We both must bear arms here now."

"Your father has become quite creative these past thirty years," the Gypsy said. "I am impressed." He took the net and several blades, then stood aside while Joss chose several implements as well.

Once he'd made his selection, Joss took up a candle, handed one to Milosh and started toward the door, but the Gypsy arrested him with a hand on his arm. "Take care," he warned. "This shan't be easy, Joss Hyde-White. Above all, avoid being bitten. These are cunning creatures. We first must find your lady and secure the Abbey, then proceed outside to join the others I have summoned."

Joss nodded. They stepped into the corridor, and he locked the chamber door. For a moment their gazes met, and a look passed between them that sent shivers down Joss's spine. More was said in that exchange than any words they might have spoken, and when Joss finally broke eye contact, he felt drained.

Milosh melted into the shadows of the second-floor hallway. There were many chambers to search, and Joss wasted no time bounding toward the back stairs and climbing to the third floor. The suites there hadn't been used in years—not since his parents had held hunting parties when he was a lad. He marveled at how the blood moon ritual had freed them to live a fairly normal life. He felt a brief twinge of jealousy that they at least knew how to combat their affliction.

Stalking the third-floor corridors, he visited the chambers in the west wing first, leaving no recess, no crevice unchecked. Nothing untoward presented itself, and he moved to the east wing, a bevy of emotions riddling him. He'd hoped to have found Cora fast; that he hadn't was driving him mad.

Outside, the howling had risen to a sinister cacophony—bestial voices out of sync; and many, judging by the rhythm. The noise had a pulse beat reminiscent of a death knell. Joss reminded himself that some among the gathering were Brothers, the redeemed, now more wolf than man or vampire—a strange phenomenon to be sure, but welcome allies.

The devil take it! There was no focus while Cora was at risk. Anger, conscience and apprehension were warring in him now, crying for supremacy. His instincts had always been infallible. This time, he could not find balance. He had to find Cora. Without her, nothing had meaning.

Nearing the attic stairs, Joss sighted something on the floor. Moving closer, he saw that a halberd had fallen from its stand beside the suit of armor stationed there. He stooped to pick it up. There was blood on the blade and on the floor. He held his candle higher and discovered drops of blood on the attic stairs.

His thundering heart rising up his throat, Joss blew out the candle. He didn't need it; his extraordinary vision, like that of the wolf, clearly showed the way. Making no sound, he mounted the narrow attic stairs, his ears pricked for any nuance of sound trickling down from the attic above.

At first he heard nothing. Then, all at once, there was a sound no ordinary man could have heard and a smell no ordinary man could have smelled. Had he been able before? He couldn't recall. Were these new gifts manifesting themselves as a matter of course, or had the situation triggered them? *Extraordinary powers,* he mused. He should be grateful for them, but their manifestation was bittersweet. His symptoms were changing. But to what level? How much of a vampire was he? He beat back those thoughts.

Cora's scent—an explosion of burgeoning roses mingled with the unmistakable scent of her blood—overtook his nostrils. Her muffled cries assailed his ears. Bursting through the attic door, he stood—feet apart, halberd raised, poised to strike he who possessed the other smell attacking his senses: a foul stench of stale blood, rot and decay that screamed Clive Clement, who indeed held Cora in a choke hold, his fangs mere inches from her jugular vein.

Tonight was moon-dark. Recalling that, Joss took a chill that almost made him misstep. He'd been born at the dark of the moon, and ever since, good or bad, all significant occurrences had taken place then. Another chill riddled him as he remembered he'd come upon the coach that fateful night when it all began in moon-darkness. Was this how it would end for him now—for them all, on a night when the only light without was reflected from the shadows in the blood-streaked snow?

In the moon's absence, precious little light filtered in from the snowy night sky through the tiny attic window. It was fitted with stained-glass patterns that cast an eerie luminosity, colored spangles on the dusty floor as the gray sky pressed heavily against it. The whole scene seemed surreal to Joss, but there was no time to analyze it, or the emotions that had brought his fangs into play.

"Let her go, Clement!" Joss seethed, carving circles in the air with the halberd.

A cold, misshapen laugh bubbled up in Clement's throat. But this wasn't Clement any longer. It was *vampir*, Sebastian's creature now, and if Joss did not act quickly, so would Cora be.

Joss's glance fell upon Cora's ankle; blood was still seeping from it. She was clawing at Clement's arm. Her tiny fingers didn't make a dent, and she bent her knee and dug the heel of her morocco leather slipper with all her might into his shin, reached behind, and thrust her fingernails into the creature's eyes. Clement shrieked. His hands clutched at one of his bleeding eyes, and his hold slipped just enough for Cora to wriggle free.

"Cora, get down!" Joss bellowed, and she dropped like a stone. Joss spun in a circle to build up momentum, then lowered the halberd with all his strength to the vampire's neck, severing its head in one fatal blow.

Cora screamed. For a moment, Joss thought it was the gruesome sight of Clement's headless corpse on the floor that had wrenched it from her throat, but no . . .

"Joss! Behind you!" she cried.

Joss spun, but not in time. From the recessed shadows beside the attic door, a younger, more agile figure sprang through the air and struck, knocking the halberd out of Joss's hand and driving him to the floor. Joss recognized his assailant at once. It was the younger passenger in the coach—Albert Clement, Cora's supposed betrothed. It stood to reason that Clement would have let his son into the Abbey. He, too, was *vampir*, his fangs inches from Joss's throat as they grappled on the musty attic floor.

The creature's strength was phenomenal, but so was Joss's. They were well matched. Out of the corner of his eye, Joss saw Cora scrabble to her feet and seize the halberd. His heart leapt. She could scarcely lift, much less wield it. She was limping as she dragged it closer.

"No!" Joss gritted out through his fangs. "Stay back, Cora!"

Whether she heard or not, she didn't obey. She dragged the halberd nearer. Try though she did, she couldn't raise it over her head, but she did manage to raise it chest-high. Albert Clement was on top of him. Joss had the strength to easily reverse positions, but he dared not with that shaky weapon looming in Cora's unsteady hands.

"Cora, don't!" he thundered, a close eye upon the shaky halberd swishing through the air. He felt the rush of air as it passed over them. "Cora! If you miss . . . !"

But Cora paid him no mind. Watching her, he almost didn't see young Clement's fangs descending. It was too late. A cry on her lips, Cora lowered the halberd. Her balance thrown off by her wounded ankle, she missed the broader target of young Clement's back, and the halberd sliced through Joss's shirt, grazing his shoulder instead. He cried out. It wasn't a deep wound, the blade having struck him at an angle, but it was deep enough to draw blood that attracted his assailant, whose fangs descended upon it.

Loosing a string of muttered oaths, Joss roared as the halberd swished through the air again. This time, it struck the creature a blow to the back of the head. Its shriek echoed from the rafters as it jerked back from the impact, and Joss scrambled out from underneath, wrenched the halberd out of Cora's hands and brought it down with all his strength, severing the neck of the writhing vampire.

"Joss—my God, I've cut you!" Cora cried, rushing toward him. "I didn't mean . . . Oh, Joss!"

He scooped her up in his arms none too gently. She had obviously struck out in a fit of blind passion, and only now realized she'd struck him.

Joss didn't speak—couldn't speak—wouldn't even if he could have. His jaws were clamped so tight upon his anger that his fangs had pierced his lower lip, and blood trickled down his chin from the wounds. *She might have been killed!* was all his addled brain could register. *What ever possessed her to leave the master suite where she was safe?* And now the scent of his blood would draw the other creatures descending upon Whitebriar Abbey, putting him at a grave disadvantage.

His jaw muscles ticking a stiff steady rhythm, Joss crashed through the attic door with little regard for the headless bodies he was leaving behind, carrying Cora below. Blind rage had made him impervious to her sobs and heart-wrenching apologies, rendered him oblivious of the pain and the blood trickling down his arm. His spine ramrod rigid, he staved on, his shoulders hardened like cold steel against her clutching fingers.

CHAPTER TWENTY-SIX

The fires were nearly out in the master suite when Joss reached it. Depositing Cora on the bed without ceremony, he chucked fresh logs into the bedchamber, sitting room, and dressing room grates, and ruthlessly stirred them to life. Snatching a length of bandage linen and a towel from the dressing room chiffonier, he returned to the bedchamber, where he spilled some water from the pitcher on the nightstand into the basin, tore off a piece of linen and began bathing Cora's ankle. It wanted one of Cook's herbal treatments, but there wasn't time for that.

Touching her delicate skin aroused him. How could that be, when he was so livid that he could scarcely see? Impossible. But there it was. He was tight against the seam. Nevertheless, his own wound forgotten, he dried her ankle and bound it tightly with the linen strip, with fingers that felt like wooden sticks for their clumsiness. Once he'd finished, he staggered to his feet, and Cora reached out to him.

"I didn't mean to hurt you," she murmured.

Joss stepped back from her. Her touch was physically painful. The warmth of it tore at his loins like hot pincers. He still didn't trust himself to speak. It was all he could do to keep from seizing her in his arms. The softness of her skin still lingered on his wooden fingertips as if they had a memory. Her rose scent, heightened from the ordeal and blended with her own essence, that sweet, earthy musk, was almost more than he could bear. But he had made his decision, and he would stick to it.

"You are still bleeding," she said. "That needs tending. Please, Joss . . . let me . . ."

"Parker will tend it," he got out through clenched teeth. The fangs had receded, though he could still feel their pressure at the ready to descend again. His only hope was to put some distance between himself and Cora, and he stalked toward the door, taking a large old key from the chatelaine he'd worn dangling from his belt since he staved that door in.

"Where are you going?" she cried. "Please don't leave me!"

"Don't let the fires go out," he said, his voice like cold steel. "Nothing will come down those chimneys with fires lit in them."

"Joss, please don't leave me like this. Not like this," she sobbed.

"I haven't time to argue with you," he said. "If you'd stayed here in these rooms, where you were safe, none of this would be. I'd have gotten you safely away before dark, and neither of us would be bleeding right now. Hah! Perhaps you are a vampire, too. You seem to have a penchant for drawing blood—*my* blood. None of this need concern you, because I'm going to lock you in where God-alone-knows-what can't get to you, but *I* must do battle now with vampires while I'm oozing blood. I shan't have any trouble finding them. They will find *me*. They will smell me a mile away downwind."

"You speak as if you believe I struck you that blow deliberately!" she cried.

"That doesn't matter. The damage is done. Do you hear that howling out there? I have no time for this. All you've done is prolong the agony."

"What do you mean?' she breathed.

"Get some sleep," he said. "Nothing is changed, Cora. Should we live, you are leaving the Abbey at dawn."

"Joss, *please*." she cried, her voice quavering.

With her sobs lingering in his ears, Joss turned the key, locking her in. He then locked the other two entrances to the suite as well, before stomping below in search of Parker in the servants' quarters. Protocol be damned!

He could bear anything but her tears, and they followed him along the corridor, down the hall clear to the landing. It wasn't his extraordinary hearing; the sound had pierced his heart. Realizing that, he almost failed to notice the tall, dark figure emerging from the shadows of the second-floor landing. It was Milosh.

The Gypsy's eyes were drawn at once to Joss's blood-soaked shirt. "You haven't been bitten?" he urged in alarm, prowling nearer.

Joss shook his head that he had not. "I found Cora," he said, "in the attic. The creature that once was Clive Clement had taken her there—"

"I've seen the carnage in the attic," Milosh cut in. "Well done! How were you injured?"

"Cora tried to help. She missed."

Milosh's eyebrow inched up a notch. Was that a smile creasing his lips? The man had no laugh lines in his angular face. But for chilling half smiles that never seemed to reach his eyes, Joss couldn't remember a single time he'd seen a genuine smile curl those lips. The expression passed almost as soon as it appeared.

"I think it was Clement in wolf form that Parker let in, and then Clement invited his son to enter. I'm hoping they were all who gained entrance."

"I smelled your lady's blood . . . and yours . . . and theirs. Was your lady bitten?"

"No."

"Are you sure?"

"She would have said."

"Would she? Where was she injured?"

Joss's brows knitted together in a frown. "The halberd fell and cut her ankle. It wasn't deep, but it bled severely. I cleaned and bound the wound and locked her in the master suite. I'll have Cook prepare an herbal salve in the morning. I was going to have Parker dress this," he said, nodding toward his shoulder. "The scent of blood will draw them."

Milosh shook his head. "No time," he said. "Is it deep?"

"No. I'm just afraid of attracting our foes."

"It's too late in any case," Milosh said. "Steady on. Young Clement was *not* the only creature the older Clement let in. Sebastian is in the house. Believe me, he already has your scent, just as I detected it. I knew he sought to gain entrance, to prowl among your father's things, to walk your father's halls as if he owned them. He is a brazen creature, is Sebastian."

"Where is he?" Joss blurted.

"I do not know," Milosh replied. "Only that he is here. I feel his power—his energy. I smell him. It's a stench unlike any other."

"What weapon will destroy him?"

"None that we possess," Milosh said. "Your parents and myself could not accomplish it before you were born. We will try again, but somehow I do not think this is the time, just as that was not the time. I also believe that when the time does come, I will be the one to destroy him, though I may destroy myself in the process."

"How do you know this?" Joss asked, his brows knit in a frown. He studied Milosh's glazed, faraway look.

The Gypsy shrugged, seeming to awaken from a deep trance. "We Gypsies know such things," he said. "I would almost be willing to make that supreme sacrifice. It has been a long fight, Joss Hyde-White, and I tire. But I also know my work is not yet done on earth."

"So, we cannot best him, yet we must fight him. We must try—how?"

"He is not impervious to fire, and your parents were able to repel and banish him with holy water. It will not destroy him, yet it has a startling effect. I believe it is because, before he was infected, he was a bishop."

"How could a bishop be so corrupted?" Joss wondered again. "And why was my father not turned? He was a man of the cloth." They had nearly reached the servants' wing, and he hadn't even realized it.

Milosh threw his head back in a husky guffaw, though no smile accompanied it. "Sebastian, Bishop Valentin, was an ambitious man, given to pomp and avarice, the perfect candidate for corruption. Your father's heart was pure. Sebastian was driven by jealousy of that, and still is."

"Sebastian wants you as much as me," Joss pointed out.

Milosh nodded. "Yes," he said simply.

"Did he infect you?

"No, we were both infected by the same creature, which I later destroyed. He did infect my wife, however. Sebastian was turned; I resisted, just as your father resisted. Many do, though not many live long as I have done. Much time passed before I learned of the blood moon ritual in Persia, and embraced it. It freed me from fighting the bloodlust so that I could concentrate upon hunting those of our kind who do not resist." He sighed. "Sebastian's infection was far too great for the ritual to help him. He was already *undead*. The blood moon ritual cannot resurrect the dead, Joss, and it cannot cure a vampire or those whom a vampire has killed that later rise up undead. What it can do is arrest the feeding frenzy, but only in those who are resistors. Sebastian has always been jealous of me because of the blood moon, and for those I have saved from the feeding frenzy with it. You should also know that in the beginning, when I first met your parents, there were some tense moments until I was certain they were candidates to undertake the ritual. If they had not been . . . Well, let us just say I am eternally grateful to Divine Providence that your parents were resistors."

"You would have killed them," Joss said, knowing it to be true.

Milosh nodded. "I would have had to," he murmured. "I would have had no choice."

Joss hung his head, thinking, and Milosh gripped his arm. "Remember—I had to destroy my own wife and unborn child," he said through clenched teeth, "because they were too severely infected. She was undead, thanks to Sebastian. Even if I'd known of the blood moon ritual then, she was too far gone for it to have helped. I pray God you are never faced with such a decision."

"There is little chance of that," said Joss. "If I must put Cora from me, I will never love another—and she is not infected. But how terrible it must have been for you."

Milosh smiled his humorless smile. "My poor young friend," he said. "How much it is that you have to learn . . . and to suffer before 'tis done."

Joss would not dwell upon that cryptic augur. His bones felt brittle with the chills ripping through him from listening to the Gypsy's tale. He'd heard much of it before, but had never really absorbed it until now.

"What are we doing down here?" he asked. The subject needed changing.

"I may not know where Sebastian is, but I will know where he isn't," Milosh replied. "He was not in the rooms I searched, nor had he ever been. If he is not below stairs, we shall secure your staff, collect more holy water and resume our search."

"Is Cora safe where she is?"

"Once Sebastian is invited in, he may come and go at will without further invitation. She is in danger. Are her hearths lit?"

"I stoked those fires myself. She knows to keep them stoked—and why."

"Will she stoke them? Suppose she falls asleep. Would it not be safer to have the maid stay with her?"

"Amy did stay with her—and Grace, when I first brought her here, but they both failed to keep that first vampire out. It either drugged or hypnotized them."

Outside, the howling and snarling voices of the wolves—almost subliminal in their constancy—reentered

Joss's hearing. He shuddered. All at once, the wolf in him responded. A low, guttural growl that resembled the roar of a lion leaked from his throat of its own volition. Something foreign roiled inside him. Was he answering the call of the Brotherhood? Or was he evolving again? Something deep inside screamed: *Nooo!* while something else embraced the inevitable with yet another roar.

"Shouldn't we be out there helping in that conflict?" he said.

Milosh studied him. Those multifaceted onyx eyes drove Joss's away. What did the Gypsy know? What did he see? What was that look—part sorrow, part something Joss couldn't name?

"Trust the Brotherhood to deal with what threatens from without," Milosh said. "Our task is here, within, where the greatest danger lies. All of the infected from that coach have been destroyed. What remains are the creatures they made before their demise, and Sebastian. If we cannot destroy him—and I doubt we can—we must drive him from the Abbey, where the Brotherhood can have their way with him. Oh, they will not destroy him, either. But they are sufficient in number to force his retreat."

"Drive Sebastian out, or let the Brotherhood in," Joss corrected him.

Milosh cocked his head to the side, his sparkling black eyes narrowed. It almost seemed that the Gypsy had not thought of letting the howling pack of summoned wolves *into* the Abbey.

"Or let the Brotherhood in," Milosh parroted. "If needs must, yes."

No, the Gypsy had not thought of that, but he was contemplating it now. Joss said no more as they descended through the green baise paneled door to the servants' quarters. There they found Parker, Rodgers and Cook huddled around the long dining table in the servants' hall. A collective gasp rose from the gathering as they entered. It wasn't until then that Joss realized what a sight he must look with his torn, blood-soaked sleeve, rumpled buckskins, likewise spattered with blood, and mussed hair. He brushed a dark lock challenging his eyes back from his brow, and made an attempt to neaten his attire.

Parker surged to his feet and shuffled to his side. "Oh, sir! How have you hurt yourself?" he breathed, taking hold of Joss's arm.

" 'Tisn't serious," Joss assured him. "There isn't time to tell you. Has anything untoward occurred here below stairs?"

A *no* voiced in unison replied to that, and Joss drew an easier breath. "Where is Amy?" he asked.

"She is with Grace," Parker said. "We thought it best to keep Grace in ignorance of the situation. Cook has been dosing her with one of her herbals."

"A wise decision," said Joss. He turned to Milosh. "What say you?" he asked, hoping the Gypsy would take his meaning. He needed to know if Sebastian was near.

He needn't have worried. Milosh read his mind, and answered: *Sebastian is not below stairs.*

Joss cleared his voice. "We have destroyed the vampire that Parker accidentally let in earlier, and another that the creature had invited to enter. . . ." A rush of murmured relief rumbled among the servants. "But," Joss said, his voice raised above them, "there is another creature inside the Abbey to be dealt with, and it would be safer if you all were closeted in one secure place until Milosh and I can flush it out."

The rumble soured, and Joss raised his voice again.

"We can do that much more quickly without worrying about you lot," he said, "so I would like you all to take whatever you need—food, bedding, whatever will see you through the night, and congregate in Grace's chamber—"

"Bedding?" Cook cried. "Beggin' your pardon, sir, but who's goin' ta be sleepin', I'd like ta know? I ain't shuttin' my eyes again for a month in here!"

"Take what you need for your creature comfort," Joss said tersely. "I want you all together in one safe place. Do it now, and lock yourselves in. This is not a request. It is an order. And stay there, no matter what you hear. Do not unlock that door until Milosh or myself comes to tell you it is safe to do so. Do I make myself plain?"

"Y-yes, sir," the group said.

"Good! Now carry on. We will wait while you gather your necessities."

"What of the young miss?" Parker said, hanging back.

"Young miss is locked safely in her chamber," Joss told him. The valet's eyebrow lifted, and Joss patted the chatelaine dangling from his belt. "This time *I* locked her in, Parker," he said.

The valet did not seem impressed. "Nonetheless, I should like to stay with you, sir," he said.

"The point of this is to have you all safely out of the way in order to have clear heads for what is to come, Parker. Besides, I need you to remain with the others to keep order. You are in charge below stairs now, old boy, remember. That is where I need you now."

"Yes, sir," said the valet emptily. He opened his mouth to speak, but the look Joss gave him closed it, and he sketched a bow and shuffled off after the others.

Joss sank into a chair at the table, and raked his hair back from a sweaty brow with both hands. "Grace's chamber is the best possible choice," he said. "It's the largest. She's shared it with Bates since before I was born."

Milosh studied him for a moment. Joss couldn't meet the Gypsy's eyes; they had the power to see into his soul. Instead, he surged to his feet and began to pace the carpet.

"Something is troubling you," the Gypsy said.

Joss loosed a mad, misshapen laugh.

"No, something other than the obvious," Milosh said. Joss hesitated. "My symptoms have begun to . . . evolve again," he said at last.

"In what way?"

"I've had extraordinary night vision ever since I was first able to shapeshift into a wolf," Joss said. "At first it only happened when I was in wolf form. Over the years it has intensified. Earlier, while I was searching the third floor, it was stronger than it has ever been."

"Go on. . . ."

"Then there is my hearing," Joss continued. "That happened when you came and spoke to me with your mind. I had no idea I could converse mentally. It may be that I always had the gift, but never needed to use it until you arrived. Or it could be something new."

"You would have to speak with your mind to another who has the same gift. You never spoke thus with your parents?"

"No."

"Is there . . . anything more?"

"My sense of smell. I could smell blood—Cora's . . . and just now, when I heard the howling, I was compelled to answer. Compelled to howl like a wolf, though in human form. Something has happened inside me, overwhelmed me. . . ."

"Your welcome into the fold—your bonding with the Brotherhood," Milosh said. "You have become one with your brothers of the blood: nothing extraordinary. And . . . the bloodlust? Have you had the urge and the appetite for blood?"

Joss shook his head. "No, not yet," he said. "But the way the symptoms are escalating . . ."

"You fear it most because of your lady," Milosh said.

"She is not my lady, Milosh," Joss insisted. "I meant what I said. As soon as it's safe, she must go."

"You are a colossal fool, Joss Hyde-White. You have the love of a lady who has accepted you as you are, unknown as that is. You may never find such a one again."

"As long as I do not know what I am, I have no right to any woman, no matter what she accepts."

"Fine scruples, but they will not keep you warm at night," Milosh said. "Like I said, young whelp, you are a fool."

CHAPTER TWENTY-SEVEN

Cora's eyes were nearly swollen shut from the flood of tears she'd shed since Joss locked her in the master suite; the counterpane was wet with them. How long had she lain there? She hadn't lit the lamps. Only the blazing fire in the hearth shed light upon her sorrow.

Darkness looked in through the window, a pearly, gray-blue darkness pressed up against the pane. The snow had ceased falling again, though airborne particles carried by the wind still hissed against the glass. There was no moon, but stars winked down like so many curious eyes. Cora couldn't bear their scrutiny. It was as if they mocked her.

Throwing her feet over the side of the bed, she moaned. She'd forgotten about her gashed ankle, and moving brought sharp, sobering pain. She cried aloud when she put her weight on it. There was no one to hear, and she limped to the window and cast her gaze down over the tor. It was alive with wolves; their terrible howling challenged the wind's deep sighs. Black ones, dark and silver gray, even shaggy russet ones, but none were white; Milosh was not among them—at least not within her range of vision.

How long before Joss would come for her? Suppose he didn't come. Suppose something happened to him. Suppose she was never to see him again! She couldn't imagine that; not after witnessing the way he felled the two vampires in the attic, as if they were young saplings, with one mighty stroke. He'd been in a blind passion when he wielded that halberd. She could still see him in her mind's eye standing, feet apart, carving wild circles in the air with the deadly weapon, wild-eyed like a madman. And there was more to it than destroying two creatures of the night. He'd been avenging her honor. He loved her—she knew he did. How could he put her from him so easily . . . as if she meant nothing to him? Why were his eyes so cold when he left her? Why was his jaw set like granite, his posture so rigid, so utterly impervious? It was as if he'd built a wall around himself that she could not penetrate.

Favoring her wounded ankle, Cora moved away from the window and limped to the door. She jiggled the brass handle, knowing it was no use. Leaning her ear against the paneling, she held her breath and listened. All she heard was the ragged rhythm of her own heartbeat. The corridor outside was as silent as a grave, and she reeled back from it and went to the wardrobe.

Her frock was spattered with blood—Clement's blood. How was it that she hadn't noticed that before? Her skin crawled at the thought, and she wriggled out of the gown until it puddled at her feet, then kicked it aside with her good foot and reached for the wardrobe doorknob. It was ajar. Had she left it that way? Cora couldn't remember. She shrugged. She was cold stand-

ing there in just her camisole and petticoat so far from
the fire; cold as ice. A bitter draft seemed to be coming
from the wardrobe—an unnatural cold. It was visible!
A crawling mist, the kind that always hovered about
the icehouse back home, drifted toward her; breathing it seemed to freeze her lungs. All at once, a blast of
frigid air rushed from it, forcing the wardrobe door
open wider. Dozens of bats rode the current out, rushing past her in all directions. The room was black with
the squeaking, flapping creatures sawing through the
air, and still more poured from the wardrobe. Cora
screamed as they grazed her arms, her shoulders. One
had fastened its talons in her long hair, wrenching another scream from her throat—a troop of screams as
she fell to the floor and groped for the frock she'd discarded to fight them off.

All at once a whirlwind collected the bats into a
swirling blur of wings and fangs and talons, and the
creatures merged into a hideous, towering entity—half
man, half bat—with acid-green, red-rimmed eyes. Its
skull scraped the ceiling and its wingspread filled the
span. It was the very same creature she had glimpsed
through the root cellar door. Soon it shrank to human
height and human form—a hideous, emaciated figure
of a man, bald-headed, swathed in yards of some anony-
mous gauze that looked like grave clothes, looming
over her. Cora backed away.

Sebastian!

Joss surged up the second-floor staircase as if his feet
had wings, driven by Cora's screams. Milosh surged
ahead of him and reached the master suite door first.
Joss had never seen the Gypsy at the height of his power,

and it rocked him back on his heels. Milosh raised his head sniffing, nostrils flared, then leapt into the air and streaked past him, lingering only briefly outside the master suite before disappearing down the staircase in a glaring, mercurial blur.

Joss was beside himself. There wasn't time for thought speech with the Gypsy. He was out of range anyway. Cora was locked inside the chamber with Sebastian, and he himself had locked her in. He was all thumbs as he fumbled with the chatelaine, groping for the key. Exasperation wrenched a string of blasphemous expletives through his clenched teeth, and brought his fists against the door with force enough to split the paneling.

"Cora!" he bellowed. "Do not look it in its eyes!"

Did she hear him? There was no way to tell. All that replied were her screams. The sound pierced him to the core, and he fumbled with the chatelaine again, seized the key and turned it in the lock.

His fangs were fully extended by the time he burst into the room. The wolf lurked just under the surface of his skin, though the chilling sound that came from him was more like the roar of a lion. The sight before him turned the blood cold in Joss's veins. The emaciated Sebastian stood before him with a choke hold upon Cora. Was that blood on her throat, on the creature's fangs? Dazed, she had ceased screaming and gone limp in its arms.

Blind passion moved Joss. A roar he scarcely recognized as having come from his own throat reverberated through the chamber. Sebastian's eyes pulsated like glowing coals. He bared his fangs as if in anticipation of a contest, threw Cora down and surged to his full height and true shape before Joss's eyes. Joss had seen it thus before, in the stables, and by the root cellar. Though it was daunting, he was not cowed. The incarnation he had just seen holding Cora when he entered was by far more frightening, its grave-clothes shroud clinging to its emaciated frame, a grotesquely aroused sex protruding from beneath.

"Run, Cora!" Joss commanded. "Run *now!*"

But she could not. She tried to rise and failed. Cursing under his breath, Joss reached her in two strides, raised her up and started to lead her toward the door, when the creature's right wing swished through the stale air and caught him unprepared, lifting him off his feet. He let go of Cora just in time, for the creature's left wing caught him on the downswing and sent him crashing into the wall.

Cora fell to the floor, a scream on her lips, and crawled into the corner beside the wardrobe. Joss lay dazed, writhing at the creature's taloned feet. Sharp, stabbing pain seared through his ribs. The distraction had nearly cost him his life. He shook his head to clear his vision. He was teetering on the cutting edge of consciousness, blinking back vertigo that blurred his enemy's image.

Over Sebastian's laughter, Joss heard the howl of a single wolf. Milosh? Why had the Gypsy left him? Where had he gone now that he was needed? Little more than seconds had passed since Joss had entered the master suite, though it seemed like hours. He groped the pocket of his buckskins for the little vial of holy water. It had scarcely come into view when Sebastian kicked it out of Joss's hand, then crushed it with one vicious stomp.

A hideous laugh came from the creature. Its breath was poison. The whole room reeked of it. "You thought *that* would stop me—that piddling drop?" Sebastian said. "You think *you* can stop me? Your father could not. Your mother could not. Not even that fool of a Gypsy could manage it, for all his labor over the years. Not even the three of them together could! What makes you so special, eh?"

It hurt to breathe, much less to talk. This was to be a battle of wits, not words, and Joss wasted no time upon the latter. Borrowing a tactic from the wolf, he turned in a flash and sank his fangs deeply into the creature's heel, the closest part of its anatomy within reach. Sebastian roared. His thrust-back head scraped the ceiling, and his wings expanded, flapping until a cyclonic wind roared through the chamber, lifting the draperies at the window and ruffling the counterpane on the bed. Cora cried out as the gust caught the open wardrobe door beside her and set it in motion, banging in its frame. She cried out again, drawing Sebastian's eyes. In a flash he loomed over her, hissing like a snake.

"Let her be!" Joss cried out, his voice like thunder. "This contest is between you and me. She is not part of it."

"Is that so?" the creature said. "I have tasted her sweetness. I always finish my meals. . . . Sooner or later, she will be mine. Oh, do not worry, Joss Hyde-White. It was only a taste . . . for now. But enough to mark my territory."

Joss took aim at the creature's other leg, but Sebastian seized him in sharp talons, lifted him off the floor and began shaking him like a dog shakes a toy. Sharp, tearing pain ripped through Joss's rib cage. He could scarcely breathe. The creature had flattened itself against the ceiling, dangling him precariously. A fall from such a height would be disastrous, and then Cora would be at the creature's mercy. Sheer willpower kept Joss's eyes from closing. He had to break free before the creature dashed him to death against the floor, the walls or the hearth, but he dared not let go. He was close to the fire; too close. The heat of the blaze narrowed his eyes. But the heat reached out to Sebastian as well, who shrank from it, sliding down the wall when it came too near his wings.

Closer to the floor, Joss fought the creature's grip with all his might, but he still could not shake himself free. The halberd wound in his shoulder had begun to bleed again during the struggle, and Sebastian focused upon the blood running down his arm.

The creature's long, pointed tongue licked at the blood glossing over Joss's Egyptian cotton sleeve. "Hyde-White blood," it warbled. "I have a taste for it. One might call it a hunger."

All at once, a rumble echoed along the corridor outside. Vibrations beneath the vampire's feet froze him momentarily, a sinister scowl spread across his face. The fireplace tools began to rattle in their brackets; the pitcher on the nightstand knocked against its basin. The crystal prisms dangling from the oil lamp began to tinkle, and a deep voice ghosted across Joss's mind. Was it real . . . or was he dreaming?

Steady on, young whelp, it said. *Brace yourself!*

A streak of silver-white light sailed through the open chamber doorway, and the great white wolf slammed into Sebastian, head on, sinking its fangs deep in the creature's enormous barrel chest. A whole pack of snarling wolves followed, pouring into the room behind. Sebastian loosed a cry so terrible that Joss lost his hearing momentarily; then, in a blink, the creature divided into a swarm of black bats. Loose of Sebastian's talons, Joss fell to the floor with a groan. He scrambled toward Cora, whose screams had nearly driven him mad. Like a man dying of thirst in the desert, he gathered her into his arms.

All around him, the room was in chaos. Snarling wolves of every shape, size and description leapt into the air, their great jaws snapping at the bats streaming through the open chamber door. Some of the bats fell prey to the lupine Brotherhood, their deaths wounding some part of the whole creature they masked, judging from the shrieks filling the air. But Sebastian would stay divided. He was far too clever to shift back into his natural state against such a formidable army. Milosh was right. Sebastian would not be destroyed today. He would be driven off to lick his wounds and bide his time until another opportunity presented itself.

None of that mattered to Joss Hyde-White at the moment. He clasped Cora to him like a madman, his trembling hands racing over her body, looking for wounds. He brushed back her long curtain of hair, exposing the puncture marks at the base of her neck, and leaked an agonized groan.

"How long did he feed upon you?" he gritted through clenched teeth as he always did when his fangs were extended.

"N-not long," she sobbed. "He . . . it overpowered me. It was hiding in the wardrobe. It must have already been there when you locked me in. When it came out, it seemed like hundreds of bats . . . then it changed . . . and bit me."

Groaning, Joss lowered his mouth to the puncture wounds upon her neck and sucked, as one sucks venom from a viper's bite, until his mouth was filled with her blood, then spat it out and crushed her close against him despite the searing pain in his ribs.

"Cleanse it with this," said a familiar voice at Joss's elbow. It was all he could do to raise his eyes from Cora's face. The blood he'd drained from her had rendered her unconscious, and she lay limp in his embrace.

Milosh's arm stretched out toward him. There was a vial of holy water in his hand. The Gypsy was barefoot, stripped to the waist, wearing only his breeches.

Joss took the vial from him and poured some of the holy water over the puncture marks on Cora's neck. She didn't move, though hot steam rose from her throat where the holy water touched her skin. Joss groaned and crushed her closer still.

"Am I too late?" he said. "Has he . . . infected her?"

"I have only seen such as this once before," the Gypsy said, obviously avoiding the question. "Your father is able to make holy water. Yet when he touches it, it boils and steam rises though he doesn't feel it. Curious."

"Yes, yes," Joss said tersely, "but *is she infected?*"

The Gypsy sighed. "You Hyde-Whites have a penchant for escaping full infection from the vampire's kiss."

"She is not a Hyde-White."

The Gypsy snorted. "She is your soulmate," he said succinctly. "However . . . unless I miss my guess, she did not resist. She *let* Sebastian taste her blood."

"Are you mad? Why would she do such a thing?"

"So you would have no more reason to send her away," Milosh replied. "So she would be as you are, whatever that may be, Joss Hyde-White."

Tears stung Joss's eyes. "If I believed that, I'd throw myself off the tor," he said through clenched teeth.

"We shall see," Milosh remarked. He lifted Cora out

of Joss's arms. Carrying her to the bed, he laid her down beneath the counterpane. "You both need tending now. The truth of my suspicions will come out later, one way or another, I'm sure."

"I thought you'd left me," Joss said, staggering to his feet.

The Gypsy smiled his humorless smile. "I did," he said. "To implement your strategy."

"My strategy? I don't understand."

"I let the Brotherhood into the Abbey. Without them, you would both be dead. I told you Sebastian was a mighty adversary. When cornered, he becomes an army. There is only one way to take him, and that is by surprise. One day I will do it, but this is not the day."

"Where is he now?" Joss asked, clutching his side as he sank down on the edge of the bed beside Cora.

Milosh shrugged. "Who knows," he said. "But not here, not while the Brotherhood is standing guard." Joss stared, and the Gypsy answered the expression with another of his curious half smiles. "Right now, they are searching the Abbey for any *vampir* that might still linger. Then, your mystic brothers will post guards at your portals. The siege is over . . . for now."

"Is she going to be all right?" Joss begged, brushing the tendrils of hair from Cora's pale, still face.

"She will," said the Gypsy on a sigh. "In spite of you."

Joss scowled, but made no reply.

"When you sucked her blood just now," Milosh said, "what was your reaction? Did the taste of her blood . . . arouse you? Did it—"

"I spat it out, Milosh," Joss snapped. "The way one sucks snake venom from a victim. That was all I could think of to do."

Milosh heaved another sigh. "A laudable effort, but ineffective in such a case as this," he said.

"I had to do *something*."

"You took no pleasure in the taste . . . in the taking of the blood?"

"Not in the way you mean," Joss said.

"In what way, then?"

"I took pleasure in her sweetness . . . and hope that whatever remained of her in my mouth, in my body, would make her mine and *not his*."

"Another symptom. You are territorial."

"I am *in love with her*," Joss seethed.

"Well, what's done is done," Milosh said. "Right now you both need rest and tending. All that blood is from the halberd wound—you were not bitten?"

"No, I was not."

Relief pulled the Gypsy's posture down. "That is something, at least," he said. "We will sort it all out. As soon as the *Brotherhood* makes a clean sweep of the house, you can release your servants. Your ribs are broken; they must be seen to and bound. If marrow taints the blood you could die, so mind whoever nurses you. I will instruct your cook in the preparation of an herbal draught that may be beneficial to you both. Meanwhile, you'd best brace yourself. . . . You have . . . company." He nodded toward the open chamber door, and Joss's head snapped toward a great black panther slinking into the room, its glowing eyes ablaze as it jumped up upon the counterpane and nudged him off the bed with a firm butt of its head and a guttural growl.

Joss straightened up and winced from the pain in his ribs. *"Mother?"* he breathed.

Milosh laughed outright, and this time it did reach his eyes. How handsome a man he was when he laughed—really laughed. But it was his mother who had Joss's attention. He rarely saw her as the great cat; the sight of her thus thrilled him.

"Come," Milosh said, leading Joss away. "Let her tend your lady. She is well able."

"Where is Father?" Joss insisted, digging in his heels.

"You father led the charge," Milosh explained.

"But how?" Joss cried. "They sent word that I was not to expect them. Where is he?"

"You will see him soon enough. Now, come. Sebastian is a fearsome entity, Joss Hyde-White, but you have no inkling of the power of the Brotherhood."

CHAPTER TWENTY-EIGHT

"Bind those ribs tighter, Parker," Jon Hyde-White barked. They were in the yellow suite. Joss was seated on the dressing room lounge, where the valet was able to doctor him with ease. A knock on the door sent Jon to answer. Amy stood on the threshold with a brimming cordial glass and a pot containing a malodorous chestnut-colored ointment on a silver salver. Joss grimaced. He could smell the awful stuff from where he sat.

His father took the salver and dismissed the maid. "You are sure you weren't bitten?" he said, setting the tray upon the gateleg table.

"I'm sure," Joss said. Conversing with a father who looked no older than he was jarring at best. It had always been thus. Making matters worse, looking upon his father was like looking in a mirror. They both possessed the same quicksilver eyes, the same mahogany hair, angular features, and expressive lips; they walked with the same swagger and carried themselves with the same deportment. They more closely resembled brothers than father and son. It was passing strange. "What I want to know," Joss went on, "is how you came here—how you knew to come. I just received your missive to the contrary."

"That was my doing," Milosh said, crossing the threshold, his thumbs hooked in the waist of his breeches.

Jon strode to his side and gripped the Gypsy's hand. The admiration in the exchange brought a lump to Joss's throat, and almost took his mind off the stabs of pain ripping through his torso as Parker tightened the bandages. Neither his father nor the Gypsy spoke. There was no need. The bond between them went back over thirty years.

"I told you," Milosh said, addressing Joss, "you have no inkling of the power of the Brotherhood. As I told you, we exist everywhere. When word is passed along the chain, a message is far-reaching."

"This all began because I went in search of you," Joss said to his father, wincing as the valet gave the linen binding one last tug.

"Milosh has told me," his father said, "that you had him to mentor you in your hour of need as he once mentored us. Such as that by far surpasses anything your mother and I could have done here." He made eye contact with the Gypsy. "And it is just one more thing for which we are eternally grateful. You could not be in better hands, son. Now, I want you to get into that bed and let those ribs mend."

"Not until I've seen Cora. I need to talk to her, Father. There are . . . issues between us that must be resolved."

"Your mother is with her. There will be time for that once you've both rested. When you are alone together. When we have left the Abbey."

"Left the Abbey? You are just come home!"

His father shot him a sobering look. "You know we cannot stay," he said. "Sebastian lives. He has crawled off to lick his wounds and regain his strength, just as he has done in the past. Once he regenerates, he will return. But not if we lure him away. We are the ones he most hungers for, Joss. Believe me, he will follow where we lead him, and that will leave you free to start a life with your lady. With the Brotherhood on guard, you will be reasonably safe—as safe as any vampire hunter can ever hope to be."

"But . . . what am I, Father? Will I age, or stay as I am? Will I wake one day with the hunger, the bloodlust? Am I man or vampire?"

Jon Hyde-White hesitated. "Your lady does not seem to care," he pointed out.

"But *I* care. What have I to offer her like . . . like *this*? What sort of life would it be for us . . . waiting for the worst, never knowing when it might happen?"

"Born of two vampires, you know what you are, Joss. That is not the question. What you really want to know is if the blood moon ritual has spared you the feeding frenzy. Only time will tell. That it hasn't happened yet is a good sign. That it hasn't happened in spite of what occurred here this night leaves me reasonably sure that it will not. I saw you. You were at your most powerful."

"And what of aging?" Joss asked.

Jon Hyde-White breathed a sigh. "I haven't seen a physical change in you since you were twenty. I believe you will not age. But we do not know that for certain. Heed Milosh's council, love your lady and above all respect the Brotherhood. Whatever you are, you are no longer alone."

* * *

"What beautiful hair you have," Cassandra Hyde-White said, running first her hand and then a silver-handled brush the length of Cora's long, rose-scented mane. They stood before the cheval glass in the master suite dressing room.

Cora marveled at how youthful Joss's mother appeared. Hearing about her condition and actually seeing it were entirely two different things. It was impossible to imagine that this beautiful woman was a vampire. She looked and acted as normal as Cora herself. Cassandra was studying her now, scrutinizing her image in the freestanding mirror. Why was the woman looking at her like that, raking her from head to toe? Was it that Cora was wearing Joss's silver brocade dressing gown over her petticoat, or did Joss's mother's interest go deeper? It was almost as if she were trying to see into Cora's soul.

"How much of what you told Joss was the truth?" Cassandra asked.

Cora lowered her eyes. "In what regard?" she hedged.

Cassandra swept her hair back, exposing the puncture marks at the base of her neck; they were ugly and red. "In this regard, my girl."

Cora hesitated. "It happened as I said," she replied.

"Not exactly, I think."

"It all happened so quickly, my lady," Cora said. "The creature seized me. I was so frightened, and it mesmerized me. Joss saw the hold it had upon me when he entered."

Cassandra looked long and hard into Cora's eyes before she spoke, and when she did, her words rode an audible breath. "You could have been killed," she remarked.

"But I was not. Joss came in time . . . and those wolves."

Cassandra took Cora's face in both her hands, and looked deeply into her eyes. "I know what you've done, what you've sacrificed for him," she murmured. "You must *never* take such a risk again. You must *never* underestimate Sebastian Valentin again, or leave yourself vulnerable to *any* vampire. My son loves you." She lightly fingered the angry puncture wounds on Cora's throat. "He must never know, Cora—"

"Your son was going to send me away," Cora defended herself. Tears welled in her eyes. She couldn't prevent them, nor could she hold them back. They were speaking of things that dared not be spoken outright—things that they both understood, though neither would give substance with words outside these four walls. "He meant to set me on a course for home at dawn," she went on, sobbing now. The mere thought of it brought physical pain. "He did not want to subject me to what he is . . . whatever he is!"

Cassandra embraced her. "Daughter," she said, "these matters are secrets of the heart—*your* heart, and that is where they must remain, if you take my meaning. Shh-hhh, now. All will be well. Joss's father is having a word with him, and this little talk we're having will be our secret, hm?"

"Y-yes, ma'am."

"I am glad to have had the opportunity to meet my son's beloved," Cassandra went on. "It may be many years before we meet again, but now I am able to live the life I must without reservations, without fear of my son's happiness. Joss is in good hands." She dropped a gentle kiss upon Cora's brow, extracting more tears, and smiled. "Now, dry those eyes and dust those blotches with talc," she said. "You have my blessing, dear . . . and my confidence. Do we understand one another?"

Cora nodded. *Secrets of the heart.* Yes, that is where they would stay. Cassandra floated out of the room then, with a wink and a nod and a finger pressed to her lips, as articulate as the words that remained unspoken.

Cora did as Cassandra bade her. She had scarcely doctored her blotches with talc and had just begun to address the bite marks at the base of her neck, when a gentle knock at the door called her to answer.

"Who knocks?" she said, shaky-voiced. It was not yet dawn, and she had made a promise to Cassandra.

"It is I," Joss said from the other side. "Let me in, Cora."

She hesitated, then threw the bolt and skittered back from the door. It came open gingerly. Cora almost giggled. Did he expect to dodge some missile? He looked as if he did. A closer look faded the smile from her thoughts, and from her lips. He was stripped to the waist, his chest tightly bound in linen strips, his shoulder also bound. Their gazes locked, he reached behind and threw the bolt. Cora almost winced at the sound it made, a rasping clang that echoed in the stillness.

For a moment they stood still, as if they'd suddenly turned to stone; then with a limp that more closely resembled a stagger, Joss reached her in two ragged strides, and crushed her into so volatile an embrace it took her breath away.

"Your ribs!" she cried when their lips parted.

"The devil take my ribs!" Joss murmured against her hair. Boldly attempting to sweep her into his arms, he winced and cried out in pain.

"You should be abed!" Cora scolded, steadying him.

"I agree," Joss said, leading her to the four-poster.

"Y-you can't mean to . . . ?"

"Oh, but I can," he murmured. Tugging the sash loose on his silvery dressing gown, he stripped off the robe and revealed her camisole and petticoat beneath. Raising the dressing gown to his nose, he inhaled deeply. "I have dreamed of sleeping in this after it has come warm from your body, laced with your scent. . . ."

Cora scarcely dared breathe. He was in earnest, and her heart was thumping so violently that she feared it would jump through her skin. The back of his hand grazed her décolleté as he removed her camisole, exposing first one aching breast and then the other. Her nipples had hardened to puckered buds, and he took one into his mouth, teasing it mercilessly. Beguiled, Cora scarcely realized he'd shed his boots and buckskins or relieved her of her petticoat until they lay together naked, ensconced in the feather bedding.

Aroused, Joss lay on his back. His hands about Cora's waist nearly met as he lifted her astride him. Cora sucked in her breath at the swift penetration. He'd plunged deeply, and her moist sex responded with a shuddering lurch that had never before occurred. Her hips jerked forward, and heat like a firestorm singed her belly and thighs.

"You are mad!" she said. "Your ribs!"

Joss cupped her breasts in his hands, his thumbs grazing her aching nipples. "If I am mad," he panted, "then you have driven me so. Once again, my love, I am in your hands. Do what you will with me, Cora."

"Does this mean I am not to be sent from the Abbey?" she whispered, afraid to ask the words aloud and break the spell—afraid to remind him that just hours before he had ended what had begun between them.

Burying his hands in her long hair, he gave a deep nod, lowered her face to his and murmured against her lips, "As soon as the roads are passable, you will indeed leave the Abbey. We shall *both* cross the border and wed in Gretna Green . . . if you will have me."

Cora gave a lurch. "If I will have you?" she asked, smothering him with kisses that drove his sex into her deeper still.

"I have tasted you, Cora," he said around the thickness of his canine teeth as the fangs descended. She could see them clearly. "I have tasted your sweetness. You are in my blood, but I am still in your hands."

Cora sucked his lower lip into her mouth. It was cut, and she tasted the thick metallic nectar of his blood on her tongue. Warm and salty, it trickled to the back of her palate and down her throat. There was no frenzy, however, only the burning desire to always join with him in this most intimate of ways.

"Whatever you are, I am one with you now," she whispered.

"And I, you," he responded, tracing the wounds on her throat with his forefinger.

Outside, the dawn was breaking, and the wolves had ceased their mournful howling. All else forgotten, the two clung to each other in mindless oblivion. Joss was indeed in Cora's hands, but more than that, he was in her heart, in her blood and in her soul. Whatever occurred, they were what they would always be, and they would face that challenge together.

The Marsh Hawk
Dawn MacTavish

Was Lady Jenna Hollingsworth's new husband the same man who had killed her father? After one night of passion, she begins to wonder. The jarring aroma of leather, tobacco and recently drunk wine drift toward her on the breeze—she remembers it so well, as well as the tall, muscular shape beneath the multi-caped greatcoat and those eyes of blue fire through the holes in his mask. Oh yes, she remembers that man with whom she shares a secret past. He is the highwayman known as the Marsh Hawk.

ISBN 10: 0-8439-5934-7
ISBN 13: 978-0-8439-5934-5 $6.99 US/$8.99 CAN

To order a book or to request a catalog call:
1-800-481-9191
This book is also available at your local bookstore, or you can check out our Web site **www.dorchesterpub.com** where you can look up your favorite authors, read excerpts, or glance at our discussion forum to see what people have to say about your favorite books.

Created at the dawn of time to protect humanity, the ancient warriors have been nearly forgotten, though magic lives on in vampires, werewolves, the Celtic Sidhe, and other beings. But now one of their own has turned rogue, and the world is again in desperate need of the

IMMORTALS

CHRISTINE FEEHAN

DARK GOLD

Alexandria Houton will sacrifice anything—even her life—to protect her orphaned little brother. But when both encounter unspeakable evil in the swirling San Francisco mists, Alex can only cry to heaven for their deliverance . . .

And out of the darkness swoops Aidan Savage, a golden being more powerful, more mysterious, than any other creature of the night. But is Aidan a miracle . . . or a monster? Alex's salvation . . . or her sin? If she surrenders to Aidan's savage, unearthly seduction will Alex truly save her brother? Or sacrifice more than her life?